"Recommended. . . . A lusty, melodramatic novel."
—*Library Journal*

———

"McMillan has this kind of novel down to perfection, snappin' on the menfolk, crying on cue, and standing tall for the Sisterhood."
—*BookPage*

———

"Warmth and down-to-earth richness . . . humorous. . . . McMillan's strong point is certainly her power of description and imagery."
—*ACE* magazine

———

"She brings out the glamour, passion, and fabulous interior design in the lives of everyday, working-class people."
—*United Autoworkers Solidarity* magazine

———

"Filled with page-turning, pot-boiling instances of deceit and vicious drama . . . equal to any of its type. Read it today!"
—*Upscale* (Atlanta, GA)

BLUE COLLAR
BLUES

Also by Rosalyn McMillan

Knowing
One Better

ROSALYN McMILLAN

BLUE COLLAR BLUES

WARNER BOOKS

A Time Warner Company

WARNER BOOKS EDITION

Copyright © 1998 by Rosalyn McMillan
All rights reserved. No part of this book may be reproduced in any form or by any electronic or mechanical means, including information storage and retrieval systems, without permission in writing from the publisher, except by a reviewer who may quote brief passages in a review.

Cover photograph by Herman Estevez

Warner Books, Inc.
1271 Avenue of the Americas
New York, NY 10020

Visit our Web site at
www.twbookmark.com

 A Time Warner Company

Printed in the United States of America

Originally published in hardcover by Warner Books.
First Paperback Printing: July 2000

10 9 8 7 6 5 4 3 2 1

This book is dedicated to my husband, John D. Smith, who began his career at Ford Motor Company as a blue collar worker, then worked his way up through the ranks as a white collar worker while going to school and receiving a B.A. in business management at the University of Northwood. "My Old Man," as I lovingly call him, is now, after thirty years of service at Ford, happily enjoying his retirement.

BLUE COLLAR
BLUES

Greed

1

The spring mornings were warming gradually. In mid-April, the sun rose earlier, and the deep cold of the Michigan winter was losing its grip. The warming rain was making mournful music for the mind. A careful ear could almost hear the song of a romantic sonnet by Byron in the steady downpour.

Khan Davis didn't have such an ear. Her mind concentrated on more mundane thoughts: money and sex.

Parking the car in her usual spot at Champion Motors' Troy Trim plant, she turned off her headlights and stole a final glance in the lighted mirror. Dabbing her pinkie in her mouth, she smoothed the high arch of her eyebrow, then fingered the right side of her short blond curls so that a few strands would just brush the tips of her half-hooded eyes.

Four feet eleven, with shiny blond hair and caffe latte skin, Khan imagined herself as a miniature Dorothy Dandridge with an attitude readying herself for a rendezvous with Harry Belafonte. But in real life, her appointment this morning was with a more dependable date, a power sewing machine that didn't give a damn how she looked.

"Damn," Khan snorted under her breath after grabbing her purse and umbrella. "This stupid weather is going to frizz up my new hairdo before R.C. gets a chance to see it." Pressing the button to pop open her umbrella, she slammed the car door and sprinted off. Halfway to the employee entrance, she could feel her hair rising like fresh yeast.

Most of the women who worked at Champion waited until they arrived at work before painting their faces in the women's bathroom, although they knew that makeup didn't make them more attractive to the males in the plant: Only the digits on their paychecks could do that.

But Khan Davis never went anywhere without looking absolutely perfect. Quite frankly, she loved to show off her petite figure. As she entered the plant each morning, Khan looked fine and dangerous. Dangerous because she already had a man.

Wearing a heavily starched pair of beige Calvin Klein jeans and a matching blouse, her gold chain belt with large loops echoing the eighteen-karat hooped earrings she wore in her ears, Khan naturally swished her hips as she walked to a rhythm from the old South that no one could hear or understand unless they'd been raised there.

The fresh scent of Cool Stream perfume oil mixed with Egyptian Musk brought attention from her male colleagues, whom she could see watching her out of the corner of her eye. Looking good and smelling outrageously different from other women was Khan's trademark.

Once inside the building, Khan was greeted by the familiar chug-a-lug noise from dozens of forklift drivers on their hi-los hauling stock in and out of the sewing units. The sharp smell of new vinyl mixed with gas fumes from the hi-lo followed, filling every molecule of air. Worse yet, she knew she was inhaling the toxic smell of burning glue coming from the laminator machines.

Reaching inside her purse, Khan removed the safety glasses that everyone was required to wear inside the plant. The titanium lights thirty feet above gave the impression of daylight, but Khan squinted as she waited in line in the break area to purchase the early edition of *The Detroit News*.

It was four thirty-five in the morning. The second shift of Champion Motors' Troy Trim Division hourly automobile workers would begin in twenty-five minutes.

The cold, high-glossed cement floor was painted stone gray. Set against the white walls, the lack of color created a stark tone that permeated every aspect of the plant. So no matter how much seniority Khan managed to tuck under her belt, she still felt imprisoned working at Champion—even if Champion was a prison that allowed her to make tons of money and then go home each day. The problem was, she made so much money that she didn't want to go home. The plant felt like a brick shrine luring its brainwashed devotees; the call of money was irresistible.

"Hot tacos. Hot tacos," Mexican José shouted as he pimp-walked into the break area. At sixty-two, José had forty-two years' seniority. He'd been selling tacos before he began his shift for the past thirty years at Champion. Rumor was that his sales totaled over a thousand dollars a week. José was living big. He drove an Incognito, Champion's most expensive sport luxury car, bought the best clothes, and had the best pussy money could buy. A few employees were jealous of the tax-free money José accumulated each week. But they weren't envious enough to stop buying his Mexican delights. Nobody made tacos like José's wife, Marisela.

Khan knew that Marisela rose at two every morning to prepare and wrap over two hundred tacos for her husband. Hours later in the plant, the spicy scent of cumin made even those who weren't hungry indulge in the hot temptations. Dozens of vending machines filled with hot coffee, cold milk, fruit juices, potato chips, candy, and other snacks were no competition for José's taco cart.

"How about you, *señorita?*" José asked in his sexy Mexican drawl. "You want two today?"

This morning Khan was tempted, but she shook her head no as she dropped two quarters into the coffee machine.

She took a seat in the break area across from the Rembrandt Imperial sewing unit she worked in. Located next to the Imperial were the Givenchy and Base Rembrandt units that took up half of the south end of the plant. Rembrandt, the top moneymaking luxury car for Champion for two decades running, was reserved for only the highly skilled sewing machine operators. Khan had begun working the unit after only one year at Champion.

In the five years she'd worked at Champion's Troy Trim plant, her routine rarely varied. In ten minutes her sewing partner, Luella, would arrive and they would head into the unit together to begin their day's production.

Several of Khan's co-workers were watching the early morning news on television sets perched high on pedestals in the break area. Khan wasn't interested. As she waited for Luella, Khan flipped open Section A of her paper, skimming more than reading. Anything was more interesting than talking to some of the other hourly workers in the plant. Usually their main topic of conversation began and ended with overtime—who got it, who needed it, and who wasn't getting any.

Sipping on a cup of black coffee, Khan turned to the business section. She began to read an article about how the Japanese were gaining market shares in the automobile industry at a faster rate than the Big Four. Because of the increased sales of utility trucks, the Japanese were implementing an aggressive campaign to capitalize on the high profit margin from these vehicles.

Mmm . . . some competition. That's something R.C. would be interested in. She missed R.C. Is that why she was reading the business section? To feel connected to him?

Khan checked her Timex, then turned to the metro section and continued reading. This morning, the comics weren't funny. And she didn't believe a word of her horoscope: *It's your kind of day. You learn secrets.*

"Bullshit."

Damn, she thought, checking her watch for the third time. It was 4:45 a.m. and still no sign of Luella, who was rarely late. Craning her neck to look down the hall, she saw familiar faces and waved hello to a few. She wanted it to be lunchtime when her shift was over. She was hoping to see R.C., who was due back in town from Japan later this morning. She needed to get home so she could freshen up and then screw his brains out.

Flipping the metro section back to its front page, she read the caption beneath a large picture in the middle of the page. The caption read: ENTREPRENEUR WEDS TOP JAPANESE FASHION MODEL. She stopped. Her heart felt as cold as a corpse. The picture was of R.C. and a woman she'd never seen before. The article read: "Mr. R.C. Richardson, 50, owner of seven Champion dealerships in the tri-county area as well as a world-renowned stud ranch in Paris, Kentucky, wed beautiful Tomiko Johnson, 22, over the weekend in Japan. The couple plan on a short honeymoon at Mr. Richardson's ranch in Paris, Kentucky. . . ."

It was as if someone had drained all the blood from her body and only the shell remained. She felt numb. Hollow. Yet her brain still functioned and was running full speed. "That lying son of a bitch!" Khan mumbled under her breath. Tears burned in her eyes like hot steam as she began to reread the article.

Khan inspected the photograph, staring at R.C.'s new

wife. In the black-and-white photo the woman, who didn't even look twenty-one years old, appeared to be of Asian and African descent. Her features were Japanese looking, but her skin tone was definitely dark.

What in the hell does she have that I don't?

Khan wadded the page into a tight ball and tossed it into the trash. R.C. had better hide, she thought, because if I see that bastard I'm going to kill him. No, killing him ain't good enough. I'm going to tie a rope around his balls, tie it to one of his cars, and drag his whorish ass down the street until he's covered with blood.

Hell yeah. That's exactly what I'm going to do. When she threw her cold coffee in the trash, her hands were shaking.

As she walked into her unit, Khan was consumed with thoughts of confronting R.C. Then again, she thought, what would be the point? She'd only lose her pride. At the supervisor's desk, a new worker was using the interplant phone— a plant no-no. Standing next to her was Valentino, Khan's first cousin.

Since early February, Valentino had been assigned to work in the Imperial sewing unit because their production volume had increased from two hundred fifty to three hundred fifty a day. Arriving at work an hour earlier than Khan, Valentino's job was to place by Khan's machine the "line-up" sheet that indicated the color and fabric (leather or cloth) and quantity of the jobs the unit would be sewing that day.

"I put today's schedule on your table already," Valentino said to Khan.

Khan swallowed back her tears and managed a small smile. "Thanks, Tino." She was amazed by her sudden, cold composure. He stepped beside her as she walked toward the front of the unit where she and Luella sewed the rear seat cushions. She stopped at her sewing table, exhaled, and talked herself into not thinking about R.C. At least not for the next five minutes. When she looked in Tino's face, she noticed his reddened eyes. "You look tired. How's Sarah and the baby?"

"Sarah's the same. But the baby is teething. We barely got any sleep this weekend."

"Didn't you work Sunday?"

"Yeah. Twelve hours in Givenchy."

Valentino was on the A-team, a clique of twelve hourly employees who worked from the front to the back of the unit and brought home anywhere from fifteen hundred to two thousand dollars a week. His job began at 4:00 A.M. chasing stock shortages, communicating schedule adjustments with shop scheduling, making sure that all of his sewers had the correct amount of stock to sew the day's production, keeping the unit clean, removing excess welt spools, thread spools, and all rubbish.

Before his day ended, Valentino would pack out all finished stock on Cooley carts, which were three-sided double-shelved metal carts that held twelve complete jobs. One job consisted of a rear cushion, rear back, two front cushions, and two front backs. He would then verify the pack-out count, submit the total to the supervisor, and finally roll the cart across the aisle to River Rouge Build.

River Rouge Build was located in the southeast corner of Troy Trim. This operation assembled the cushion covers to the front and rear cushions onto foam rubber pads and steel track frames for three of Champion's luxury car lines, Rembrandt, Syrinx, and Remington. Once they were put together these items were sent on to River Rouge Assembly to be added to the cars.

Ten years earlier, when several jobs were being sent to Mexico, Champion lost some of their main car lines. But at the same time the River Rouge Assembly Plant, which was a subdivision of Champion, was expanding. Troy Trim was always eager to bid on new jobs for Rouge Assembly. Just this year, Champion had bid on a job to house the very profitable Facial Operations, which consisted of pouring color-keyed plastic into molds that produced the facial bumpers.

As for Valentino, River Rouge proved highly lucrative for him as well.

Because they were freefloating workers, the A-team tended to get most of the overtime. Supposedly, that favoritism had stopped because of the complaints from other employees, but everyone knew that the same group of people were still getting the majority of overtime.

And Champion's hourly workers lived and fought daily for overtime. But the price was high: it reduced them to beggars. Even though the workers may not need the money, they were as obsessed with getting overtime as an angry drug addict always needing more.

Khan placed her purse beneath her table, unlocked her cabinet, and took out her sewing tools. She looked at Valentino and said, "No wonder you look beat. You're going to kill yourself working so much overtime."

It was a shame to see such a pretty man so worn out. Tino was just over six feet tall, with wide-set shoulders and a narrow frame. Most of the women in the plant thought Valentino was beautiful. Especially Luella. Until Valentino matured, Khan had never realized that one man could spend so much time apologizing for being so pretty. Even behind his glasses no one could miss the indecent length of his lashes.

As she focused on her cousin, Khan felt her own hurt over R.C. move out of the way. She and her cousin had always been close. Khan was also close to Valentino's father, Uncle Ron, who was the union boss at the Troy Trim plant. "Now, show me a picture of that baby. I know you got some new ones."

Valentino's face lit up like a river of gold when he flipped out a new photo of Jahvel from his wallet and handed it to Khan.

"Tino, if this boy gets any prettier, I'm personally launching his modeling career."

Tino flinched. A man didn't want his son to look pretty. Tino especially hated the idea that his son would inherit his problems. Being a man, and being respected, was more important—especially for a black man.

Two years ago, Valentino had been hooked on the crack pipe. He lost his job at Champion, then was fired from a bussing job at a low-end restaurant. During that trying time, his wife, Sarah, stuck with him. But when Uncle Ron finally kicked them out after Valentino stole money from him, Valentino and Sarah were homeless. Sarah soon found out she was pregnant and moved back in with her parents. They tried to convince her to abort the baby and divorce Tino. Sarah refused, and this proved to be Valentino's wake-up call. He went through drug rehab and kicked his habit. Sarah stuck it out.

"Sarah wants Jahvel to go to Harvard. Neither of us want him to become the third generation of Lamotts working in a factory." He smiled at his cousin. From the center aisle, a hi-lo driver blew his horn and signaled for Valentino.

"Hey, it's time to get to work."

"Yeah," Khan mumbled, snatching her thoughts away from R.C., "and my partner's not here yet."

Tino slid off the table. "When Luella gets in, tell her I put that stack of white front cushions on her table. I need them repaired as soon as possible. Rouge River's on my ass."

It was a typical Monday morning. Tired workers grunted their hellos and good mornings, followed by the angry whirring sound of power sewing machines gearing up. Even the machines had an attitude this morning.

Fifty-five minutes later, Khan was hunched over her machine, sweating like a mad dog poised for the kill. It had taken her less than an hour to sew up most of her float.

The power of the machine's humming vibrated from her fingers to the tips of her toes, but it hadn't done much for the throbbing pain in her head. Where was Luella? It just wasn't like her to be so late and not even call. Then Khan's thoughts returned to R.C.

Fuck it. That bastard owes me an explanation.

She reached beneath her table and retrieved her purse in search of change for the telephone. As she did so, she inhaled the unpleasant odor of a man who thought he could camouflage not taking a bath with an overdose of cologne—her supervisor, James Allister. So much for the phone call.

Scratching his head with a pencil, Allister stood by her machine with the time sheet in his hand. "Mornin', Davis. I need you to pick up two hours of production to cover Luella's job until she gets in."

Khan looked at the time sheet and rolled her eyes. Thirty years ago the union and the company had agreed to let each unit monitor the amount of overtime granted to their employees. The rule was that, while one employee might get more overtime than another, no one should ever get more than thirty-two hours ahead of the other people in the unit. Everybody kept an eye on everyone else by watching the postings that the supervisors put up near their desk every Monday. If one worker was posting eight hundred hours and another posted eight hundred and fifty, everyone knew there was a problem.

The thirty-two-hour spread was agreed to because everybody's job was so different that it was impossible to main-

tain the overtime spread any closer. The agreement was
rarely enforced until the late 1980s, when overtime started
becoming scarce. Now, everyone watched the postings like
a Budweiser lizard watching a frog. And everyone knew that
if they were offered overtime and refused it, the amount of
the hours they refused would still be added to their total
overtime hours. If someone was twenty-six hours ahead of
the others in the unit and was offered six hours of overtime,
it would put them at the limit whether they accepted the
hours or not.

The cold coins in her hands felt like hot metal against
Khan's sweaty palms. They burned with the fire she felt in
her teeth and gut. "Not today, Allister. I've got plans this
afternoon." Of course she didn't tell him that her plans had
suddenly changed: instead of spending a romantic day with
R.C., all she wanted to do was go home and cry in peace.
"Give her a few minutes. I'm sure she'll be in."

"Can't wait. I've got Rouge on my back and you're low
on hours. If you don't want the overtime, I'll have to charge
you." Allister made no attempt to hide the smirk on his
chalk-white face.

Khan turned to see that Chet, who ran the listing and welt-
cord machine in front of her, was almost out of work.
Luella's absence was stopping progress.

The scent of Allister's cheap cologne sickened her and
she turned up her nose. "Sorry. Not today," Khan said,
silently cursing Luella under her breath. Khan just couldn't
deal with more hours. She needed some time to herself.

Turning back to her machine, she sewed a few stitches in
the plastic cording, then pushed the button for the arm to cut
off the excess. Swiveling to her left side, she placed the
cypress-cloth cushion and leather facing between the welt
cord, then pushed the knee pedal to lift the foot and shoved
the stock beneath it. She could feel the thick, smooth texture

of the luxury body-cloth against the tips of her fingers as she lockstitched the top, following through to the end of the 5/8-inch sew seam. After clipping the threads, she spot-checked her work, then tossed it on the cart beside her table and noticed that her watch said six A.M. Where the hell was Luella? Khan just couldn't deal with working overtime today, of all days. She felt like she could barely make it to quitting time.

There were four more cushions left. In two minutes Khan would be out of work. Without Luella moving work down the line, Khan, like Chet, would be cooling her heels.

No such luck. Khan looked up to see Mary Kemper, a sewing operator from the Syrinx unit, sitting down at Luella's machine. Khan sighed. Mary could sew triple production, but half of it was usually garbage. The quality curve on their line would plummet today. Any other day, Khan would care. But right now, she couldn't worry about quality. She felt her problems were greater than Champion Motors.

At that precise moment, Luella was driving like Road Runner passing Wile E. Coyote on her way to work. When Luella had tried to start her car this morning, her DieHard had been as dead as yesterday. She'd waited fifty minutes for a tow truck to give her a jump, and when she finally took off for work, she was furious. At the corner of Big Beaver and Alpine, she was just a mile away from Champion. It was still raining and she was driving too fast. Her bald front tires caught an unexpected puddle and she skidded off the road, losing control. Luella crashed into the pole that supplied electricity to eight city blocks as well as to Champion Motors. The pole went down and the lines were cut, dancing in a crazy spray of deadly white light.

Khan was forcing the last two pieces of rear backs

beneath the sewing foot when the foam edges of the stock stuck on the side of the foot. With her left hand holding the stock in place, she yanked the wheel with her right hand, then pressed down on the foot pedal.

Immediately, the plant went on emergency backup power. The system provided electricity for the emergency lights and certain strategic computer systems, but no production operations.

Khan heard the sound of the generator and looked up at the blinking lights. Even without electricity, her powerful sewing machine was still moving from the force of its own momentum, sending size-ten needles piercing through her left middle finger, again and again, making a trail up past her knuckle and stopping at the center of her hand. The coarse green thread felt like a wet whip against her tender skin. Blood began to seep through the stitches, each a sixteenth of an inch apart.

"Ahhh." Khan sucked in her breath and turned her head away. "Oh Lord, what have I done! Oh my God!" She screamed.

The bluish tinge from her engagement ring was the last sparkle of light she saw before losing consciousness.

Chet hollered for a mechanic. He and Valentino worked for fifteen minutes to dismantle the machine and release her hand.

Still unconscious, Khan was whisked off to William Beaumont Hospital.

When Khan opened her eyes, it took her a moment to get her bearings. Everything around her was beige. She couldn't be in the plant. Then she inhaled the sharp smell of disinfectant and, looking around, remembered what had happened. She looked down at her hand, which was covered with blood and throbbing.

She heard the sound of footsteps coming toward her and prayed that it was R.C., that somehow he had heard of her accident and realized the mistake he'd made. Even though she knew this was foolishness, her heart sank when the doctor entered. He mumbled some medical terms to her that she didn't try to understand. What did it matter? She was injured and in pain. And the man she had loved for five years wouldn't be there to take her home.

Damn you, R.C.! her mind screamed as she felt a hypodermic needle piercing her skin.

She watched through squinty eyes as the doctor worked on her hand. Since the shot they gave her for pain didn't work, she felt every one of the thirty stitches he looped through her swollen hand. But that ordeal was nowhere near as intense as the pain in her heart.

The doctor tried to soothe her with comforting words. Still, Khan tuned him out. Her thoughts ran back to the day several years before when her Uncle Ron had told her that R.C. would never marry a factory worker. He had been right.

A spasm of pain seared through her fingers, and Khan winced in agony. By the time the shot finally began to work, the doctor was finished and her hand was bandaged.

Four hours later, Khan was back at the plant. The doctor in the medical office at Champion provided her with a slip that released her from work for the remainder of the day and put her on temporary disability until she had her stitches taken out. Though she was excused from working, she still had to report back to him on Tuesday.

By 11:40 A.M., Khan had parked her car at the Virginia Park Townhouses—home. It was nearly fifty-seven degrees and the sun was just coming out. A small wind lifted the budding branches in the front of her condominium complex, then let them fall again. The warm breeze carried the scent of spring as she placed her key in the lock and opened the door.

Once inside her compact condo, she was greeted by the sensual fragrance of French mulberry displayed in decorative wrought-iron pedestal bowls.

Wincing at the pain in her hand as she hung up her coat, the anger she had felt earlier flushed through her again like the hot flash of a woman going through menopause. She felt confused. Exactly how, she wondered, was she supposed to feel?

Disgusted with herself, she clicked on the television set and turned to BET, Black Entertainment Television. The top ten videos were on. Maybe that would change her mood.

"Ha! Ha!" the choir said.

I don't see a damn thing that's funny, Khan thought as she shed her work clothes and slipped on a pair of diamond-patterned silver and pink cotton pajamas.

"Put your hands together," she heard the choir shouting from the television at the opposite end of her apartment. They were stomping on the devil. In her mind, she envisioned R.C. Her knee twitched in anticipation. Hell, she thought. I can do better than that.

Khan tried not to look at the picture of R.C. on her dresser. The harder she tried not to look, the more it kept drawing her eyes like a magnet. Yet she couldn't put it away—not yet.

She snatched off her engagement ring, which the doctor had thoughtfully switched to her right hand, placing it in the top drawer of her dresser along with all the expensive jewelry R.C. had given her. All of it glittered and gleamed and looked as vulgar as she felt.

The photo of R.C. and his bride flashed through her mind. She removed the heavy antique silver locket from around her neck. Inside was a picture she and R.C. had taken when they were in Las Vegas.

Khan picked up the phone and dialed his home to see if his flight from Japan had arrived. She knew he was scheduled to land at 9 A.M. His maid, Bonnie, recognized Khan's voice the second she grumbled hello.

"Mr. Richardson isn't here, Ms. Khan," said Bonnie.

"When do you expect him?"

"I can't tell you that."

Of course Bonnie knew exactly where the bride and groom were. And of course she wouldn't tell Khan. Things were going to get ugly and there was no way of avoiding it.

"Tell him I called." She spoke between clenched teeth. "And Bonnie, I suggest you pull R.C.'s coattails to the side and whisper in his ear that if he doesn't call me today, I'll be on his doorstep tomorrow to kick his rusty black ass." *And that half-breed he married instead of me.*

Tears welled in her eyes as she hung up. "Ha. Ha. The joke's on me."

Her stomach grumbled and ached when she went into the bathroom to grab some tissue. Whatever pain medication they'd given her made her tongue feel thick and dry. Just then, the telephone rang.

"Hello," Khan said hesitantly, praying that it was R.C.

It was Thyme.

"Hey, girl. I heard about your accident this morning. How's my little friend faring?"

Khan felt her shoulders sinking. "Oh, okay I guess." She wiped her eyes with the tissue but the tears kept falling.

"Stomp! Stomp!" the choir said louder. "Church, are you with me? Put your hands together."

Khan punched the remote and turned off the television set. She'd had enough of feeling ridiculed. Especially by a group of folks who didn't even know her.

"Hey," Thyme said, "you sound funny."

"It's the medication," Khan lied. She inhaled and pulled herself together. "Have you heard anything about Luella? Allister told me while I was in the medical office that she was in a car accident."

Thyme laughed. "The pole she hit is in worse shape than she is. It took Detroit Edison nearly four hours to get the lights back on inside the plant. We were just about to send everyone home."

"I can imagine what all those folks were doing up there in the dark." Khan managed to laugh. "Screwing like gerbils."

"Be nice now, girl. Everyone's back to work. Even Luella."

"Great. Now Allister's probably having her do my job as well as hers. And he'll still probably charge me four hours today," Khan huffed. "Maybe if I bought that stinking bastard a bottle of Cool Water cologne he might get the point. Then again, he might try to fire my broke ass."

"Loosen up, Khan. Get some rest, and I'll be over as soon as I can. Need anything?"

"I hate to ask, but do you mind stopping at the Somerset Collection to pick me up a half-pound of Mrs. Fields oatmeal-and-raisin cookies?"

"You hate to ask? Girl, when are you going to grow up? You're just like a little kid. Just tell me what you need—I'm your friend."

Khan felt a tear touch her smile, and tucked her pajamaed legs beneath her. Never, she thought, I'm never going to grow up. That's what R.C. loved about me.

2

Thyme Tyler unlocked her desk drawer and removed the FedEx envelope. The name and address of the sender had been omitted. For at least a month she'd been waiting for this information. She could feel the perspiration itching on the tips of her fingers as she ripped open the top and removed the contents.

Inside was a list of people who worked for Champion Motors and their salaries and bonuses. Thyme's breath stalled in her throat when she heard a knock at her closed door.

With fingers as nimble as an eel, she quickly covered the FedEx package with the monthly costs sheets from the maintenance department that she was supposed to be going over.

If she couldn't trust this information being delivered to her own home, she certainly couldn't risk her secretary finding out about it.

"Dr. Tyler?" her secretary, Elaine, said as she entered after the second knock. "I'm leaving now." Elaine handed her a pink memo slip. "Your husband called while you were meeting with Mr. Lamott." Her husband, Cy, also worked for

Champion, but he worked at World Headquarters in downtown Detroit. Thyme was the plant manager at Troy Trim.

Thyme could have sworn she saw Elaine blush when she mentioned Ron Lamott's name. She'd heard there was something romantic going on between her secretary and her friend, Ron, who also happened to be union boss at the Troy Trim plant. But lately Thyme felt as if Elaine had begun spying on her. For the past month, Thyme knew, rumors had been circulating around the plant that she was going to be replaced as plant manager by the first of the year. And her secretary's actions of late made Thyme feel as if Elaine were somehow checking up on her. Would Elaine be stupid enough to put her own job in jeopardy? After all, Elaine was a single mother with a small son to raise. Could Ron use Elaine to gather company information that Thyme was privy to before she got canned? Didn't they both know that Thyme was as much in the dark as the hourly workers? She made a mental note to keep a careful eye on Elaine.

Thyme and Ron were good friends and had always respected each other—despite the fact that she was the plant manager and a non-union salaried employee. It was as if he were a Democrat and she a Republican. At the plant, Thyme and Ron were on opposite sides of a clearly drawn barbed-wire fence, but in the private sector they were friends. And although she and Ron had butted heads in the past, they had weathered many union versus company storms.

"Thanks, Elaine."

At that moment, a loud crash echoed from the company parking lot outside of Thyme's window. From Thyme's office they could see Ethel Adams' red Illusion truck just backing out of her parking spot. As both Thyme and Elaine looked on, Bill Elliot hit her from the rear with his white Algeron. After twenty-three years working in the automobile industry, Thyme identified employees by the cars they drove rather than by their names.

When Thyme turned her attention away from the scene, she noticed Elaine's eyes roving over her desk like lasers scanning, and when they met Thyme's gaze the connection was combustible.

"Is there anything else that I can do for you?"

"Call the Troy police," Thyme sighed. "Knowing Ethel, she'll be cussing Bill out until they get here. She just bought that truck last month. Then feel free to go."

Elaine smiled and left.

Thyme smelled frightened sweat—her own—and felt it slide down between her breasts as she uncovered and began to reread the material she'd so carefully hidden.

Behind her, the clock on the wall ticked like a death-watch, reminding her of the past, the present, and all that was to come.

Just before the weekend, her boss had advised her that Allied Vespa was interested in letting Troy Trim bid on a new job, and tomorrow twenty of their bigwigs were arriving to tour Thyme's plant.

She had made sure every crook and crevice in the 550,000-square-foot plant was meticulously stacked, packed, cleaned, and organized. The gray cement aisles had been waxed twice over the weekend, and all employees had been warned to keep their workstations spotless.

But Thyme couldn't shake the feeling that there was something strange going on. Ordinarily, she knew about the tours at least a month or two in advance. This was too hurried; it just didn't make sense. I smell a tamale, Thyme thought, alluding to the growing trend for Champion to siphon off Troy Trim's work to their Mexican operations. Her instincts suggested that the two situations were somehow connected.

When she questioned Cy, he seemed vague, almost evasive. As a division manager of three Champion trim plants, Cy should know what was going on. Would he keep something from her?

Twenty questions and no answers, she thought to herself.

Thyme hated Tuesdays. At least a quarter of the hourly workers who had worked fifty to eighty hours the previous week would show up Monday but take Tuesday off. Those who did show were too tired to work overtime to make up for the missing workers.

Tuesday was also the day the weekly cost meeting with all the department managers was held. Quality Control, Engineering, Production, Material Control, Accounting, and Salary Personnel all sat around the table presenting their costs for the previous week. Each department was required to operate within an allocated budget. Quality Control would often borderline on running in the red. Production was the main player, and they were in the red. Luckily, the rest of the departments usually ran in the black.

Before Thyme's trying Tuesday would end, she had to try to devise a plan to improve Production's profitability as well. It was a feat that appeared more impossible as each year of her tenure passed. But there was no way she'd quit trying; she was determined to find a way to put her plant in the black.

Thyme's job also consisted of forming product teams with at least one employee from each of the six departments. Under her supervision, those teams would work toward bringing in new jobs to Troy Trim, balancing labor costs and the cost of raw materials coming into the plant and monitoring the quality of the product going out the door. In doing so, she had to make sure that labor costs didn't exceed twenty-five percent and production costs didn't exceed seventy percent of her budget. Capital expenses took up the remainder.

Thyme resented the hierarchy at Champion. Despite her advanced degrees, she truly identified with the blue collar workers. Even though they made what the white collars referred to as "stupid money" by performing mindless tasks, they earned it twofold. Still, Thyme felt that what they sacrificed in lack of sleep and time with their families, no amount of money could replace.

Satisfied that the FedEx letter had everything she needed, she picked up the cost sheets for the potential Allied Vespa job and began cutting and pasting the figures.

Just about the time she was ready to call it quits, the telephone rang. It was Frank at River Rouge Assembly Plant, and he didn't have good news. The plant was off-line because the Delta bolts were snapping and breaking.

With the plant off-line, if the seats required for a particular vehicle were not available at the installation location for the final stage in assembling the automobile, the car had to be held in a repair area instead of moving on to Fit and Finish. Champion estimated that it cost approximately two thousand dollars per car each time this situation occurred. And Champion wasn't in the car business to lose money.

The Delta bolts they used in the passenger-side recliner arm of their luxury cars were designed to bear a certain amount of torque. But now the bolts were breaking at twenty pounds less than the required spec, and no one knew why.

As she listened to Frank complain about the costs, Thyme searched her computer and found that it was possible the entire shipment of bolts received in Troy Trim's system on Thursday was defective. That meant at least one thousand seats couldn't be fitted.

"How soon can you get another supply of bolts?" Frank asked Thyme.

"I'll have to make a call to our supplier in Georgia, then get back with you."

When she hung up, she dialed the supervisor in Rouge Build. "Cindy, we've got a problem with the Delta recliner bolts. Check the lot numbers 47,555 through 48,555 and pull them out; they appear to be defective."

Next she called Quality Control. They took forever to answer. "Hello, Sam. Problems with the Delta bolts. Send a couple people down to Rouge Build to remove the defective bolts. Cindy has the lot numbers. Then take them to rejected parts in the holding area. It's late, so I won't be down there until tomorrow."

Damn! The tour tomorrow! By then there would be dozens of luxury seats lined up in the east aisleways, blocking all who passed.

When she finally got the Georgia supplier on the line and told him that she needed a shipment tonight, he politely told her that they couldn't possibly be flown into Metro Airport until seven in the morning.

Thyme needed the bolts by four A.M. Everybody was always in a rush. Time was money.

She called Frank back and told him when the bolts would be in.

"We've got seats stacked up in the warehouse that will have to be refitted," Frank said.

Thyme could hear the frustration in his voice but there wasn't much she could do at this point. "Frank, the best thing I can do is send two utility workers down in the morning to retrofit the seats. That's the best I can do." This would mean sending workers to an out-of-line location—another loss of money. The pressure was building.

Thyme was exhausted. She took a deep breath, closed her eyes, and said a silent prayer. After a few minutes she began gathering her papers and put them in her briefcase. She looked up at the plaques and awards that covered all four of her office walls. From associate to doctorate, every aspect of her education and employment with Champion was documented. Filling in the spaces were dozens of pictures of Thyme as she received awards for service and charity work. Only one photo showed her private life: the wedding picture of herself and her husband, Cy, that occupied the left corner of her desk.

Was it all worth it? she wondered. In a few months she would know.

She turned off her computer and put on her London Fog trench coat. With the contents of her future tucked between her breast and her armpit, Thyme left her office and headed down the hall toward the exit.

Located just adjacent to the door leading outside to the parking lot was the ten-bay truck dock where they loaded and unloaded purchase parts. The heavy scent of gasoline was a constant reminder of where she worked: in an automobile plant.

Ordinarily, plant managers were required to put in or be accessible for at least twelve hours daily. Today Thyme had worked thirteen. It was 6:01 P.M. when she backed her silver Presidio out of the spot bearing her rank and name: PLANT MANAGER—TYLER.

As she drove toward Khan's neighborhood on the west side of Detroit, Thyme's thoughts ran back to the tour in the morning. Apparently, Allied was interested in having Troy Trim build the front seat components in their 1999 Pantheon sports car. Okay, but why Champion? Thyme knew that General Motors had already submitted a good bid for the same job. It didn't make sense that Allied would also come to Champion.

After Thyme purchased cookies for Khan, she called Cy

at his office and then at home. He wasn't at either. She'd try again later.

It was dark as a thief's pocket when she parked by the neighborhood party store close to Khan's house. She could smell the thick fragrance of rain in the air the moment she stepped outside the car.

Once inside the party store, she paused to view a new selection of wines: Medalla Real Private Reserve Cabernet and a Rodney Strong Sonoma County Chardonnay. Out of the corner of her eye, she noticed two rough-looking men enter the store. Their eyes seemed riveted on her clothes and jewelry. Suddenly nervous, Thyme gave them a Don't-fuck-with-me-today-boys stare until they finally turned away.

Thyme purchased the Medalla and Rodney, a fifth of Chivas Regal for her husband, and also a bottle of '92 Beringer Cabernet Sauvignon Private Reserve, her favorite, and left the store. The tension of tomorrow's meeting had caused her body temperature to rise above normal. She could feel the edges of her neat wrap hairstyle rolling back like Buckwheat's in the *Little Rascals*.

Slow down, girl. You don't have time for a trip to the beauty parlor in the morning. And you know you can't perm or hot-comb your own hair.

Turning down Virginia Park where Khan lived, she could see half-dressed young men from fourteen to thirty running, cursing, and shouting along the lighted basketball court. It was a sight Thyme rarely saw in the suburbs, and it brought back memories of when she was in high school.

Even though the evenings were cool for April, the sound of kids in the neighborhood seemed to warm the early spring air, and the excitement of the young voices was infectious. And as Thyme shut her car door, she breathed in the sweetening air and tried to let go of some of her heavy burden.

Was she really going to be forty-five in August? Lately she felt as if she were turning sixty.

With packages in hand, Thyme took a final glance over her shoulder at the young men playing pickup ball. Turning away, she climbed the short set of stairs and rang the doorbell.

Khan opened the door, wearing the exact pair of pajamas that she had given Thyme for Christmas.

"Hey, girl," Thyme said, hugging Khan. She stood back and appraised her, then reached for her friend's arm. "Are you still in pain?"

"Naw. Just a little sleepy from the painkillers," she said, yawning and beckoning Thyme inside. "Mmmm," Khan said, grabbing the familiar red and white bag of Mrs. Fields cookies from Thyme's hand. "I can smell the raisins and brown sugar."

"Good. Dig in. I need to make a call." Thyme removed her coat and tossed it on the chair.

Moving toward the small kitchen area, Thyme followed Khan and watched her count our four cookies and pour herself a glass of milk. When Thyme removed a bottle of wine from the other paper bag, Khan didn't hide her displeasure. Thyme knew that Khan had become particularly sensitive to other people drinking alcohol because R.C. had a bit of a problem.

"You know I don't own any wineglasses."

Noticing a stack of paper cups near the refrigerator, Thyme removed one while she dialed her home number. "It's okay—I'll just pour it in one of these." After four rings, the voice mail came on and Thyme's frown mirrored Khan's. "Cy, this is Thyme, honey. I'm at Khan's. I'll be home around nine. Love you, baby."

When Thyme hung up, she noticed the forlorn look on Khan's face. From their years of friendship, Thyme knew that Khan was suffering from something more serious than a hurt hand. It appeared to be more like a hurt heart.

From the narrow kitchen, Thyme admired the beautiful aquarium in Khan's eccentric apartment. She knew that the aquarium and the exotic tropical fish were a prized gift from R.C. to Khan. The enormous glass case took up half the west wall. Though Thyme had never met R.C., she had drawn some conclusions about the man Khan was so hopelessly in love with. R.C. had always seemed a bit flashy, and Thyme got the sense that he hid behind his big gifts.

Thyme looked around at Khan's brightly colored apartment and smiled at her friend's indomitable spirit. Mango and tangerine walls made striking statements next to the strawberry, electric grape, and lemon yellow furniture. Not even the bathroom was spared. The clawfoot tub was painted a ripe persimmon, leaving the feet white, against one wall of deep purple and another painted in a diamond pattern of dark and light violet. A yellow-and-white-plaid shower curtain stood out boldly beside coral and purple towels.

Every time Thyme visited Khan's home, her heart said "Wow," and her mind wished that she felt comfortable with so much color. Thyme had to give her friend credit; the fruity hues juiced up the tiny condo and seemed to capture the ever-present child in Khan. For all of Thyme's success, she envied her friend and wished that she had the nerve to paint her walls in lively colors and decorate her place with so much freedom.

Thyme and Khan settled into the lemon-colored loveseat in the living area to enjoy their treats, Khan with a glass of cold milk and cookies and Thyme sipping on a second cup of wine.

Feeling herself relax for the first time that day, Thyme kicked off her red pumps and eased back into the soft cushions. "Before I could even read the incident report about your accident today, your uncle Ron was in my office with a health and safety violation."

"Uncle Ron. Why? It was my fault. I wasn't paying attention to what I was doing."

"Not necessarily. This is the fifth incident we've had in two weeks with the Zori sewing machines. Ron believes that the foot on the Zori three-elevens—"

"Are poorly designed," Khan finished. "When Chet and Valentino got my hand out, they said the angle of the foot came out too high. It should be more level. Anyway, Uncle Ron wrote up that grievance. I didn't tell him to—"

"Don't worry about it. Right now safety is the second biggest concern at Champion. Overtime, as you know, has always come first. But by the end of the month the national negotiations with the unions will be getting underway and we don't need all these safety problems adding to the pressures of local bargaining issues. They give you blue collars more chips to play with." Thyme didn't mention what she felt was her other big priority: the increasing number of violent outbreaks among the blue collar workers.

Thyme and Khan had always managed to have a close friendship despite their differences. Thyme was especially grateful that their relationship transcended the chasm between white and blue collar workers. Thyme had met Khan at a barbecue at Ron's house when the girl was just sixteen. Khan was visiting her uncle from her home down South. Thyme had immediately been impressed with Khan's clear ambition to succeed in life; so much about her had reminded Thyme of herself at that awkward age.

But ever since Khan had dropped out of college, lured by Champion's high wages for hourly work in the plant, Thyme couldn't help but feel that Khan wasn't working up to her potential. Thyme did her best to hide her disappointment from Khan and instead gently encouraged her to go back to school and finish her degree. Khan was just too damn smart to work in a factory.

Thyme worried for her young friend. Khan seemed especially distracted tonight, which made Thyme even more concerned. She watched as Khan looked again at the phone, as if willing it to ring.

"Thank God Luella's accident wasn't on company property," Thyme said.

"So Uncle Ron has a legitimate gripe?"

"Always. He's well informed. Ron's the best plant union chairman we've had. He's a tough negotiator, but he's fair. He really cares about his union members. I'm not just saying this because he's your kin."

Khan set the remainder of cookies and milk beside her on the side table, and when she glanced in Thyme's direction, her beautiful face was streaked in pain.

"Khan, is something else bothering you? You don't seem like yourself, and I don't just mean the accident."

Khan's voice was flat. "Remember I told you about the first time I knew I was in love with R.C.?"

"Yeah, your exact words were: 'The love I feel for R.C. calls me like the scent of a budding magnolia tree calls to bees.' "

"You remember?"

"Certainly. You were only nineteen, and I was convinced that you had no idea what love meant."

"That's what Mama Pearl said, too," Khan said dejectedly. Thyme had heard Khan speak many times of her grandmother, Mama Pearl, who had raised Khan after both her parents died when she was just a child.

"That was five long years ago. Maybe both you and Mama Pearl were right. Mama Pearl thought that R.C. was too old for me. She said that if we ever had children, the baby girl would be born gray-headed, or the male child would come out with a full beard and mustache." Khan laughed. "And of course they'd be wrinkled from head to toe." Her huge dark brown eyes darkened and her voice became more serious. "I didn't really care, though."

Thyme kept silent. One subject she rarely broached was having children. It was a touchy one between her and Khan. Neither agreed with the other's point of view. Thyme had never wanted children; Khan felt that a woman's life was incomplete without motherhood. Cy tended to agree with Khan. When Thyme would tell him that she needed more time to be somebody, he'd tell her that having a child would never take away from what she wanted to do with her own life. But Thyme didn't trust that; she believed that children would always come first and her own goals would get lost in the shuffle.

Silence enveloped the two women while they pondered their own thoughts for a moment. Then Khan went over to the aquarium and watched the graceful movements of the brilliantly colored fish.

"I know y'all thought that Mommy forgot to feed her babies," Khan said to the fish. "Come on up here, Felix—it's time to eat. Hurry up now, Slowpoke, before the rest of 'em eat up all the food." She sprinkled the food on the water.

Thyme could see the reflection of Khan's serene smile.

"Did you know, Thyme, that fish are the only backboned animals with two-chambered hearts?"

Thyme wasn't sure why, but she couldn't answer. Maybe it was the wine. Maybe it was the fish that Khan seemed to love like her own children. Then again, maybe it was her heart trying to tell her something.

"Imagine that. And that bastard I was in love with tried to break the only one God gave me." Khan paused and then turned and faced Thyme. "There's something I've wanted to tell you. Last Christmas, I found out I was pregnant. Four days later, I turned twenty-four. Some birthday gift, huh?"

"Why didn't you tell me?" Thyme asked, trying to push away her hurt feelings.

Khan shrugged. "What was the point? R.C. hadn't asked me to marry him. And when I told him that I didn't believe in abortions, our relationship began to change. I saw less of him then. That is, until I miscarried last month. Still, things just weren't right between us."

"I take it R.C. doesn't want any children?"

"No." Khan moved away from the fish tank and sat down opposite Thyme.

Thyme reached for her friend's hand. "But I thought things between you and R.C. were good—you always talk about how much in love you two are."

"Two weeks ago, when he was getting ready to leave for Japan, I started giving him a hard time about our relationship. The night before he left, he presented me with a small sapphire engagement ring. There was no fanfare, no kisses, hugs, no lovemaking. I was expecting a diamond solitaire—a big one." Khan stopped. Her voice was quivering when she spoke again. "I should have known then that something was wrong. When he gave it to me, he said, 'Hey, pretty girl, you start looking for the skimpiest little wedding dress you can find. It's hot as hell in Kentucky around August.'"

"And?"

"Haven't you read today's papers? R.C. got married."

"Are you kidding me?"

"Hell no." Khan looked toward the phone. Her eyes seemed to be begging it to ring. "He married some cute chick while he was in Japan. They're spending their honeymoon at his ranch in Kentucky." Reaching for another cookie, Khan frowned, and tossed it back into the bag. "I know that Uncle Ron, Mama Pearl, and even you didn't approve of the relationship. But I saw something in him none of you did. We were good for each other. And I'm not just talking about the bedroom, either."

"I know what you mean," Thyme said. "No one thought that my marriage to Cy would last this long either. Especially Sydney." Sydney was Thyme's sister-in-law, Cy's twin sister. Thyme's thoughts drifted to Sydney, who was unaware that prejudice squints when it looks and lies when it talks. Then Thyme looked at Khan and said, "Now it's my turn to confess: I've filed a discrimination lawsuit against Champion."

"Really? Why?" Khan looked surprised.

"When I was promoted to plant manager at Troy Trim four years ago, there were twenty-five hundred employees. I was hired to bring in new business to increase production. Now there are only twenty-one hundred employees at Troy Trim. The rest have been permanently laid off."

"Tell me about it. It's all you hear about at the plant. Everyone's scared they're going to be next."

"Your Uncle Ron's always on my back to do something about Troy Trim's obvious streamlining." Thyme sighed. "I realized after a while that I was being pressured to increase production and reduce people. How could I satisfy you union people and still make money? It's a squeeze play: there is no way for me to do my job successfully. I began to wonder if I was given this position to get rid of me, force me out."

"Damn, Thyme, you can handle it. Every time I see you in the plant, you're wearing a bad-ass suit, some bad-ass shoes, and shaking that bad-ass wrap hairstyle of yours. I tell some of my co-workers in the unit when you walk by, 'See that fine sister? She's my friend. And one day I'm going to be just like her.'"

Even though her skin was a deep shade of chocolate, Thyme was sure she blushed.

"You know how hard I've pushed you about getting your degree so that you could get ahead in the business world. A degree counts. It states who you are. How hard you've worked to become who you are now. All that's great, but in my ignorance I thought that a degree and hard work alone would gain me access to Champion's upper echelon. I know now it won't. Get this: Ten years ago management stipulated that salaried employees who were seeking a promotion should have a college degree."

"So what's the problem? You've got a Ph.D.—"

"It hasn't done me a damn bit of good. Somewhere someone wrote in that policy that everyone with a B.A. was eligible except for Thyme Tyler." Thyme needed to be careful here. Although Thyme wanted to tell her the facts, she didn't want to discourage Khan from finishing her degree in communications. "I've lost several promotions over the past ten years. The company isn't aware how much I know about the salaried employees they've promoted over me."

"What I'm hearing is that even though you're qualified, they've promoted less qualified folks than you?"

"Exactly."

"Then it's a race issue." Khan paused and then said, "And why are you pushing me to go crazy over a piece of paper that could possibly have no meaning?"

"Because you need it. We're not given the proper respect without it. Not out there in the white world where it counts." Thyme downed the last of her wine and went into the kitchen crumpling her paper cup. "And if my attorney is as good as he says he is"—she tossed the cup into the trash can—"I'm going to get paid big-time because of it." A basket. She made it.

"You're going public?"

"Amen."

"How does Cy feel about this?"

Thyme hedged. "We discussed my being pissed off about the promotions a while back. He thinks it's a mistake. Cy feels that to make a fuss would ruin my career."

"You said the suit was big. I'm assuming we're talking a million dollars?"

"Maybe. Most likely between seven hundred fifty—"

"Fuck the career. With that much money, you can quit Champion and do something on your own."

"The money is not the point. I grew up at Champion. Besides, Cy works there too."

"The perils of plant life," Khan said, sighing dramatically. "The whole company seems to be turning on its head. Tell me, Thyme, do you think we'll strike in September? Uncle Ron won't say."

"I doubt it. As you probably know, *Motor Trend* picked the Chrysler Incognito as the car of the year and now they can't build that car fast enough. The waiting period is nine months for all new orders. My guess is that Chrysler is going to be the next strike target because they'll be under so much pressure."

Khan tried to whistle, but her mouth was stuffed with cookie crumbs.

"But haven't you and Cy ever argued over the fact that even though you have a Ph.D. and he only has a B.A., he makes twice as much money as you do?" Thyme and Khan had always been remarkably open about money. And occasionally about issues of race.

"No."

"Even though you know it has to do with the fact that he's white and you're black." This was a statement, not a question. Before Thyme could answer, Khan spoke up. "I'm sorry—just because my relationship is over doesn't give me the right to try and create problems in your marriage."

Thyme knew that Khan had learned to be especially attuned to racism, having grown up in Itta Bena, Mississippi.

"What did Mama Pearl used to tell you?"

Khan smiled and said, emphasizing her southern drawl, "If you ain't light, bright, and damned near white, you ain't worth nothing."

"And you know your Mama Pearl don't speak unless she knows it's the truth."

The silence between them was awkward for a moment while Thyme put her shoes back on. "Look, Thyme, you've always been everything that I want to become." Khan paused and took a breath. "But when I wanted to come by for a quick visit the other day, I was stopped at the gate."

"I've been meaning to talk to Cy about it. I've got to get you the code so that won't ever happen again."

"Hell. You know I'd love to be living large like you two in the Bloomies. Waking up to birds singing good morning. Crickets whispering good night. Hell, last time I was there I thought I'd entered never-never land. But now since my man done left me, I don't stand a chance. I'll never be able to afford that shit."

Khan sounded bitter and a touch resentful. Thyme hesitated before saying anything. This was touchy ground between them, and Thyme didn't want to seem defensive about Cy being white.

Khan shook her head and then said, "So how's the white brother holding up in the bedroom?"

"My mama told me to never discuss my man's theatrics in the bedroom with another woman. I'd live to regret it." Thyme tried to smile and defuse the tension between them.

"But girlfriend, I don't have no interest in a white man.

Nothing personal, but I don't believe that a white brother can come nowhere near to making love correctly." Khan cupped her buttocks with her good hand. "I'm talking about fucking, not oral sex."

"Someone gave you the wrong information, my young friend. White men hang as long and as hard as black men. Don't be fooled by myths." Thyme went back into the kitchen and placed the half-empty bottle of wine in a bag. "I know I'm acting like a ghetto girl, but since you don't drink, it would be stupid of me to leave it." She smiled, then became more serious. "Sex is the least of what's between me and Cy. It's much more than that."

Thyme couldn't help but smile as she watched Khan, who wasn't even five feet tall, move around in the kitchen, cleaning off counters and washing out the few dirty dishes left in the sink. She looked like a child trying to play house, a miniature Barbie.

"So . . . getting back to the lawsuit, do you think you're being discriminated against because you're a woman or because you're black?"

"To tell you the truth, Khan, I'm not sure, but I can hear the question you're afraid to ask: Why did I marry a white man? I think what we need is to come together in a joint effort—black, white, men, women—and to fight for what's right: equality." Thyme laughed and then said, "That's the bullshit I tell everyone else. The simple fact is Cy has *pash*. He could flirt with an entire room full of women at one time, and each woman would feel special—which doesn't bother me, because I know he only has eyes for me."

Khan was frowning, a sure signal that it was time for Thyme to go home. Thyme got her car keys out of her purse, saying, "Maybe I should go. It's been a long day for both of us." She moved toward the door and cracked it open. The fresh air felt invigorating and she could smell the rain in the darkness.

"I'm hearing two things, Thyme. First, apparently Cy doesn't know you're going forward with the lawsuit. And second, he doesn't realize how strongly you feel about the discrimination issue at Champion. If your marriage is so secure, how can you keep secrets like that? Secrets are as bad as lies."

Thyme's voice broke. "It's the first time I've ever lied to him about anything."

"I don't know, girl. I think you should clue the white brother in. This type of shit may come back to haunt you one day," Khan said in a warning voice.

Thyme said solemnly, "Sometimes you got to eat a little shit and act like you like it."

3

As the moon fell behind the clouds, the first signs of dawn lit the Kentucky sky with hints of purple, orange, and yellow. Some of Kentucky's finest thoroughbreds, housed in R.C. Richardson's stables, were sniffing the early morning air, breathing in the honey-sweet of April apple blossoms.

Tomiko lay asleep, her cheek resting against her husband's shoulder blade, her arms making a necklace around his waist. They'd been at R.C.'s Paris, Kentucky, ranch for almost a week, and each night felt like their first together. Last night they'd made passionate love in a new way.

The first words out of her spouse's mouth the night before had been "Baby, there ain't no directions."

Placing her empty champagne glass on the fireplace mantel, Tomiko had presented R.C. with the Let's Celebrate Kit—For Lovers Only, a good-luck gift she'd received from her girlfriend in Japan. Tomiko wanted to impress R.C. and show him that she could be adventurous in bed.

Tomiko had been dressed in a sexy red satin teddy, and R.C. wore matching red satin boxers. They'd sat down on the bedroom floor in front of the blazing fire and R.C. began to look through the cleverly wrapped box, which contained wild berry body dust; pina colada warming oil; tropical fruit love gelee; strawberry kissing potion; lickable cherry body paint; strawberry whipped creme; China musk massage oil; aromatherapy bubble bath; a bag of confetti; a red, heart-shaped candle; a white feather; and two balloons.

"Come on, Tomiko," R.C. had said impatiently, "let's get in the bed."

"This stuff smells good," Tomiko had said in a throaty whisper as she'd sprayed the strawberry whipped creme into two pink clouds over both of R.C.'s nipples.

Looking down at himself, R.C. had laughed. "Is it my turn now?"

Before she knew it, R.C. had sprayed the remainder of the can of whipped creme all over his wife, then proceeded to sprinkle her with the wild berry body dust. Minutes later, they were having a ball, but the room had been a wreck.

"Are we through playing?" R.C. had said fondly as he picked confetti from Tomiko's hair. "Can we fuck now?"

"Only if I can get on top," she'd said, popping the yellow and blue balloons taped on her breasts. As they'd made their way to the bed, they'd left a trail of red underwear along the floor.

"Wait," she'd said in a husky whisper. "I forgot something." She had gone back and retrieved the white feather tickler and teased the length of his eager sex. "We might need this."

Once in bed, R.C. had taken Tomiko in his arms and kissed behind her ears and down the nape of her neck, arousing her. As R.C.'s tongue had slid inside her mouth, still sweet with the taste of wild berries, she'd reached down and caressed his hardened member.

Opening her eyes now, then slowly closing them, she was reminded of their lovemaking once again as she pressed her nude body closer to her husband's. Oh my, Tomiko thought, as her thoughts drifted back to the feather, who would have thought it could do so much. . . .

Suddenly, her reverie was interrupted by a harsh knock at their bedroom door.

"Mr. Richardson! Mr. Richardson! Get up!"

R.C. jumped out of bed and began searching for his red satin robe.

"What is it, Caleb?" he shouted as he stumbled over one of his slippers.

Tomiko knew that Caleb was the man who worked with R.C.'s prized horses.

"Got a problem out at the stables, boss."

As her eyes adjusted to the darkness, Tomiko slowly made out the shapes of the room: the lovers' kit littering the floor, the empty champagne glasses, the scented joss sticks on the nightstand, her red satin teddy a few hand prints away. Tomiko also noticed the still-nude form of her husband. Looking at him now, she almost laughed. She hadn't noticed before how oddly his buttocks were shaped. His broad, heart-shaped rear end with strong, narrow legs and dark-chestnut coloring looked much like those of the horses he bred. From the waist down, R.C. was the color of an ashy Andalusian. Even his wide, bulbous nose was shaped like a mare's buttocks. Yet her husband, who had just turned fifty years old, was devastatingly handsome.

Struggling to slip on his robe but not quite making it, R.C. poked his head outside the door.

Tomiko raised up cautiously on her elbows and listened with her eyes as well as her ears.

"Wicked Widow is in labor."

"Did you call the vet?"

Since her father also bred horses, Tomiko had grown up around the beautiful animals and knew when she heard the sound of the groom's voice that something was wrong. She also knew it was unusual for foals to be born on a farm set up to breed studs. A horse breeder's primary business was to use his stud's talents by impregnating mares for a large fee. Apparently R.C. was more ambitious than most. He owned two top thoroughbreds: Reverse Richard and Oxford's Fool. Both were the foals of recently retired Triple Crown winners. Their stud fee was fifty thousand dollars. One prize stud could accommodate over one hundred mares in a season. Since he became the sole owner of the Paris farm eleven years earlier, borrowing money from his old buddy Oxford, he'd told her he'd purchased five broodmares for his private use. He planned on racing the two-year-olds sired by his own studs in Japan. It was clear to Tomiko that between the horses and the car dealerships, R.C. couldn't help but make loads of money.

"It's bad, R.C. The birth is breech. The mare is straining real bad. You could lose both the mare and the foal."

Wrapping the sheet around her, Tomiko jumped from the bed and threw on her clothes. "Is the foal early?"

"Yes."

Caleb explained to them that the regular veterinarian was out of town and his office was sending his replacement.

Within minutes, they were at the stable door, roughly three hundred feet from the main house.

Standing sixteen hands high, Wicked Widow was a black beauty. Her coat the color of expensive black mink, the horse was a testament to her pedigree. The Wicked in her name was an allusion to her temperament.

"We can't just watch her die," Tomiko said, alarmed. "She's suffering."

"Where the hell is the vet on call?" R.C. asked as he paced the floor outside the stall.

Caleb shrugged nervously as he tried to calm the mare.

"He was on his way over an hour ago. Shoulda been here by now. It's nearly six A.M."

"Can I help?" Tomiko asked.

No one paid her any attention.

"Don't worry," Tomiko said, easing into the stall and dropping to her knees, "I know what to do."

R.C. looked frantic. "What if the foal doesn't make it?"

Tomiko wasn't sure whether R.C. was worried about the mare or his financial investment. She tried to think about what her stepfather would do at this moment. She knew that the mare was a side issue, and that she had to focus on delivering the foal. Once the foal was taken care of, then her stepfather would tend to the mare.

"Let me help you," Caleb said to Tomiko.

Tomiko stroked the mare's neck. "You can hold the mare steady while I turn the foal around." She eased down on the bank of hay to lie next to the horse. Tense minutes passed as Tomiko worked feverishly with the mare, her hands up the birth canal.

For a moment, she locked eyes with R.C. They both understood that Tomiko was fighting to save the foal's life. It was going to be the mother or the child. There was no way they would both live.

When the mare began to groan and kick, R.C. looked away. Seconds later, when the mare's screams heightened, he turned back again. "What's taking that damn doctor so long?" R.C. snapped at Caleb.

"He's already too late." Caleb's jaw muscles flexed as he struggled to hold the mare's head still. "There now, girl. Hold steady now," he said as he watched Tomiko work inside her.

Wicked Widow strained and trembled, her movements becoming increasingly restless. She groaned and convulsed in severe pain. Her shiny coat was swathed with sweat.

"You should leave, R.C.," Tomiko whispered. "You're scaring her." Her arms were coated with blood and she could see both fear and disgust in R.C.'s eyes. "This is your first birth, isn't it?" she asked him.

R.C. didn't bother to answer. At this moment, his clothes were soaked clear through.

What difference did it make now? she thought. The foal was almost here. He would either faint or leave. She pushed away her own disgust at her husband's reaction to his beloved horse.

And just as the sun rose on that early spring morning, a beautiful black foal was born, and its finger-warming breath caressed Tomiko's cheek.

Wicked Widow blinked twice, groaning a sigh of relief. The struggle was over.

Tomiko looked at her husband and saw not a hint of compassion in his eyes. It made her sad to think how cold he could be toward something he treasured—at least financially. When their eyes met, he looked away.

R.C. checked his watch. "Time to go, baby. I've got to be out of the house by eight. I'm hoping to make a million today at the Blue Grass Stakes at Keeneland."

At that moment, the mare collapsed, her eyes glazed over in a dead stare.

"Have her body taken away as soon as the rest of the men are in, Caleb. We might get a hundred dollars for her. And tell that vet when he shows up I'd better not see this visit on my bill."

Tomiko's eyes filled with tears as she looked from the dead mother to her newborn child.

Gripping the teat between her index finger and thumb, Tomiko offered the foal a milk-soaked finger, moistening its lips to give it a taste of the milk. She felt the foal give a tentative suck against her fingers. The eager foal stretched out its tongue and bent the edges upward, forming a channel.

Tomiko grabbed the bottle left at the top of the stall, which Caleb must have seen to in case of just such an emergency. Gripping the makeshift teat between her index finger and thumb, she squeezed and produced a dribble of milk, persuading the foal to get accustomed to bottle-feeding.

When she returned to the house, R.C. was showering.

Tomiko retired to their bedroom, exhausted from the morning's events. She knew that R.C. expected her to accompany him to the seventy-fourth running of the Mishimoto Blue Grass Stakes in Lexington, an event that was sponsored annually at Keeneland Race Track. One million dollars was guaranteed to three-year-olds on a 1⅛-mile course.

"Tomiko," R.C. said, shaking his wife's narrow shoulder. She had fallen asleep. "It's time to go."

Tomiko looked at the clock and saw that it was nearly eight o'clock.

"No, no. I can't," Tomiko mumbled.

R.C. urged, running his hand over the expanse of her hips, "Come on, baby. We can't miss the first race. I can feel it— my luck is high."

"You go," Tomiko said in a thick voice, "I want to check on the foal. What if she stops feeding from the bottle? Her mother's gone. One of us needs to be there."

Angrily, R.C. said, "Caleb can take care of the foal. Come on, Tomiko. Get dressed. We could win enough money today to buy ten more Wicked Widows."

Tomiko remembered what she had been taught: It is the duty of the wife to obey her husband. She got up, showered and dressed quickly and quietly, and left with R.C. for the racetrack.

On the way, she tried to feed off of his energy, but wasn't successful. She kept thinking of the mare's dead eyes.

The moment they entered the lower level of the racetrack, Tomiko could tell that her husband felt at home. At ten A.M., the grandstand was over half full. Anxious, middle-aged, blue collar men and women stood in lines at betting windows fifteen to twenty deep, waiting to hand over most of their paychecks for tickets that wouldn't be worth a copper penny in five minutes. "We'll get our seats first, then come back down to place our bets," R.C. told Tomiko as they climbed the stairs to the second level, clearly the more exclusive area, reserved for heavy bettors.

Inside the stadium, where bets were placed, Tomiko watched as men stood in front of eight television screens screaming, entranced by the action. Their faces changed from hopeful to hesitant to desperate to despairing. Tomiko had seen it all at home in Japan.

Tomiko could hear their voices debating the odds. The serious bettors hunched over papers, track records, lineage, jockey history, reports on the track conditions, owners, trainers, and so on.

How could R.C. enjoy this? These people were empty.

Fans were filling the stadium faster than roaches running from a housefire. Even though it wasn't quite eleven A.M., the smell of fresh popcorn, peanuts, and bitter beer filled the air.

"I don't want to bet, R.C." Tomiko's words were lost in the sound of pre-race chatter.

Over a million and a half dollars were being bet today, R.C. had told her. What Tomiko couldn't know was that R.C. counted on winning, in fact had to win, at least two hundred thousand dollars. After buying Tomiko a large diet Sprite, he left her to place his bets.

When he returned, the horses began lining up in the starting gate, and R.C. and Tomiko took their seats near the window on the second level.

Next to them a man with a program clenched tightly in his hand spoke through gritted teeth. "Let's do it, Ice Chaser!" he yelled.

Tomiko felt R.C. tense beside her. "Did you bet on her, R.C.?"

"Damn right. Seventy-five grand. And if that bitch loses today . . ."

Tomiko whistled under her breath. "I didn't know you'd risk that much on one horse."

R.C. was smiling now; the mare was steady at the gate and the race was about to begin. "You might as well know now. I bet big and I win big."

"And when you lose?"

Her husband ignored her as the crowd stood and shouted. Have No Doubt was ahead at the quarter mile, Only Action was in second, and Ice Chaser was close behind. By the time they reached the half-mile, Ice Chaser was coming from behind to battle Have No Doubt. R.C. was jumping up and down like a five-year-old on a pogo stick.

In a wink of an eye, Ice Chaser pulled out in front by a head. The screaming escalated. Just as suddenly, the mare stumbled and fell, the jockey tumbling off the horse. Silence fell across the stadium. The tickets R.C. had been clutching so feverishly slipped from his fingers and scattered like lice on the cement floor. Simultaneously, R.C.'s cell phone rang.

Though he spoke in whispers, Tomiko heard R.C. explaining to the person on the other end of the phone that he'd make up the loss before the day was out. Tomiko couldn't believe that he wasn't concerned about the mare or the jockey. It was like a repeat of earlier this morning. Was she the only one who saw the horses as breathing beings rather than pieces of profitable meat?

Tomiko watched R.C. as he spoke frantically into the cell phone. Was this who she'd married?

R.C. was more than twenty-five years older than she, but they'd known each other since she'd been a young teenager. He'd come around to her stepfather's stables, wanting to get into the horse business. She had followed the handsome black man around the horse farm and he had paid special attention to her.

When he visited three years ago, she had become a woman and suddenly R.C. looked at her differently. At first they had dated in secret. He had swept her off her feet. She'd never before met a man who was both so romantic and sophisticated. All the young Japanese men she'd dated had been stiff and formal. Tomiko had clung to R.C.'s expansiveness as if he were a life raft in a cold dark sea.

He'd told her tales of America, the rolling hills of his horse farm, his beautiful home in Michigan, and she'd become entranced. She shared with him her dream to become a fashion model and he promised her that, with his help, she could be a fashion star in both the United States and Europe.

R.C. was the first person she'd become close with who shared her black heritage: her mother had kept her away from her black father's parents, her grandparents. Tomiko knew her mother was ashamed that her daughter was half black. R.C. was the first man to make her feel beautiful rather than strange with her deep olive skin tone and wild, crinkly hair.

Up until then, she had only felt different. Most of the people in Japan shunned her. She remembered a conversation she'd had with her mother when she reached puberty.

"You're not a baby anymore, Tomiko. Soon you'll be old

enough to marry a fine young man. Possibly someone from the Sugimoto family."

"The Sugimoto boys don't like me. They tease me because of my dark skin."

"Oh, but that will pass. They will soon see how beautiful you are. And all else will be forgotten."

"But Mother, why can't I marry someone of my father's race? A black man."

"Now you hush. Don't you let your stepfather hear you talk that way. You are Japanese. Not black."

"Then why do we speak English, Mother?"

"Because we make our living with horses and must deal with the Americans." Her voice was insistent: *"Shumatsu ni nani o shimasu ka."*

"Nichi-yobi ni tomodachi to kabuki o mimasu," Tomiko answered.

"Ii desu ne." Her mother smiled. "See? You haven't forgotten our language."

"No, Mother." She lowered her eyes before speaking. "But I'd still love to go to America one day."

Her mother's voice was bitter. "Listen to me, Tomiko. I regret marrying your father. Never will I agree to let you sell your soul to those black devils."

"Is that why the kids at school ask to see my tail? Because they think that black people are devils?"

"Tomiko! Why do you tell such tall tales!"

"I speak the truth, Mother. They tease me about how long my tail is. Especially the Sugimoto boys."

"They're just jealous. You listen to your mother. You are beautiful and someday you will be successful because of it. Then these children will beg for your friendship."

But Tomiko had defied her mother. She kept her relationship secret until one day her mother confronted her.

"Tomiko, Mrs. Hashimoto has told me that she has seen you with Mr. Richardson. Is this so?"

With her eyes to the floor, Tomiko said, "Yes, Mother, it is true. We love each other and we are going to marry."

"How can you do such a thing!"

"Mother, I am not a young child anymore, I am a grown woman. I love him and he loves me."

"You will be unhappy, my child. You will go to your beloved America and you will see that you will feel just as different there as here."

Thinking back, Tomiko grew wistful at her mother's words. Was her mother right? Was it possible that marriage to R.C. and life in America still would not fulfill her dreams?

R.C. ended his phone call and put his arm around Tomiko. "We'll do just fine. You'll see." But Tomiko knew he was talking about money again.

"I don't like it here, R.C. This isn't the way I planned on us spending our honeymoon. When are we going to see your home in Michigan?"

"Be patient, baby." He kissed her softly on the mouth. "Today's important. A lot depends on how much I win today."

"Why?" Tomiko asked suspiciously.

"Don't worry. Leave it up to me."

"As your wife, don't you feel I should know what's going on?"

R.C. quickly eased her back in her seat and patted her on the knee. "We'll talk about this later at home. Right now I've got business to take care of."

"But how soon can we leave?"

"Don't push it, Tomiko."

"But R.C., when are we going to Michigan so I can start

my modeling career? You told me they were waiting for
me."

"Who was waiting for you?"

"The modeling agency!" Tomiko said in frustration.

They had discussed this issue before they left Japan, and
R.C. had promised he could pull some strings. Was R.C.
reneging?

"I told you I'd get you an agent," he said. "Now leave me
alone. I've got money on these horses. As soon as we get
back to Michigan, you'll be working with a top agent. You
have nothing to worry about. You're going to be the biggest
thing since Naomi Campbell."

"But I look too Japanese!"

"Listen, Tomiko, I can't tend to your insecurities right
now."

They were interrupted by a second call from R.C.'s bookie.

"R.C. here." R.C. stroked Tomiko's face.

At five foot ten, Tomiko knew she had the figure to make
it as a runway model. But she worried that her looks were
too exotic. Her wide-set almond eyes were offset by raven,
wild, center-parted hair, and she'd often been told that her
full lips gave her a certain voluptuousness often missing in
the models.

He cupped his hand over the phone before he spoke.
"Don't worry, baby, you're nothing short of gorgeous.
Everything will work out fine. Just leave it to me. America
hasn't seen anything until they've seen you."

Tomiko felt paralyzed. Just leave it to him? Could she
trust him?

The following day, Saturday, it was back to the track. R.C.
was again consumed by the races. Tomiko may have been
young, but she wasn't stupid. She calculated his bets as the

day went on and realized that he had bet over two hundred thousand dollars. She figured that he'd lost as often as he'd won, but she knew for certain that if he continued to gamble this way, they'd either be using one-hundred-dollar bills for toilet paper or stealing cardboard boxes from the homeless. Her mother had taught her that women should be in charge of the household income, and Tomiko knew it was her job to be prudent with money.

Sunday she came up with a plan to get his attention back on her.

"Will you be ready soon?" R.C. asked Tomiko in a hurried tone. "The races start in an hour."

"No, I thought I'd dance today." Tomiko knew how much R.C. loved to watch her perform the Butoh dance. She had learned the dance as a child, in the years when it was being fine-tuned as an art form, having only been developed in Japan in the 1960s. As an expression of artistic individualism, the themes of the dance strike deep, ranging from personal suffering to fear, mortality, and wonder. As a child, she would think about her father when she danced. Since he had died when she was very young, she had found no other way to experience her sense of loss.

Tomiko hoped that if she kept his interest with her dancing, R.C. would change his mind about the races and he would stay home today. R.C. always got aroused when he watched her dance.

But when she beseeched him to stay, telling him of the day she'd planned, he only said, "I'd like to watch, but can't you wait until this evening?"

She was already wearing her dance costume, the exposed parts of her body powdered and her thick hair wrapped in a printed scarf. "I'll dance for you tonight if you'll take me shopping this morning."

Kissing her gingerly on the mouth, R.C. opened his

locked desk drawer and wrote Tomiko a check for five thousand dollars. "Here, why don't you go shopping instead?"

It was a clear dismissal.

"Caleb will drive you downtown. You can trust him."

"R.C.?" she began, then stopped. The check felt like fire in her hand when she accepted it—dangerous, seductive. Easing her hands behind her back, she tore the check in half. "Oh . . . nothing."

When he walked away, she crumpled the paper in her hand and tossed it in the trash. No, she wasn't kidding herself about the value of money, but she knew that one day she would be able to give it to him. She would always remember a valuable lesson that her mother had taught her:

"Money spent on yourself may be a millstone around your neck; money spent on others may give you wings like the angels."

4

Sparkling glass panels flanked the corridor of Champion Motors' new World Headquarters in the heart of downtown Detroit. Thick-piled, violet wool carpeting and expensive, rose-violet coordinated furnishings accented the plush entryway into the building, welcoming the visitor into the world of commerce and money.

At 7:45 A.M., dressed in a silk-on-silk navy pin-striped suit, white shirt, and red tie, Cyrus Tyler stepped off the elevator that led to his office on the fourteenth floor. Wet Paint signs were still affixed to the walls of the hallway, and Cy turned up his nose, but not at the smell of paint. The company reeked of contradictions. The swank interior of the plush building only underscored the humiliations suffered by the hourly employees working for Champion.

Cy suspected that maybe ten out of the tens of thousands of hourly employees who worked in the surrounding metropolitan plants had ever gotten a glimpse of the interior of the posh World Headquarters. If only they knew, they would quit, he thought.

Some men's egos are greater than their ability to understand differences among people. Cy would one day realize that most of the hourly workers didn't give a damn about visiting or working at World Headquarters. As a matter of fact, the annual incomes of the hourly employees exceeded those of many of their white collar counterparts.

The new facility had just been completed last month. It had taken almost a year for Champion to move three thousand salaried employees into the twenty-story global office, and the finishing touches on the first-class building had had to be completed around the employees.

Champion Two Thousand was less than twenty months away. The company's plan to realize Champion's promise to its stockholders to save billions of dollars each year had not boosted the company's stock since the program was first implemented three years earlier. The only way they were saving money was through the early retirements and voluntary buyouts of thirty-two hundred salaried employees in the United States. A series of merciless cost-cutting mandates had eroded morale in some divisions of Champion's white collar workforce of 52,400 rather than increasing sales. Those with common sense feared for their jobs.

Cyrus Scott Tyler was one of them. Cy shook his head and then thought about the news he'd heard over the radio that morning. A Champion plant had been plagued with quarreling workers. Thank God it wasn't Troy Trim, his wife's plant. The slayings were today's top story.

"There was a triangle going on there," said one of Champion's maintenance crewmen. "Coltrain warned the other guy. He told him that if he wanted to see his wife, don't do it in front of him."

Cy thought about how Thyme would not listen to his advice and leave the automobile industry altogether. Now things were getting too violent. Working at General Electric would have been a better choice. But she had been at Champion for twenty-three years. I'd be wasting my time to try to convince her to quit, he told himself. Besides, he knew that she was as devoted to Champion as he was.

The radio host had continued.

"It began at five A.M. Sunday morning, as workers filed into the Van Dyke plant to earn some overtime making heaters and air-conditioner components for the new Syrinx car line. Witnesses said that less than a half hour into the shift, Alvin Coltrain pulled the automatic pistol and confronted his estranged wife and her lover, Sean Zion, in a passageway in the rear of the plant, known as the heater area. Coltrain first shot his wife, then fired at her lover, who apparently was trying to stop him from shooting her. Coltrain then put the gun to his head and pulled the trigger."

Cy was sick of the violence. Stress at the plants was at an all-time high.

Everywhere, in all the plants, there was violence—much worse than on the streets. If Champion's hourly workers were this stressed now, it was going to be an all-out war when they found out the company's plans for Troy Trim. Company against union. Hell, worker against worker, for that matter. And Thyme would be right in the middle of it.

Pushing open the glass doors, Cy said good morning to his secretary. "Get my wife on the line, will you, Geneva?" Cy asked before retrieving his messages and walking into his office.

"Certainly, sir."

As Cy unlocked his briefcase, he heard Geneva's voice over the intercom. "Your wife's out of the office at this time, sir. Elaine said to try back in an hour."

"Try calling her then, Geneva. Thanks," he said, hanging up the phone. Aggravated, he changed the channel on the radio in his office to a smooth jazz station.

Cy's office, newly decorated in cherrywood, silver, burgundy, and black, was well lit, with tons of shiny recessed lights around the perimeter. A black-lacquered Champion clock was located on the wall behind his desk. Thick burgundy carpeting covered his six-hundred-square-foot floor space as well as his private bar and bathroom. Silver-framed pictures of Thyme, his twin sister, Sydney, and his nephew, Graham, sat beside his phone. But Cy's most treasured items were the bowling trophies that were displayed throughout his office.

Champion Motors was taking drastic measures to remain competitive with General Motors, Ford, and Chrysler. Since Champion had started developing the trim operation for its new luxury car line, Syrinx, in Mexico, sales had increased. The corporation was seeing less and less of a need for trim business in the United States. Syrinx, as well as ten other top-selling Champion lines, was now being sewn in Matamoros, Mexico, and fifteen other lines would be moved to Mexico next year. By that point, American production would be cut by a third.

His throat felt dry as ashes and he tugged at his tie. He removed a stack of files from his briefcase and headed for the refrigerator that his secretary was considerate enough to keep supplied with fresh sparkling water. A wave of nausea swept over him. The Perrier temporarily cleared his head as he chugged down three-quarters of a bottle.

He was on the phone when he heard a knock at the opened door.

"Come in," he said to his boss, John Sandler. "Have some coffee. I'll be finished in a minute, John."

Sandler declined the coffee and, with a broad smile fixed on his face, waited until Cy completed his call. When he did, Sandler handed Cy a sealed envelope.

Inside, Cy knew, was his yearly performance bonus check. Champion paid bonuses at the start of the new fiscal year in April.

"You'll notice this year's bonus is substantially higher than last year's."

"That's good to hear." Cy stood and briskly shook Sandler's hand.

John Sandler, a slim, deeply tanned, white-haired man of sixty with a falsetto voice, was one of five top officers at Champion. His division was Financial Services. He reminded Cy of an aging choir boy trying to sing his way into heaven, never able to make it. Sandler was known around the company as one of the biggest liars in the business.

Cy wondered why Sandler had personally brought him his check. Usually he allocated that menial job to his secretary. Something else was going on. Cy knew that the only way to find out was to ask questions and try to gauge which answers were lies. "Does Senator Reese still plan on accompanying me on the Mexico trip next month?"

"We're completing the final details of your meeting with the senator and the Mexican ambassador. I feel this new business venture with the Mexican government is going to prove very advantageous for Champion."

Cy felt the hairs on his neck rise. He knew that Sandler was once again reminding Cy that if he valued his job, he'd keep his mouth shut about the company's plan to sell off its Troy Trim plant. Sandler knew that Thyme was head of operations at the plant, but he was banking on Cy's loyalty to Champion and to his paycheck.

"When the dollar represented gold, it was just as good as gold," Sandler continued. "But now it's only as good as the current state of inflation. The lower Mexican wages give us an opportunity to hold on to a little more of that gold."

Cy was becoming more and more uncomfortable with withholding vital information from his wife. Keeping secrets about the coming changes at Champion had begun to keep him awake at night. If Thyme ever found out how much he knew, there was no telling how she'd react. Cy had many friends, hourly and salaried, from whom he was keeping important information that could profoundly impact their jobs. But this was business. Big business.

"I've been at this company for thirty-five years, Cyrus. I've seen the automobile industry bounce back and forth and go through hills and valleys. Champion Two Thousand was not designed to be a short-term palliative. Changes are occurring because we are reengineering the company."

Cy was sick to death of hearing the strategy behind the destruction of thousands of autoworkers' lives. How could Champion treat husbands, wives, mothers, and fathers like numbers? How could Champion ask him to decide who should be cut from employee rolls?

Sandler continued, "We need you to expedite Champion Two Thousand. As you know, this program is Champion's strategy to remain the leader in the automobile business now and in the future. We need to anticipate global market changes."

Sandler's words echoed in Cy's mind throughout the long day.

It was 10 P.M. when he left the office. As he drove home, Cy kept going over his conversation with Sandler: it was clear that Champion was throwing him a bone to keep quiet. But how long would his own job be safe? Didn't he owe it to himself and to Thyme to be honest about Champion's plan to dump hundreds of jobs? And how had he gotten stuck with the job of streamlining?

Cy knew he was partly responsible for Champion's development of Mexican production. He had used his own ties in Mexico to help Champion pave its way into the Mexican market. After he graduated from high school, Cy had spent a year living in Mexico City; he had been lured there by its culture and language. After college he returned to Mexico to work in the General Motors plant in Matamoros. It was in Mexico that he had first fallen in love.

Cy's thoughts turned to Graciella, the woman who had been his lover now for over twenty years—before, during, and after his marriage to Thyme. Cy and Graciella had two children together, and despite his love for Thyme, he still hadn't been able to give up his relationship with Graciella.

He had met Graciella when they were both working at the General Motors plant, but it had been their mutual love of bullfights that ultimately brought them together. Graciella still kidded Cy that what he had between his legs was as strong as a bull. For reasons he couldn't explain to himself, he felt more virile with Graciella than he ever had with Thyme.

Though he knew that he satisfied Thyme sexually, he always worried that there was something missing in their relationship. Was that why he clung to Graciella? He couldn't let go of the myth that the black man's penis was better hung than the white man's and it bothered him. Though they never discussed it, Cy felt a racial wedge between himself and his wife that he had overlooked as a newlywed but which grew as maturity crept in and life's knocks hit them. And then there was always Thyme's resistance to having children.

When Cy opened the door of the elaborate master bedroom, Thyme was already asleep. He knew that if he didn't wake her, she would complain in the morning.

The soothing ambience of their bedroom was perfect for relaxing. There were a few steps up to the main area, which was dominated by a round revolving bed that was eight feet in diameter. Behind the bed was a twenty-foot rectangular portrait of Thyme, her nude body draped seductively with pale pink silk. Rose petals were sprinkled in her hair and at various spots in the sheer fabric. She had been thirty-five when Cy had the portrait commissioned. She was more beautiful to him at that age than ever before.

"Wake up, Thyme. I'm home."

Cy pressed the remote to turn on a CD. Thyme sat up on her hindquarters like a praying mantis.

"Turn that shit off. I thought we agreed on the music we were playing this month? No country."

"Oh," he said, massaging her slender thighs, "am I supposed to listen to rap, like Tupac Shakur's Makavelli tape you love to listen to?"

"Yeah. And Lil' Kim."

"Kim, like Cy, has one syllable. Translated to needing only one nut tonight. One good fuck."

"Don't be crass, Cy."

"Just ghetto. I thought you liked it like that."

Thyme turned away. "That's not fair. I don't ridicule white folks' music. I just don't want to hear it when we make love. It screws up my rhythm."

"Hey. I love black soul."

She smiled. "But you can't dance. You don't have any rhythm."

"Excuse me," Cy said, rotating his pelvis on top of her.

"Except between the sheets."

Cy reached beneath the covers and removed her gown. He could hear her weak protests but ignored them. "You know you want it. Don't fight me. It only makes me work harder."

"Stop. I'm tired, Cy."

Ignoring her weak protests, he kissed her softly on the lips. When he felt her mouth open to welcome his tongue, he kissed her more deeply, as if he were drinking in her whole mouth, tongue, and breath into his. His tongue grew more and more thrusting, as if it had become a sex organ itself.

Reaching down, he massaged her breasts, then released

himself from her kisses to suck each breast gently before tenderly tugging at her hardened nipples with his teeth.

His fingers reached lower to caress her narrow waist, curvaceous hips, sliding his pressed palms around and down until he felt her soft mound. He could feel her hairs curling around his fingers as he gently teased the entrance to her moist womb.

"Cy," she sighed, reaching out to grab his throbbing penis. "Put it in, baby. I can't wait."

He kissed her above her navel, then putting his hands on her shoulders, he turned her around. Lying his body over hers, he took pleasure in rubbing his flesh against hers, feeling the softness of her buttocks pressing deep into his abdomen. He moved in circles, pressing his penis deeper into the crevice of her buttocks, pinning her arms above her as he did so.

He felt her moving beneath him, lifting her head to feel his neck curling around her cheek and slide down to rest at her shoulder. Together they moved to a snakelike rhythm until their bodies became moist with desire.

"Put it in, baby," she moaned.

"Not yet." He teased her further, pushing his penis down the bottom of her buttocks to part her lips. He dipped the tip a half-inch inside, and felt her pushing up against him, demanding full penetration. When she pushed up and he felt himself sliding deeper inside, he eased back out.

He would not take her.

"Please, Cy. I need it now, baby."

"Not yet."

He turned over onto his back and positioned her on top of his penis, easing her down slowly, a half-inch at a time. He lifted his buttocks moving ever so lightly, until their pubic hairs met for a brief kiss. They rotated their hips in reverse, building the tempo, gradually, faster and faster, clicking their pelvis bones until they were out of breath, then moved slower in one direction, plunging deeper, her vagina clasping his penis like a mouth.

He pushed down to the very depths of her womb, and felt the juice on his thighs pouring from her. As he pushed, he could hear little sucking sounds as all the air was being drawn from her womb as his penis filled her. In and out he moved swiftly, admiring the way his penis glistened from the juice of her love.

When her orgasm came, he followed seconds later. Still, he wanted more. The strains at Champion today made him want to make love to his wife all night.

They lay together panting, her body on top of his, until their breathing slowed.

Thyme rolled over onto her side and sighed with pleasure.

Cy left the bed, standing nude in front of the wall of glass in their bedroom, which looked out on the Lower Straits of Lake Bloomfield. He opened the French doors and inhaled the fresh, cool air. He heard her stirring in bed. "Thyme, we need to get a boat to place out on the lake. A pontoon. They're not terribly expensive. In fact, one will be delivered this weekend."

"You must've read my mind. I'd been thinking about the same thing." Thyme reached for her housecoat at the foot of the bed. "Now close the door, Cy—it's freezing!"

"There's not a place in the world that's more beautiful."

"Once again," she said, joining him, "I couldn't agree more."

"Remember when you first showed me the house? I wasn't too impressed."

"Yeah. You thought it was too big."

"Nine thousand square feet of custom living space on three levels. I didn't think we'd ever furnish it all." He appraised the elegant room now, but his eyes were always drawn back to his prized possession: the portrait of his wife. "Now, I love this house. But not without you, Thyme. I hate this house when you're not in it."

It was more than the average worker, blue collar or salaried, could ever hope for. The lake's beauty served as the inspiration for the theme of the decor, with water inside as well as out. One slate-colored two-tiered waterfall greeted guests; a pyramid-shaped fountain stood in the living room. Silver-blue wool carpeting was set against the palest blue walls, with touches of burgundy to show the richness of the woods. There were two staircases on each end of the mansion, recessed lighting throughout, and three types of wood. Located on the lower level of the two-story house were a sunken hot tub with ceramic tile and a steam room. There were three kitchens, including one in the mother-in-law suite in the east wing—it was a part of the home each knew they would never use.

But it was the view of the lake that had sold Cy on 2300 Cyprus Cove. It was a symbol of success. Cy was not satisfied with accumulating money; he wanted to show how successful he was.

After Thyme fell back asleep, he walked through the dining room, admiring their heirloom china, which had been left to him by his parents. His great-grandparents had purchased the porcelain in the early 1900s in Beijing, China. Thyme had cried tears of love and affection after his mother offered the china to them on her only son's wedding day. It was a legacy that should be passed on to his children.

Maybe it wasn't too late for Thyme to change her mind. Stranger things had happened.

Neither color, circumstance, nor Champion could come between them. The love they shared for each other was stronger than the elements that threatened them—like race, like his disapproving sister, Sydney, like his mistress, Graciella, and the children they shared.

When he went back into the bedroom, he could hear Thyme exhale, a faint smile still on her lips. He admired his wife's beautiful black body glowing in the semidarkness; even in her sleep it was disturbingly provocative. The thought of waking her again entered his mind. He went to lie beside her and his hands stroked her delicate flesh softly, as if she were a flower. He kissed her earlobe, then whispered, "I adore you."

The familiar smell of her perfume enveloped him, on the sheets, the pillow—even his body had caught the scent. He snuggled closer, breathing in the aroma of her scent lingering on the sheets.

5

Their plane landed in Detroit Metropolitan Airport at 7:40 on Tuesday night. Ten minutes later, Tomiko and R.C. were met at Northwest baggage claim by Herman, one of R.C.'s drivers. With tons of luggage finally stowed, R.C. took delight in pointing out to Tomiko all of the interesting sites along Interstate 94 as they drove east toward home.

A full moon bulged low in the sky, its face turned toward them, lighting the cars whizzing past them like silver phantoms. At least six late-model vehicles, some wrecked, some just with flats, were abandoned on the right side of the highway. Tomiko observed houses so close together that if someone dropped a match on one, another would catch fire. Before she could organize the zillion questions she wanted to ask R.C. about her new surroundings, she felt a jolt, and fell against him.

"It's nothing. Just a pothole," R.C. said reassuringly. "It's one of the things Detroit is famous for."

Tomiko could hear Herman snickering.

"It's not like I pictured it would be, R.C.," Tomiko said, adjusting her antique Japanese jacket and stealing another glance out the window. She had looked forward to seeing

Detroit as her new home, but the landscape she saw out the window did not feel welcoming.

"Did you get in touch with your advertising person about using me in one of your dealership commercials?" She and R.C. had agreed that they would use a commercial about one of his dealerships featuring Tomiko to attract more work for her. That way, she'd better her chances for being accepted by one of the top modeling agencies.

"Not yet."

"But why not? You know this is important to me. You promised."

"You don't have a green card yet, Tomiko."

"I don't understand. You promised me that you had already set up everything before leaving Japan. I married an American citizen—doesn't that automatically get me a green card?"

"No. This is real life. The green card isn't even green anymore. It's pink and it makes you a 'resident alien,' not a citizen. We're going to have to be very careful with this, Tomiko. People get deported every day."

"I know. But we haven't done anything illegal."

R.C. paused and then said, "Tomiko, do you remember the papers we signed before we left Japan?"

"We signed a lot of papers."

"I know, but I'm talking about one in particular; the immigrant visa. Remember, we were in a hurry . . . well, I was in a hurry to get back home and I suggested that you come in as a tourist on a visa waiver. We filled out a form called an I-Ninety-four. That meant that you had to lie and tell them that you were just coming to the States for a visit and would not be residing here permanently."

"I don't see why Americans make it so difficult for people to work here. They should be glad that I'm not applying for welfare."

She could hear R.C. chuckle. "It's a long story, Tomiko. But as your employer, I can file an I-Nine form for your permanent residence card. I know all this sounds confusing, but you'll have to trust me. I've got some smart people here working with me on this. Be patient. Everything will work itself out."

R.C. touched her chin with his fingers, pulling her face back toward him, then let them run across her lips. He kissed her. "Don't let small things upset you. Detroit is a great city. Once you see the house, you'll love it here. Especially the food. Are you hungry, honey? I'm starved."

"Can we stop by the market? I'd like to cook dinner tonight."

"Are you sure? I can have a steak and lobster dinner delivered by the time we get home."

Tomiko smiled. "Have you forgotten how much you loved for me to cook for you when we were in Japan?" The warm look in his eyes told her that he remembered, and remembered also what they had shared afterwards.

Since she had left Japan, she hadn't had an ounce of decent food. Sure, R.C. took her to the most exclusive Japanese restaurants, but it wasn't the same. The food was high in presentation but low in taste.

The one and only talent that Tomiko seemed to have inherited from her mother was cooking. Everything else she'd learned on her own.

R.C. checked his watch. "Take the Fenkell exit, Herman. Make a left on Fenkell, take it three miles up to Evergreen. Make another right at Evergreen. Kisoji's Market is on the west side of the street."

The glass-fronted market sparkled with bright lights. Beige laminated walls showed off the artfully displayed products. Once inside, Tomiko could smell the familiar

scent of soybeans and sesame-flavored bean curd as well as
the flavorful assortment of teas and exotic seasonings.

Several other Japanese women shopped inside the market, and they greeted her warmly—more warmly, in fact,
than her Japanese compatriots did in her home country.

A small line was forming at the fish counter as the women
studied the day's selection of fresh octopus, *maguro, ebi,*
and *hamachi.* They were out of one of Tomiko's favorites:
akagai, or red shellfish.

She spotted the noodles with which she could make *soba*
and *udon* dishes, her favorite main dishes, and purchased
fresh vegetables, grains, seafood, fish, chicken, and a small
portion of pork.

She was happy to find the Japanese foodstuffs plentiful.
Her mother had warned her to resist the heavily spiced and
greasy foods that the Americans loved; they were saturated
with oil and butter and would make her fat.

Satisfied that she'd selected well, Tomiko motioned for
R.C. to come in and pay for the groceries. R.C. handed her
a brochure from Kisoji's. "They have a delivery service."

Gushing like the newlywed she was, Tomiko hugged her
husband. She had begun to feel homesick but was ashamed
to tell him. But now, having been surrounded by the familiar sights and smells of Japan, she felt less estranged. "Are
we far from our house?" Tomiko asked once they were back
inside the limo.

"About twenty miles. But there's another market you'll
like on Seven Mile Road. You can walk there from where we
live."

"I'm going to surprise you with something special for
dinner."

"Tomiko. It's late. We're both tired. We can order in and
you can cook a meal tomorrow."

She ignored the impatience she heard in his voice. Even

though she was a size six, she still loved to eat. She was fed up with the American food and she'd been barely able to eat. Tomiko was positive she'd lost an unnecessary five pounds. She had to take care of her body if she was going to make it as a model—and she would.

"You'll see. I'm going to serve you the best Japanese food you've ever eaten."

They debated about the logistics of cooking at such a late hour until the white limo stopped under the arch of the Italian-style ranch on Gloucester Drive in Palmer Woods. The front entrance was lit up like a palace. It was one of the most impressive homes Tomiko had ever seen.

Tomiko watched R.C. unlock and open the arched front double doors with beveled glass that led into the thirty-four-foot-high clerestory atrium and foyer.

"Hello, I'm Bonnie. Mr. R.C.'s maid." The light-skinned black woman with rich red kinky hair and freckles extended her hand to Tomiko. "Welcome to Michigan."

Tomiko shook the other woman's hand. Bonnie appeared to be appraising Tomiko, and her gaze seemed a little menacing to Tomiko. Still, Bonnie's voice was neutral when she said, "I'll check on you later to see if you need anything." R.C. was giving instructions to Herman, seemingly oblivious to the exchange between the two women.

Even though there was so much to see, R.C. took Tomiko around the house in less than five minutes.

The interior was airy and had a tropical feel. The thirty-foot-high ceilings created an impressive but inviting welcome. Recessed lighting wrapped around the ceilings. The floors in the living room and lower level were made of polished limestone from Italy. R.C. had told her that the carpeting in eggplant, teal, and plum was custom made to offset the neutral tones. A columned archway framed an elegant elevator, whose facade was accented by a hand-tooled copper dome. Six thousand square feet of luxurious living were packed into two levels. The lower level, accessible by either stairs or elevator, opened into a lower loggia.

Tomiko was surprised by such luxury. "This is where you live?" she asked.

He took her arm and led her back upstairs. "This is where we live."

With only a few of her suitcases unpacked, Tomiko asked Bonnie to press the matching batiked black silk kimonos she and R.C. had purchased before leaving Japan. Soon she was serving her husband dinner: grilled chicken on skewers that were dipped in a thick, sweet peanut sauce. She had prepared a clear soup containing two or three white beans, a slice of red ginger cut in the shape of a starfish, two pieces of twisted kelp, an ear-shell, and a sliver of pink fish. The rest of their meal consisted of grilled seafood and steamed vegetables. Though it was nearly ten-thirty, the meal was light enough so as not to disturb their sleep—or anything else.

Tomiko had learned early on that the appearance of food and the manner of serving it was as important as the food's taste. Food presentation was an art designed to nurture the spirit as well as the body. Therefore, her every thought during the preparation had been attuned to the spirit of the body, a fact she hoped would reach R.C. where it counted.

She served the meal in the lower-level dining area, which R.C. said he preferred. R.C. had brought a simple, flower-painted pottery flask and cups for sake. She wondered who had stocked the elegant chinaware and flatware. As for the interior decor, it was obvious that her husband had hired the very best talent in home design. Hungry, they both devoured the dinner.

Afterwards, they retired into the sitting area to watch the late-night news.

"I don't believe this shit." R.C. turned up the volume on what was obviously a commercial for a Champion dealership. He dropped the crossword puzzle he'd been working on in his lap and leaned forward for a closer view of the show. A regulation-size boxing ring appeared to have been airlifted and planted in the middle of a canyon. Shadowboxing inside was a well-known country western singer, who was dressed in a pair of oasis blue Everlast boxing shorts trimmed in silver. Sydney stood just outside the ring, leaning seductively against the new 1999 silver Rembrandt. Behind them was an unidentifiable mountain. A close-up shot panned the truck, then the singer's superstar smile. The music started and the singer crooned the catchy jingle, "Once a champion, always a champion; if you get stuck, we got the truck."

"Sydney Tyler, you white witch, you do have class."

Tomiko watched as her husband's eyes were glued to the commercial. There was no denying that the woman, obviously the owner of the dealership being featured, was beautiful, with her petite body, striking wide-set blue eyes, and cleft chin. Her voice as she spoke her lines was sultry and soft.

Was this competition? Tomiko wondered.

The phone began to ring.

"R.C., are you going to get that?" Tomiko began collecting the empty plates and putting them on the tray.

No answer. Heading for the kitchen, she answered the phone on the third ring. "Hello?"

"Hi. I'd like to speak to R.C."

"Who's calling, please?"

"It's Khan."

In a flash, Tomiko remembered R.C. calling out this name in his sleep. She thought quickly. "Now is not a good time. Can you call back later?"

"No. Put him on the phone."

"Is this business?"

"No. It's private."

"Call back tomorrow, please." Tomiko didn't wait for an answer. She hung up.

She decided that she wouldn't give this woman named Khan another thought, whoever she was. What did it matter? R.C. was her husband now.

She imagined how delightful it would be to take his shaft between her lips and slowly fill her mouth with every last inch of him. How she would love to feel his orgasm with every pull of her mouth, and then tell him how much she enjoyed the ambrosia of his juice. Oh, how she would pull him down even deeper to the small of her throat, tightening her lips around his head so he could feel the tenderness inside her mouth once again. She knew that she would bring him to the exquisite edge of orgasm, then ease back and admire the glistening energy of his shaft throbbing at her.

Alone now upstairs, her vagina began to pulsate with the thought of feeling him inside of her as she removed her personal items from her suitcase. She knew that she couldn't bear to fantasize further. She hurried to finish her task of organizing her toiletries and cosmetics in the bathroom.

Afterwards, she showered and perfumed her body with Nude cologne and came to bed wearing her sexiest nightwear: nothing. R.C. had come upstairs quietly to join her and was already turned over on his side when she slid into bed beside him. But when she did, she sensed that he was tense about something. She flicked off the TV set he had been watching and snuggled closer. Kissing the back of his neck and shoulder, she moved her hands across his torso, then reached up to thread her fingers through his hairy chest. He turned over onto his back and removed his briefs. And when he did, Tomiko took him inside her mouth, and she could feel his body relaxing. But for some reason, the more she enjoyed the taste of his flesh, the softer he became. So soft in fact that finally his penis folded in half like a wilted dandelion.

Tomiko couldn't imagine what was wrong. She couldn't decide if she should say something or try something different. So, without another thought, she released him and began to kiss and lick his lower torso, then continued farther up and over the slight swell of his belly, which was soft on the surface yet taut with muscle. She stopped only for a second to rotate her buttocks and straddle him.

Before she knew it, he flipped her petite body off of him with a strong shrug. The tone of his voice was harsh. "That's enough."

"R.C.? Is something wrong?"

He kept his back turned from her when he spoke. "No. I've heard about young people your age believing in voodoo sex."

"Voodoo? What do you mean by that?"

"People who are expecting magic in their sexual relations." He reached for his briefs and slipped them back on. "I'm fifty years old, Tomiko. I'm not a sex machine. You should have known there would be limitations."

"But . . ."

"Now go to sleep. I ain't performing no magic trick tonight."

Tomiko turned over onto her side and curled her body into a fetal position. Silent tears stung her eyes, then fell like rivulets of molten lead, the torrents burning a passage to her heart. He turned away from her and again pulled the covers over himself. Minutes later, he was snoring.

Eventually, she fell asleep, her mind struggling with the pain that was most difficult for her to bear: the deadly pang of shame.

*   *   *

The morning sunlight woke Tomiko. The spot beside her was empty, which was no surprise. R.C. must have already left for the office.

The spacious master bedroom was airy with views of the outdoor landscape through a wall filled with high windows that angled into skylights. The cool atmosphere was enhanced by wallpaper made up of mottled lavenders, aquas, and teals that gave a soft, impressionistic feel to the room.

Rising from the bed, she stood by the window, stretched, and peered outside. As she stood there a small flock of colorful butterflies came into view. She could almost hear their wings as they fluttered by. She felt surrounded by beauty indoors as well as out.

It was a lovely morning. Resting her forehead against the warmed glass, she closed her eyes, trying to forget the hurt of last night, and chose instead to pretend that it had been just a bad dream. She imagined instead that she and R.C. had made delirious love.

She was so caught up in daydreaming that she barely heard the phone.

"Hello," she said. Nude, she lay across the bed.

"Hi. Are you finding everything you need in the house?" It was R.C.

"Sure."

"Are you upset about last night?"

Of course she was. But there was no point in mulling over it now. Instead she asked, "R.C., when are you going to teach me to drive in Detroit? I don't like the idea of Herman driving me around the city every time I want to leave the house."

"We'll start this weekend. Now, I've got to go."

Tomiko thought it very clever the way R.C. managed to

be so attentive toward her and brush her off at the same time. She supposed that, with a little patience, she would one day be as cunning. Tomiko knew that once R.C. saw her in action, at work, competent and professionally put together, his admiration for her would grow, and their love, like fire once again kindled, would soon blow into a flame.

It was nearly ten in the morning by the time she had showered and changed, and she could smell freshly brewed coffee in the kitchen. Tomiko had little use for the chauffeur, but to her Bonnie was essential. Bonnie knew the truth about what went on in the house. Tomiko had felt an odd tension when she met the woman the night before, but she was confident she'd eventually find a way to get through to her.

When she entered the kitchen, Bonnie obediently poured her a cup of coffee, then went back to cleaning out the refrigerator.

"Do you know a person named Khan?" Tomiko's voice was calm as she sipped her coffee.

"You should ask Mr. R.C. about that. That's none of my business."

Tomiko noticed how hard Bonnie was looking at her. "Is something wrong, Bonnie?"

"Listen, I respect you as Mr. R.C.'s wife. But I expect you to respect something about me, too. I've been running this house for years, just the way Mr. R.C. likes, and he's never complained. Not once. He likes his privacy. I don't cater to no one coming in here asking about Mr. R.C.'s personal business. Whatever you need to know, you should be asking him, not me."

Tomiko stuttered. "I . . . I . . . just thought . . ."

"Leave the thinking, child, for the grown folks."

Thus the ground rules of the home were set: Do it Bonnie's way or there would be hell to pay.

For the next couple of days, Tomiko surreptitiously kept

close track of Bonnie. She watched her make out the dinner menu for the week, an eye on her laundry schedule as well as the schedule she kept while cleaning the house. Tomiko was sure that Bonnie was watching her as well. Finally, Tomiko figured out a way to forge a bond with Bonnie. She was a clothes fanatic.

R.C. had followed through on setting up an interview for Tomiko with his advertising agency, and on Friday she had an interview at eleven at the Penobscott Building. Deciding what to wear, she thought, was a good way to ask for Bonnie's advice. After scouring her closet, she selected her best outfits and spread them out over the sofa and chairs in her bedroom.

Soon enough there was a knock at her door. It was the time when Bonnie removed the dirty clothing to begin her morning's wash.

Tomiko noted the fascination in Bonnie's eyes as she spotted the tailored tweed by Marc Labat, the chocolate coatdress by YSL, and the featherweight printed crepes by Cécile et Jeanne. One especially caught her attention, and she came a little closer to inspect a new silk by Edouard Rambaud.

"My Lord," Bonnie said, shaking her head, "this sure is fine." She touched the hem of the fabric. "Don't see this type of quality silk around here much."

"Thank you. R.C. bought most of my clothes in Paris. But this one," she said, touching the fine silk, "he purchased in Kyoto. I have an interview today with an advertising agency," she said casually. "What do you think I should wear?"

Bonnie looked at each of the outfits carefully and chose a navy blue silk suit with celery green leaves embossed on the lapels and cuffs. "I think you'd look beautiful in this, dear."

"Perfect choice." Tomiko smiled warmly at Bonnie. Then

she paused and thought for a moment before she spoke, "Bonnie, I realize that I'm a stranger. But soon you'll know me better and maybe even trust me. I'll be around a long time." She measured her words carefully. "I can see how much you care for R.C. I can't be the best wife to him if I don't know what's going on." She paused, looking Bonnie dead in the eye. "Of course I don't expect you to tell me all of R.C.'s private business. But I worry about this woman, Khan. Were they lovers?"

Bonnie was silent.

"Were they lovers, Bonnie?"

"Yes." She stopped, and began collecting Tomiko's clothes off the sofa. "For nearly five years."

Bonnie began hanging Tomiko's clothes, leaving out the outfit she would wear to her appointment. Once she was finished, she began to tell Tomiko a little about R.C. and Khan. All the while she talked, she continued to do her housework. After all, she was on a schedule and she had shopping to do this afternoon.

Before long, Tomiko knew all she needed to about Khan. She told herself it really didn't matter. The bottom line was that R.C. had married her and not Khan.

While Bonnie removed the sheets from the bed, Tomiko hung on to every word. Afterwards, Bonnie sat down on the edge of the bed to take a short break. They were just about to get to the best part, Tomiko thought: what Khan looked like.

"Can't say she wasn't pretty. She was. Blond hair and all, 'cepting she had one of those looks like Buckwheat on the *Little Rascals,*" Bonnie said, "and the cutesy facial expressions of Darla."

"Who's Buckwheat?" Tomiko asked.

"I forgot—you don't know. Anyway, Buckwheat's hairstyle was the seventies Afro. The Afro was the black man's secret weapon then because the black man had hair. Afro Sheen used to come in colors. Black Mist would make women follow a man around. Afros gave the black man back his self-esteem. And that made the black man *fine* in the seventies. But later on in that decade, they came out with the super 'fro. That's what turned all the ladies' heads—even the white ones. If the Jackson Five had had Quovadises, nobody would have noticed them. The super Afros were it then. They made men look fine even if they were ugly."

Tomiko and Bonnie laughed together. If there was one thing she knew about, even in Japan, it was the Jackson Five. "I love this, Bonnie. I've never learned about black people before. They're so racist in Japan. No one speaks of them except to insult. Please don't stop."

Bonnie smoothed back the loose strands of her fire-red hair and smiled. "Next it was the TWA: the teeny-weeny Afros. Then there were the men who wore hats like Marvin Gaye and Sidney Poitier. Sidney's hair has been the same length since nineteen sixty."

"R.C.'s got a TWA." Tomiko glanced at his photo on the nightstand.

"And I imagine he's had it about fifty years, too."

The two women laughed.

"I've got to rent you some movies so you know what I'm talking about. In the days of the TWA, no black man sat in first class on an airline. Well, Sidney Poitier was first class. But Bill Cosby could never sit in first class, because in those days, he had an Afro. And that was when porkchop sideburns were in style. With those looks first-class passengers would stare at him, maybe think he was a radical or something. Even if he was famous, they'd probably not recognize him, seeing as he was black.

"Anyway, the same bald-headed man in the sixties became your husband in the seventies. And that's when my generation came into the picture. The women like me with thick nappy hair got tired of Mama sitting by the stove, spitting on the pressing comb. The thicker the oil, the nappier our hair. We suffered then. Our small children suffered, too, when we combed their hair. They cried for hours."

Tomiko noticed that Bonnie had stopped smiling.

"I know a child that ran out into the street to keep her mama from straightening her hair. You couldn't see a part on her scalp. It looked like her entire head was colored with black Magic Markers."

"That's so sad. I would never let a thing like that happen if R.C. and I ever had a daughter."

"You wouldn't have a thing to worry about. Times have changed. Mr. R.C.'s money makes him a part of a new breed of black. You know, Tomiko, they have an ethnic selection at Blockbuster Video. You can go find your roots."

Tomiko treasured Bonnie for acknowledging her black blood and embracing it. "I need to rent the whole section, I'm so ignorant."

"Child, just listen. You can learn what you need to know by just witnessing. Black people have their own ten commandments. We're religious, but we're proud. When we get a little money, we don't even start with a Chevy. We say, 'No, I got the brougham. I want the lights to blink, I want the remote that talks, and I want the loudest audio system that you can install in that sucker.' "

Tomiko had to wipe the tears away, she was laughing so hard. Bonnie had her groove going.

"Black folks have a Cadillac in the front yard, and the house don't have no windows. They just left Jax's Car Wash this morning, and they're going back tomorrow. Half of them don't even have a bed. They're sleeping on a dirty pile of clothes for a mattress so they can make that next month's car payment.

"We've got a new breed of black people here in Detroit: the Chaldeans. Even though they've come here from Lebanon and Iran and have only been here a short while, they own most of the gas stations, the party stores, the liquor stores. We're too stupid to see what's happening. They got everything now. They are interested in buying up what black people are interested in.

"The Chaldeans are trying to be like us black folks these days. Twenty-four-karat gold jewelry is the main attraction for the women. All they want is gold jewelry. They put a jewelry store on a dress. Don't even bring them a plain dress. They need weight. They'll get a whiplash holding up that dress, but they won't listen if you tell them the truth; that it's too garish.

"And talk about their homes. Where they live, it's usually not far from a black neighborhood. The Chaldean men try to model their women after black women. First of all, their favorite color is black. Oh yeah. They tell their women to get blackonized: 'I want you to look like a black woman.' They find the best-looking black woman and say, 'Make yourself look like her.' They want their woman stylized and jazzed up. They want them independent. Yet they expect their women to keep quiet. They mimic us. They go and get the finest. They may start at Payless, but they end up at Neiman's."

"How do you know so much, Bonnie?"

"I read, I listen, and I gossip."

"I don't know how R.C. found you, Bonnie, but I'm so glad that I met you."

Bonnie tossed the dirty sheets out into the hallway. "I ain't finished yet, girl. Let me tell you about the white women. These white whores that now are the rich white man's fifth wife are the same whores that screwed them when they were married to their fourth wife. I remember one woman in particular who starred on a stupid game show we have here. She was called a home-wrecker. Her pictures were on the front page of the *Enquirer*. And now that same girl is in trouble, her rich mate is screwing around on her. Even though she's on her third face-lift, and her teeny-weeny anorexic body fits into a size zero and her fake teeth shine with the whitest Pepsodent smile, she's as miserable as a hound dog when his master leaves the house. She's twenty years younger than his last wife and she still can't keep his whorish ass at home.

"She knows that she's going to be right up there with the rest of the whores. Welcome to the dog pound. These are the dogs. The Atomic Dogs. Remember that dance?"

"No," Tomiko said timidly.

"I keep forgetting you ain't from around here."

"What about the second, third, and fourth wives? Where did they go?"

"Girl, they went to the old wives' camp."

Tomiko laughed until her small belly ached, and with that laughter, she began to feel brighter and more hopeful that her life with R.C. would get better.

6

"If I don't do this now, I never will," Thyme said to herself as she applied a third coat of mascara. All night she'd been thinking about her upcoming meeting with her attorney. Look at me, she thought, stepping back from the mirror and assessing herself. I look like a professional, speak like a professional, and conduct business like a professional. Why should I have to fight for the respect I deserve?

Not even her husband understood how she felt. How could he? He wasn't black and he wasn't female. He'd supported her in the beginning when she'd first begun to agitate over not receiving promotions, but his support didn't seem to go very deep. How could she tell him she had taken the next step toward filing the lawsuit?

When she had interviewed for college, Thyme had been asked: "As an aspiring black American about to enter college, what do you want?" Her stock answer was "To be a black face in a high place." That was still her answer.

As valedictorian of her high school class in 1971, she had delivered the commencement speech at graduation. Even though blacks represented less than two percent of her graduating class in West Bloomfield, she had structured her speech as a message to her fellow pioneers. She ended with: "I believe racism is a fundamental form of human evil. And I believe we cannot hide from evil. I feel that racism can be changed, reformed, ameliorated, even restricted. But racism will always take some form in society today and we can't ignore it."

She was to learn later that the five-minute-long ovation she had received was unprecedented. The irony was that as an outspoken black female during her high school years, she had kept silent about her relationship with one of the most popular white athletes, Cy Tyler. Even though her classmates accepted her as the valedictorian, she knew that they would never condone interracial dating.

Cy's twin sister, Sydney, had discovered their affair right before graduation. She threatened to tell the Tyler family, which would have been disastrous for both Cy and Thyme when her parents were alive. Like Cy, Sydney was a natural blue-eyed blond. She was the homecoming queen. With wide-set eyes, a narrow nose, full lips, a center cleft in her chin, and a prominent jaw, she was a female version of Cy. And as twins, they were as close as one second is to the next.

Ironically, if Sydney hadn't played her hand, Thyme might not have had the nerve to prepare a speech about being black and being proud of it. And she might have never discovered how much Cy truly loved her when, later that night, he had slipped an engagement ring on her finger.

At that young age she had never questioned Cy about how he felt about her race. They weren't concerned with the prejudices of the world; their only care was how much they loved each other. In truth, she was always so conservative, so neat, so proper, so unblack, as to appear color-less despite her deep chocolate skin.

To Cy, she felt, color hadn't mattered. And for a long time it hadn't mattered to her.

But now, more than twenty-five years later, race did matter. It factored into every aspect of her life, and it was time she did something about it.

After spraying a touch of oil sheen on her hair, she brushed her wrapped hairstyle until every strand was in place. She gave her makeup a final check and glanced at her watch. Turning out the lights in the bathroom, she hurried into the bedroom to say good-bye to Cy. "Call me, honey." She kissed his groggy head, and flew down the back hallway. It was twenty minutes to five in the morning. Cy didn't have to get up for another hour.

She grabbed her purse and keys. Halfway down the hall, she made a U-turn back to the kitchen. She'd forgotten to write out the weekly check for her cleaning lady, Sonia.

All during the thirty-minute drive to work, she scrutinized every year of her and Cy's marriage. She hadn't realized until now how easily she made excuses to condone their interracial relationship. It all seemed to be coming to a head now.

In the first five years of their marriage, she'd held firm in her conviction not to have children. Had God been trying to tell her something even then? She'd told Cy and herself that she wanted and needed to concentrate fully on her education and career, that she believed that would prove most fulfilling. It took Thyme eight years, while working full-time at Champion Motors, to acquire a master's and Ph.D. But truthfully she was afraid to bring biracial children into this world. She felt she was able to handle the prejudicial treatment of being black, but how could she be certain that she could protect her offspring from the prejudice—from both black and white races?

God had been kind. In the early years of their marriage, Thyme had failed to conceive, which provided a natural cover for her true feelings. Children could come later,

Thyme assured her husband. But as time went by, she and Cy had fallen into a stiff silence on the subject.

It was hump day, Wednesday, the day to get over and ride downhill toward the weekend. Thyme made it to her office at precisely two minutes to five. A truck was just pulling out of the dock, filled with seat cushions from Rouge Build, heading for the assembly plant. She thought back on the Delta bolts problem at Rouge Build last week. Thyme had planned on sending two workers to Rouge Build to install the bolts so the cars could move on to the assembly line at River Rouge. But the situation was so critical that she'd had to send four utility workers. Valentino had been one of them and it hadn't been long before Ron told her Luella was complaining about Valentino's getting overtime.

Luella was worse than a computer virus. Intent on infecting the minds of her fellow workers against one another, she was a time bomb. Thyme was certain that one day Luella would explode on her.

Thyme was relieved that the major ordeal of last week, the tour with Allied Vespa, had gone well. Initially, the group of minority businessmen refused to see how they could benefit from switching their business to Troy Trim. Skeptical of Allied's intentions early on, Thyme had done her research and felt comfortable with any questions asked her. She still didn't understand why management had her going through the motions, but she was certain they could match GM's bid.

This week had started smoothly enough, but the day before an hourly employee had threatened to kill his supervisor. As Thyme began sorting through her desk papers, Elaine knocked and then handed her a mound of faxes. "Doug Bierce from Security just called and asked if you would give him a ring when you had a moment."

"Did he mention what it was about?"

"Yeah. A supervisor's car was broken into."

"What's the matter with everybody?" Thyme frowned and started sorting through the faxes.

Turning on her computer, she checked her propfs mail. Propfs, an electronic mail used by all salaried workers at Champion, was the primary method of communication within the company. After answering her mail, she went to work on the mounds of problems that were a daily part of her job. She found a moment to call Doug in Security, who brought her up to speed on the incident, just before Elaine buzzed her.

"Dr. Tyler," Elaine said, over the intercom. "Your meeting with Ron is in fifteen minutes."

"Thanks, Elaine." She organized the folders on her desk and headed out of the office. She dreaded going to the meeting with Ron to discuss the case of the homicide threat. Any discussion with Ron on the matter seemed bound to end in an argument. How could Ron defend the actions of an employee who had threatened the life of a supervisor? The employee had to be fired; there was no other resolution. Champion's policy was clear and, friendship or not, she would not bend the rules.

The meeting took two hours, and was just as rough as she'd predicted it would be. It turned out that the incident Doug had called her about was part of this same situation. The employee who had threatened the life of his supervisor was the same one who had broken into the car this morning. The incident was further complicated because of race: the employee was black, the supervisor white. When Thyme announced she would fire the employee, Ron looked at her with bitter disgust. She knew that the subject of her white husband wasn't far from his mind.

Glancing at the clock on the wall, she now felt relieved to have to leave for her appointment with her attorney. Her attorney's office, on the sixteenth floor of Cadillac Towers, was located just three blocks from Cy's new office building. Wearing a wide pair of dark sunglasses and scurrying into the remodernized structure, Thyme felt like a convicted criminal. She moved to the back of the elevator and waited until the car stopped on the tenth floor. Once she announced herself to the receptionist, Thyme was escorted into her attorney's office.

"Good afternoon, Mrs. Tyler."

"Afternoon," Thyme said tentatively. She was still nervous.

Stephen Kravitz's office was expensively furnished. From the gilt-framed paintings to the polished mahogany desk, the atmosphere smelled of success and old money.

"I've been discussing your case with my partners. Chances are Champion will settle before ever going to court."

"Why?"

"Union negotiations." He put his hands behind his head. "This is contract year, Mrs. Tyler. You've picked an opportune time: the company can't afford any more bad publicity."

"I hadn't thought of that."

"Your situation appears to be a solid case of blatant discrimination."

Thyme smiled, and her body relaxed. She eased back in her chair and listened, releasing the buttons on her jacket and crossing her legs. She'd written Spielberg, Baum, and Kravitz a retainer check for ten thousand dollars. No matter what, her reputation and self-respect were worth the money. Now if only she was able to make Cy understand.

"I'll read you a copy of the deposition that we plan to present to Champion. There are six counts in the lawsuit." He leaned forward and shuffled through the stack of legal documents.

" 'Count One. That the Plaintiff, Thyme Tyler, is, and at all times relevant to the allegations contained herein was, a resident of the City of Bloomfield, County of Oakland, and State of Michigan . . .' "

As he continued to read, Thyme felt the tears slipping down her cheeks. This was serious. She hadn't wanted it to get to this point. She had prayed that Champion would promote her. There was no turning back now. Thyme heard him add:

" 'Four. That the Plaintiff, Thyme Tyler, has been and continues to be an employee of the defendant Champion Motors, initially hiring in as an hourly employee on May twenty-two, nineteen seventy-five, at Defendant's Rouge assembly plant.

" 'Five. That the Plaintiff, Thyme Tyler, was first promoted to a position as a salaried employee on or about August thirty, nineteen eighty, the position being that of a Manufacturing Clerk, Salary Grade o-three.' "

Thyme listened to her history at Champion Motors. Count by count, the lawsuit didn't miss a beat. Every position she had held was accounted for. She'd forgotten some of the events that had occurred in the twenty-three years she'd worked at Champion. A part of her felt old. Another part of her felt as if she'd just arrived.

Later that day Thyme called Khan. "Hey," Thyme said, trying to be cheerful, "the Kentucky Derby is on this weekend. How'd you like to watch it with Cy and me?"

"Cool."

She felt Khan's hesitation before she spoke. "Thyme?"

"Yes?"

"Cy isn't planning to try and hook me up with some white guy, is he?"

"Of course not."

"Hey, I've got a right to ask. We're friends."

"I wouldn't set you up without telling you. I don't keep secrets from my friends."

"Just your husband."

"That's unfair, Khan."

"Damn. That shit sounded real personal. I think I'll write in for us to appear on the *Ricki Lake* show."

"Stop, Khan. I'm serious." Thyme was bothered by her friend's sarcasm; she wasn't in the mood.

"Oh, don't get too serious, girlfriend. Cy hasn't done anything to make me want to come over and kick his ass, has he?"

"Naw. Nothing like that." Twin tears rolled down Thyme's cheeks. "So you'll come? We're going to put the pontoon in the water and watch the Derby while we sit and sip on spirits. And of course I've got plenty of gourmet cookies for you."

With all the stresses she'd been dealing with lately, Thyme couldn't wait to spend some fun moments with her young friend who could always make her laugh. "Hey, have you got a pencil handy? I've got the code to get in the gate so you don't have to be announced."

"You kidding?"

Thyme could tell that Khan was pleased. There were only seven homes in their small section of Bloomfield. Culturally speaking, it was a zip code that meant you'd arrived. And Khan would feel more accepted having their code—to hell with Cy and his paranoid need for security.

"No. It's one-three-nine-three. Got that? Just bring your swimsuit. It might get hot enough to dive in."

"Just tell Cy to get the chessboard out. I'm going to kick his ass."

"See you on Saturday."

*   *   *

By Friday night, Thyme was exhausted. She and Cy were putting up the dishes while they listened to ABC's *World News Tonight* with Peter Jennings. Then a local reporter gave an eloquent spiel on the day's hot story, reporting from just outside the picket line at Chrysler's Mack Avenue plant in Detroit.

"Eight Chrysler assembly plants are shut down, including those that build the two-seater sports car, the Incognito, Chrysler's car of the year. If the strike continues, Chrysler could lose a million dollars a day."

"Wow," Thyme said. "I'm worried about our upcoming contract. If things have gotten way out of hand at Chrysler, it may affect things at Champion." Thyme turned up the volume.

"Hell, they should go back to work. They won't win," Cy stated matter-of-factly.

Thyme was stunned. "How long has it been since you were a union brother? Don't answer that, because I know. It's been twenty-five years. What happened to your sympathy for the blue collar worker?"

Cy shrugged his shoulders. "When a strike breaks out, nobody wins. The company loses money, the union loses money. The company can recoup their losses by raising the cost of cars. But the union loses ground with the company in any upcoming negotiations. Therefore, neither side goes away happy."

"I don't agree with you." She frowned. Spraying with Fantastik, she wiped down the Corian counters with a vengeance. For the next two hours they argued over hourly versus salary.

In the past two days, wildcat strikes had broken out at General Motors, Chrysler, and Ford. For everyone in and around Detroit the strike issue was as important as the price of chicken is to Perdue.

Thyme was surprised at how loyal she felt to the union even though she hadn't worked hourly for almost eighteen years. Before now, it hadn't mattered. Now it did. It was just what she needed to work off some angry sweat.

Thyme changed into her exercise clothes and went downstairs. She ran ten miles on the treadmill and put in twelve minutes on the weight machine. She took a shower afterwards and sank her weary body into the comfort of the hot tub.

She could hear Cy's familiar footsteps coming toward her before she opened her eyes.

"I'm sorry, baby," he said, sitting down beside her. In his hand he held a yellow and white packet. Their photo album was tucked under his arm.

"Remember when we took these?" He showed her pictures of the two of them at Niagara Falls taken last year, on their twenty-first anniversary. "Handsome couple, I'd say."

Thyme smiled. "I'd forgotten how much fun we had. When did you get these printed?"

"The other day. We're so spoiled by our computer-ROM we haven't taken the time in years to put pictures in our album."

Thyme turned the pages, smiling at the memories, each more precious than the last. There was a section near the back filled with pictures of Graham from birth to age three. Thyme remembered telling Sydney that if she sent them any more pictures of her baby, she'd better send a photo album along with it.

"Let's not argue." He kissed her apologetically.

She glanced at the album. The moment had passed for her to mention the lawsuit. There was no way he would ever understand how powerless the union people felt, and how powerless she felt, unless she stood up against Champion for blatant discrimination.

"I love you so much, Thyme," Cy said as he stepped down into the circular sunken hot tub. When he began to remove her bathing suit, she helped him.

Thyme loved him. She couldn't deny those feelings. They came regardless of their differences—and there were many. "I love you too, baby," she said as she gave in to him.

They began to make love, though for her it wasn't so much desire as need. The secret she was keeping from Cy was weighing on her. Was she just imagining that Cy seemed to cling to her? Was she just on edge out of her own guilt or was he more needy lately? This tension only heightened the intensity of their lovemaking. They dabbled in the sexual delights of the Kama-sutra, as well as Japanese erotica, and yet both wanted more. How much farther could they go?

Saturday afternoon Thyme couldn't wait for Khan to come over for the Derby event. Thyme had been jittery, distracted by the pending lawsuit and wrestling with whether to confide in Cy. Could she trust him to stay by her side even if he disagreed? Even if it put his own job in jeopardy? She wasn't ready to risk it.

The Cirrus Boat Company had just delivered the open-air boat, and Cy was in the midst of planning how to get the pontoon into the water.

The weather was perfect. It had been topping seventy degrees all week. The wind was mild and there wasn't a cloud in the sky. Thyme arranged the lawn furniture on the lower level and put out the chess game and cards—their afternoon activities. Since the Derby only lasted a few minutes, they would have the rest of the day to fill.

Just then, Khan arrived, kissing Cy on the cheek and

handing him a bottle of Chivas Regal. "I figured you could never have enough scotch in the house."

"Hey, girl," Thyme said, hugging Khan. "You look good in those shorts. You two chat while I cut up some veggies."

"How's your hand, Khan?" Cy asked.

Thyme hoped Cy wouldn't bring up the subject of Khan's love life. Cy had always loved to tease Khan about her sexual exploits with men, especially her voracious appetite for R.C. Like Thyme, Cy had never met the infamous R.C.: he'd just heard the stories.

As Khan flexed her fingers back and forth, she said, "I can still feel a slight tingling in my hand when it gets tired. Unfortunately, this is the hand I use for more personal matters." She winked at Cy. "But enough about me, Cy. Tell me about your new boat . . . I mean pontoon."

Thyme smiled as she brought the tray down the steps. "Don't get him started, Khan. He won't shut up talking about his latest toy."

"It's an Eight-twenty-four Special Edition and floats smoother than the flight of a dream."

Surprisingly, Thyme thought, Khan seemed genuinely interested in Cy's explanation of the seats, tables, and cooler that outfitted the pontoon.

"Okay already. What I want to know is, when do I get my turn to drive this sucker?"

"Right about now," Cy said, slipping on his boat shoes and handing Khan a pair. "Let's grab some music."

"What you got? I don't go for none of that Spice Girls bullshit."

"I'm way ahead of you, Khan." Cy selected some music from the entertainment unit. "Which do you prefer: Lil' Kim, Solo, Ginuwine, or Erykah Badu?"

"All of 'em. But let's start with some Badu."

Cy turned to his wife. "Coming, honey?"

"I'll pass. I've got to check on the Jell-O. I think it's about ready for the fruit cocktail. Remember, we only have an hour before the race begins."

When Cy and Khan returned, Thyme had just turned on the television set and was sipping a glass of Chardonnay. She fixed Cy a shot of Chivas and poured Khan a glass of pink grapefruit Crystal Light.

The broadcasters were introducing some of the Derby's past winners, and Thyme felt excited as clips from last year's race dashed across the big screen.

The horses were at the starting gate.

Cy, Thyme, and Khan had each picked their favorite and placed a five-dollar bet among them.

Boom. They were off.

The camera zeroed in on the strong front runner, named Livewire.

"I should have bet on him," Cy exclaimed.

"It's a she," Khan spoke up.

"How do you know?" Cy asked.

"I just know," Khan said quietly.

Thyme looked at her and realized that Livewire must be R.C.'s horse. Khan looked miserable.

Less than five minutes later the race was over. Livewire was the winner. All three of them had lost.

As the camera zoomed in on the winner's circle, Khan sighed audibly. "Oh, God."

"Damn, who's she?" Cy asked. "She's gorgeous."

Khan began to collect their plates and glasses. Thyme looked at the television screen and saw a beautiful woman dressed all in black with a peach rose attached to her bosom. A large hat covered the side of her face, but her beauty was unmistakable.

"What?" Cy said as he half turned from the set and looked at Khan.

The two women said nothing as they looked each other in the eye. Then the owners' names flashed across the screen: MR. AND MRS. R.C. RICHARDSON OF PARIS, KENTUCKY.

R.C. Richardson and Tomiko stood with their jockey next to their horse, accepting the wreath of roses in the winner's circle.

"Khan, are you okay?" Thyme asked her friend.

"Yeah. But there must be a huge mistake. Weak studs finish last, not first," she said bitterly.

7

Settle down, ladies, settle down," Khan said from her seat in the midsection of the Bel-Aire Theater. *The Revenge of Cleopatra Jones,* starring Tamara Dobson, had just ended, and the women had been screaming and hollering throughout the two-hour movie. Damn, there are some ghetto folks up here, Khan said to herself, shaking her head.

It was a typical Tuesday movie night out, Khan's weekly treat to herself, and she'd never before thought about asking for her money back. But tonight she could barely enjoy the picture for the noise.

As the audience filed out of the theater, Khan followed slowly. Like a trained hound dog sniffing out the perpetrator's scent, Khan spotted R.C. a few feet ahead of her. It had been a few weeks since she'd seen him on TV at the Kentucky Derby.

At that moment, R.C. turned, and when he did Khan felt herself melt like a mother at the sight of her baby's first tears. He wore a powder blue Nike jogging suit, a color that Khan had always loved on him. He'd never looked so handsome. Oh God, how she missed him.

"R.C.?" she whispered under her breath.

R.C. narrowed his eyes at Khan and turned away quickly, disappearing into the crowd.

"She should have fucked that motherfucker's brains out," a woman said a few steps behind Khan, referring to the movie.

Khan sniffed back tears. "Damn right, girlfriend." Khan's eyes were glued to the spot where she'd last seen R.C. "He deserved to die."

Walking with the crowd, she exited and felt the cool night air kiss the tears on her cheeks good-bye.

Minutes later, she slipped inside her cranberry-colored Phoenix sports car and started the ignition. In the parking space beside her was a face she didn't recognize.

The man with dreadlocks had pearl-white teeth that sparkled spectacularly in the darkness.

She turned her head and turned up her nose. *Freaky bastard!*

His dreadlocks rested on his shoulders. Khan hated them. To her, dreads looked hideous. Being black didn't mean being ignorant. She couldn't understand why it was necessary to show America that blacks were from Africa when ninety-nine percent of the black community had never even been there. It didn't make sense.

As she started up the ignition, she yawned. *This is one damn night I wish I had gone to bed instead of going to the movies.* The image of R.C.'s cold face burned hotly in her chest.

Once home, she considered calling her Mama Pearl, but realized it was too late. Her next thought was calling Thyme, but she shrugged that off, not wanting to invade her friend's privacy. Her final thought was to call her Uncle Ron. No, she figured, he and Aunt Ida could be getting it on just like Thyme and Cy.

She needed to be consoled by the wisdom of those older.

To them, her troubles were probably trivial. She could hear them preaching:

"Wait till you're married. . . ."

"You think you got problems. Wait till you have a husband. And children . . ."

Which was exactly what she wanted: a husband. A family. Children.

Why had R.C. ignored her?

Without thinking, she went straight to the phone. He must have been expecting her call, because he answered on the first ring.

"R.C. It's me."

"I figured you'd call."

"You could have called me. I deserve at least that."

"I thought it would be better this way."

Khan wanted to scream "You cowardly son of a bitch!" Instead she said, "Hey, maybe you're right. I've met someone my own age and my Mama Pearl is pleased as plum pudding. You know how old-fashioned she is."

It wasn't entirely a lie, she thought. Julian Anderson, a computer analyst at Champion, had been bugging her to go on a date for months.

"Yeah."

"Whew." Khan wiped the lying sweat off her forehead. "So how's your health?" *Has your new wife been able to convince you to use lotion on your ashy ass yet?*

"Cut the shit. I've got it coming. Go ahead, cuss me out."

I guess not. You're still ornery as hell.

Her voice was low, cunning. "Why?" She took a deep breath. "I thought we were going to get married. Why would you have given me the ring?" She heard him stutter.

Khan continued, "Well I've been thinking that we're better off friends than lovers. So, R.C., now I'm your friend. And I know you're still my friend." Her eyes brimmed with tears. "Don't trouble yourself worrying about me. As I said, I've found someone too."

"Khan."

"No." She tried to keep her voice even, gulping back tears. "I think it's better this way. We weren't meant for each other anyway. . . ." Her voice trailed off.

"Baby—"

You son of a bitch. How dare you call me baby when you've got a wife? Does she wear colorful kimonos to bed? Is that what turns you on? She took another deep breath. "I wish you and your wife all the happiness that you deserve." *You both deserve a six-day-old case of the clap.*

"Please let me explain—I had to marry her. It's an arranged marriage to get her out of Japan. She had to leave the country. I'm just helping her out—"

Khan didn't let him finish. "Stop, R.C. I don't want to hear it." She knew he was lying. The truth was that R.C. had gotten a smell of some young Oriental pussy and he wouldn't let go till Gabriel blew his horn. "I've got to go," she said casually. "Bye, R.C."

Click.

Speaking of horn, I'm going to get some motherfucker to blow mine.

Rushing to the bathroom, she washed her face with ice-cold water. "You're okay, girl. You're just fine. Don't let that bastard get his rocks off on your pain." She splashed more water on her face. "Okay. Okay. You're okay now."

Lifting her face, she looked into the mirror. Even though her face was coated with water, she could still feel the tears.

Khan leaned her head back, raking her fingers through her two-inch haircut. Her roots were a half-inch long. "Bitch. What you need is color." Bending down, she reached beneath the sink cabinet and sifted through the piles of junk for a box of L'Oreal hair coloring.

Mixing the white developer with the nearly clear coloring until it thickened, she stood before the mirror and said to herself, "Okay girl, you're 'bout to be a pretty bitch tonight. And you too, missy," Khan said, patting her crotch. "Fuck R.C. and his young bitch. You can do without him. He's doing just fine without you. Somebody gonna tell you that you fine. That you all that she is and more." *I can't help it if the stupid bastard didn't know I was the best damn woman he would ever have.*

She washed, washed again, conditioned, and blow-dried her pretty yellow hair. It was Ice Gold, the exact color of her lipstick and new nail polish.

As she dressed in satin pajamas, dried flowers rustled on the sill. The mellow May air was still cool as it rushed in through the half-cracked bedroom window.

It was 10:00 P.M. She was itching in places she couldn't scratch, tossing and turning, and trying to concentrate on Julian. Wrapping the cotton coverlet over herself, she turned on her side.

Tossing and turning, Khan kept replaying her conversation with R.C. Should she have told him to fuck off? Why had she been so gracious, telling him they were friends? Could she really be his friend?

The clock on the nightstand said 1:10 A.M. and she wasn't even close to sleep. She kicked the covers to the side and tucked the sheets beneath her chin. Shortly thereafter, she tried to dream about Julian fucking her brains out, something R.C. rarely did. Then Khan tried to remember R.C.'s deficiencies: he was so old, he had a problem fucking and staying hard. As she continued struggling to sleep, Khan tried to picture R.C. as a tired, withered old man. Finally she fell into a dreamless sleep.

*   *   *

Khan was almost finished with her day's production. Her new partner, Jeremy Stannapolis, was working out well. Khan smiled smugly as she watched Luella swishing down the aisle. Luella had insisted on a new partner when Khan had been out with her injured hand. At first Khan had felt hurt. As much as Luella was a pain in the ass to work with, Khan had grown accustomed to their teamwork. Now, Khan was glad; her new partner was much easier to get along with.

Just then, her cousin Valentino came by her workstation, dressed in a pale lavender sport suit. Beneath his suit, Tino wore a tight white T-shirt. Khan thought, With a body like his, how could he hide it?

"Hey there, cousin. How you doin'?" Valentino said affectionately. Nodding in the direction of Luella, he said, "I'm sure you don't miss being partners with Luella."

Khan instinctively rose to Luella's defense even though she was pissed at her. She knew Luella was a good person underneath. "She's a pain in the ass, Tino. But we worked well together. Don't diss her. It's only natural I see a side of her that you don't."

"Next thing you know people around here are going to be calling you a whore, too."

"Tino, Luella's a good wife and a good mother. She works hard to put her two boys through college."

"A good wife, hah! She's the kind of wife that asks her husband to pull out the broken stove and once he fixes it, doesn't mop the floor behind it before he pushes it back."

"Hm." Khan cocked an eyebrow at Tino. "What if it wasn't dirty?"

"It was dirty all right. Look Khan, every man around here knows that the broad has had more pricks than a secondhand dart board." He sneered. "And them fools are still standing in line to screw her during lunch in the company parking lot."

"You lying."

"Get real. The women around here call her Skunk Butt behind her back." Tino's eyes grew in amazement. "Where you been?"

"Shhh, here comes your dad."

Tino mumbled, "And he knows all about her too."

She could hear the sharp intake of breath from Tino as they walked toward Ron, who had been stopped midway in the aisle by a man and woman.

Khan noticed the woman eyeing her uncle's crotch during the entire conversation. She was positive that Tino observed it as well.

"Well, Ron, it's just like Millie was saying," the man spoke up. "Cordell Mitchell, the supervisor on midnights, worked Saturday and Sunday afternoon in Maintenance moving machines out of the Illusion truck unit. I don't know what's going on around here, but that's a carpenter's job and he knows it. He thought he was slick, but my Millie spotted him all right." Millie, still eyeing Ron, nodded in agreement. "Are you going to write up Cordell or not? We've been getting the runaround from the other committeemen for over a week now."

"I'll speak with Cordell this evening," Ron said patiently.

"You know he's going to deny it," Millie harped, still giving Uncle Ron's body the once-over.

"I can't just take your word for it, Sam," Ron said, as he shifted a stack of papers from one arm to the other. When he caught sight of Khan, Ron ended any further discussion. "I'll get back with you by tomorrow. That's the best I can do."

Khan thought the woman was tacky, checking out Uncle Ron so blatantly. But apparently her uncle didn't agree. His eyes sparkled from the woman's attention. And in those eyes she saw a certain sexiness that she'd never noticed before.

She had to admit, at fifty-six, and with thinning gray hair and a thick mustache, her uncle was still quite a sexy man.

"Hi, Ron," Khan said after Sam and Millie had left. "I've been meaning to stop by your office. It's been so long since we talked." She gave Ron a quick conspiratorial wink, then smiled. "Will you give my best to Aunt Ida?"

"Sure."

"Ron," Valentino said, nodding hello to his father, his tone more formal than usual.

"Hey," Ron said, not bothering to add anything more— not even a "How are you," never mind a "Hi, son."

Khan felt torn. The tension between father and son was almost unbearable. Even though she loved them both, she didn't want to get involved in whatever battle Ron and Tino were duking out.

Ron looked at Valentino, hard. "How're Sarah and the baby?"

Valentino gave his stock answer, and Khan wondered why Ron seemed to know so little about Tino's family.

Just then Luella approached them.

Luella was wearing the teeniest top possible without risking being written up by her supervisor. Hell, the weather had barely stabilized at seventy but already the diva of Champion was ready to show off her huge breasts and flat stomach.

Khan was often shocked by Luella's scanty attire, but she had to admit that even at forty, Luella had a body worth showing off.

Luella's long, luscious legs on her five-foot-seven-inch frame made her hard to ignore. The wild, crinkled, shoulder-length hair she had weaved and wore to perfection only added to her sexiness. And Luella had a natural mesmerizing presence about her that reminded Khan of Marilyn Monroe.

If truth be told, Luella made Khan keep her own shit in check. Khan didn't want to be outdone in the looks department by a woman sixteen years older than she was.

"Did you take care of my grievance?" Luella asked in the throaty voice she used for flirting.

Valentino rolled his eyes and Khan smiled.

What's up with these women checking out Ron's crotch? Khan wondered. He couldn't be raising that much hell at his age. Or could he?

Ron avoided her eyes. "The meeting is on for next week, Luella. You'll hear from a member of the committee. You know I don't handle those negotiations."

Luella's ripe body was inches from Ron. "But I want *you* to handle it," she said in a whimpering voice. "They don't know my situation like you do."

Khan could feel both Ron and Valentino cringe.

"I'll talk to you later, Khan, Dad," Valentino said abruptly.

Khan could almost hear Ron scream when Tino's "Dad" echoed down the aisle.

Luella extended her nude leg and cocked her shoulder back before turning her gaze toward Tino. "I'll see you later, junior," she said.

"Sure." Valentino rushed off.

Usually during work hours, Valentino addressed his father as Ron. The policy had been established since Valentino was first hired in at Champion. He hadn't broken Ron's harsh rule until now.

What was up with this triangle? Khan wondered. You could cut the tension between Tino, Ron, and Luella with a knife.

It was lunchtime, and only a few people were in the unit. Generally, Khan ate by herself, having no desire to join the others in the cafeteria. Khan was about to leave and go eat when her uncle stopped her with his hand on her arm.

"Come up to my office for a minute." It wasn't a request; it was a command.

Passing all the committee room offices, Khan followed Ron into his office, which was the largest on "committee row," as the workers called it. Unlike the other cookie-cutter rooms, Ron had color in his office. His visitors' chairs were dark teal, his desk and bookcase a dark walnut wood grain. Two large fern plants, courtesy of Ida, were balanced in opposite corners.

Once inside he asked her, "Do you have money in the bank?"

"Sure I do," Khan said nervously, taking a seat across from his desk. In her head, she calculated her small amount of savings but her weak smile didn't betray her.

"You know there is bound to be a strike soon."

"I thought you said we weren't going to strike, Uncle Ron," she said. "We can't afford to strike."

"Mexico's stealing our jobs, and the company is letting them do it."

"Mexico? How could they compete with American workers?"

"Blue collar workers hired by Champion in the fifties were able to buy new homes, put money in the bank, and even send their children to college. Now the company is hiring our brothers and sisters at six dollars per hour." Khan knew this was way below union scale.

She kept silent.

"The wage in Mexico is even smaller, so now some of our union sisters and brothers who have been laid off are working at small plants where unions have no power. They sign up at ten dollars an hour and less." That was ten dollars less than they would make if they worked for the Big Four, Khan calculated.

"So you think we should worry about the contract in September?"

"We have a little time, but Mexico's automobile production has more than doubled over the past five years. Do you understand what I'm trying to say, Khan?"

She jerked her head up and said, "I'm not sure."

"I'll give you an easy example. I think Champion's going to offer us a buyout. Eight years ago Champion pulled this same stunt. We had young workers with families waiving their recall rights and accepting fifty-thousand dollars in severance settlements. One man in particular took a job at a small welding factory for eleven dollars an hour after he took his settlement and left. This was eight dollars less than he made at Champion. Just over a year later, he was laid off from that job. The fifty grand was gone, and his wife filed for a divorce."

"You're scaring me, Uncle Ron." She was finally beginning to pay attention.

"What's happening is that we're losing thousands of jobs to Mexican labor. I'm not just speaking about our black brothers and sisters. I'm talking about the UAW. Color doesn't matter. It's been increasing steadily for ten years. Sure, Champion tries to deny it, as do the other automobile companies. But they're lying. Our president claims that increased trade with Mexico will create jobs on both sides of the border. He believes that, in thirty years, America will benefit from expansion into Mexico. Meanwhile, thousands of families employed by the automobile companies, especially in the state of Michigan, will be the first casualties of that free trade."

"Where'd you hear this, Uncle Ron?"

"Read the papers, Khan. And not just the society section.

Over the past seven years alone, the Big Four Detroit-based automakers, Champion, General Motors, Chrysler, and Ford, have reduced their production in Michigan to one-point-six million cars from two-point-eight million. Obviously, they're reducing workforce as well. You don't hear too much about it because we're not laying off people. The company is reducing the head count through attrition, death, retirements, and firing. Now where do you think that leaves you and me in a few years?

"Champion just eliminated six hundred salary workers in their Flat Rock Operations. An unspecified number of hourly workers is expected to follow. No. Our company's not playing fair. They're not telling us the truth about how they're doing business, what their picks are. Just lately, I learned that in this plant all the small parts are grouped together now under Plastic Products and Trim Products Division and Allied Products Organization. Champion plans on grouping everything together now and eliminating more jobs. I've been trying to find out just how many more jobs they're going to eliminate. You better stop spending every dollar you get your hands on and stop taking this overtime for granted."

"Do they really only make ten dollars a day in Mexico?"

"They make less and they feel like Rockefellers," Ron said, shaking his head. "Soon everyone will start feeling the pinch. The blue collar jobs will be the first to go, but they won't be the last. The suburbanites are not immune, and neither are the bankers. Everyone in Michigan is tied somehow to the automobile industry."

"Are you talking about Thyme?" Khan knew Thyme and Ron had a complicated working relationship.

"For sure. But she and her white husband don't got a damn thing to worry about: they know what's going on at the top, so they're probably planning their escape. But people like you and me, we will cease to matter if the American manufacturers run their business the way they feel is most cost effective."

"My goodness, Uncle Ron. I never thought about it that way." *How in the hell am I going to pay my mortgage if we strike? Fuck the car, they can take that shit back. But I can't sleep on the streets. Damn!*

"You have to realize how much Detroit has declined since nineteen sixty-eight. Its population has slipped below a million for the first time since the early nineteen hundreds. There's nothing but liquor stores on every corner, and vacant premises. Detroit has yet to recover from the riots of the nineteen sixties. We're in trouble here, babe."

"Well it sounds like a strike is inevitable."

Ron looked pensive. "I can't say what the union's planning. A lot of changes are being made. Membership is way way down, just like I predicted."

The merger of the top three unions that was announced in 1995 by the Big Four was close to being implemented. The steel workers, the automobile workers, and the machinists would soon be under one umbrella union. The result would be a two-million-member behemoth. As the transition had occurred, many workers had lost a sense of their own voices being heard and had begun dropping out of the union altogether.

No one had thought it would happen so soon—no one except hard-line union officials like Ron. Ron had reiterated over and over again that the unions would merge. He had been right on target.

Although it was the unions who won the wage gains of the 1960s and 1970s and led American blue collar workers into the middle class, those same workers were now losing ground to inflation, cuts in benefits, and the attrition of manufacturing industries. They had begun to lose their foothold in the middle class.

"I think if you're smart you'll start putting away some cash," Ron said, slicking down her blond hair. "And I must admit, your hair *is* real pretty."

Khan blushed. "Stop, Uncle Ron." Few of the other workers knew she was Ron's niece. It was better that no one knew she was related to a union manager. If people knew that Ron was her uncle, some of the assholes would jump to conclusions and think she was getting an extra hour of overtime.

"Like I said, you're smart. Smart people have money in the bank."

Khan plastered a wide smile on her face. Her Visa as well as her MasterCard were over the limit, and Neiman's had confiscated her card the last time she shopped there. I'm as broke as a sick, limp-dicked dog, but ain't nobody but the bill collectors got to know, Khan thought to herself. R.C. had always told her that money was made to be spent. She just wished she wasn't such an expert. Hell, she thought, who could afford to save money these days?

Maybe only those at the top. Like Cy and Thyme.

8

"Wow! That's hot!" Luella said, blowing the smoke off the mug of coffee her husband, Omar, had just handed her. She popped a Dexatrim into her mouth and downed half the scalding coffee.

It was four in the morning and at least seventy-five degrees outside on this late May morning. Despite the temperature, Omar, the same man who wouldn't dream of leaving his bed when there were ten inches of snow outside, had insisted on warming up the car for her.

"The air's working fine, sugar." He went through the motions of checking the oil, gas gauge, and tires.

Like I didn't know that already, fool. She got into her car, set her mug in the holder, and slammed the door shut. She turned on the headlights, put the car in reverse, then let the window down.

"Omar, make sure that the trash is taken out." She could see from her rearview mirror that her neighbor's was already on the curb. "Today's Friday, you know."

Their three-bedroom ranch was situated on Six Mile Road near Hubbell. Omar drove eighteen-wheeler refrigerated semis for a living and was gone twenty days out of the month. The least he could do, she figured, when he was home, was take out the damn trash.

"I won't forget, sugar."

As soon as she pressed down on the gas pedal, she could see him giving her his familiar puppy-dog look. "What is it?" she asked, poking her head out the window and frowning.

By any woman's measure, Omar was a good-looking man. His skin was the color of rich mahogany. His irises were black and unreadable; a woman could see herself in the depths of them. Of average height and build, Omar's sexiness was his nonchalant attitude toward his all-American-boy good looks. At forty-five years old, his hair was still so thick he cut it himself twice a week. All combined, he possessed the attributes that made women want to follow him to the ends of the earth.

"Will you be home by three? I've got to get my rig loaded—"

Luella looked bored. "Look, Omar, I know you're going to California. And I know you'll be gone for a week." *Thank God.* "Now what is it? You need to get loaded up on pussy before you leave?" She forced a smile. Stupid bastard. You would think after twenty-two years of marriage, he would have figured out by now why she ever married him in the first place.

"Sugar, we ain't spent no time together since Easter and that was over a month ago."

"I'll do what I can," she mumbled, then screeched out of the driveway. Their two sons were in their third and fourth years at Columbia University. She and Omar had worked hard for the last twenty years to save enough money for their children to go to a top college. But ever since they'd moved away, Luella no longer felt the need to keep up the pretense of being the good wife. She wanted her boys to finish school so she could retire early and have some real fun. But now she had to go to work and fight for more overtime—after all, Columbia was expensive.

When Luella arrived at work, she was disappointed to find that Valentino had been transferred out of their unit for the day. With no one to distract her, Luella finished her ten hours of production by eleven o'clock.

Just as she was leaving, dreading going home to her husband, Allister offered her two more hours of overtime, which she readily accepted. An hour later, she cruised by the new job postings listed on the bulletin board. Although she hadn't mentioned it to anyone, Luella had bid on a job for a receiving inspector in Quality Control, which would take her out of production altogether. The position paid $1.10 more an hour and there were fewer people to fight with about overtime.

After checking in the front office on the status of her application, she stopped back by Khan's machine. It was a quarter after twelve and the noon news was on.

"Pull up a seat, Luella. There's a story on about Oprah's new movie, *Beloved*."

As they listened to the female anchor reel off all of Oprah's accomplishments, Luella squirmed with envy. Luella popped another Dexatrim, chasing it with sixteen ounces of water. She didn't realize that Khan was watching her.

"Is that a diet pill, Luella?"

If I didn't like you, I'd cuss your Barbie-looking little ass out. What the hell you think it is? "No. Vitamins." She felt her stomach bubbling and thanked God that she would soon be excreting the fig bar she'd so foolishly eaten earlier. The sound of applause from the television brought her attention back to Oprah. Luella rolled her eyes at the slim television sensation as she began to describe her new movie.

"I remember back when they were calling her Okra."

"Stop, Luella. You know you ain't right," Khan chastised.

"Hell, I'm tired of them talking about that bitch like she's the greatest thing since Johnny Carson. I remember when she wore a three-x. So now Okra's skinny and wearing designer clothes 'cause they don't come in alphabet sizes," Luella huffed.

Khan turned off the TV and said to Luella, "Hey, what you doing for Memorial Day weekend? Will your boys be driving home or are they catching a plane?"

"They can't," Luella said sadly. Perhaps that's why she was in such an ornery mood today. She missed her sons.

"You know how much I love to look at pictures, Luella. I ain't seen them babies' photos since they graduated from high school."

Luella blushed. "They ain't babies, child." But Luella couldn't resist showing them off. Khan and Luella both knew good and well that Khan had seen pictures of them at her sister's wedding last year and had commented on how handsome they were. It was Khan's love of family that had tied the bond of their working friendship from the very beginning.

"My, my, these are some sexy-looking dudes. Are they both still making the dean's list?"

"Yep. Cole's a four-point-o, majoring in pre-law, and Reese is holding steady at three-point-seven in archaeology. They both have real good jobs this summer in New York City." Luella looked at the photos of her sons. "I don't know how I ended up with such brilliant children." *At least Omar was good for something.*

Just as she was about to insert the photos back into her wallet, two more pictures fell out. Khan grabbed the one closest to her foot.

"Luella, what you been hiding this fine-ass man for? I

ain't never even heard you talk about him. You think some of these women gonna steal him?"

Luella quickly took the picture from Khan. "Who, Omar? Not really."

"His name is Omar? He don't look like an Omar. Mmm, girl . . . and I thought Valentino was handsome—Omar's a fox."

"Granted, he's good-looking, but he can't fuck worth a damn. Got an itty-bitty dick. His tongue is longer than his shit is. That's how I ended up with his sorry ass. As usual, I was the last one in high school to find out."

"You lying, Luella. Even so, you still got a husband. Shit, I wish I had one, especially one this damn pretty. I think I'd get an orgasm just lying in bed beside him."

"I've tried everything. Nothing's worked. He ain't satisfied me in years, but he don't know it. You think he's pretty. A lot of women do. But nobody knows that I have to get out the Pine Sol after his stinking ass leaves the bathroom. Nobody knows that I have to put Spray 'n Wash in his drawers before I wash them." Luella paused, turning up her lips in a mock smile. "And when he wakes up in the morning with crust all around his mouth and his breath smells worse than dog shit . . . girl . . . he ain't pretty all the time."

9

The iridescent bronze patent-leather pumps Thyme wore hurt her feet. They were brand spanking new, along with the silk and linen cream silk suit she wore. Last week, in preparation for Thyme's meeting today with Champion's division managers (the group who mandated all production decisions that affected Champion's various plants), Cy had taken Thyme shopping. Thyme loved it when her husband picked clothes for her; it was the one indulgence he never refused. He had selected the empire-waist three-quarter-length jacket with matching skirt at Sherri's in Bloomfield and had even chosen the bronze and cream print scarf, which she had casually draped around the jewel-necked collar. A Mikimoto Cherry Blossom gold brooch held the scarf in place.

At this moment, the confidence she wore on her face was more important than the clothes on her back. Thyme felt certain no one could tell she was nervous when she stepped inside Champion Motors' new headquarters. She felt a trickle of sweat slip down between her breasts as she clutched her briefcase and pressed the elevator button.

Since Troy Trim had lost the bid for Allied Vespa's new business, Thyme had put together a proposal to address production issues. In the meantime, Thyme was told that three of the car lines sewed on the afternoon shift would be leaving Troy Trim; one of Champion's other facilities would be assuming those jobs. She received no explanation as to why, nor did any new business come into Troy Trim to replace the loss. Without wasting any time, Thyme decided to be proactive and develop a proposal that would anticipate any more cutbacks at Troy Trim.

She had discussed her proposal with Cy, and he felt that she'd done an excellent job figuring out how both to increase production and cut costs—without eliminating jobs. Discussing her proposal with Cy had made Thyme feel closer to him than she had in weeks. She still had not summoned the courage to tell him about the lawsuit, hoping that she might not have to; if the managers supported her proposal, they would surely give her a promotion.

Her meeting was on the fourteenth floor—the same as Cy's office. Of course, as one of the division managers of Trim, Cy would be at the meeting.

"Hello," Cy's new secretary said. "And you're here to see . . . ?" she asked, while offering Thyme a seat with an outstretched hand on the beige leather sofa.

"I'm Mrs. Tyler. Mr. Tyler's *wife*." She put a heavy accent on the "wife." "I'm sure he's expecting me."

Thyme watched the woman's attitude change as she turned red and paged Cy. "Of course."

You look surprised to see me. And of course you couldn't tell by the tone of my voice that I was black. At least I've solved one mystery today. She's about as attractive as an anteater.

Three minutes later Cy was standing in front of Thyme. They hugged and Thyme felt temporarily soothed.

"Good morning. You look beautiful, Thyme," he said,

kissing her on the cheek. "Are you ready? Everyone's waiting."

"Wait, honey." Setting her briefcase on the floor, she faced her husband and straightened his striped tie. "There. Now it's perfect." She raised her eyes slowly toward the secretary, who was watching them out of the corner of her eye but trying her best to be discreet. "Show me the way."

Once in the conference room, Cy gestured toward a chair across the table from him. Eleven other division managers were gathered around the burled wood table. There was only one other woman in the room: Mrs. Candice-Marie Avery, the fourth wife of the financier Allen Jeremy, whose firm, Nelson, Avery, and Goldberg, owned Fairlane Town Center as well as several other multimillion-dollar businesses in Dearborn. Thyme knew that Mrs. Avery had been a division manager when she married her husband, and, to everyone's surprise, continued working. Rumor had it that her prenuptial agreement kept her from Allen's millions. Now she sat beside her husband on Champion's board of directors.

Introductions were made, and then it was Thyme's turn to make her pitch. "As you know, Champion Trim is seeking new business—"

"What happened to the Pughmont Corporation that toured Troy Trim last month?" Candice-Marie cut in.

"It was Allied Vespa, not Pughmont. Unfortunately, we were outbid by General Motors." Thyme looked at Cy, whose face was expressionless. She was certain that everyone in the room knew what had happened with Allied, so why was Candice-Marie asking? Thyme continued without pausing. "We're running full on one shift, and half on the second. Several of the luxury units are piggybacked, but we have room for at least four more car lines."

Looking at the stoic faces around her, Thyme suddenly realized that everyone in this room, including her husband, knew why the jobs had been taken away from Troy Trim, but clearly they weren't going to tell her what was going on.

"This is what I suggest," she said, keeping her voice steady as she handed each of them a copy of her proposal to sew headrest covers in Troy Trim. Thyme went on to explain the ideas that she planned to bring more business into the plant. The proposal included information on the cost of raw materials and the product they could produce for other facilities.

"How exactly can you secure new business?" one manager asked.

Without waiting for her response, another manager asked, "How do you plan on staying competitive?"

No sooner had she started to answer that question, another question flew at her. She was being railroaded. A sudden sense of betrayal came over her. Something made her keep her eyes away from Cy's.

"Can your plant handle that much new business and still keep the same level of quality and maintain our Q-one rating?"

"I'm trying to do the job you pay me for, gentlemen. Run a profitable plant and produce a quality product." She ignored Candice-Marie, who wouldn't even look her in the face when she spoke to her. "Bringing in new business at Troy Trim is first and foremost."

Cy hadn't spoken a word since the meeting began. He hadn't asked a single question or commented on her proposal. What was going on? She wrapped up her proposal and summarized her ideas. As she shook hands with everyone and thanked them for their time, she fought back tears. Glancing over her shoulder, she caught Cy huddled with his boss, John Sandler. He didn't make a move toward her.

Why hadn't he stuck up for her? They'd talked about her

proposal several times at home and he'd agreed with her ideas. Why not now? Why not here?

Thyme walked out of the meeting without showing the least bit of tension. As she got on the elevator, she had a broad smile pasted on her face for everyone to see, including Cy.

Once in her car, she began to drive, going nowhere in particular, radio tuned to 97.9 WJLB. She found herself cruising around Palmer Park, still trying to unwind. What had happened in there? Why hadn't Cy warned her about how the board would react? What was going on?

Was he keeping something from her? Why wouldn't he have hinted at the board's position if it was so steadfastly against developing any new business at Troy Trim? Why would he purposely set her up to fail?

For the rest of the afternoon, Thyme drove around Detroit. She and Cy had made plans to go to an elegant dinner in Bloomfield that evening at Giovanni's Supper Club. Thyme went to get a manicure and then a pedicure—anything but go home and confront Cy.

In part to lift her spirits, in part to shock Cy, Thyme dressed that evening in a body-plunging black evening gown, which highlighted the deep curves of her body while starkly underlining the nakedness of her skin. She'd never had the nerve to wear the dress before.

Giovanni's was filled to capacity. There was a slight traffic jam at the front desk where other expensively dressed patrons hoped for a table. Cy and Thyme were seated beneath a beautiful Impressionist painting by Joaquin Mir Trinxet. Several other paintings, including works by John Singer Sargent, Max Liebermann, and Mary Cassatt, added drama to the high-ceilinged room. But not as much drama, Thyme ascertained, as the glances she was receiving from some of the men in the room. Throughout the evening Cy pretended not to notice, while Thyme enjoyed the fine wine and rich food.

"I made a call to Hasbro today. They're sending me some additional information on my G.I. Joe pricing lists. I have big plans that one day my collection will be worth hundreds of thousands."

Thyme looked up at him for a moment, paused, and grunted, "Uh-huh."

"Yeah, sweetie, the more I get involved with this G.I. Joe stuff the more impressed I am from a financial standpoint."

With today's events still fresh in her mind, Thyme didn't want to listen to her husband's pleasantries. Instead, she found herself admiring the cute shoes the little girl across the room had on. She could tell the child was well mannered by the one tiny hand that rested in her lap while she ate.

"What do you think about those vintage comic books I just purchased?" Cy asked.

"I'm sorry, Cy. What did you say?"

Cy and Thyme spent the remainder of the evening discussing safe subjects: their pontoon, the landscaping in their backyard. Even the neighbor's new dog seemed to be a delightful topic for Cy.

The next day, as Cy was getting ready to leave for his bowling tournament in Reno, Nevada, Thyme backed out of accompanying him on the trip at the last minute. She just wasn't up for it. She was sick to death of their faux politeness with each other. She was ready to argue. Dammit, she wanted to scream at Cy. Hell, she wanted to slap the shit out of him.

The moment Cy left for his trip, Thyme picked up the phone and called Khan. Before Thyme could speak a word, Khan broke in with her own problems. "I'm sick of this shit. It's on every television station, the main topic of conversation over the radio."

"The strikes?" After the strike at Chrysler, the union had ordered strikes at several more Chrysler plants around Detroit. The pressure between the hourly workers and the company chiefs was building.

"Yes, and now more violence." The violence at the various auto plants had become a regular feature of plant life ever since January, when a worker at Ford shot his wife, her lover, and then killed himself after a heated argument. Then on a Sunday in March, a skilled tradesman killed a security guard, then himself, because the guard had been harassing the tradesman's daughter. Next, a thirty-year-old female employee shot and killed her nineteen-year-old lover after he threatened to end the affair.

Nearly every day for the past two months, the headlines had read: SHOOTING AT CHRYSLER. SHOOTING AT FORD. TWO DEAD AT GENERAL MOTORS. How long until there'd be shooting at Champion too?

What was even more alarming to Thyme was that all the crimes occurred during overtime hours. It was becoming more and more clear that as the workers sought the increasingly elusive overtime, the increased tension between them led to violence. There was an unmistakable pattern. And the fact that the violence went unchecked meant that none of the plants provided enough security and the corporate hierarchy refused to respond to the situation. It was as if the corporate offices encouraged tension among its hourly employees.

"It'll be over soon," Thyme said to Khan, not quite believing herself. Three days earlier, eighty-eight hundred Menzi Packard electrical system workers who made wiring harnesses for virtually all Champion cars and trucks built in North America walked off their jobs. The labor relations between company and union continued to worsen. A strike by Local 2207 of the International Union of Electrical

Workers in Lorain, Ohio, could shut down all Champion assembly plants in the United States, Canada, and Mexico.

The walkouts came as a strike occurred by six-thousand United Auto Workers at Champion's pickup and truck plant in Wayne, and as the forty-two hundred workers in Lawton, Oklahoma, entered their third week on the picket line.

"That's not what Ron says. He says the UAW has to strike or we'll lose everything," Khan said nervously.

Thyme's retort was swift. "Someone always has to make that sacrifice for others to reap the benefits."

"Girl, you sound like one of us," Khan commented.

Thyme wondered again whose side she should be on—white collar or blue collar. What did it all mean anymore?

Thyme said good-bye to her friend, promising to check in with her over the weekend. It was early June and still not too hot to lie outside. All Thyme wanted to do for the next two days was lounge on her back patio and finish the novel she was reading. Without Cy around, she might even be able to get some rest.

Monday morning came all too quickly. It was only eleven and already Thyme had a raging headache. She gulped two Excedrins and hoped her headache would retreat. Today she wore a knee-length silk chiffon dress, the upper half teal, and the lower a bright orange, with variations of gold dots imprinted all over it. Sometimes wearing brightly colored outfits helped lift her spirits.

"Dr. Tyler?" Thyme heard her secretary say over the intercom. "There's a Mr. Richardson here to see you."

Checking her appointment book, she saw that all she had on it was an afternoon appointment with the employee involvement (EI) group out in Annex B.

Ordinarily, the foreman of the sewing unit conducted this weekly grievance meeting, which was usually attended by twenty employees. But Thyme knew that the overtime equalization situation had gotten out of hand. Ron had asked her to join the group this afternoon to discuss the issues. The tensions were so high among the workers, Ron thought Thyme's presence alone might help the employees resolve their issues. It would take her at least five minutes to drive over there in the electrically powered motor cart she used daily. She didn't have time to meet with anyone right now.

"Mr. Richardson doesn't have an appointment," Thyme snapped. "Tell him to make an appointment." The name Richardson sounded familiar.

Even though the door to her office was closed, she could hear Elaine fencing with the man about getting in to see her now. If she didn't get rid of him in five minutes, they'd run into each other.

Just as she was collecting the keys to her motor cart, the man burst into her office.

"How dare you come in here!" she shouted. "Get out before I call Security." It took her a second to recognize him. She knew exactly who he was: Khan's ex-fiancé, R.C. Now what did he want?

"Hold on," R.C. said softly. "We can settle this without any problems. I only ask for two minutes of your time, Mrs. Tyler."

Tucked beneath his arm was a Presidio front seat cushion. Suddenly, she realized why he was there. These dealers were always trying to hustle the factory. But, Thyme thought, we're always two steps ahead of them.

Their eyes met and Thyme's flames subsided. Though they'd never been introduced, she was very familiar with this man and had been for the past five years. Khan loved him.

"It's okay, Elaine, go back to work. I can handle this." She sat back down and pushed aside the papers she'd been looking at. She could tell that he was very angry but trying his best to hide it. Clasping her hands in front of her, she checked the clock on the wall, then said, "How can I help you, Mr. Richardson?"

"This morning I received several crates of seat cushions at my dealership that were sent back unrepaired." He tossed a sample on her desk and took a seat in front of her that she hadn't offered him.

Thyme barely glanced at the cushion before she spoke. "I'm quite aware of the repairs, Mr. Richardson." She spoke fast. "The seats were returned because this problem is not a manufacturing defect. I'm sure you're aware that Champion's policy is to fill and return all orders within seventy-two hours. You know that we don't repair knife cuts, cigarette burns, and splotches of paint."

"But—"

The phone rang. It was her attorney. "Excuse me. Mr. Kravitz, I want to talk to you. Can I call you back?"

Turning her attention back to R.C., she inhaled. "As I was about to say, in the past we've repaired the seat cushions. We can't afford to do business that way anymore, Mr. Richardson. Our budget has limitations."

Per her order, Champion had sent the crates of seats back to R.C.'s dealership with pieces of tape attached to the problems that were not covered by their factory warranty.

"I do a lot of business with Champion. And I know several other dealerships that won't be too pleased about this new policy either."

Gathering her keys and purse, she said, "Come with me, Mr. Richardson. I'd like to show you something."

Thyme led R.C. out of her office and, after stopping by her secretary's desk to give her a quick message, led him through the salaried offices and out into the plant.

They were greeted by the thunderous sound of hi-lo drivers loading and unloading stock from the backs of suppliers' semis at the truck dock and by the peculiar smell of uncut roll goods.

Once they were seated in the motor cart, Thyme could tell by the way R.C.'s eyes bulged at the sight of the huge knitting machines they passed that he'd never been inside a factory before.

Presidio had three sewing units: luxury, base, and signature. It took Thyme less than seven minutes to show him the repairs that they received daily from other dealers. Every repair was a serviceable one, and under warranty. Even though the cushions were disposed of and replaced with a new component, each repair was individually inspected and recorded.

R.C. didn't utter a word as Thyme stopped their cart near Irvin Miller. She checked her watch. "Right on time, Irv. Can you give Mr. Richardson a ride back to the salaried offices? We've finished our business."

Starting up the motor, she turned when she felt R.C.'s hand touch her shoulder. "Excuse me?"

"Truthfully, Mrs. Tyler, I really need to get these cushions replaced."

Thyme knew that Richardson was in a quandary. Champion Trim was the only company that sewed Presidio cushions. The luxury leather trim set cost eleven hundred dollars, each component costing just over two hundred and fifty dollars. Thyme did a quick calculation in her head of R.C.'s repairs. His cost would be roughly twelve thousand dollars.

Thyme put the cart in gear. "We'll repair the cushions, Mr. Richardson. But at your expense. Ship the crate back to us, along with a check, and we'll return them in seventy-two hours. Good day."

She smiled to herself. It was about time they put an end to

that shit. R.C.'s dealership had cost them thousands over the years. And without new business, they couldn't afford to continue doing business that way. It had to end.

By the time the employee involvement meeting was coming to an end, most of Thyme's afternoon was gone. The whole thing had been a disaster. Her headache had not retreated. Angry accusations about the select few on the A-team elicited heated shouts from both hourly as well as salary. As the meeting wore on, the accusations about workers receiving special treatment became intolerable. Ultimately, Thyme was about to make a suggestion that everyone agreed with. She would personally monitor all overtime allocated by the foreman during the next ninety days. There would be no exceptions.

But when she got back to her office, Ron was hot on her heels.

"Bullshit! It's pure bullshit, Thyme. You knew about it all along," Ron began shouting at her. "You've been lying, covering up that our jobs are all going to be moved to the Mexican plants."

"I have no idea what you're talking about," she said calmly. "When you settle down maybe we can talk." But as she spoke the words an eerie feeling came over her, and her thoughts were of Cy's frequent trips to Mexico.

"Champion's selling us out, Thyme." He hesitated before he added, "Maybe even you."

Thyme tried to find the words to soothe the tension between them, but Ron refused to sit down, and stood by the window glaring at her. "It seems the whole time we've been friends, I've been new collar and you've been blue collar. This fact has never come between us before. Why now?" She was trying to be diplomatic.

Even before he spoke, a part of her knew. Reported in today's papers, next to the story of a Bloomfield bank robbery, was the latest dictatorial stance by the Big Four on their outsourcing policies. They couldn't have picked a worse time to be selling out the American workers so boldly. There was nothing but strikes and trouble everywhere you looked. Who headed their public relations committee, anyway—Dumbo?

The executives from all four corporations said that even though they would like to maintain their operations in the Detroit area, they must keep costs in line with other competitors. And that meant transferring production to the southern United States, or Mexico if taxes, land, and labor costs were lower there.

Fury was written all over Ron's face when he launched into his spiel. "You tell me how the average working American, namely the automobile workers, should react when the president decides to provide the Mexican government with financial support and the Mexican worker with jobs—our jobs!"

"Ron, you know I don't support that agreement."

"And your white husband. Does he?"

So that was it.

"That's not fair, Ron. We've been friends for years. What does our friendship have to do with Cy?"

Without Ron saying so, Thyme knew what Ron thought: She and Cy were above this fight.

Ron lived on the east side of Detroit, in the same neighborhood as the poor working men who were constantly being evicted because they couldn't pay their rent. Most of them were laid-off automobile workers. Obviously, his neighborhood was a far cry from where she and Cy lived. Yet it had always been Ron's staunch advocacy of the working man that was the single thread stitching their friendship together over the past twenty years. They respected each other. White collar or blue. If Ron thought Thyme was holding out information on him, their friendship would be shattered.

"How can the working man win? How can the black man win?" Ron was overwhelmed with emotion. "I was here during the 'sixties riots in Detroit. That was damn near forty years ago, and most of the businesses that have reopened since are liquor stores."

"Ron?"

He was at her desk now, with his huge hands pressing into the varnished wood, his face inches from hers.

"No—think about it. On damn near every corner in Detroit, there's a liquor store. When you drive to the suburbs, where you live," he sneered, "you can't hardly find one. You got to drive to another county." His voice was quivering with emotion and his eyes filled with tears. "Why is that, Thyme?"

He reared back and returned to staring out the window at the workers from the second shift parking their cars and heading toward the east hourly entrance.

It hurt her to see tears in his eyes. She had to look away. What could she say? She knew he was right. The unasked question was: Even though you're married to a white man, even though you live in the suburbs, have you forgotten about your black brother? The brother who gave you life in the first place.

"I understand what you're saying, Ron. And you're exactly right. But I have no control over how Champion chooses to do business."

"Understandably so, Thyme. But my point is this: Troy Trim jobs are being sewn in Mexico at this very moment. Don't ask me how I know. It's my job to know. And if I know, why don't you? You were once an hourly employee—blue collar like one of us. Have money and white power changed you that much? No matter who you're married to, you're just as black as the rest of us."

"But Ron, you know how hard I worked for my promotions. My marriage had nothing to do with where I am today."

When Ron walked out of her office, Thyme broke down in tears. How much did Cy know? Was this why her proposal was a moot point as far as the board was concerned? What information was Cy keeping from her?

Thyme tried to push away her thoughts about whether or not Cy had been aware of Troy Trim's jobs going to Mexico. He would have told her, wouldn't he?

Before leaving the office, Thyme returned her lawyer's call.

"This is Thyme Tyler; I'm returning Mr. Kravitz's call," Thyme said shortly. She didn't have the energy to be polite to Mr. Kravitz's secretary. God, she was tired.

Mr. Kravitz came on the line quickly. "Thyme. How are you?"

"Fine," Thyme said without enthusiasm.

"I wanted to let you know that the subpoenas will be delivered in two weeks."

"Does that mean I have two weeks if I want to change my mind?"

"Change your mind? You have a strong case—why are you hesitating?"

"I'm not. I guess I'm just a bit scared."

"That's natural. But I'd like to remind you that you're in good hands."

"Thanks. So what happens after the subpoenas?"

"Then I take the depositions, from which we build the evidence for your case. Have you been able to obtain that evidence we discussed in our last meeting?"

Kravitz was referring to information that Thyme needed from her friend and colleague Vicky Kress. Thyme had befriended several new collar employees on her way to the big league, and Vicky was one of them. Vicky had moved up in the ranks before Thyme and left Troy Trim in 1995 to work at World Headquarters, but they had remained friends.

Thyme knew that Vicky had access to documents that detailed all of the promotions of the salaried employees over the past fifteen years.

As soon as she was done with her lawyer, the phone rang again.

"Thyme, honey, I just found out I have to leave for Mexico tonight."

"But baby, you just got home. Why now?"

Cy had arrived home from Reno late the night before and Thyme had been asleep. This morning she was out the door before he'd even opened his eyes. Were their schedules just conflicting or was Cy avoiding her? They still hadn't talked about the meeting last week regarding her proposal, and she wanted a chance to talk to him about Ron's accusations about moving all trim production to Mexico.

"I can't explain right now, Thyme. But these trips are important to the company at this time."

"Are you telling me that you can't tell your wife about your job?"

"Let's not get into this over the phone, Thyme. Someone could be listening."

"Oh, now we've got spies in the company. What's going on, Cy?"

"Thyme, stop. As long as the company makes money, we make money. Now hush. Get my suitcase out for me. I'll be home by six-thirty."

But when Cy came home that evening he was running late. He guzzled down the half tumbler of Chivas, then kissed his wife quickly on the cheek before snapping his suitcase shut. "You know I hate leaving you. I'll be back in a few weeks. We'll have a chance to catch up then."

Following Cy into the foyer, Thyme said, "Why do you have to go? Why can't someone else go in your place?"

"We've gone over this before, Thyme," he said, rolling his eyes as he jerked his head around to stare at her.

Thyme felt her headache returning.

"I have a good rapport with the Mexican workers, and I speak better Spanish than the other managers. Besides, I'm sure a promotion is forthcoming. Sandler's given me every indication that I'm the new man to oversee all Plastic Products, and Trim. Then the trips to Mexico will stop," he said, with a fatigued tone in his voice. He hugged her tightly. "Okay?"

Every instinct in her body told her he wasn't telling the truth. Yet she smiled her best smile and hugged him back. "Okeydokey."

Reaching into his jacket pocket, he handed Thyme a pager. "I've got a new pager. Can you put this old one on the dresser for me?" he asked. "I forgot to turn it in before I left the office." Then he added, "I still have the same phone number."

He checked his watch against the time on the wall clock. "Shit, I'm going to miss my flight."

"Cy?"

Busy scrambling in the front closet for his Detroit Pistons cap, he spoke hurriedly. "I'll call you this evening, honey. I gotta go."

Thyme felt his cold kiss on her lips as he hurried down the hallway and unlocked the door to the garage.

"Cy?" There were a million things she wanted to say, to ask, none of which would ease the pain she felt.

His handsome face smiled at her as he slammed the trunk, storing the small pieces of luggage, then jumped into the car and started the ignition. "What, Thyme?"

"Nothing." She felt her heart sink. For some odd reason, she felt a sense of abandonment. "Call me."

Thyme felt too troubled to cry. Tears wouldn't be enough. She didn't get into bed until midnight. And when she did, the sight of his empty side of the bed made her ache with loneliness.

Just as she went to dial Khan's number, the phone rang. "Yes?"

"It's Sydney, Thyme. Is Cy there?"

Thyme felt her body cringe like a cat about to fall in a pool of water. "He's away."

"Where'd he go?"

Again, her body shivered. That demanding tone. Thyme hated it. "He's out of the country. He'll be back next week."

"Do you have the number where he can be reached? Graham's not feeling well." Graham was Sydney's three-year-old son.

"Can't this wait until he gets back? Cy *is* away on business."

"But his family means more to him than his stupid job. Now are you going to give me the number or not?"

Her voice was firm. "I've made it clear, Sydney, that this can wait until Cy gets back. I'm sure Graham will be fine. Why don't you call his father?" Jarrod, Sydney's fourth ex-husband, lived in London.

"That's none of your business. Really, Thyme, I'm disappointed in you. You know better than to cross me. Cy's not going to appreciate hearing about this when he comes home. I really don't think you've learned your place yet. Have you?"

Thyme felt the hard click penetrate every vein in her body.

"Bitch. You white bitch!" Thyme shouted to the empty room, all her anger and frustration from one day falling into her rage at Sydney.

Lust

10

Cy took the shuttle from Mexicali Municipal Airport to the Hertz rental car station, still somewhat disoriented from the turbulence of the flight. He found the lettered spot where his midsized vehicle was parked and popped the trunk to put in his luggage. Ordinarily Champion provided a car and driver to pick up executives at the airport and take them to the hotel, but Cy had always declined. He liked to have the freedom to move around as he pleased. He'd requested a Champion car but none were available. Good news for the company!

As Cy drove to town, he noticed the sparkling new Chevrolet Suburbans passing him. Most of Mexico's new elite were politicians and drug dealers, and their burly bodyguards were never far behind. Meanwhile, ragged laborers roamed the cobblestone streets of Matamoros, sipping *pulque*, a cheap fermented drink, from plastic cups.

American cars were as popular as ever. Especially trucks. Chevrolet Suburbans? Lincoln Navigators? Hell yes! But there didn't seem to be as many Champion Illusion trucks. The FM radio waves thundered with U.S. rock-and-roll and rap. He knew from all the time he spent there that Mexican television was inundated with shows like *New York Undercover* and *Murder She Wrote*. American feature films packed the theaters. What was next? he wondered. A women's basketball team?

Cy parked his red Taurus in the Radisson's rear parking lot and paused to listen to an interview on the radio. "I'm not ashamed to say that I prefer U.S. products over Mexican ones," said Tiara Navarro, who was introduced as a housewife who loved to shop at Wal-Mart. "They're better made," she finished. What was Mexico coming to?

Certainly it was not the way he remembered it from the early years he'd spent here. Had he changed—or had Mexico? Where was that boy who had met and fallen in love with the beautiful Mexican girl? So much was different now.

Cy checked into the hotel, then waited until Frederico, the clerk he was used to doing business with, came on duty. "My calls—"

"I know, Mr. Tyler. They are to be forwarded to the usual number."

Eleven years earlier, Cy had had a private line installed in the home he shared with Graciella. It was just after Juana was born.

He drove away from Matamoros on the highway that ran parallel to the rolling hills. Graciella and their children resided about thirty miles south in a growing suburban area. As he drove, he admired the beauty of the countryside. With his window open, the unique smell of Mexico emanated from primitive family-run cafés, which were nothing more than exterior kitchens with crude tables. The aroma of dried jalapeño peppers, so different from anything Michigan had to offer, filled the air. It brought him back to old times. Good times.

Cy thought back to the first time he and Graciella got together. Always he remembered first the yellow ribbon fixed to her jet black hair. He'd been a skinny kid of nineteen working for General Motors, and Graciella had been just fifteen. They'd had so much fun together. She was shy but he had brought her out. They enjoyed going to the bullfights, eating tacos, and then making love. Cy was not a virgin, but he'd never experienced such warmth and passion as he'd found in the arms of Graciella.

When he returned several summers later on company business, Cy told Graciella that he loved a woman back home and they would soon marry.

For the next several years, he tried not to contact Graciella when he traveled to Mexico on business, but after they both began working for Champion, he would see her at the plant. They continued to be drawn to each other, and eventually Cy was unable to resist the temptation. And then Graciella became pregnant with Juana.

Back home, Thyme had finished her Ph.D. dissertation over three years since. She'd put off having children, and Cy had come to the conclusion that she never wanted them. That was more than eleven years ago. Juana was turning twelve soon, and their son, Gregor, was almost eight.

He had no idea where the years had gone. Maybe each year the affair continued with Graciella, he lost one with Thyme.

Cy knew he should have ended their relationship before Graciella became pregnant again—either that or told Thyme the truth. But he couldn't leave Thyme. He loved her. Not even the birth of his son almost eight years ago had diminished his love for Thyme. How could he reconcile the love and passion he felt for both women? He had married the most beautiful woman in the world—Thyme—a woman who captured his soul, quenched his thirst, and made beautiful love to him. Yet there was still something missing, something he seemed to find with Graciella. But soon, he knew, one of the relationships had to end. And in his heart he knew it would be Graciella he had to leave—in spite of their children, whom he loved deeply.

In recent months, Cy had been preparing for this break with Graciella. In fact, with the promotion he was counting on, he would no longer have to come down to Mexico on business. He would make a renewed commitment to Thyme and never be unfaithful again.

Cy knew that with Champion essentially shutting down its trim operation in the United States, his job would shrink. He had to get out of Trim, and Cy was counting on being promoted to Plastics, covering all of North America. After twenty-five years he was still devoted to Champion, even though Sydney insisted that it was time for Cy to think bigger and leave Champion. Sydney had continually offered him a partnership in her Champion dealerships. His annual salary, she said, would triple what he made now at Champion.

He thought back to their conversation just the other day, when she told him about the upcoming merger. Champion planned on replacing its St. Louis dealerships with several superstores. The plan was the closest any of Detroit's Big Four had come to regaining control of the sale of their automobiles from a network of long-established dealerships. According to Sydney, she was sitting in the catbird seat. In order for the Big Four to accomplish this, they had to settle with the current dealerships—like Sydney's. He could almost hear her meow at the amount of money she figured Champion would offer to purchase her dealerships. She was certain it would be so high she couldn't afford not to sell.

The plan had to be approved by the city's twenty-two Champion and Atlantic-Pacific dealers. Sydney and R.C. Richardson's combined dealer ownership in the metro area amounted to twelve. Their compliance was critical. The superstores and a network of auto care service centers would be owned by a newly created company that Champion would control. Several of the big dealers, like Richardson and Sydney, would then retain an equity interest in the company.

Cy hadn't mentioned any of this to Thyme, of course, upon Sydney's insistence. Anyway, Cy wasn't ready for that big a change yet. First things first. Now he had to focus on cleaning up his life with Graciella.

When he arrived at his modest home in Reynosa, Graciella was waiting for him, having taken the day off work. She looked beautiful. No, irresistible. Her full face was tanned a deep brown. Her voluptuous figure was as ripe as the sap that turns to nectar in the velvet of the peach. Hundreds of twinkling dark curls caressed her brows, cheekbones, lips, and neck. He allowed himself one embrace, mindful that before the visit was ended he would break her heart.

"I've missed you, Cy. I'm so glad you're here. The children can't wait to see you."

"Graciella, we need to talk."

"Nonsense. Stop being so serious all the time." She touched the lines around his eyes and smiled. "It's making you old."

Cy withdrew her hands from his face and held them in his. "But I am serious, Graciella. This is something not to take lightly."

She pulled away. "Can't it wait until tomorrow, Cy? After all, we've got days and days."

And nights too. Cy couldn't stop envisioning them together in bed: Graciella's huge, chestnut-brown nipples. Sweet sweat dripping off their nude bodies as they moved together, satisfying their own needs first, then each other, and finally cresting their pleasures together as one. He was afraid to lose the pleasure of such an intense lover.

Just then, Juana and Gregor came tumbling into the room. Seeing his children always brought tears to his eyes. Juana resembled both her parents, whereas Gregor was all Graciella in face and body, but borrowed his father's china blue eyes. Cy made a silent promise to himself to treat them right and always be there for them, even if he wasn't their mother's lover any longer.

Dinner was a feast. Tamales, filled with fruit, chicken, pork, and beef, were warming on the stove.

Graciella placed a heaping helping of Cy's favorite dish before him: shredded pork tamales seasoned with slivers of jalapeño peppers and studded with raisins. He thought his belly would burst. It was the closest he came to feeling like a kid again. But that didn't prevent him from taking one last tamale before leaving the table.

Later, in the living room, Gregor had fallen asleep on his lap. Throughout the evening, Juana seemed quiet, almost hostile toward Cy. But he didn't want to press her. She was entering puberty and Cy knew she was sensitive. But when Juana took her brother's hand to take him to bed, Cy couldn't miss the disdain in her overly polite voice as she said, "Good night, Father. Sleep well."

Graciella had been in the bedroom, laying out Cy's clothes for work the next day, and hadn't heard the exchange.

"Come, Cy," she called out. "It's time for bed."

Reluctantly, Cy entered Graciella's bedroom. The lights were dimmed, and fresh flowers scented the air. She wore a short orange nightgown and sat poised on the side of the bed, her skin glowing like the sunset.

He moved toward her, his clothes suddenly feeling hot on

his back. Stopping a few feet in front of the bed, he met her eyes as he spoke. "I can't do this anymore, Graciella."

Suddenly he could hear Thyme's voice saying "Call me tonight" as he'd driven away from the house last night. He felt awful that he had only left a message on their answering machine before leaving the hotel. And for the first time he could remember, Cy felt a numbness in his penis.

"But why? I don't ask you for much. Is the love we feel for each other so wrong that we cannot share it?"

Cy turned away. "No more, Graciella."

"I don't believe you. You care for me. And it's not just because of the children."

He could feel himself weakening. She spoke the truth. "It's late. We both have to go to work in the morning." Cy, trying to hang on to his resolve, started to leave the room.

"Where are you going?"

"To sleep on the couch."

"Nonsense, Cy. You can sleep here with me." Her voice was tempting, alluring. "I won't touch you."

If he gave in, he knew a worse hell awaited him.

"Please stay with me tonight," she pleaded.

"No, Graciella," he said firmly. He retired to the couch in the living room. Later, as he lay in his shorts and covered with a thin sheet on the sofa, he could hear her weeping softly throughout the night.

The following day Cy had a meeting at the Champion plant in Matamoros. He and Graciella rose at dawn and drove to the facility, which was just fifteen minutes away. Graciella had barely spoken to him. Her shift started at 6:00 A.M. Over the twenty years they'd known each other, Cy had helped Graciella move from sewing operator to supervisor.

Just outside the plant, they passed through a small town, built by Champion to stop the exodus of their unskilled employees. The employees in Mexico could, and often did, periodically quit their sewing jobs at Champion because they knew they could come back next week and get rehired. They could quit again the following week and come back a month later. In America, if you quit, there was no coming back.

Unskilled Mexican workers were notorious for obtaining training from the American-run factories and fleeing across the border to America for a job that paid more than four times as much.

Partly because of the irregularity in the workforce, the quality of product from the Matamoros facility had deteriorated during the past three months. The trim parts were being rejected by the assembly plants, and it was Cy's job, as division manager of Trim, to intervene. At this point, Champion could not afford to have any slowing in Mexican production. For the life of him he couldn't understand how the Mexican supervisors, including Graciella, allowed the workers to turn out so much garbage.

Graciella was supervisor of the Paladin sewing unit, which was one that Cy was investigating. The Paladin was a new sport utility truck that was due to debut in September. The assembly plant was having a fit because the front back seat cushions didn't fit.

Cy was sitting at an empty sewing machine. Sitting just in front of him was an attractive young woman who kept turning around to smile at him. Seventy percent of the workforce were women between the ages of fifteen and twenty, and many of them were looking for mates.

"Ms. Perez?" he called out to Graciella. "Could you come here for a moment?"

Graciella rolled her eyes at the woman as she came toward him. "Yes, Mr. Tyler?"

"You're aware of the problems the assembly plants are having with the front back seats?"

"Of course. But my operators are doing their best with what they have to work with. They work hard every day—"

He stopped her. "I'm not suggesting that they aren't working hard. After speaking with the mechanics, I've realized there's a problem with some designs and the machines."

"Why don't you get the situation corrected?" Her voice was hard. "You expect us to do excellent work with inferior equipment?"

Around him several workers giggled.

Graciella had never spoken to him like this before. And, to be honest, Cy was turned on by her attitude.

"New machines aren't necessary. The gauges are the problem."

Graciella hissed. "You know that's not the truth. Champion is just trying to get off cheap. These jobs should be sent all the way back to the drawing board."

Graciella had a point. The machines in the Mexican plants weren't as new as the ones in the American plants. Still, the machines were built to last fifty years, and had a lot of life left in them. "Call a mechanic over here, Ms. Perez, and I'll prove my point."

It turned out that the main problem was with the gauges. The tack sew seams were supposed to be one-quarter of an inch and the finish seams were set up to be five-sixteenths of an inch. Even the mechanics mixed up the metal plates once in a while when they installed them—which is how the sewing operator ended up using finish gauges on tacking machines.

Having discovered the problem, Cy made a call to Plant Engineering to get the gauges color-coded to distinguish one from the other.

Cy also learned that with only three mechanics to service eighty people, oftentimes the workers had a long wait to have their machines repaired. Sometimes, one mechanic told Cy, the workers would try to repair the machines themselves. Also, with the high temperatures in Mexico, the machines were always breaking down. It was a common problem that needed to be addressed.

Once the mechanics carried out Cy's instructions, he returned to Graciella's station and asked her to bring everyone under her supervision back to the unit. With everyone standing around him, he removed his jacket and sat down at the machine. He sewed the entire seat cushion from start to finish. When it was completed, he compared the cushion he'd sewed to those they'd done the day before. He took the whole group and the cushions over to the build area. The builder first tried to put on the cushion that Graciella's team had made. It didn't fit correctly. Then the builder placed Cy's cushion on the mock seat, and it fit almost perfectly. With a minor engineering change, the problem would be solved.

Cy left early that day so that he was home to greet his children when they returned from school. But still Juana hung back. Nothing he did made her warm to him. She was old enough to understand that her mother and father's relationship was a sin. And her mother's sin seemed to be irreversible.

"Anybody want pizza?" Cy asked that night.

Gregor plopped his chubby body on Cy's lap. "Me, Father. I want Domino's like the TV says. Can you buy that for me?"

Cy realized that his son was now proficient in English as well as Spanish. Cy cringed inwardly when he thought about the day he'd have to explain his other life to his son. Would his children ever forgive him? How could he explain to his son that he lived in another country with another woman?

"Gregor," he said, slipping him off his lap carefully, "let's ask Juana."

But Juana ignored them.

"I've got a thought, Gregor," Cy said, trying to deflect Juana's chill. "Would you like to go to the bullfights this weekend? Your mother and I used to attend them all the time."

"Cy," Graciella said, smiling nostalgically, "that was so long ago."

"Let's do it."

There were cheers from Gregor and Graciella, but not from Juana.

After dinner when the children had gone to bed, Graciella and Cy were in the living room sitting in a stiff silence. Graciella interrupted Cy's reading to tell him that when he had taken Gregor out for pizza, Juana had asked her a cutting question. Juana had said, "How do you know how well his wife is living? You only know what he tells you. You don't even know his address. All you have is a pager number to contact him by. It's like he is spitting in your face."

Graciella had slapped her. But it was obvious to Cy that their daughter's question had lingered.

Early Saturday morning, the six-hour drive to Tijuana for the bullfight was fun, though Juana was silent all the way. Gregor made up for it with his high spirits. Caesar Castanéda was fighting. His rare appearance in the Plaza Mexico was being hailed as *"¡Buena suerte!"*

Cy purchased the best seats, at $35.25 American, and they were well worth it. The action they witnessed at the ring was incomparable. Every second was filled with colorful matadors and the huffing and snorting of the black bulls. Even the noticeable smell of bull manure didn't dampen the excitement.

Glancing at Graciella, Cy felt like he had been transported twelve years back in time when he and Graciella had attended their last bullfight. The action in the ring had prompted more action later, a night of beautiful sex. His instincts told him that Juana had been conceived on that memorable evening.

They returned to the Villa Vera Hotel, and Juana and Gregor collapsed into sleep in their own room. Cy and Graciella had gotten a suite, with adjoining rooms. Now, as they prepared for bed, Cy felt himself weakening. The memories were too strong between them, and he found himself powerless to resist Graciella.

In the semidarkness, Graciella's brown body gleamed as if she were wet, coming out of the sea. She moved slowly toward him and he felt her sweet breath encircle his neck, like a necklace of honeyed berries. He could feel her breath against his face, his chest, his stomach, his hips. Graciella stroked his throbbing member so gently, so lovingly, Cy thought he would scream in exultation. When she lowered her head and closed her hot mouth over his sex, he clutched the sheets and pushed his hips forward. Carnal pleasure rippled through his body from the balls of his feet to the top of his head as she began feathering kisses along the length of him with the tip of her tongue. Soon he felt the bed dip slightly beneath his buttocks as she straddled him.

Cy shuddered and released the fluid that expressed his pent-up passion.

In the dark, Graciella smiled and said, "Now, my darling, I will make love to you tonight in such a way that you have never experienced before . . . not even with me."

What had happened to his promise?

11

As slowly as shadows creep at the setting of the sun, weeks passed in the Richardsons' household. It was now mid-June, and in some ways Tomiko felt more adjusted to Detroit. R.C. had finally taught her how to drive, so she wasn't as dependent on Herman and Bonnie to do everything for her.

With Magic Markers, R.C. highlighted the best shopping centers, the supermarkets and hairdressers, on her map. She practiced daily, and before long she knew exactly where to go and how to get there. R.C. was proud of her for insisting on her independence.

And he'd also come through on her working papers. She hadn't yet received her so-called green card, but she had been doing some commercials for R.C.'s dealerships. She liked the work, but she was more worried about her marriage. There was something seriously wrong and Tomiko didn't know what to do.

Tomiko felt out of sync.

R.C. had been spending more and more time out of the house. He talked nonstop about his horses, especially Livewire, who had not placed in the Preakness. Most weekends Tomiko didn't even see R.C., and sometimes he wouldn't come home until the wee hours of the morning, when she'd already gone to bed.

Tomiko had only Bonnie to brighten her weekends. Yesterday had been a perfect Saturday in June. The sun sparkled like the color of burnished brass, and Bonnie suggested that she and Tomiko go shopping. They dressed in their most colorful outfits and went to all the best stores. Bonnie even took Tomiko to Birmingham's Bishop & Company, style and wardrobe consultants. When Tomiko noticed that the proprietor's name was Sydney Bishop, she raised an inquisitive brow.

"Bonnie, isn't she the one who stars in the Champion commercials?" Sydney had just walked into the store, and immediately the workers scrambled to greet her.

"Sure is." Bonnie turned, browsing through a rack of silk dresses that were similar to the ones that Tomiko owned. "Pretty smart lady, that one is. She also owns a chain of Champion dealerships."

"Oh, so that's why R.C. is so interested in her. She's his main competition." How interesting, Tomiko thought.

This morning, Tomiko couldn't budge from bed. R.C. hadn't even come home last night. They were making love less and less often. Now he was shutting her out again. Things were so strained between them that Tomiko was beginning to wonder if he was seeing another woman. Worried, Tomiko talked with Bonnie, who assured her he'd come around.

Tomiko couldn't reach R.C. He talked about the Derby race day in and day out. He ran the tapes over and over. It was an obsession, the kind of obsession that Tomiko wanted to be for him. Though she had no idea how much he had won or lost gambling on the thoroughbreds, she knew their marriage deserved more of a shot.

Dawn's shell-pink fingers reached through the tightly closed blinds, unlatching a new day. Tomiko turned over, then stretched her long body. Turning her head to her right, she noticed that the pillow beside her bore no sign of use. It was the third time he'd done it. What was going on?

The sound of birds chirping merrily outside her window gave her the motivation to leave the bed. Looking in the mirror as she brushed her teeth, she stopped in midstroke. After washing her face, she went into the kitchen and scavenged the cabinets. She found what she was looking for and put on a kettle of water.

Everyone kept telling her how young she was, she thought, as she placed chamomile tea bags over her puffy eyes, but she wasn't stupid. Lately, she looked like shit. She couldn't help but wonder if her husband was avoiding her because he was having a problem performing sexually.

Tomiko spent most of Sunday cooking a special dinner for R.C., waiting for him to come home. At around two in the afternoon, he sauntered into the house without so much as a word of explanation. He looked terrible. His shirt was unbuttoned, his pants unzipped, and his eyes were bloodshot. He went downstairs to his private study and Tomiko didn't see him for the rest of the afternoon.

After they ate her elaborate dinner quickly and in silence, the phone rang. R.C. picked it up and Tomiko heard him laugh as he'd never laughed with her.

Trying to keep herself busy, she flipped through the newspaper to the movie section. She loved American movies. By watching movies, she could learn more about Americans in two hours than she could reading a four-hundred-page textbook. Bonnie's advice to rent ethnic movies had turned out to be a fantastic way to learn about African American culture.

Later, she heard the hearty sound of his laughter, and

assumed he was still using the phone. She quietly picked up the extension and listened. But the only gossip she gleaned was a dial tone.

"Dammit, Bonnie!" he shouted. "Where's my whiskey?"

"Let me fix it for you, R.C." Tomiko ran to the head of the steps.

"Never mind. Bonnie'll get it." The tone in R.C.'s voice sent chills down her spine.

Tomiko couldn't bear any more. "I'm going to bed. I'll see you in the morning. Good night, R.C., Bonnie."

Tomiko was in a deep sleep when the phone awakened her. The voice mail answered before she could.

Sensing that something was wrong, Tomiko got out of bed to check the voice mail.

"This is Sergeant Peters at the Seventeenth Precinct in Detroit," the message said. "We have Mr. R.C. Richardson in our custody." She could hear him clearing his throat. "R.C.'s been charged with a misdemeanor and is unable to make this call himself. I suggest you contact his attorney." Tomiko had no idea who R.C.'s attorney was. She knocked loudly on Bonnie's door, waking her. Sleepy but calm, Bonnie located the number for R.C.'s attorney.

"Tomiko, I think we should wait until at least seven A.M. to call."

"Okay, okay," Tomiko said nervously.

When the clock struck seven Bonnie dialed the home of Mr. Bellows. No answer. They waited another hour and called Mr. Bellows's office. Bonnie spoke for Tomiko. It took a few minutes before they were referred to the cell phone of his personal secretary, then his voice mail, then back to his secretary again.

"This is very important," Bonnie screamed into the receiver. "Mr. R.C. Richardson, one of Mr. Bellows's biggest clients, is in jail in Detroit. I would appreciate it if you had a forwarding number."

Bonnie rolled her eyes. "Mr. Bellows is out of state until Wednesday," she repeated to Tomiko. "She wants to take a message."

"Can she connect us with Mr. Bellows's associate?" Tomiko asked.

When they finally reached Mr. Bellows out of town, he assured Tomiko that he would have R.C. released that morning.

Exhausted, Tomiko went back to her bedroom. She took a seat on the sofa. A new movie had just begun: *Indochine*. The countryside reminded her of home, and it made her so sad she began to cry. Before the movie ended she dialed her parents.

"Hi, Dad. Did I wake you?" It was 10:00 A.M. here, the middle of the night in Japan.

"It's okay, Tomiko," Mr. Sugimoto said, his voice thick with sleep. "You know we love hearing from you. Anytime."

"How's Mom and the rest of the family?" When he said everyone was asleep, she asked, "How are things over there?"

"The economy is suffering here, Tomiko. We're all a little nervous."

"Are you in trouble, Dad?"

"Oh, we'll be fine. The commercial horse business is on its way back up. If things continue this way, we may turn a profit this year. How are you?"

Tomiko wanted desperately to tell her parents of her trouble, but she was afraid her mother would only give her a critical "I told you so." So she didn't say anything.

"I love it here." She forced herself to sound cheery. "Wait until you see the lovely pictures of our home in Michigan and the ranch in Kentucky." She felt like a hypocrite, lying to her parents. Fighting back tears, she ended with "I love you, too. I'm so happy."

When she hung up, she turned to view herself in the mirror. Her skin was blotchy in spots. The exotic eyes that she hoped would win her a career were red rimmed. She looked terrible. She remembered that her mother had always told her how important it was to keep your husband happy. But the traditions she'd been taught in Japan didn't work for her in America.

Hurrying to the bathroom, she splashed her face with cold water until she felt her skin tingle with pain. Once again she looked in the mirror.

You will not embarrass your parents. You will not judge your husband. It is not your place.

Close to five o'clock that day, R.C. was released from jail. His clothes were wrinkled and dirty, and his breath smelled like white lightning whiskey. His little Afro looked like it was in the beginning stages of growing dreadlocks. In short, R.C. looked like an old man. Tomiko tried not to be repulsed. She had never seen him like this before. He looked not only old, he looked beaten.

He had been incarcerated for gambling at Blind Pig, an illegal joint. R.C. never discussed his arrest, and Tomiko knew that meant it could happen again.

Two days later, R.C. was still acting as if nothing had happened. Yet she knew R.C. felt guilty when he presented her with a brand-new bright red Algeron convertible. It wasn't what she would have selected. It was so flashy she felt self-conscious driving it.

12

Twenty dollars!" Khan said scathingly. "Shit. How come so much, Melanie?" She opened her wallet and handed Melanie her last juice . . . a lonely Andrew Jackson. "You know no one has any extra money these days. For God's sake, we may be the next strike target!"

"We're planning a big retirement party for Huey," Melanie explained as she handed her the card to sign and added, "We want to give him an all-expense-paid trip to Egypt."

Khan wanted to say, "Hell, I'd like one of those vacations my damn self." Instead she said, "That's so sweet."

Melanie held an old bobbin box taped on the sides with a small slit cut on top. Huey's name was written all over the box in bold black marker. "We're asking everybody for twenty dollars instead of the usual five, otherwise we won't have enough money for everything we planned."

Khan didn't hear Julian Anderson come up behind them. "Hey, Khan, Melanie. What's up?"

At least once a month, Julian asked Khan out on a date, and she kept putting him off. Momentarily, Khan thought back to the lie she'd told R.C. about being romantically involved with Julian.

Melanie spoke up. "Do you know Huey Spear?"

"The gentlemen who's worked over forty years in the carpenter shop and who is always, and I mean *always*, smiling? Who doesn't know him?"

"Then get your money out."

After Melanie left, Julian started in on his spiel. "I came to ask you if you'd like to go to Second City Saturday night. Solo is supposed to be appearing on stage to sing some songs from their new album."

Khan thought for a minute. She studied him up and down in a matter of seconds. He was no Billy Dee Williams, that was for sure. But the brother was good-looking, dressed exceptionally well, and obviously had cachet. But for some reason, he turned her off. Maybe it was the large gold tooth always shining at her when he spoke. *Shit, he didn't ask me to marry him, and Lord knows I could use a change of scenery.* Hell, she could use a real date right about now. And a quick fuck wouldn't hurt either. Still . . . "What time?"

Just as he was about to speak all hell broke loose behind them. Luella and Valentino were inches apart and the spit was flying.

"Excuse me, I've really got to go," Khan said to Julian, then scribbled her number on a piece of paper. "Call me later?"

Luella, with one hand on her purse as though reaching for a weapon, was all up in Valentino's face. Valentino had a fist balled up and was pointing a finger in her face.

Oh hell, let me stop these fools before someone gets hurt.

"Look guys, this shit ain't funny." Khan clamped her hands on her hips and leaned her small body in between Valentino and Luella. She was getting fed up with refereeing their constant bickering. All they ever did was argue about who got overtime. Didn't anyone enjoy going home to see their family every once in a while?

It's too damn hot to be fighting, Khan thought.

Two weeks earlier, Luella had been returned to Khan's sewing unit, and every day since, Valentino and Luella had been at it like Popeye and Bluto.

At first, Khan had welcomed her back. But now she had to admit that, even though it took her longer to finish, she had been less stressed out working with her other sewing partner. And here was Luella now, proving Khan right. Luella loved drama.

The three of them were two machines back from the front of the unit. Luella was always teasing Valentino, with her forty-four-D breasts bouncing off him like beach balls, watching his penis rise as she did it.

It was Friday afternoon and their foreman, Allister, who also ran the knitting operation, had gone home before lunch with a stomachache. He had left specific instructions as to who was to work the two hours of overtime in the unit today, as well as the ten hours Saturday on the knitting machine. The hourly workers worked at different stages to inspect the raw yarn that was woven into the knitted vinyl. Most of this product was sold to other businesses for stadium seats, lawn furniture, and boat seats. It was in such high demand that Champion needed workers to do overtime on Saturdays and usually Sundays.

"Luella, are you on your period? Or do you just need a good fucking?"

Luella rolled her eyes at Khan, her huge chest heaving up and down. She didn't respond.

"Tino, are you on yours?" Khan looked at him as if she weren't kidding. He didn't answer. "Fine. Since ain't none of y'all on the rag, forgive me for saying that I'm on mine, and I'm in an ornery damn mood. Don't get me in the middle of this shit today."

"We don't need you." Luella began pulling her hair back into a rough-looking ponytail. "I told you before, blondie—stay out of this. 'Cause somebody's going to get hurt up here."

"And I told you to stay out of my business, Luella." Valentino pointed his cocked finger in front of her heart and let it rest a hair's breadth away. "You got a problem with my overtime, take it up with the boss."

Khan could smell the smoky scent of Luella's Eternity cologne rising from her breasts like steam. "Look, guys—"

With her arm curved like a shovel, Luella pummeled Khan back out of the way. "I'm not going to tell you again, Khan—"

Khan saw the anger on Tino's face before he spoke. "You keep your hands off of her." Tino yanked Khan toward him. "I don't want to have to hurt you, girl. I don't fight women. But you keep this shit up, and I might change my mind and put my foot up your ass."

Half the unit had left, but the people who were still around were now sitting on top of their sewing machines watching the argument. Khan yelled, "Brother, sister, hold on for a minute!"

"I'm warning you, bring your sorry butt two inches farther this way, and I'll show you how Luella can kick some ass." Luella was standing in a fighting position, her weight on the balls of her feet.

"Luella! Tino! Y'all know better than this shit. Let's try to resolve this without violence. Do y'all want to get fired for fighting?" Khan implored.

Neither said a word. But Khan could see that both were contemplating her words. Company policy stated that employees were automatically fired for fighting. Usually the union could get their jobs back, but the company made them suffer between two and four weeks with no pay.

At least eight inches shorter than Luella and a foot less in height than Valentino, Khan stepped between them. With one palm pressing into each chest, she shoved them back a foot. "Settle down," she said, wiping the sweat off her forehead. "Just settle down." It was eighty degrees outside, and at least a hundred inside the plant. Only the break areas and cafeterias were air-conditioned.

Valentino looked at Khan and then said, "It's over."

Luella agreed with a slight nod of her head.

As Luella started walking away, Tino turned back to Luella and said, "I work every Saturday, Luella. And you know it." His voice was tight with anger.

Luella reached her hand back inside her purse, clutching it to her bosom. "That's exactly why nobody else can get any overtime around here. You and your A-team buddies are sucking up all the overtime. The rest of us are tired of the politics going on behind our backs. It's bullshit!" She moved closer to his face, shouting, "I got bills, too!"

"Maybe we should talk to Ron," Luella said in a mocking voice. There was a tense pause before she continued. "He can straighten this out."

"Bullshit," Tino fumed.

"You sure you two ain't fucking?" Khan asked, knowing that sometimes you had to go out on a limb and confront people on their shit. Khan had learned from her Mama Pearl that oftentimes what was really going on between a man and a woman was masked.

Luella's only response was to turn and charge off toward Ron's office.

"This is a bad time to talk to Ron, Tino," Khan said, falling into step with her cousin. "Maybe you should let her have the overtime. One Saturday won't make or break either one of you." She wanted to say more, then stopped.

Several strands of Luella's hair were sprinkled along the floor ahead of them. Valentino glanced at Khan and began to laugh. He whispered, "Luella makes enough money to get a better weave than this, don't you think?"

"She stopped getting weaves; she's started this new infusion shit that glues the hair on." She tried to stop Valentino as he broke out again in laughter. "Shhh, she'll hear you."

"Ron better fix this shit, otherwise I'm taking it higher," Luella said over her shoulder. "The A-team is bullshit. They shouldn't get special treatment when the rest of us need overtime just as bad." She was climbing the steps to Ron's office, swinging her hips and bitching all the way.

Valentino followed a few feet behind her, reaching down and picking up the hair as it continued to fall. He held a handful now. His cheeks bellowed out like barrels as he tried to control his laughter.

Khan was following close behind, still trying to stop the confrontation from escalating. Khan felt nervous for her cousin; she knew how serious Valentino was about overtime. "Listen, y'all," Khan broke in. "None of this is necessary."

Stopping at the top of the steps, Luella turned around to face Valentino and Khan. Khan kicked Tino, and he switched the handful of hair behind his back. But when they turned to look at Luella, they both froze in disbelief. Her face was slightly reddened, and her eyes were beginning to swell. They hadn't realized Luella was crying. Her hair was wild and sticking up all over her head. She looked like a tigress ready for a fight. "Nobody takes my overtime," she huffed, disappearing into Ron's office.

This is going to be fucked up. I can feel it coming. Damn.

Just then Ron came out of his office. "Luella just told me

about what's going on," he said accusingly. Before either
Tino or Khan could explain, Ron said, "Tino, Luella's going
to work eight tomorrow."

"But Da—Ron. I haven't missed a Saturday in six years."

Neither Khan nor Tino missed the smirk on Luella's face.

"Ron, I'm working tomorrow. Can Tino have my hours?"
Khan offered.

"No. Tino, you can take this up with Allister on Monday,
and I don't want to hear another damn word from either of
you."

As pugnacious as a pit bull, Tino threw the handful of hair
in Luella's gloating face and stormed out of the room.

Khan sat down for a moment to catch her breath, all the
time thinking to herself, I don't need this shit. It's hard
enough for me just being here—two old gray motherfuckers
acting like kids. Let me get my ass out of here.

R.C. had already given her enough high drama to last a
lifetime.

13

Silhouetting her against the back wall, the headlights from a car parking in front of the motel made Luella's body look exquisite. She was on her knees in a crouched position with her head tilted back, her huge breasts pointed proudly like an ad for implants. She had positioned herself over her lover's mouth, and, looking down, she could see his tongue darting up and down, in and around her sex like a hypnotized pink snake.

"Ron, baby," she softly screamed. "I'm ready to come."

When she looked down at him masturbating himself, she reached back and replaced his hand with hers. Circling his penis with a tightening grip, she rotated slowly in practiced strokes, coaxing him to come. She felt Ron's teeth tenderly biting her clitoris, signaling her as if they'd been screwing for years, until a final, surrealistic shudder passed through their bodies. The sensation lingered for a few blissful seconds, and Luella was overwhelmed with a sense of power.

Ron rubbed a finger down the crack of her ass, then slapped it. "That was great." He left the bed and poured himself a shot of Seagram's gin.

Luella lay back leisurely on the bed and assessed their

night of lovemaking. She was sore, and she usually didn't feel that way after having sex with him. But Ron hadn't touched her in nearly a year. The last time, he'd had a problem. He hadn't been able to get hard. Now, after his second orgasm, he still appeared to be rock solid.

It can't be a piss-hard.

"Okay, Ron. We both know you ain't Superman. You've done something with your dick. What is it?"

"Nothing. What's wrong? You ain't been fucked good lately?"

"Judging by your actions tonight, you haven't been either." She caught his smile and went to the table to join him. She unscrewed the cap of a diet Dr Pepper from the 7-Eleven bag they'd brought with them and took a long swig. "Mmm, that felt good. Now tell me, Ron. We've been friends a long time—what's the deal with your dick?"

His smile was cocky. There was a twinkle in his eye that hinted he was proud when he said, "I've got an inflatable penile prosthesis." As he talked, he began to deflate it.

When she looked down at his penis now, it somehow looked deformed. Luella couldn't help it. She burst out laughing. Then she asked, "Hey, can I try it?"

At first he refused. But on further coaxing, he let her. Taking her hand in his, he guided it along the left testicle until she told him that she could feel a small, ridgelike ball. Luella jumped. "Doesn't it hurt?"

"Not a bit. It did for the first three weeks, then the pain went away. Anyway, the pain is subjective. Here," he said, taking her hand. "Let me show you how first." He held his penis in his left hand, and with his right thumb and fingers on each side of his testicle, squeezed the small ball until his erection grew to full size.

When Luella tried it, her eyes grew wide with disbelief. Artificial or not, the thing felt damned good inside her.

"How does it deflate? I thought I heard a sound before."

"No. It was your imagination. There's a release bar right here . . . feel," he said. Placing her hands on his balls again, he guided her until she felt the protruding bar just above the pump.

"Does Ida enjoy it?"

"We're having the best sex of our married life," he said with confidence. "As for the others . . . let's say they think I'm John Holmes. They don't know because it's not visible. It's entirely inside my body. If I hadn't told you, you wouldn't have known, either."

You should have kept your mouth shut; you might have stood a chance of getting another piece of pussy. "Isn't it a bit vain to have that done?"

"Positively. Just like the women who have breast enlargements. If the man and woman feel better about themselves, they're more likely to give and receive greater pleasure." He paused. "And judging by your actions tonight, I'd say you were extremely pleased."

Luella didn't know what to say. On the one hand he was right. On the other, she was a little repulsed. She could only smile in response.

"The doctors say that erectilely impaired men should opt for penile prosthesis as a last resort. This is the third one."

She finished her drink and reached down to touch it again. Turning it over, she probed every inch, like a whore examining a new trick's dick. "Hmmm . . . I must say it's interesting. What happened before? Did it break?"

"No." He laughed. "The first one caused a small infection. Once I got over that, I got a hematoma."

"Which is?"

"A collection of blood in the incisional area." He pointed to the spot. "See, right here."

"Damn, Ron. And you weren't afraid to do this again?"

She refilled his empty glass. "You know what kind of man I am. Without a steady piece of ass, I can't keep my mind on my job." He began massaging his penis as if she weren't even in the room. "So, next I tried a different kind of implant; a vacuum erection device with a type of banding and medicines that have an aphrodisiac effect, with some kind of medicines like testosterone, yohimbine, isoxsuprine—"

"Isox—yoh—what? What kind of shit is that?" Luella was feeling a chill and went back to the bed to cover up.

"Shit that didn't work." He finished his drink and came to the bed to join her. "I was back to square one. Changed doctors and went back to the penile prosthesis."

"And you haven't had any problems with this one?" She was praying that he didn't think she had gotten back in the bed because she wanted to fuck again.

"Well, because of the length of my penis"—he smiled— "I sometimes experience some degree of flexion when it's erect. That means the tip sometimes raises and bends when I'm moving my hip or pelvis joints. Otherwise, it hasn't given me any more problems."

She looked down at his penis. It looked six inches soft, and must be at least nine pumped up. "That shit must be pretty expensive."

"Damn right. First two cost me sixteen thousand bucks. This last one was fifteen grand alone." He tapped his penis, sliding the skin back to expose its full length, and began to squeeze the pump casually to make it erect again. "But this baby has a lifetime replacement policy."

"Whew," Luella whistled. "That's an awfully expensive dick you wearing, brother." She started to laugh again. She slung the sheets back, picked up her things, and headed toward the bathroom.

But what she didn't say out loud was how Ron's condition made her think of her own: Before she was hired at Champion, she'd weighted two hundred and ninety-eight pounds. Getting close to Ron now seemed only to remind her of her own deformity.

The following Monday, Luella spotted Ron passing by their unit. She skipped over to him and began a casual conversation about the wrong stock on her machine, until she was sure that Tino saw them.

Within Tino's earshot, Luella said to Ron in a sultry voice, "Why don't you meet me at the Filling Station Lounge after work?"

Ron looked up at Tino. "I'm a married man, Luella," he replied in a harsh tone. "I don't go that way."

"Oh yeah? That's not what you said the other day."

He reached inside his pocket, took out a Salem, and lit it. "Luella, let's talk about this later. I've got business to attend to," Ron said quickly and walked away.

Luella sauntered over toward Tino, who was talking to another worker, telling a story and gesticulating effusively. Luella zeroed in on the lazy way Tino flexed his wrist. Her eyes scanned his clothes, tight pants, showing the bulge, and his obvious effeminate ways. She smiled and said, "Brother, I don't know how I missed it before." Her half-closed eyes lowered to his crotch. "Now . . . I . . . understand."

"What are you talking about, Luella?" Tino asked in a bored voice.

"Uh-hm," she said, nodding her head. "I think you may be one of those married men who sneak out at night with his penis pulled back and taped beneath his butt." She paused, smiling. "I must be slipping. Don't know how I ever missed it before."

Tino's lips tightened. He took a step back and pushed his

cigarettes into his back pocket. He neither denied nor acknowledged her accusation.

"But you know what?" she continued. "I'd love to try it anyway. I've never slept with a he-she before. Probably be the best orgasm I'll ever get. Come on, Tino, we can leave now. I'm getting all warm just thinking about showing you how a real woman can make you bust a blood vessel."

"Rumor around here is that cunts like you don't come like normal women. I hear it comes out of your ass."

"One thing about rumors," she said, turning to leave. "The one who started it probably enjoyed it most."

14

Even though he'd asked her on short notice, Khan accepted Valentino's invitation to dinner Saturday night. His wife, Sarah, prepared an excellent meal. Exceptionally shy, Sarah hardly said two words while Khan was there, but she seemed to enjoy the attention Khan paid to their beautiful baby boy, Jahvel. It was evident by the way Valentino and Sarah touched each other, anticipating each other, that they were deeply in love.

After dinner, while Sarah prepared the baby for bed, Khan and Valentino found a moment to talk. She followed him downstairs to his small hobby room, where he repaired television sets. Khan could tell from the tension in his gestures that Tino had something on his mind.

Tino handed Khan a diet Coke from the small refrigerator and unscrewed a Boone's Farm Strawberry Hill wine cooler for himself.

"My mother's been putting up with my dad's other women for so many years! I don't understand why she hasn't divorced him. He's given her plenty of grounds."

She grabbed the arm of the chair and seated herself slowly. "Haven't they been together since Aunt Ida was fourteen years old?"

"Yeah, and she's fifty-three now."

"Sometimes I think she and your dad are more like brother and sister than husband and wife. How can you divorce your own family?"

"Haven't you heard? Kids are divorcing their parents these days. Anyway, my mother's good-looking enough to get another man."

"You don't get it, Tino." Khan took a breath, then exhaled. "Your mother doesn't want another man. Mama Pearl always told me that a marriage goes through three stages. First there's lust, then love, then devotion. Your mother and father are in the third stage."

"Mother might excuse Dad's other women, but if she ever found out about Luella, she'd shoot Dad's balls off."

"Luella?" Khan's voice was a whisper. "Uncle Ron's screwing her?"

Tino crossed his legs and clasped his hands in his lap. "Yeah. What a disgusting piece of shit. I heard that Luella also broke up Cheryl Rhodes's marriage. All for overtime. Luella is a vulture."

Khan nodded. Who wouldn't remember Cheryl? She planned and organized the huge Christmas party Champion held every year. No wonder the party had flopped last year. "Damn, that's some shit. Cheryl is good people."

Khan just shook her head. The bickering between her cousin and Luella, then, went deeper than politics. "How'd you find out?" Khan asked quietly.

"The guys I work with. I overheard her speaking to Dad." His eyes flashed angrily around the room and back to Khan's disturbed face. "Someone needs to stop her; all she does is cause trouble."

"Take it easy, Tino. I know Luella is impossible to deal

with. But everyone is under so much pressure, now is not the time to seek revenge."

Tino was shaking his head, obviously not listening to her warnings.

Khan rose to leave. "So am I going to see you and Sarah at the Fourth of July picnic next week?"

"No fuckin' way. I can barely stand to see my father's face, never mind go to his house."

After Khan left that night, she suddenly felt overwhelmed by the pain and hostility within her own family. As always, at times like these she missed Mama Pearl and her calming wisdom.

Khan drove through the silent darkness until she pulled into a parking space and dragged her tired body up to her condo. As she inserted her key in the door she heard a man coming down the steps from the condo at the end of the complex.

She turned and froze. "Do I know you?" A snarl came across her face. She remembered the dreadlocks. "Wait. I've seen you at the Bel-Aire Theater."

"Exactly." He didn't try to come closer. "We seem to have the—"

Khan cut in. "Are you following me?"

"No, no." He held up both his hands in defense. "Look, I'm Buddy. My Aunt Viola lives here. We usually go to the movies together, but lately she's been sick and I've been going alone."

"Sorry." Khan relaxed. She knew the elderly woman was a friend of her Aunt Ida's and realized she hadn't seen her lately.

Buddy said, "It's late. I better get going. See you around."

He's got some nerve! What makes him think I want to see him again? Buddy didn't wait for her to reply as he hopped into his car and sped off.

As she entered her apartment, the telephone was ringing. Just as she picked up the phone, the line clicked off. He'll call back, she thought to herself while stripping off her clothes and heading for the bedroom. The light on her answering machine was blinking. As she sat on the bed in bra and panties, she listened. "Khan. I've got to see you. Call me." It was R.C.

He wants to fuck me. I don't think so. Blood, she thought as she turned on the shower jets, you ain't hardly the Mack daddy you think you are.

Work the following week was strained. Khan kept a close eye on Luella, Ron, and Tino, watching them like a rattlesnake ready to strike its prey. Allister asked, and Khan accepted, working twelve hours a day for the entire week. She couldn't help but notice that Luella seemed to be purposefully inciting Valentino every chance she could get. Luella not only flirted shamelessly each time Ron came into the unit, but she also started mimicking Tino when he'd walk by. Khan felt that Luella was being cruel.

Leaving the plant one day, Khan ran into her Aunt Ida, who had always reminded Khan of Louise on the television show *The Jeffersons* because of the way she spoke without moving her lips.

"Tino told me that you stopped by last weekend for dinner. Now you know I'm jealous. You come and give me a big hug."

"I'm sorry, Aunt Ida." Khan hugged her back, and the serene smile on her aunt's face reminded her of her Mama Pearl.

"You ain't been by the house since last July. You better be comin' to our picnic this coming weekend. What you been into, child? Your uncle tells me that you and your friend have broken up."

She should have known that her uncle had seen the article in the papers about R.C.'s wedding. Why hadn't he said anything? "Yes. It's over." Khan was instantly embarrassed. "But you look good, Aunt Ida," she said brightly. "What's your secret?"

"Your uncle, honey."

Khan felt a pang of guilt. How would Aunt Ida feel if she knew Ron was sleeping around? And with Luella of all people. Is that what devotion meant? No matter what the other did, they'd remain together for a lifetime? Shit, it wasn't fair.

Later at home, Khan thought about how, as much as she had to let go of R.C., she hadn't. As she fed her fish, she made a decision not to allow herself to even think about R.C. again. The hell with him.

As the devil would have it, seconds after she'd made herself this promise, the phone rang.

"Hello?"

"Khan, it's me. Please don't hang up. Please. Just give me a minute. I'm begging you."

Her heart lunged. She'd never been able to deny him anything he'd asked for. "What, R.C.? Make it quick."

"Can we meet?"

"Why? I didn't see no news of your quickie Mexican divorce in the papers."

"Don't, Kahn. I'm serious."

"So am I. Go to hell." She hung up. And when the phone rang again, and then continued, she turned the ringer off, said good night to her fish, and went to bed.

The next day, Khan finished work by one. When she pulled up in front of her condo, she spotted a UPS truck parked near the curb. The driver was already ringing her bell and she hurried to sign for a small package. Once inside her little front hall, she ripped open the box and was shocked by what she saw.

She was tempted to put it on. She then remembered that she had chores to do. She walked past the couch and casually threw the small box on it, then ambled to the laundry room and started on a load of clothes.

As she sauntered around her small, colorful condominium, Khan thought about the gleaming diamond ring and note R.C. had sent her: *You'll always be my baby. Do you forgive me?*

He wanted her forgiveness. And, actually, part of her understood that it's possible to love more than one person at a time. She wanted to open her heart to R.C., but she just didn't want to get hurt again.

She finished spraying the necks and arms of her white shirts with Spray 'n Wash, then heard the rinse cycle finish and peeked inside. She removed the plastic bubble still filled with fabric softener and frowned. "I knew this damn thing wouldn't work."

Just as she was inspecting the bubble, the phone rang. Her hands were wet with cold water. She shook her hands and let the machine pick up until she heard Thyme's voice.

"Hello, Thyme," she said after picking up the phone. "Do you know how this fabric-softener bubble works?"

"I have no idea."

Khan balanced the cordless phone beneath her chin and went back into the laundry room. "What a rip-off," she said, lifting the top of the washer and dropping it back into the darkened water.

"So what are you up to?"

"Not much. What about you? Is Cy away again?"

When Thyme called Khan on a Friday, it usually meant Cy was traveling.

"He's in Mexico," Thyme said dejectedly. "He comes

home Sunday night. I still haven't told him about the lawsuit."

"You better, girl. Aren't the subpoenas going out soon?"

"Yeah, my lawyer called last week and said they'd be delivered the week after next."

"So you'll be alone on Fourth of July weekend?"

"Yeah."

"You know you're welcome at Ron and Ida's."

"I know. Maybe I will."

"I have an idea. Wouldn't it be fun to spy on R.C. and his new wife?" Khan asked. "I heard R.C.'s having some grand opening celebration for his seventh dealership in Bloomfield this afternoon."

"And why would you know what R.C. is doing?"

"Oh, I make it my business to read the papers," Khan said, laughing. Khan had also been watching Tomiko in the commercials. The ring from R.C. had bolstered her spirits, made her feel impish. "Let's go."

Hundreds of multicolored helium balloons were released into the sky just as Khan and Thyme arrived. Loudspeakers touted Champion's sport, midsize, and four-by-four pickup trucks.

Tomiko, with a seductive smile plastered on her face, was wearing a violet evening gown, getting in and out of shiny new trucks while cameras filmed her every move.

"The bitch has got good taste," Khan mumbled, observing the skimpy dress. "In clothes, that is."

Thyme drove past the action and slowed down. "The commercials don't do her justice. Even you have to admit." Thyme nosed her silver Presidio into a vacant spot and parked.

"Yeah, and I bet her vagina dentata is pretty, too."

"What's that?" Thyme asked.

"A pussy with teeth." Getting more serious, Khan said, "Don't park here," and pointed to a parking space three rows back. "We can see everything from over there."

"I didn't think he'd pull it off," Thyme observed, peering through her rearview mirror as she backed out of the space. "I guess the laid-off Champion workers didn't follow through on their threat to picket."

"Thank God. Our fight is with the Mexicans, not the Japanese."

Thyme finished parking, then turned toward Khan. "Look! Here she comes."

"She may be smiling, but the bitch don't look happy." Khan was easing back on the front seat and cocking her shoulders back in mock black attitude. She pushed the wide sunglasses she wore down low on her narrow nose. "Something's up with her."

"Give the girl a break, Khan. I'm sure she had no idea about you and R.C. She's not at fault. R.C. is."

"You're right. Where is that conniving bastard?" Khan fumed. "He's not out here. I can spot that asshole a mile away."

Stunned that she hadn't seen it before, Thyme asked, "What's that on your finger?"

Khan reared her right shoulder back and smiled. "Just a little something." Her mouth turned up in a smug smile as she admired the emerald-cut diamond ring. "Isn't it just perfect?"

Thyme pulled Khan's hand closer to hers. "My goodness, that must be four carats."

"Four-point-three." She flipped her hand in a half arc. "Before you ask, I'll tell you the dope, okay." Her hand went back up. "Now don't say nothing. I know the brother is married."

"Have you talked to him? Why didn't you tell me?"

"Look, Thyme. I was mad. Okay? I'm still mad. I don't like the brother. Okay. But he called and begged to see me. I refused. Okay. Then the brother sent me this *bad-ass* ring to show me how sorry he was. Okay? I still may send the shit back, but this is a *pretty* bitch." She blew on the stone and shined it across her lap.

Thyme frowned. "You've got to be kidding me."

"Look, I don't know about you and Cy, but R.C. and I got memories, you know." She laughed. "I remember when we went to Las Vegas for New Year's. Girl, we had a ball. We stayed at the MGM Grand Hotel. Our room was on the fifteenth floor. You shoulda seen me looking like Spider Woman, butt-naked up in the window screwing R.C.'s balls off with spotlights shining all over us." She laughed so hard tears fell.

Thyme didn't join in on her laughter. Instead, she looked down at Khan's ring, then directly into her friend's eyes. "I'm disappointed in you."

"I haven't done anything yet. But I'm thinking about it. My pussy is throbbing so bad, like it just wanted to reach out and grab something. Shit! I ain't been screwed in ten weeks. And I'm used to having regular sex, okay?" She opened her legs wider. "I just can't think about doing the dating scene again. The ring makes me feel respected. It'll take months before I feel comfortable enough to go to bed with a new man." She exhaled deeply. "I'm sorry—I can't wait that long."

"Is sex that important to you?"

"Damn right. Don't tell me you and Cy ain't shaking the sheets every time the lights go out."

"Khan." Thyme blushed. "Cy's a busy man."

"Too busy to *fuck*?" Khan mumbled under her breath. "That's the *first* thing a black man takes care of." Khan could feel Thyme's silence.

"As I said, he's busy." Thyme's voice was defensive. "But it's not like I have to worry about him being out with another woman. Cy's completely faithful."

"How beautiful," Khan said with intentional sarcasm. "Let's go."

Thyme started up the engine. "Oh, so you don't believe me. You're saying that my man is cheating on me like yours did?"

Khan paused, trying to control her growing anger. "I ain't saying nothing like that. What I'm saying is that like you, I love my man. And when a woman loves a man like I love mine, you're liable to believe anything."

The two friends let the radio keep them company as they drove home.

The beginning of July was vacation time for most hourly employees at Champion Motors. It was a time when many filled their children's plastic pools with water and ice cubes, set out plastic palm trees in their backyards, and pretended they were in Jamaica. Salaried workers took real trips to exotic places. Last year, Khan remembered, Thyme and Cy had taken a ten-day cruise to Alaska. Not this year, Khan thought. Thyme and Cy were supposed to have left for Martha's Vineyard before Cy had to go away to Mexico on business.

Now, as Khan got ready for the annual barbecue, Khan hoped that Thyme would come by the party. They'd been friends too long to let a silly misunderstanding come between them. That day Khan dressed in the gold crocheted top she'd been working on for months, and a pair of skin-tight black jeans. She rolled the top back on her sunroof Saturday morning and drove toward her uncle's home on the other side of town.

When she entered his yard through the back gate, she

could see the lusty smoke from the grill curlicuing in a haze of whitish gray, then disappearing into thin air. Neighbors on both sides of Ron and Ida Lamott's home stood by the fence, smiling, talking like they couldn't wait for the show to begin as they watched Ron perform his yearly magic tricks.

Khan had to admit, her uncle Ron's crib smelled like paradise. Hickory coals smoldered beneath two-inch steaks and quarter-cut chicken parts, and beautiful cuts of baby back ribs bubbled a cinnamon brown on another grill. Ron Lamott wore a smile on his face as wide as the colorful apron tied around his broad behind. She tried not to think of Ron cheating on Ida.

The backyard was filled with people, most of whom worked at Champion, including the deejay, Angeldust, who worked in the roll goods warehouse. Positioned at each corner of the backyard, four speakers blared B.B. King's blues.

As Khan walked through the thick crowd waving, smiling, and saying hello, she didn't see Valentino and Sarah anywhere. Not that she was surprised. Valentino had sworn they wouldn't go.

Looking at her uncle Ron now, Khan had to smile. She loved to see him this way. He was in his element. The lines of tension were gone from his face. He was calm. Cool. His secret barbecue sauce, which he gave as gifts every Christmas, was simmering on a burner next to the ribs. She inhaled the bomb sauce and felt her stomach cry out in need.

"Hey, Uncle Ron," Khan said, giving him a strong hug. "Are those ribs going to be ready soon? I'm ready to grub."

She felt him taking stock of her tiny body in a gentlemanly way. "Girl, you need to eat a slab all by yourself. Then maybe you can stop buying your clothes in the children's section at Neiman's."

Khan turned around, modeling her skin-tight jeans. "You have to agree, Uncle Ron. They fit well."

Ron snapped a dish towel against her buttocks. "Stop being so fast. You know damned well Pearl wouldn't like it."

Though she barely tipped the scales at one hundred pounds, Khan was certain that the men who whistled at her petite figure didn't view her as a child. Khan knew that Mama Pearl wouldn't exactly approve of her outfit.

Removing another dish towel from the rail, she popped her uncle in the head when he turned back around to the grill. He let her have her way for a minute. Then the tables turned. He snapped the towel tight, whopping the small of her back repeatedly into a weakened state until she surrendered. Now it was clear who was in control.

"I give. I give," she whimpered. "Where's Aunt Ida? I haven't seen her yet."

Khan felt her uncle releasing her. His head turned in the direction of a younger woman, not outwardly attractive, but turning heads all the same, near the back of the yard. She was introducing herself to other guests.

Khan recognized Thyme's secretary. Just as Elaine turned to catch Ron's eye, Khan caught hers. Khan's antennae were instantly raised. Something in the air between Elaine and her uncle made Khan suspicious. *Damn, Ron, do you have that much action left in your old ass to pass around to three women?*

Khan smiled without sincerity at Elaine, then at Ron. She was suddenly tired of the games men played. "I'm going inside to check on Aunt Ida. Tell the DJ to play an oldy but goody will you? Like 'What's Goin' On.'" Not waiting for an answer, she entered the kitchen through the back door.

Ida was cutting up celery and bell peppers. She was in the process of making a tubful of potato salad. After they hugged and said hello, Ida released Khan's hands, avoiding her eyes. Khan followed her gaze outside, where Ron smiled at everyone and turned over smoky slabs of meat. Elaine had stepped up beside him and was whispering in his ear.

"I'm not going to put up with this shit." Ida's hands shook and her bottom lip quivered as she chopped up the peppers and scraped them into the large bowl.

"Oh, Aunt Ida." Khan placed both arms around her aunt's wide shoulders. She thought about Luella and Ron, and now this. "Don't pay any attention. It's probably nothing." Inwardly, Khan cringed.

Her aunt shuffled over to the refrigerator and filled a glass with bubbly liquid. Khan could smell the barley from where she stood. Her aunt downed half the glass of beer in one gulp. A foam mustache coated her upper lip. She tried to wipe it off and missed half of it. "Pressure. Ha. Nothing would take his mind off his penis. I ain't never seen a man so in love with his private. It's the first thing he washes when he gets in the shower." Ida's eyes were laughing, but her face was stern. "When he was younger it was cute." Ida hiccupped. "Now I want to tell him so bad how much his face stinks."

Khan couldn't hold her laughter.

Ida finished the glass of beer. "I'm tired of smelling a penis face, Khan."

They both looked out the kitchen window. Her aunt was watching Ron, and so was Khan, until she saw a familiar face—or should she say head? There was Buddy, dreadlocks down, talking to people as if he knew them personally.

"Do you know him, Aunt Ida?" Khan asked, pointing at Buddy. "I've seen him a couple of times at my condo."

Ida's eyes were still glued on her husband when she spoke. "That's Viola's nephew. He's a nice boy—even with that hair. Viola was supposed to come, but she wasn't feeling too well this morning."

When Khan looked back, her aunt had opened a cupboard and took a sip of the drink that she had concealed behind the huge Tupperware bowl. Khan could tell Ida was getting tipsy. Ida then went to the cutting board and began cutting up the boiled eggs. Khan removed the knife from her aunt's hand. "I'll finish making the potato salad."

Her Aunt Ida mumbled a few words under her breath. "No, I can do it. Ron'll be mad."

It took a few minutes for Khan to convince her aunt to take a nap. When Khan tried to help her to the bedroom, Ida said that she had to use the bathroom first.

Khan was positive that her aunt hadn't gotten the rest of her cry out.

The oven was turned up to 450 degrees for the baked beans, which weren't ready. She checked inside the refrigerator and noticed that the cole slaw was chilling and covered it with Saran Wrap. Cole slaw and barbecue weren't enough for a meal. Khan knew that with as many people as there were outside, they'd be ready to chow down soon.

When she heard her Aunt Ida exiting the bathroom, Khan left the kitchen to help her. Ida continued to mumble as Khan forced her tired body into her bed. "He promised, Khan. Ron promised we'd be married before the Fourth." Her voice was heavy and filled with pain. Even though it was hellishly hot, she pulled the covers over herself before closing her eyes. "He lied. I can't live like this no more."

Forty years together, and they weren't even married! *Oh, my God!*

Just when Khan was about to leave the room, Ida reared up and whimpered, "That son of a bitch brought his lowdown tramp to our party." Tears rolled down her face and she closed her eyes and fell back against the pillow. "Does he take that much pleasure in humiliating me?"

After Khan got Ida to sleep, she cut up the onions and finished the potato salad. Next, she cut up the broccoli, cauliflower, carrots, and zucchini. She breaded and fried half of them, and used the other half for a vegetable tray with ranch sauce. Afterwards, she placed everything in ceramic dishes, then put the food on the picnic table outside. She ignored her Uncle Ron's questioning eyes.

When Buddy waved to her, Khan used his appearance as an excuse to cut away from Uncle Ron; otherwise she might have been tempted to ask him about his bogus promise of marriage to her aunt.

"Hi, Buddy. How's your aunt?" Khan couldn't help but stare at his clothes. Didn't he own a decent outfit? But on further inspection, she noticed the brilliance of his smile. Every tooth in his mouth was even and perfectly shaped. She wanted to ask him if they were real. One thing was for damn sure: apparently he spent all his cash on his mouth.

He was a bit odd, but he definitely had more sex appeal than Julian.

She and Buddy talked for a while, and their conversation turned to a subject they both loved: movies.

When everyone else had served themselves, Khan dug in. Ida never appeared. By late afternoon the food was gone and the guests had left. On her way home, Khan felt lonesome. She missed the sound of Buddy's laughter. Watching the wandering clouds that floated high above valleys and hills, she felt an inner longing to connect with someone. It wasn't just sexual; it was more out of need to be a part of someone else's world. Even if it were just for a moment.

When she got home, the branches outside her door whipped in the wind as though they were dancing. R.C. seemed a bitter memory.

15

I love to hear you say my name when you reach an orgasm." Thyme slowly released her fingers from Cy's buttocks as he lay on top of her. Sweet joy rushed through her as his lips closed over her breasts, still swollen and sensitive from their lovemaking. She felt his soft breath against her bosom as he buried his face in her cleavage, then rolled over on his back.

As he turned toward her, his face was aglow with a sweet smile of affection and understanding. "I know," he said in a sultry voice.

It was late Sunday night, and Cy had just returned from his trip to Mexico. Thyme was so relieved to have him home again that she'd seduced him as soon as he walked in the door.

"Cy? Can we get serious for a minute?" She felt nervous but she was determined to go ahead.

"Mmmm, I feel too good. Getting serious might spoil my mood. Especially if it's about Champion Motors."

Her voice was low. "Please, there's something I really need to talk to you about."

"All right." He folded his arms behind his head and raised a brow. "Go on. I'm listening."

"I'm filing a lawsuit against the company claiming discrimination. Some of the people you work with will be subpoenaed next week. They might not be so friendly toward you."

"What? How could you? You did this behind my back?" He swiveled his legs over the side of the bed, sitting up straight. He sat there silently, then stood up, revealing his toned buttocks. He walked swiftly to the chair in the corner of the room and gathered his clothes in his arms.

"Behind your back? I've been trying to talk to you for weeks. You've been away for the past month. It's as if you've been avoiding me!"

Thyme stared deeply at the pearl blue walls, the silver carpeting, her pastel portrait. They seemed a collage. Her eyes burned, straining not to blink. Tears filled them.

"I can't believe this. Do you know what you're doing? You'll put both our jobs in jeopardy!"

It was like their union had never occurred. Suddenly Thyme felt vulnerable in her nakedness and pulled the sheet to her shoulders. "That's all you care about. You can't for a minute think about my side of it. I'm beginning to wonder if you colluded with Champion and stopped them from promoting me!"

"You sound like a crazy person. You're totally paranoid."

Crazy for marrying you?

"I would never do anything to hurt you or your career. How could you think that? Don't we have any trust in one another?" Cy continued.

Thyme looked at Cy, her eyes brimming with tears. She wished she could say yes, that she still loved and trusted him as she always had, but something deep inside had been shaken.

Instead of answering Cy, she turned and looked out the window at the starlit sky. When she heard the sound of the shower jets in Cy's bathroom, she dragged herself into her own, trying to believe that he loved her enough to support her, that he would come around, hoping against hope that she hadn't put too great a burden on too small a soul.

When Thyme finally called Khan the following Monday, she was glad she did.

"What's up, girl?" Khan asked in a cheery voice.

Thyme felt relieved. "How was Ron's barbecue?"

"Fine. Is that why you called? Why do I sense you have something on your mind other than slabs of meat on a grill?"

Thyme said quietly, "I finally told him."

"You told Cy about the lawsuit?"

Thyme felt tears filling her eyes. When she trusted herself to speak, she said, "I told him last night when he got home. All he seemed concerned about was Champion."

Khan kept silent.

Say something, Khan. I don't care if you call me a fool. Just tell me your true thoughts. I need to hear them. Please! "I know you think I should never trust Cy, but you don't know him. He's always been there for me before." Thyme was glad that her friend couldn't see her tear-streaked face. She never wanted her to see her so humbled. Especially by a man.

"Thyme, I'm sure he loves you very much. But this situation is complicated. I don't think there's any getting around the race issue."

"You're right. I'm not sure how I'll feel about our marriage if Cy won't support me in this."

"Cross that bridge when it comes. For now, remember where you are in your career: right at the top. And remember that you're a strong, smart, proud black woman. Can't no man take that from you. Even a white one." Khan paused. "And most importantly, Thyme, I want you to remember that you've always got a friend. I love you, Thyme. You're doing the right thing."

"I am?"

"Sure you are. It's just that the right thing isn't always easy."

That afternoon, Thyme met Cy at their financial planner's office to discuss their investments. Removing his Mondo di Marco sunglasses, Cy embraced his wife. He kissed her lightly on her cheek as she sat in the seat beside him. What a day for it, thought Thyme.

As they waited for the financial planner, Thyme admired her husband's clothing as she glanced down at his slamming chocolate alligator shoes. Again, she felt a pang of contrition. He was so fine, but how come he couldn't be more supportive? He wasn't like the typical white male. Dressed in a chocolate brown Hugo Boss suit, silver pink shirt, and silver print tie, he looked like a mannequin in a Saks Fifth Avenue window.

When they had dated in the late sixties, Cy had only worn moderately priced clothes, but once he started earning money, his attire reflected it. His ties were always Fumagali or Robert Talbertt, his suits by Hugo Boss, Armani, or Richard Tyler, shirt and shoes by Gucci. She remembered kidding him about his three pairs of alligator loafers— unheard of for a Caucasian male.

"Tired?" Cy said gently.

"Exhausted." She wanted to stroke his face and plant a kiss on his soft lips.

Luckily, before last night's argument came up, the door opened and a young woman called their name. She led them to Mr. Aldinger's office.

Expensive artwork was the backdrop for expensive furniture. Keith Aldinger commanded high fees, and he was worth it.

He handed each of them a prospectus for how to diversi-
fy and invest heavily into more retirement programs. Thyme
listened with one ear. Based on their past history with Keith,
they had nothing to worry about. She was certain that he
would protect their money the way he did his other clients'
who left his office smiling like angels.

Then he handed them a two-page statement, listening
their incomes so far this year. Thyme snapped to attention.

"Let's get down to business, Cy and Thyme. You both
know why you're here."

Thyme nearly choked when she read the bonus that Cy
had listed beside his name. He had lied to her by twenty
thousand dollars. Why? He knew she'd find out eventually.
She gulped hard as she read the rest of the report, not daring
to look at her husband.

"It's clear that you two need to move some investments
around. Champion stock is declining fast, given its shift to
Mexico. My suggestions are as follows. . . ."

Afterwards, Keith walked them back to the reception
area. "You know, if you two could adopt a couple of kids,
you'd come out a lot farther ahead," he said jokingly. "Uncle
Sam loves couples like you." He shook their hands and was
off.

When Thyme looked at her husband, he looked away.

That same night Thyme longed to slip into a pair of pajamas and sip on a glass of wine. But no, Cy had already made
a commitment to have dinner at Sydney's house.

When they arrived at Sydney's, it was jet black outside,
but her home was lit up like a palace. Located on Southlawn
Avenue just two miles from Woodward in Birmingham, her
home was a showcase with over fourteen thousand square
feet of living space.

Situated on 4.34 acres of professionally manicured
grounds, the house afforded privacy as well as security. A

Gunite swimming pool, spa, and tennis court complemented the lush grounds. Inside, there were five bedrooms, five bathrooms, and four half-baths. The master suite alone was over twenty-five hundred square feet.

Cy parked the car on the outer curb of the driveway and they walked to the entrance. When they rang the doorbell a black maid opened the door.

"Hello, Mr. Cyrus, Ms. Thyme. It's so good to see you two. Ms. Sydney is in Master Graham's room."

Master Graham! The boy was only three years old and already she was calling him "master." How low would Mildred go?

"Thanks, Mildred," Cy said.

Before they could take a step, Graham ran toward them and hugged his uncle around the legs. "Hi, Unc C." Graham could only say a few words. Yet "Unc C" was one of the phrases he loved to roll off his tongue. And Cy adored him.

Cy had explained to Thyme the feeling of immortality Graham provided. There was nothing Cy wouldn't do for him. Even though Sydney could afford it, Cy had already put aside a considerable amount for Graham's education. Thyme felt no resistance whatsoever to her husband looking out for his nephew. If she hadn't presented him with a child, how could she prevent him from loving his own blood?

As Cy picked up his nephew and swung him around in his arms, Graham instinctively reached out for his Aunt Thyme. His color blindness was only one of the things Thyme loved about him. Most children don't know about prejudice unless their parents teach them.

Thyme couldn't help being drawn to Graham, despite her less than warm feelings toward his mother. Graham's innocence was accentuated by his chubby little arms and legs and his soft cheeks.

Just as Thyme reached out to hug the child, Sydney came

down the hall. Quickly and awkwardly, Thyme withdrew from Graham, who looked a bit bewildered.

"Cy," she said, hugging her brother tightly. Her voice lowered an octave when she said, "Thyme, it's so good to see you." Sydney placed her arm through Cy's and led him toward the dining room, leaving Thyme to walk behind them.

"I'm starved. What's for dinner?"

"I thought we'd start with onion soup, then Caesar salad, and the main dish is pheasant with wild rice stuffing and curried beets." Sydney, who wore no lipstick or any other makeup, blew back a lock of hair. "I've been cooking all day. But what other way could I show my brother how much I missed him while he was away?"

"Mmm and strawberries, Unc C," Graham said, holding up his red-stained hands for Thyme and Cy to see.

Graham's tiny chubby hands were covered with red blotches. Well, Thyme thought, maybe Sydney made dessert, but I'll be damned if she cooked the rest of the meal. Thyme knew that Sydney's lack of makeup and dress-down attire was a ruse, a costume to make her fib about cooking credible.

As they dined on course after course of soup, salad, breads, shrimp appetizers, and pheasant, Thyme became more and more convinced that Sydney hadn't spent more than ten minutes cooking. Mildred, she bet, had cooked it all.

Just to check it out, Thyme said sweetly, "Sydney, how did you ever learn to make pheasant? Why, it's superb."

Sydney hesitated and said, "Ah well, our mother used to serve it at her fancy dinner parties. Isn't that so, Cy?"

Cy grunted noncommittally and filled his mouth with food.

"So how do you make it?" Thyme continued.

Sydney looked at her hatefully. Thyme had blown Sydney's cover. She smiled to herself. It made the evening worth it.

"More sauce, Cy?" Sydney asked, jumping up to wait hand and foot on Cy and change the subject at the same time.

"No, this is fine."

"Come, come. I know how much you love my special sauce."

How sickening, Thyme thought.

Dessert was worse. Thyme knew Sydney made the dessert because it was too sweet and the only bad part of the meal. Sydney piled so much whipped cream and so many strawberries on Cy's shortcake that it would take a mouth as wide as the Detroit River to swallow it.

By the time they headed home, Thyme had had enough. "I don't care if she is your sister," Thyme shouted in the car, "she's one of the most miserable bitches I've ever met. Imagine the nerve of that whore treating my husband as if you were her man!"

"She was just being—"

"Who do you take me for? And that wimpy-ass black maid. My Lord, where did she find her? She acts like she's still on a plantation. Don't ask me to go back over there again!"

"Give her a break, will you? You know her divorce was just finalized. It's only natural that she would—"

"Bullshit! Which divorce is this? The third? The fourth? I don't blame them, I'd leave her frigid ass, too."

"And where did that come from?"

"Excuse me. My Lord . . . are you that stupid? The only time that bitch heats up is when she's around you. Now you figure that shit out."

16

Cézanne once said: "The landscape thinks itself in me. . . . I am its consciousness." He would often ponder for hours at a time before putting down a single stroke. If he were alive today, he would be touched by the beauty of mid-July, and within it he would capture the natural beauty of a young woman named Tomiko.

The critics loved her. At five foot ten and a shapely size six, the cameras loved her too. She looked absolutely bewitching in close-ups. Her deep olive skin tone showed that she was a woman of all cultures—a plus on the contemporary modeling scene. Her high forehead represented royalty. Her slightly long nose and chin with small, full lips inspired comparisons to the timeless beauty of *Mona Lisa*.

After signing with Clara Clarke, a hot young agent in West Bloomfield, Tomiko's schedule was jam-packed with several high-paying modeling stints in New York, California, and, in the fall, London and Paris. These jobs would take Tomiko away from home for one and two weeks at a time. She didn't like traveling that often, but who could turn down twenty-five thousand dollars per shoot? Regardless, Tomiko was tired.

Without the help or interference of R.C., Clara had secured for Tomiko the position as Champion's national model, in addition to being the spokesperson for her husband's dealerships.

It was the middle of July, and the projections for which new auto would win *Motor Trend*'s Car of the Year were a main topic of conversation in Detroit. The two top choices were Champion's luxury Atlantic sport coupe and Mishimoto's Verve. Marketing was at a fever pitch, and models like Tomiko, who made cars look good, were in high demand.

"Ms. Richardson," the makeup artist snapped, "if you don't keep still, I'll never get your face on right."

"What do you expect? I've been sitting in this chair for over an hour." Swiveling around, she looked into the mirror facing her. Her jaw tightened in anger. "Dammit, Betty, look what you've done! My eyelashes are crooked, my foundation is too dark, and my lips look as if you've doubled them. I could do a better job myself."

"Then why don't you!" Betty threw her palette on the counter. "You women expect us to perform miracles."

There was a hard knock on the door and the director's assistant, Emery, marched in. "Tomiko should have been on the set five minutes ago. What's the problem now?"

Before Tomiko could speak, Betty cut her off. "I quit. She claims I fucked her face up. You deal with her."

"She just wants to make me look as bad as she does." Tomiko covered her face with cold cream, cleaned it, and began redoing her makeup. Betty continued trying to get the assistant to see her side of it.

Tomiko said, "Give me five minutes and I'll be ready to shoot."

Betty angrily gathered her things and started to follow the assistant out of the dressing room. "One more thing,"

Tomiko said over her shoulder. They both stopped. "I'll be doing my own makeup from now on. I'll have my agent contact you." She pointed at Betty. "And I want her salary added to mine."

True to her word, Tomiko was on the set in five minutes. The admiring stares she received from the men on the crew confirmed that she'd done a good job on her face. But Tomiko didn't feel so glamorous now. It was six o'clock in the morning and the hot lights beaming down from overhead felt like violent sun rays. The crew was antsy and so was Tomiko. Everyone had been at the studio since four.

The commercial they were filming today was at R.C.'s used-car dealership. It held over two thousand cars and trucks from both the Mishimoto and Champion car lines. The lot was one of the largest in the state. This commercial would spin off into a radio ad.

All of R.C.'s marketing ideas had worked, and his dealer-ships were thriving. And although Tomiko was glad for R.C., she couldn't help but feel a touch of resentment. R.C. was able to consume himself with his car dealerships, his horses, but not with her.

She hated getting up this early, especially for only five thousand dollars. (Even her husband paid a fee.) Once she'd started making money, she wanted more and more. She'd had it with these cheap local jobs.

Suddenly Tomiko noticed R.C. watching her from the trailer. Even from that distance, he looked annoyed and tense. She tried to catch his eye, to no avail. He rarely showed up at shoots, so she felt a bit off kilter. When the assistant director called "Action!" she was all business.

Suddenly everyone on the set was moving. The extras hired to move around the parking lot strolled into place. Tomiko was supposed to be a saleswoman trying to con-vince a buyer to purchase a car. Just as she was about to deliver her lines, she caught another glimpse of R.C. out of the corner of her eye and, for some reason, she felt nervous.

Tomiko missed her cue and the director called "Cut!" This occurred a number of times. Each time the director called "Action!" Tomiko would flub her lines.

Over and over, they repeated the silly scene. Tomiko couldn't believe her own stupidity. The more they shot, the worse she got. Then, at last, they made an almost perfect scene. The director assured her that the next one would do it. By then it was 8:30 A.M. Tomiko was so tired she could barely keep her eyes open, let alone smile and focus her practiced gaze in the camera.

R.C. came up to her before the next take. "Tomiko, what's going on? Each take you screw up is costing me a fortune. Please. Try to do it right this time. I can't afford to blow this right now." He wiped his sweat-streaked brow, then gave her a perfunctory kiss on the forehead.

Tomiko felt chilled to the bone.

"On one, on two, on three," the director said, then paused a second and screamed, "Action!"

Tomiko plunged into the scene, and when the director called "Cut!" Tomiko knew it was her best take of the day.

Finally! A wrap.

Tomiko looked around for R.C., but he'd left without a trace.

When she returned home, it was only ten-thirty in the morning. No one was home. Bonnie had gone grocery shopping, Tomiko assumed, and Herman, the chauffeur who lived over the garage, appeared to be gone as well. Where was R.C.?

Certain that R.C. would at least be home by dinnertime, Tomiko changed into her exercise clothes and worked out for two hours. Afterwards, she took a hot bath and made a cup of lemon tea. By then it was nearly two. Bonnie still hadn't made it back and the house was as quiet as a woman the first day and a half after she's married. Tomiko fell asleep.

The doorbell awakened her. The room was flooded in darkness. She had no idea what time it was. She stretched out and waited for Bonnie to get the door. When the ringing continued, she lifted herself up from the sofa and saw by the clock on the nightstand that it was midnight.

Where was R.C.? Had he made it home?

"Bonnie? R.C.?" Tomiko called out after exiting her room. Now the person was knocking on the door. She was starting to get pissed that Bonnie wasn't attending to her duties. "Hold on," she said, turning on the lights.

Opening the door, she saw one of their next-door neighbors, his hat in his hand. "Sorry to bother you this late at night," the man said, "but my wife insisted I bring this letter over tonight. It was delivered to our home by mistake last week."

When she read the return address on the envelope she was confused—the sender's name, Johnson, was unknown to her.

"Sorry for the delay," the man said, turning to leave, "but we've been out of town."

"No problem. Thank you."

Closing the door, she stopped, listening to the sound she heard coming from down the hall. But by the soft shuffling footsteps, she knew it wasn't R.C.

Normally wide awake until one in the morning, Bonnie looked tired and haggard. "Evening, Tomiko. Did someone ring the doorbell?"

"Yes. I took care of it." Tomiko tucked the envelope in her pocket. She had a terrible feeling about it. It terrified her. She immediately decided to put it from her mind.

"What's wrong with folks these days coming to your

home all times of the night?" Bonnie turned off the lights. "And before you ask, Mr. R.C. ain't home. And don't ask me where he is because I don't know."

Tomiko thought about how nervous he'd been at the shoot and wondered if there was a connection. "I'll see you in the morning, Bonnie. Good night."

Once inside her room, Tomiko fell face forward on the bed. *Where are you, R.C.? I need you to hold me.* She thought about their upcoming trip to the ranch and hoped that spending time there would help bring him closer to home, closer to her. As tender as her falling tears, she hugged herself, and closed her eyes.

Right before she fell asleep, the phone rang.

"Hello, may I speak with R.C., please?" It was a friendly male voice.

"He's not here. May I take a message for him?"

"Yes. This is Oxford, an old friend of R.C.'s. Is this Bonnie?"

Tomiko laughed, happy that her accent was fading. "No, this is Tomiko, R.C.'s wife."

"Wife? What wonderful news. When am I going to meet you? When are you two going to visit me in Seattle?"

"I'll have to talk to R.C. about that."

After Tomiko hung up the phone, she fell into a heavy sleep.

Later that night, Tomiko was awakened by a whisper.

"This is the last time, I promise. I'll never do it again. God, please help me win. Please. Goddammit! Please. Just this one last time!" R.C. hollered out in his sleep.

Tomiko turned over onto her side and shook her husband. "R.C.?" He huddled on the edge of the bed, clutching the sheets tightly. His body trembled. As she tried to massage his face, she felt wet tears on his cheeks.

"I don't have it. I swear." He was crouched in a fetal position now, his eyes and teeth clenched together tightly. "You can't take—!" He was shouting, then began tossing and turning.

"R.C., wake up," she said, shaking him gently.

Tomiko sat there, waiting a few moments until he became still. Then she put her chin into his muscled arm; the smell of sweat and Catalyst cologne filled her nose.

R.C. continued to dream. "I'm sorry, Oxford. I didn't mean it."

She started to shake him again, but instead pulled the covers over him and lay her head on his shoulder, knowing that if he awakened, he would feel her loving arms around him, holding him safe.

Oxford? Who exactly was Oxford?

17

"As you know," John Sandler began, "we've been very pleased with your performance. You've done an excellent job in Mexico." Sandler paused. "We'd like to show our appreciation by promoting you."

Cy stood with confidence. His wine-colored Armani suit fit him well. Gold cuff links sparkled against platinum shirt cuffs.

"We haven't figured out exactly when or where the position will be, but we're looking at two possible areas that will further showcase your expertise as a top-level manager."

They were in Sandler's office. He had called a meeting this morning with Cy and a man to whom Cy had not yet been introduced. The gentleman was expensively dressed and sitting in the background. He only nodded in Cy's direction when Sandler made his announcement. Cy had expected his promotion to be announced in this meeting, but he was a bit disconcerted by the presence of the stranger.

"Congratulations, Cyrus," John Sandler said, shaking his hand. "No one deserved this promotion more than you."

Cy was smiling as he shook Sandler's hand. Before Cy

could say anything, Sandler continued: "However, there is a condition."

Suddenly Cy caught sight of an imposing file on Sandler's desk with Cy's name on it.

"There's another matter we feel that we need to discuss with you, Cy," said Sandler. He signaled toward the unknown gentleman. "This is Brian Manning, one of our attorneys." His voice was resonant. "He has a few questions to ask you."

Cy took a seat on the sofa. He felt the anger rising in his gut.

Brian accepted the brown and gold file handed to him by Sandler. "We're very concerned about a lawsuit that was recently filed. As you no doubt are aware, Mr. Tyler, your wife has filed a discrimination suit against the company. Several of our high-level executives have been subpoenaed."

Cy felt himself turning as red as the rains of hell. *So that's what this is about. Why didn't she listen to me? I knew this would happen.*

"At this point, there are several plants on strike. The company is losing millions because of the labor disputes. We feel that a lawsuit by one of our plant managers will reflect poorly upon everyone concerned and give us negative press. With the upcoming contract negotiations, we can't afford that."

Cy finally spoke up. His voice was measured. "I'm not aware that a suit was filed, gentlemen." If they could sling bullshit, he might as well get his shovel out, too. "I know nothing about this issue."

"We're hoping that you can convince Mrs. Tyler to drop the lawsuit," Manning said. "That way, we could go through with processing your promotion."

Cy received the gazes of the two men as if he were in front of a firing squad.

Without hesitating, Cy said, "Certainly. I'll see what I can do."

Back in his office, Cy loosened his tie. He tried calling Thyme. Elaine said she was visiting another plant and wouldn't be back in the office that day. Damn, he'd forgotten. Thyme had mentioned it to him this morning before she'd left for work. Now he'd have to wait until this evening to speak with her.

How could Champion do this to him? After all his years of service?

Since Champion planned on selling Troy Trim by the end of the year, half the jobs were going to Mexico, and the other half would be farmed out to the new buyer. Cy became suddenly aware that he had not mentioned any of this to Thyme. In his mind, he'd been protecting her. Up to this point, Sandler had guaranteed that Thyme would be given a position at World Headquarters. Now, with her filing the lawsuit, that promise was as good as a Confederate twenty-dollar bill. And so was his promotion.

Damn!

It was a fact that Champion Two Thousand was predicated on the company's succeeding at the huge risk they'd taken in developing their Mexican factories. If things went right, the company could save a half-billion dollars when all the Mexican operations were in place.

There was no denying on Champion's part that the Mexican operations could provide that much in savings. The Japanese automaker Kutani Motor Co. had just reported a $690 million profit. Because of the improved earnings from their subsidiaries in Mexico and Europe, Kutani was able to post the highest group profit in five years.

But what Champion wasn't disclosing, Cy knew, was that not just Troy Trim, but all the trim operations in the United States would eventually be lost to the Mexican workers. That meant the assembly plants here in the States would be affected as well.

Looking up, he noticed that the sky had turned dark. A storm was brewing. It would rain soon. He made a few phone calls, checked his e-mail, and sent out two faxes to the Mexican plant. There was very little else for him to do, and with each passing second, he felt less and less like faking being busy.

Fuck it. He was too keyed up to do any more work today. After letting his secretary, Mary, know that he would be gone for the remainder of the day, he grabbed his briefcase and walked out the door.

There was little traffic at that hour of the afternoon. He headed down Jefferson Avenue and then exited onto Interstate 375, which would turn into Interstate 75 and take him home to Bloomfield.

His thoughts turned to the evening he and Thyme had planned for tomorrow night. They had box seats at the Fisher Theater to see *Titanic*. Thyme had told Cy that even though everyone knew how the play ended, she'd heard that the gripping fate of the passengers on the ship still moved the audience to tears.

Ironic choice. With both of their futures at Champion possibly ill fated, maybe they were on their own *Titanic* voyage.

His anger at Thyme returned and Cy pressed down the accelerator. How could Thyme be so selfish?

He needed to talk to someone, so he punched in Sydney's number on his car phone as he changed lanes. The line was busy. He and Sydney were so much alike; professionalism and getting ahead in the business world were their prime motivations in life.

He thought again of Sydney's offer to go into business as her partner in a Champion superstore. He knew that his and Thyme's combined yearly income paled next to Sydney's. Maybe now was the time.

For some reason, this line of thought made Cy feel even more sullen than he had felt earlier, and he was glad in a way that he hadn't reached Sydney. As he parked his sports car in the third slot of his garage, Cy sighed.

Once inside, he shed his business clothes and changed into a pair of shorts and a T-shirt. With three hours to kill before Thyme came home, Cy decided to go downstairs and work out. That would keep his mind off his confusion about what to do about his career. After pouring himself a cold glass of orange juice, he listened to the phone messages. It was no surprise there was a message from Sydney. "Cy, we need to talk. Please stop by today—without Thyme."

He knew that tone—it meant trouble.

He called Sydney again, and this time she picked up. "Cy, you should come over. I don't want to discuss this over the telephone."

"What is it, Sydney? I was just about to work out." Cy could hear the note of confrontation in his sister's voice. He wasn't in the mood for a fight.

"About your other family in Mexico."

Her words lay flat in the air between them.

How in the hell had she found out?

"Cy, don't worry. I'm not going to say anything. I never thought Thyme would satisfy you anyway. I just want to know how you could think that you could keep a secret from me."

"Sydney, it's a long story and I can't talk about it right now. Who told you about Graciella, anyway?"

"When you want to tell me the whole story, I'll tell you how I found out about Graciella."

"I'm warning you, Sydney, this isn't a game of poker with you holding the winning hand. Back out now while you still have time to fold."

"Just listen to me, twin brother: You better start cleaning up your priorities."

Cy hung up the phone. He knew what she meant. In Sydney's mind, Cy should have only one priority: her.

After working out, Cy went to the deli and purchased dinner: cold cuts and a couple of pasta salads. As he began setting the kitchen table, he told himself that his sister loved him too much ever to hurt him. He had to trust that love now and concentrate on getting his relationship with his wife back on track.

When Thyme walked through the back door and saw him working in the kitchen, she smiled.

He studied her face as if it were a key to a mystery yet to unfold. "How was your day, honey?" he asked, helping her remove her suit jacket.

Thyme didn't even meet his eyes as she said, "I had a bad feeling about the plant the moment I saw their shipping facilities." She paused to shake her head in disbelief. "Can you believe Patterson Trim only had one truck dock?"

He followed her down the hall to their bedroom. He'd heard about Patterson, a family-run minority business.

"Actually, I can. Most businesses, especially minority businesses, can't afford to retool their plants."

Cy sat back on the bed and watched her remove her clothing. Her beautiful chocolate skin looked sumptuous against the red silk suit she wore. He loved her in red. He also loved to watch her undress. Cy felt himself getting aroused.

When she sat in front of the vanity and removed her nylons and red pumps, Cy forgot all about the lawsuit, Graciella, his promotion. He reached inside his shorts and pressed his hands against his erection. Once again, he wanted to erase the problems between them with sex.

She was nude now, and the provocative curves of her shapely hips pressed deeply into the soft satin stool as she removed her makeup. "I assume they still use railcars?"

"Exactly. And we don't. One hundred percent of our business is handled by trucks." Thyme tossed the tissues she'd used to clean her face into the trash can. "I explained how all of our business was handled by truck. I tried to get him to understand how the just-in-time procedure frees up floor space and avoids storing excess inventory. But he wouldn't listen."

It was well known that most companies making money today handled their business the same way. While it would take a railcar up to five days to make it from the Troy plant to the plant in Lorain, Ohio, a truck took a maximum of four hours to deliver. But minority businesses could seldom afford such a cash outlay, and without the equipment, they couldn't ship their supplies just-in-time. As a result, they were losing money.

"They said it would cost them millions to install new truck dock facilities." Thyme turned on the shower. "I can't understand it. The Japanese instituted this same JIT practice in the 'seventies. And it's the primary reason why they're so cost effective today. Why are minority businesses so slow to do the same thing?"

"But why do you think the UPS strike crippled so many businesses? Because everyone is using trucks." He had her attention. "The UPS strike proved how many companies no longer keep large inventories. They depend on trucks and air freight to conduct business—especially trucks."

She stepped into the shower hollering, "And UPS as well as FedEx are expanding now. Patterson's transportation practices make even less sense."

When Thyme stepped from the shower, Cy was waiting for her in their bed. A colorful plastic tablecloth was spread on top of the bed, accompanied by their beautiful china and sterling silver flatware. The dinner was laid out on a platter and cut into small sections.

The mind-soothing music of Yanni played softly in the background.

He loved the look on Thyme's face when she came back into the room and saw where they would eat their meal. Minutes later, they were giggling and laughing like the days when they first met. Cy just hoped all of the tension would disappear forever.

When he fed her a slice of fresh pineapple, they juice ran down his fingers. He felt Thyme take his hand and slowly lick off the sweet nectar.

He wanted to make love to her so badly he could scream. But when he heard her yawn, he knew she'd be too tired to enjoy it.

Placing her hand in his, he said, "Your birthday's tomorrow. I haven't bought you anything yet." He ran his fingers through her hair, stopping to touch her lips with his finger. "Tell me what you'd like."

She looked up at the picture of her behind the bed and frowned. "Oh, I don't know," she said, creating tension lines around her mouth. "I really don't need a thing. Maybe we could take a trip since we missed our vacation on Martha's Vineyard."

"We can't leave right now, sweetheart."

"What about Thanksgiving? We could take the three days off before vacation begins and spend a week abroad—what about in Rio?" Cy couldn't help but notice Thyme's animated voice; he realized he hadn't heard her excited in months. Maybe he hadn't heard her at all.

"Rio? Why Rio?"

"I don't know. Never mind. What about Africa? You know, check out my roots. My history." She turned to him. "I'm not sure why, but it feels especially important to me right now."

Without her saying so, he knew there was a correlation between her age and wanting to get back to her roots. Though she never discussed it with him, Cy knew Thyme had been dreading her birthday and hated getting older. The signs had been evident all year: the change in her clothes, hairstyle, worrying about her weight. "I'd love to go to Africa with you, sweetheart. I'll take care of the arrangements tomorrow." He lifted her chin to hers. "And by the way, you're the youngest-looking forty-five-year-old woman I've ever seen in my life."

He needed her comfort. He brought a bowl with hot water and soap to bed and washed her hands and mouth like a baby. "Baby," he said, after removing the tray and tablecloth, "let me rock you to sleep. I know you're beat." He kissed her softly on her lips, along her cheek, and then moved to her ear, whispering, "Let's not talk about business, work, or birthdays any more tonight. You and I are more important." Thyme was already fast asleep in his arms.

Cy awoke early the next morning. Thyme was still asleep. He left her a note saying that he was going to Time Travelers in Beverly Hills to purchase some things for his G.I. Joe collection, and would be back by three. He added a postscript that he hadn't forgotten about their *Titanic* tickets this evening.

When he returned home, he had in his possession a 1965 Deep Sea Diver G.I. Joe in its unopened box, one of the original brass models of the Japanese Nambu pistol, and a French Resistance fighter that was handmade by Walter Hansen. They were priceless. Thrilled by what he'd bartered and bought, he set up his treasure in the library, taking care to position them by the rest of his extensive collection.

Afterwards, he couldn't find Thyme anywhere. But when he opened the patio doors on the lower level, he saw Thyme and Khan floating in the middle of the lake on the pontoon. Moving to the end of the dock, he waved. But he sprinted back to the house when he heard the telephone ringing.

"Hello," he said, out of breath.

"Hello. Mr. Tyler, this is Krandall Jewelers. The items you ordered for Mrs. Tyler are ready for your approval. Can you stop by this afternoon?"

Cy paused and looked back at Thyme and Khan still relaxing out on the water. He checked his watch. He still had another hour. "Certainly."

Fifteen minutes later he parked in Krandall's parking lot.

"Mr. Tyler." Riley Blackwell, the head jeweler, extended his hand. "Won't you have a seat?"

Cy had wanted to surprise Thyme with the diamond necklace and earrings, but he'd forgotten until yesterday to confirm the order. The store had to have them shipped from its safe. Mr. Blackwell was known for his unique bejeweled creations and historical designs. Looking at the jewelry, Cy was amazed. The precious diamonds were set in an intricate lacy web of white gold. Thyme would be speechless. Mr. Blackwell handed the pieces to Cy, and Cy nodded his approval. Cy then filled out and handed the jeweler his personal check and asked that the package be wrapped.

By the time Cy made it back home, Khan had left and Thyme was sitting on the edge of the platform in their bedroom, wearing a lavender bra and slip, polishing her toe nails. She looked at him and said, "Where've you been?"

"To the jeweler's." He brought the package from behind his back and handed it to her. "It's a birthday gift."

Thyme sat, continuing to paint her toes, not really looking

at him. Finally, she looked up and said, "Is there something you want to tell me, Cy? You look like you have something on your mind."

For a minute, Cy thought about telling her about his promotion and its condition. But when he saw the tired, worn face of his wife, he decided against it. Another time.

"Here, Thyme. Open your gift."

After opening the package, Thyme said nothing. He assumed that she was overcome by the beauty of the pieces. But when she finally spoke, her words startled him.

"I'm surprised by your extravagance, Cy."

Tightening the top on the polish, Cy eased himself up to see that Thyme's face was now void of a smile. In fact, she looked angry. "Don't you like them? I was certain that you'd—"

Thyme stood, the diamond necklace dangling off the tips of her fingers as if it were made of candy. Her voice was ice cold. "Did you think two pieces of jewelry would make me withdraw my lawsuit? Not on your life."

Cy was dumbfounded. What had he been thinking? Suddenly, Cy realized how far apart they'd become. His brow lifted slowly as Thyme began to speak again. "I've been talking to Ron Lamott. He seems to think that Champion is keeping secrets from the workers about the plants in Mexico. Do you know anything about it?"

Cy measured his words before he replied. "Not really. It's possible that you may know more than I do about company secrets. Ron seems to know everything about everybody beforehand. You keepin' an eye on that secretary of yours? Elaine's probably a leak."

"Elaine?"

Cy continued in a calm voice. "Thyme, you're jumping to conclusions and placing too much trust in your friends."

"Oh," she said, standing. "Do you mean my black

friends? Maybe I've missed something. I'm not supposed to believe them, but I can believe the white scum that run Champion Motors? The same white scum that have stopped me from getting where you are today?"

Cy spoke slowly. "Thyme, you have to understand something. Champion's not about color. It's about business. Do you understand what Champion Two Thousand really is?" She was silent. "Tomorrow—no, today—take the time to look up the word *oligopoly*. That means a market situation in which each of a few producers affects but does not control the market. In laymen's terms it means that it's all the same product except for the outer skin. Therefore, what will happen is this: GM makes the best seats, Chrysler the best wiring harnesses, Ford the best drive trains, and Champion is known for its quality in audio systems. They'll all buy from each other," Cy explained.

"I don't get it. How will each company make money if they're all working together?"

"Whoever markets the best will be the company that prevails. Toyota has been doing this for years. The Lexus is a marketing phenomenon. It's about time the Americans caught up."

"I don't feel comfortable about any of this bureaucratic bullshit," Thyme responded. "The only thing I care about right now is the fact that I probably won't have a job at Champion in two years. But you will. That's because you know what's going on and I don't." Her voice began to rise. "Oh, yeah. I get it. They can still get rid of people like me if they decide they want to. Because I don't belong to the old boys' club like you do."

"Stop it, Thyme. This is business. That's how it's run."

"No, goddammit. It's about time we discussed—everything. My discrimination lawsuit against Champion is solid.

I'm sick and tired of white people with less education and less skills being promoted over me."

"Thyme, you don't—"

She raised a finger. It shook as she spoke. "Don't go there with me, Cy. I love you. You know that. But don't make me choose between what's right and what's white. You might lose."

18

Screwing wasn't this much work, Khan thought, wiping the sweat from her forehead. Crouching in the middle of the kitchen floor, she stopped, pulled up her baggy jogging-suit pants, and sat back on her knees. She then tightened an old black scarf tied around her head. With an earnest expression on her face, she picked up the scrub brush and dipped it into the bucket of warm pine water. Perspiration dripped from her temples. Even though it was August and the heat was sweltering, Khan needed to wash her floors—it was a form of therapy.

Lifting her head at the sound of the phone, she was thankful for a break. From the number displayed on her caller ID, she knew it was her Mama Pearl. She hadn't spoken to her since July, and Labor Day was a month away. How could she tell her that this would be one more vacation she wouldn't be able to make it down to see her? What words would spare her feelings?

She didn't yet know that her guilt didn't diminish the hurt her sin caused.

"Hey there, baby," Mama Pearl said. "How you doing? I been worried about you."

"I'm sorry, Mama. I've been meaning to call you." The cleanser she had sprinkled on the floor made her sneeze.

"Now you watch what you're saying. Don't put me in the same category as those bill collectors you hate calling. You know Mama's not here to judge you. I can feel when things ain't going right in your life. That's the purpose of this call."

Oh Lord, Khan thought, her Mama Pearl had always been able to read her mind. And always, always, she made it so easy for her to talk over problems.

"How come you know me better than I know myself, Mama Pearl?" She went back to her task. Holding the receiver of the portable phone between her shoulder and chin, she dipped the brush back into the bucket and started where she'd left off.

" 'Cause you ain't full grown yet. You been wasting your time up there in Michigan searching for the wrong things—"

"Do you mean a man?" She sniffed, then wiped her nose with the back of her hand.

"Naw, I ain't saying that. What I mean is that when you truly grow up, I won't have to call you. You'll be calling me. Now you tell your Mama Pearl what's troubling you."

Khan exhaled. She stood, finished with the floor, and went to empty the dirty water into the laundry tub.

She didn't know where to start. Everything was screwed up, from her job to her bank account. "To tell you the truth, Mama Pearl, I don't know where to begin. Everything needs fixing. I'm broke, for starters."

"I'm listening."

Removing her scarf, Khan took a seat in the living room. The soft cushion felt good against her back. "Thank God they picked General Motors last month for the strike target. Otherwise I don't know what I'd do."

"I'm still listening."

"I've been paying my tithes, though, when I can. The

church down the street is Methodist. I haven't been able to find a good Pentecostal one yet, though."

"What's the pastor's name?"

"Uh . . . Reverend Wright. I been meaning to ask my friend Thyme to come along with me one Sunday. You remember my friend Thyme, don't you?"

"Of course. She's the person you've been trying to imitate since you left Itta Bena."

"Now be nice, Mama. You'd like Thyme—she's helping me make more of myself."

"And amen for her." Mama Pearl took a deep breath. "All right, Khan. Now you told me that you're broke, you probably won't strike next month, and that you're not going to church every Sunday. Now tell your Mama Pearl the real problem."

She felt naked as December's earth.

The green light in the fish tank glowed, showing off the bodies of tropical fish squirming around in the water.

"R.C. was married in April and he didn't even bother to call me. I knew you never liked him, so I couldn't bring myself to say you were right about him."

"When you gonna learn, child? I ain't here to judge you. That's what the Lord is for. What I'm here for, Khan, is to help steer you in the right direction, and maybe"—Khan could almost hear her smile—"maybe out of love give you my opinion about a few things."

"But you told me that R.C.—"

"Wasn't for you. I know. And one day you'll find that out for yourself. What I think you should concentrate on is yourself. You are a wise, talented girl, and I am proud of you. You owe it to yourself to do something with your life. Be important; make yourself important."

After she and Mama Pearl hung up, it took Khan another

hour to finish cleaning her small home. She could still hear her Mama Pearl's words.

It was Saturday night and Khan made a vow that she could do at least one thing to make her Mama proud. She would drive over to that church on the corner of Seward and Delaware tomorrow morning and attend a service.

Resolute, she went into her bathroom and turned on the bathtub faucet full force. Pouring three capfuls of fresh woods–scented bubble bath into the water, she lit all five peach magnolia candles that were perched on the shelf above her and turned off the lights. She inhaled the sweet scent as she shed her clothing. Not only were the candles pleasant to smell, they were also beautiful to look at. Pressed almost to translucence around the pretty peach-colored circumference of the heavy candle were dried white magnolias, their pale green leaves and small buds meeting at the center and base of the flower.

She hit the remote on her small television as she stepped down into the water. When she did, bubbles covered her chin, and she laid her head back on her bath pillow and watched *The Pretender.* As soon as she got comfortable, the phone began ringing. Khan let the machine pick up. She heard Thyme's voice, asking about lunch tomorrow. When Khan heard how distraught Thyme sounded, she got on the line.

Khan shortened her much-needed thirty-minute soak and ended up on the phone for almost an hour. The problems between Thyme and Cy had gone from bad to worse. They were barely speaking to one another now.

As soon as she hung up, her Uncle Ron called. Ida was threatening to put him out; could Khan come over and talk to her? Ida refused even to speak to Ron and was drinking herself into a stupor every night.

Finally, Valentino called, asking if she would baby-sit for Jahvel on Sunday.

It seemed that everyone needed her. Except the man she needed the most.

She had to hurry; it was almost eleven o'clock, and she didn't want to miss the opening of *The Keenan Ivory Wayans Show*. Jada Pinkett was one of the guests.

Khan went into the kitchen to grab a glass of milk, and tucked four cookies into a napkin. On her way back to her bedroom, she could hear Jada being introduced. Then she heard a soft knock on the door. *Who in the hell is it now?* she wondered in irritation.

Peering through the peephole in her front door, she saw the back of his head first. Even with such a small glimpse she knew who it was. She opened the door and let him inside but kept the door cracked open. Instincts told her to send him away. But for some reason, she couldn't. *Shit, could Lauren Bacall turn away Bogie? Hell no.*

"Come in," Khan said, opening the door for R.C. She hadn't seen him in so long, except in her imagination. Now the sight of R.C. in the flesh was shocking. His skin looked gray. Shining through the eyes that she had always loved so much, as she looked up at him, she saw a look of surrender. She'd never seen him so vulnerable. And it weakened her.

Khan closed the door behind him. Even though nothing was said, and nothing was offered—no matter what—she felt helpless.

"Khan," he said so softly she thought it might have been the wind whispering her name. The warmth of his voice ran straight through to her womb, and she felt her knees weaken. The screenplay for the night was already written, and there was no way to edit the script.

Without knowing or understanding why, she reached out

her hands as he came quickly toward her. They slid to the floor in the entryway.

She gave in to R.C. with everything she had, even though a voice in her head whispered that she'd pay for it later. What did it matter? They were together now.

They kissed.

She felt his tongue slide into her mouth and linger. She felt full, unable to breathe. "R.C., blood. I need you," she panted as he began to rotate his hips deliciously against her. "Don't stop. Please don't stop."

It's a rule of life: Things get better with time. Khan and R.C. were no different.

His first orgasm was quick. Khan came frequently and each time with a thrilling tremor, which shook her from head to toe. She could feel R.C. holding back so that they could enjoy another round of pleasure. It thrilled her that he still maintained such restrained skill.

Khan bathed in the scent of him, a musk that she luxuriated in and could never find in a bottle of men's cologne.

And now, as she lowered her head below his navel to please him the way he loved most, she tasted the sweetness of their love, as heady as wine. As delicious as it had ever been.

She clasped the head of his penis in her hand and, with her fingers as tightly closed as the buds of a flower, roughly kissed and bit the stem of his organ.

"Khan, baby, that shit feels so good." R.C. pressed his hands on the sides of her head and rotated his pelvis. "Please baby, do it like you used to."

Even with half of him inside her mouth, Khan smiled. She loved making him feel good, and she loved the exquisite taste of his penis inside her mouth. At that moment, she took even more of him inside her mouth and closed her lips tightly. She felt him clutching at the carpet. Then pulling with her lips as if she wished to entice his organ away from his body, she continued the pressure.

Khan knew he was seconds away from an orgasm. Encouraged by his response, she took him more deeply into her mouth, pressed his penis with the back of her tongue, then suddenly withdrew. She held his hardness in her hand and gently bit the perimeter around the tip. Next, she caressed his entire organ with her tongue, concentrating on the long vein that ran column-wise along the length of him.

R.C.'s penis stretched out like it had stilts. She pushed the entire organ into her mouth and pressed on it with all the might she had up to the root, as if she wanted to swallow it whole. Khan luxuriated in the feel of him within her and took pleasure in bringing him to an intense climax.

He came like an ambulance driver, fast and in a hurry, as Khan stood back and watched the white show. It was an act of nature that she never tired of watching. "Damn, R.C., that's the prettiest dick that I ever saw," she said, watching the whitish liquid squirt from his pulsating tip.

"Don't you want to get in bed?" she asked.

She led him back to the bedroom and turned on the pink light on the nightstand. In his touching and retouching, she recognized that making love with R.C. was better than she remembered. Their lovemaking continued for another hour. By then, Khan had forgotten all about his wife.

Her eyes were closed in bliss, reliving every second, every sound, every scent of the man she'd longed to love her, lying next to her now. Close to two hours had passed. When she felt him slipping from beneath the sheets, she opened her eyes.

"R.C.?"

He hesitated, then said in a pitiful voice, "I got to go."

Go? You couldn't wait to get your ass over here, now you gotta go? He seemed to be saying everything in two directions and the intersection was in her head. He was leaving now and would never return.

"Blood, I don't want you to go." Khan clung to him, afraid that his leaving would starve the fever of their lust. "It's never been this good between us before." Her eyes frantically searched his until he turned away.

She clasped the sheets over her body.

Nothing else was said between them as he dressed, then left, abandoning her.

Hearing the door slam softly behind him, Khan cringed. Old tears streamed down her face. She felt used. Why did she keep making this same damn mistake? Mama Pearl had taught her better. Khan knew she hadn't used her wisdom tonight. Tonight would be the last night.

Khan stood by the window stark naked. She pulled open the drapes in her bedroom. She wanted to be seen and judged for who she was.

Up above, a million stars sparkled in the black night sky. Khan felt a chill. She had the weirdest feeling, as if the stars were eyes. A million eyes staring down on her. Condemning her for what she'd done.

Tenderness

19

Tomiko hummed a Patti LaBelle song. Her eyes opened and closed as her body swooned to the soft beat. She felt so fluid, so soothed and relaxed. It was as if the music were two warm hands massaging her entire body. Tomiko felt carried away as she imagined Patti climbing a mystical staircase to a higher plane of feeling. Tomiko twirled around in a circle, snapping her fingers up high.

Outside the hot August air clung to every tree, car, and body. But inside Detroit's Jazz West Club, Tomiko felt cool, oh so cool.

Pumping her arms in the air, Tomiko worked her buttocks from left to right to the beat of the soulful music. It was her first time at the club, where all the patrons were younger than thirty. Beautiful black young men and women from chocolate brown to ecru were popping their fingers, having a good time laughing and dancing in the packed nightclub. Tomiko was beginning to feel like one of them.

Her dance partner was tall and lithe. When the record was over, she headed back to her table. Just then, she noticed a good-looking brother, his eyes focused on hers, coming toward her.

"Hi, I'm Nathan," he said, staring at her mouth. "That's some pretty lipstick you're wearing."

Tomiko blushed. "Thanks. I'm Tomiko."

The tempo of the music suddenly changed. "For You," Kenny Lattimore's hit song from the previous year, had just started. It was still one of her favorites. Her thoughts traveled to R.C. Where was her husband? Once again she wished he were with her tonight, holding her close.

Earlier, Tomiko had refused several offers to dance to the slow love songs the DJ played. She really wanted to try slow dancing, but she hadn't been able to build up the nerve. Slow dancing was so sexy, especially, she'd observed, when dancing with a black man.

"Care for another dance?" He held out his hand.

Accepting him, she said, "Sure."

"Your raven wild hair and olive brown coloring say you're black, but your exotic slanted eyes and small nose and chin say otherwise. Are you Oriental?"

"Japanese and African American."

"It's a good mix, Tomiko. You're gorgeous."

"Thank you." She smiled. Her cherry lips sparkled. Her shoulder-length hair, falling down into thick rows of gentle waves, was as black as a raven's feathers. Unadorned by jewelry and wearing very little makeup and all black, Tomiko was the definition of simple elegance.

Bonnie had taught Tomiko the American black dances. Tomiko's parents had been very strict and had never let her go out to dance clubs in Japan—not that there were any near the family's home and horse farm outside of Kyoto. But Bonnie had shown her how to dance to the funky tempo of Usher, Maxwell, Ginuwine, and R. Kelly. R.C. had promised her he would take her to a nightclub once she was ready.

Earlier this evening, Tomiko had been completely dressed

and wearing a new pair of chunky dancing shoes, but R.C. was in his pajamas and complaining of a migraine. She had been ready to stay home with him, in a way relieved to have him home at all. But to Tomiko's surprise, R.C. had suggested that she go alone and, dying to dance, she had reluctantly agreed.

Now she was glad she had come.

From the moment Nathan placed his arm around her waist and pulled her next to him, to her amazement she felt her heart beginning to pound. His face was just inches from hers, and she could smell the cool mint on his breath as he made small talk, asking her if she lived in the city. By the song's second verse, she knew that he worked for a software company in Dearborn and lived on the west side of Detroit—and that he was single.

Turning to her right, she observed some of the other couples kissing, women resting their heads on their partners' chests. The music was building, the love song making you feel as if you wanted to be in love with the man you were dancing with, right at that moment. She felt the music touching her heart, then gravitating down to her hips, which reacted naturally to the lovely melody.

Tomiko felt her partner relax and pull her closer to him as he guided her around the dance floor. The scent of his cologne was so fresh and sweet she almost asked him the name of it. Slow dancing with Nathan was like having sex on the dance floor. Tomiko could feel the sweat between her legs. There was no way she could deny the attraction between her and Nathan.

When the song ended, Tomiko knew she better go home. She wanted her man to make her feel the way this man made her feel. Her body tingled with the anticipation of making serious love to her husband.

"Thanks," Tomiko said, loosening herself from his enticing arms. The next tune started up. By the tempo of the music she knew it was another slow song. The DJ announced that he was playing "If Only You Knew," a love song by Phil Perry, for all the lovers in the house tonight . . . one more time.

No, I won't, Nathan. You're fine, but you better find a young woman who's single. It's time for me to go home.

Making her way through the crowd she left the dance floor and headed for the pay phones. It was ten minutes after eleven when she called home.

Bonnie answered.

"Hi, Bonnie, it's Tomiko. Is R.C. still asleep?"

"No . . . I don't know," Bonnie stuttered.

"Never mind. I'm on my way home." She was certain, from Bonnie's tone, that R.C. wasn't home.

Driving home, Tomiko remembered how hard it had been at the ranch when they had been there in July. One of the stallions had broken a leg and was suffering badly. He had to be shot. R.C. had been in a rage; he'd had big plans for the stallion. From that point on, their stay at the ranch had gone downhill. R.C. seemed to be having a problem staying hard when they made love, and he refused to discuss it with her. She could barely remember the last time they'd had a good night of sex. When was it? Early June? Before his arrest, certainly.

She remembered that their evening had begun as it always did, with a game. It was called An Enchanted Evening.

The mood had been set on the veranda outside their bedroom. Tomiko had marinated raspberries in a special liqueur and placed the fruit in champagne glasses. White chocolate–covered Godiva raspberries were in a bowl beside them along with a cold bottle of Cristal champagne.

The object of the game was to win a wish. Each player was supposed to take a blank card and write down a secret wish that the player wanted fulfilled by or with each other, one that could be fulfilled the same evening. Without disclosing the wish, they set the cards aside until the end of the game. The players move around the board, drawing cards that direct their actions. Some cards ask for verbal responses; other suggest gentle touching or playful advances; others are more subtle and ambiguous.

Tomiko had insisted that they play this game totally nude.

"Have you written down your wish?" Tomiko had asked R.C. She had sipped on her champagne, then said, "I've written down mine."

"I read the rules. I'll go first." When she'd nodded, he had drawn a card from the deck and asked, " 'Lines, curves, bends, turns—what is it about your partner's body that you find alluring?' "

Tomiko had thought for a moment, then reached down and stroked his toes. "I love how they feel when you're on top of me and they curl over mine." She'd smiled, then said, "My turn." She had read the card to herself first then had begun to move her body into a comfortable position as she read it aloud. " 'Think of your partner as Michelangelo, Rodin, or Picasso. Pose for him.' " She'd extended her chin and head high, and, turning her body slightly to her left, had cocked her left leg up, placing the tip of her finger at the mouth of her vagina. "You like?" she'd asked, seeing from the corner of her eye his growing erection.

She'd sat there feeling his eyes ravishing her body. He'd never looked at her that way before. "Do you want to stop, R.C.?"

"No. One more." He had drawn, then read, " 'Using the tip of a finger and your most flowery style, trace your name somewhere on your partner's body.' "

R.C. had set his glass to the side and leaned over beside

her. With his index finger he'd begun to write along her thigh.

"That's awful long for R.C."

"My birth name is Richard Charles Richardson."

The game had turned out better than she had ever expected—especially since he had shared something with her that was important: his name. But she had had to wait long for the rest of An Enchanted Evening. R.C. had taken her hand, lifted her up, and carried her to the bed.

"Now I'm going to fuck you tonight like I ain't never fucked no woman before." He had reached down and placed her hand on his penis. It was hard as iron. "Not because I desire you. But because I love you, Tomiko."

That night had begun with the thought of them having an innocent night of fun and ended with more pleasure than she had ever dreamed possible.

And thinking about that night now warmed her with so much love, she wanted to rush home. She only hoped R.C. was there to greet her.

Sure enough, R.C.'s car was missing from the garage. She needed to talk. The great weight of her loneliness had descended upon her once again.

She went into the bedroom she shared with R.C. and lay, fully clothed, on top of her Mikimoto duvet. She opened the drawer of her bedside table and looked at the letter she'd received last month. She still hadn't read it. Unsure why, Tomiko felt afraid, as if the letter contained a Pandora's box that might affect her future in a negative way. She'd opened the envelope and several snapshots had fallen out. She'd looked at them quickly and then returned them to the envelope. But now she wanted to satiate her curiosity. With the letter in hand, Tomiko walked down the hall toward Bonnie's room.

"Bonnie, are you asleep?" she asked through the closed bedroom door.

"Just about."

Tomiko could hear the springs of the bed squeak lightly seconds before Bonnie opened the door. "I didn't mean for you to get up."

"Don't give me that, Tomiko. You got something on your mind. Where have you been, girl?"

"I went out dancing."

"And did you remember all those steps I taught you?"

Tomiko imitated the latest dance, the Chinese Checkers.

"You work it, girl," Bonnie praised. "Did you do okay, then?"

"Great, I think. Especially with this one guy."

"And?"

"Well, he wasn't R.C."

"Girl, sometimes it's better to get attention from somewhere else than wait around and feel sorry for yourself." Bonnie paused and looked at Tomiko. "But you've got something else on your mind, don't you?"

"Well, yes. I received this letter and I wondered if you would read it with me."

"Hold up. You're telling me you can't read it alone? What on earth is the problem?"

"I'm just nervous."

Bonnie stared at her a moment, then sat up in her bed and took the envelope from Tomiko. She opened it as Tomiko sat beside her. The three pictures fell out.

"Who's this?"

"I think the baby is me."

One picture was of a black man holding a baby. Another photo was of four adults: a black man and a Japanese woman (Tomiko's mother) seated in front of an older black couple. There was also a young girl who appeared to be about four years old.

"And these other folks?" Bonnie stopped. "Hey, we should stop right now and read the letter first. Otherwise none of this makes sense."

"Will you read it to me, Bonnie?"

"I understand, honey," Bonnie said, hugging Tomiko to her.

Opening up the carefully folded pages, Bonnie read:

" 'Thank God we've finally found you. You probably don't remember us, but we're your grandma and grandpa Johnson, your father's parents. We haven't seen you since you were real little. We've missed you so much, Tomiko. Don't think a day's gone by when we haven't thought of you.' "

Bonnie and Tomiko looked at each other. Tomiko's hands trembled as Bonnie read the letter.

" 'We don't know how much you were told about us, but after your father died and your mother remarried, we weren't allowed to see you anymore. We tried so many times to change your mother's mind. But she refused. She said she planned on raising you as Japanese and she was going to make you forget your black heritage. Your father wouldn't have wanted that. He was our only child, Tomiko, and we loved him so. And you are our only grandchild.

" 'You might be wondering how we found you. We never gave up hope that we'd find you. And when we saw your picture in the paper with your husband a few months ago, we knew immediately it was you. Our Tomiko. Your grandfather did some checking and found your husband's address. We know it was a true sign from God that you're here with us at last. We love you.' "

It was signed by both her grandfather and her grandmother, Albert and Diane Johnson.

"My Lord," Bonnie said, looking again at the pictures, "these are your grandparents!"

Bonnie read the postscript. " 'Please contact us.' " Their telephone number was listed beside it.

"I . . . I . . . don't know—" Tears caught in her throat.

"It's okay, honey. You go ahead and cry." And for a full five minutes she did.

Bonnie went to get tissues and when she returned, Tomiko was able to speak.

"You know, Bonnie, it's odd. I haven't thought about my father in years." She sniffed, then wiped her nose. "My memory of him is so blurred it's almost as if he never existed. But the letter and pictures prove that he did. I don't hate my mother for the decision she made, but I do resent being denied a part of my heritage. I have never thought of myself as black before—my mother wouldn't let me."

"But you married R.C.," Bonnie pointed out.

"Yes. But I don't think I was so aware of why I was attracted to R.C. Now I feel like I have found some sort of key to myself." Tomiko sighed in relief as she looked up hopefully at Bonnie.

"Tomiko," Bonnie said, rising. "I think it's best if you were alone now. You've got a lot to think about. Decisions to make. You sleep on it tonight, and if you want to, we'll talk about it in the morning. Okay?"

Tomiko nodded, rising from Bonnie's small bed. As she walked back to her own room, the tears once again formed in her eyes. Tomiko's aloneness crashed around her. *Where are you, R.C.? Again I need you to hold me. And again you are not here.*

20

The day of the depositions had finally arrived and they were being held in the offices of Thyme's attorney, Stephen Kravitz, who had subpoenaed several Champion division managers, including Cy's boss, Sandler.

It was ten in the morning. They'd begun the depositions at nine. One by one, fifteen unwilling witnesses were being interrogated relentlessly by Thyme's attorney. And as each witness gave his or her testimony, Thyme felt her hopes for winning wane.

Mary-Elizabeth Wright, who worked in Salaried Personnel, was now on the stand. Her brows were furrowed and her nostrils flared as if she smelled something foul each time she looked at Thyme.

"Could you please tell us, Ms. Wright, if there was an opening last year for the position of plant manager at an A plant in Lake Orion?"

"Yes, there was."

"And who received that promotion?"

"Ed Bolton—"

"Whose previous position was . . . ?"

"He was an accounting mana—"

"And was a grade what?"

"Eleven."

Stephen turned and faced the judge. "Let me preface my next question to Ms. Wright, Your Honor, by explaining the difference between an A plant and a B plant. The plant manager at an A plant is usually a grade fifteen or above; a plant manager at a B plant is a grade thirteen."

Scratching his head, Stephen pondered his thoughts out loud as he turned back to the witness. "So you're telling us this morning, Ms. Wright, that Champion Motors is in the business of hiring a grade-eleven accounting manager for the position of plant manager over my client, an experienced plant manager, who is a grade thirteen, for a grade-fourteen position at an A facility?"

"Well . . ." she began, stumbling.

"Your Honor, let me explain that my client presently is the manager at Champion's Troy Trim plant, which is a B plant. The Lake Orion facility is an A plant that has approximately five thousand employees and over a million and a half square feet of manufacturing floor space. Because the pay scale for A plant managers is substantially higher than at a B plant, it would be advantageous for any employee trying to advance her career to seek employment at that facility." Stephen turned back to Ms. Wright. "Aside from her obvious qualifications, could you explain to us to the best of your knowledge why my client was not even interviewed for this position?"

"Mrs. Tyler's DIS reflected her preference for remaining at Troy Trim. Her unwillingness to relocate to another plant was the primary reason we didn't consider her a candidate for a promotion at the Lake Orion facility."

The DIS, the development interest survey, was filled out by every salaried employee. This survey was updated year-

ly by the employee and was crucial in determining whether
he or she was eligible for a promotion.

Thyme was fuming.

*How could Wright sit in front of my face and tell such a
huge lie? Everyone knew I fought for that promotion at the
Orion plant. Why would I give up a job fifteen minutes closer to my house that paid twenty-five thousand dollars more
a year?*

Sitting up tall in her seat, Thyme could see a small flutter
of triumph flash across Mary-Elizabeth's face. Thyme had
known Mary-Elizabeth for over ten years. She'd always flirt
with Cy at company picnics in front of Thyme, which infu-
riated Thyme and merely made Cy laugh.

Thyme wanted to cover her face with her hands so badly
her eyes ached. She felt degraded and humiliated. But she
sat there tall and proud while her heart and soul felt as if a
volcano had erupted within her.

The depositions were signed and numbered as exhibits as
each person Mr. Kravitz had subpoenaed gave testimony.

Next was a notice of deposition and request for production of documents. Thyme knew this was where she had
Champion by the balls. Her friend Vicky Kress had come
through with the documents that detailed all of the promotions of the salaried employees over the past fifteen years.
Out of the two hundred seventy-five promoted, only one
was black. There was no way Thyme would disclose her
source of information, not even to Kravitz. The point was
that the information was correct and that was all that mattered.

It was now eleven forty-five. Thyme knew they'd have to
break for lunch soon. Stephen had just introduced plaintiff's
deposition exhibit number fifteen. Audrey Hall, a white
woman who'd recently been promoted to a grade fourteen,
was now being interviewed.

Thyme's mind wandered. She knew the story. Audrey was Candice-Marie Avery's niece and had been hired her first year out of the University of Illinois. Thyme had read her résumé. Audrey was no slouch, but she had very little hands-on business experience. Apparently that hadn't gotten in her way to be promoted to manager of the Electronics Engineering Division.

When he finished with Audrey, Stephen came over and whispered in her ear. "Would you consider bringing your husband in? He could be crucial to our case."

"No."

"But he could supply us firsthand with the emotional damages that you—"

"Forget it, Stephen. It may or may not help our case. But it could destroy my marriage. No way am I calling Cy in to testify. If we can't win with all these witnesses, let's cut our losses and fold." Thyme knew it wasn't rational, but she couldn't ask Cy to appear as a witness. She was still waiting for him to volunteer.

Thyme wished he had been there to support her. Though she knew she still loved him, she felt more distant from him than ever. How could they patch up their differences now? Was it possible? Does love really conquer all?

If I win or lose, Thyme thought, at least I tried. At least I showed these white folks that they can't treat black people this way. We'll fight back. They must think I'm a real fool if I sit back and let them promote people less qualified than me and think I won't sue their ass for racial discrimination.

At this moment, Stephen was interviewing the last witness. All through the process Thyme had pointed out the contradictions or blatant lies in the testimonies of the witnesses. She'd say to Kravitz, "It didn't happen like that. This is what really happened." And Stephen would listen and come back with a slamming rebuttal. Looking over to her left, she could see that Champion's attorney was coaching his witnesses as well.

What a joke. It was like everyone was playing a game of shuffleboard. You could move here. Then I'll move there, and we'll assess the situation. And finally whoever tossed out the best question would certainly win. *How stupid.*

Stephen threw back his shoulders when the next witness took the stand. It was John Sandler, Cy's boss.

"Mr. Sandler, are you familiar with Champion's policy to promote only those employees that have attained a bachelor's degree or higher?"

"I don't recall."

"Mr. Sandler, are you aware that some of your salaried employees in a grade nine or higher have merely an associate's degree?"

"I don't recall."

"Mr. Sandler." Stephen cleared his throat. "I'm told that you have a master's degree in business management. Is that true?"

"I don't recall."

Stephen turned around and smiled at Thyme. "Is your name John Sandler?"

"I don't recall."

Champion's attorney, Brian Manning, was so frustrated he tossed all his papers up in the air in disbelief.

This time Thyme met Stephen's smile.

John's arrogance and unwillingness to cooperate with Thyme's attorney or even answer simple questions had lost him the case.

His pathetic smile was broader than Stephen's; John Sandler *still* didn't get it. He gave Champion's attorney a bewildered stare and shrugged his shoulders.

*   *   *

Thyme whistled as she showered Saturday morning. Kravitz had assured her that there was no way Champion wasn't going to settle. Thyme's case had forced them into the corner. At that moment, Thyme felt that nothing could upset her today. Not even her husband's distance.

But her joy was short lived. The devil was no idle spirit but a vagrant renegade that never stayed long in one place. Perhaps he'd followed her home from the courtroom on Friday and was trying to make his presence known today. The motive, cause, and main intention of his walking was to ruin her. Just before she opened her eyes this morning, one of the devil's helpers must have shown up full of smoke and fire.

It was eighty-two degrees by six o'clock in the morning on this day in the second week of August. The humidity made it feel like a hundred. Even with the air conditioner set to kick on at seventy degrees, Thyme felt uncomfortable.

Cy was still asleep in the guest room. He'd managed to avoid her the entire week, and Thyme had been grateful. Each was hiding something from the other. But now, she thought, it was time to bring things out in the open—she felt she had very little to lose at this point.

She slipped into a cotton robe, pulled her hair into a pony-tail, brushed her teeth, and started the coffee.

Moments later, the mind-awakening scent of fresh Colombian coffee filtered through the house. From the kitchen, she could hear Cy getting up as she removed two large rolls from the freezer.

"Cy!" she hollered a few minutes later. "The coffee's brewing, and I've got cinnamon rolls in the microwave." Cy was dressed only in boxer shorts when he came into the kitchen, his silver hair spiked in spots. "It's muggy in here. Let's have breakfast out on the water," Thyme said, suddenly nervous.

Cy was still slowly awakening. "Mmm, smells good," he said.

"They're almost ready. So—are you coming?"

"Give me two minutes and I'll meet you at the dock."

Thyme balanced the coffee, rolls, newspaper, and napkins as she walked to the dock.

Catching up with her, Cy released the boat from the dock and jumped inside, then held out his arms for the breakfast tray. The seductive lure of the rhythmic waves was so relaxing that Thyme considered passing on the discussion and taking a quick nap.

There was only one other boat on the lake as they sipped their coffee. Thyme braced herself. She needed to hear from Cy's own mouth if what Ron had told her about Troy Trim was true and whether Cy had known all along.

She spoke slowly. "Cy, I talked with Ron earlier this week. We were discussing the labor situation in Mexico. Tell me that it isn't true that you've been personally involved with the Mexican facilities that sew Troy Trim's stock." Her eyes drilled into his before she spoke again. "Tell me that isn't true, Cy."

Thyme could see that he was struggling. A few moments later, he sat back against the pontoon's gunwale.

"All I know is that some of the production is being shifted to Mexico. Champion has other plans for Troy Trim."

"Other plans?" Thyme bored her eyes into his.

"Yes. Don't worry; everything will be all right. Champion takes care of its own. The company is just trying to clear the way so that Troy Trim can develop new business." Cy smiled now. "Isn't that what you've been trying to accomplish, honey?"

"Cy, that doesn't change the fact that you lied to me. You told me that Champion wasn't going to do any outsourcing to Mexico."

"Baby—"

The water around them began to lap the boat, creating a subtle motion. "I'm your wife, Cy. I'm not your baby. We should talk when we've both had more time to think."

"I agree."

Thyme realized in her heart that we hate some people because we do not know them; and we do not know them because we hate them. At that moment of revelation with her husband, she hated the Mexicans. She hated Champion Motors for lying—for making her husband lie to her. With all her heart, she did not want to hate her husband. Because after loving someone so much, her hatred toward him, she knew, would be far deeper than her love.

When Cy docked the boat and went into the house, Thyme had the worst cry she'd had in years. *What about me? What about us? Does that company mean more to us than we mean to each other?* A part of her didn't want to know the answer. But one thing was clear: Cy had indeed lied to her.

The devil had had his day.

21

This was a mistake, Randy," Luella said, frowning. She hadn't noticed before how long his nails were. Nor how dirty. "Maybe you should take me back to my car."

They were at Slappy Joe's Bar on the corner of Seven Mile Road and Grand River Avenue. It was just past midnight on Saturday night and the bar had been steadily filling up since eleven. While he consumed shot after shot of Hennessy, Luella had kept watch on the door for fear that someone from the plant would recognize her. She'd met Randy one night after work in the parking lot; his car had a flat and she'd helped him.

But now she suspected that her date had had a little too much to drink.

"Hold on, girl. The room is just down the street, and it's already paid for."

Already paid for—already paid for—already paid for. She didn't like the sound of that. It was the first time Luella realized how cheap she must look to this man. "I'll give you your money back, Randy. Just take me to my car and let's call it a night."

Randy's face distorted into an angry smile. She was positive now that he'd had too much to drink. "I don't want your money," he said, squeezing her arm, his thick nails leaving a lasting impression. "I want sumpin' else." He left a tip on the table, took her arm, and damn near pushed her outside.

She wore a skin-tight devil-red catsuit. A matching long sheer sheath showed off every inch of her voluptuous curves and highlighted her ravishing red hair. She knew she looked fine, but tonight it was the wrong choice of clothing for all the wrong reasons.

The Dorcheshire Motel in Redford was just eight blocks down, and they were there in five minutes. The Dorcheshire was an establishment that had a Jacuzzi with blue mood lights embedded on the sides. They also offered king-sized water beds and free adult movies. But most people frequented the motel because of its "short stay" policy: four hours for a mere forty-five dollars.

Luella had always wanted to go there, but not under these circumstances. The moment they stepped inside the room, Randy began stripping off her clothes, not even bothering to take off his. He merely let his pants drop to his knees when he pushed her nude body down on the bed.

Randy didn't screw her; he abused her. He didn't want oral sex or regular sex. He wanted it from the rear. Luella loved sex, but she'd never done it that way before. He hurt her so bad she screamed in agony. She prayed that someone heard her. He didn't even bother to use lubrication. When they left the room, tears streamed down her face. She could barely walk. Without even looking, she knew that he had left bruises on her. How would she explain bruises to Omar when he came home next week?

They'd only used two hours. And "used" was exactly how Luella felt.

Just as she opened the door to his car, she heard voices from the motel's upper level and turned toward the noise.

"Bitch! You come back here!" the scantily dressed man hollered.

Then she saw another man bolting down the corridor a few feet away, sprinting down the steps. His clothing was ripped in spots, and when he reached the lower level Luella could see that blood oozed from his mouth. She could also see that the man was Valentino.

"What the fuck are you doing here?" she asked as he headed in her direction.

"Luella, let's go," Randy said impatiently.

She could see that Valentino was trembling, anxiously looking at the man upstairs, who appeared ready to run after him. Tino's eyes were wide with horror. A tear trembled down his face. "He tried to—" He clasped his hand over his mouth, muffling a cry. "Nothing." He didn't bother to look back as he ran down the street.

When she turned back around, Randy was frowning. "What was that shit all about?"

"Take me to my car, Randy," Luella demanded, not bothering to answer him.

All weekend she soaked her bruises in Epsom salts, rubbing down her body afterwards with cool cotton balls saturated with witch hazel. She'd never felt so violated before. In all her years of sleeping around, nothing like this incident with Randy had ever happened. Was this a sign for her to stop and settle down? What was she getting out of the sex if she came home battered?

On Monday, Luella went to work calmly. She avoided eye contact with everyone and went straight to her station. At one point, on her way to the break room, Luella bumped into Tino, who was packing the Rouge Build Cooley carts with

Remington luxury seat cushions. She could smell the aromatic sweat gleaming against his muscled arms.

"Tino? How are you?" Luella realized she sounded a bit nasty.

Tino gave her a hard look. "Luella, stay out of my face. My life is none of your business. I'm warning you: Don't fuck with me."

Luella decided to change her tack. "The thought of the three of us in bed together is turning me on."

"You couldn't pay me enough money to fuck you, Luella." Tino flipped five front backs onto the top shelf.

"I love it when you talk to me like that," she said, handing him the rear cushion that completed the set. "I'll give you one more chance to prove you're a man. And if you don't, I'm going to have to resort to different tactics. You know, like tell your wife you been giving up more ass than you been getting."

"You low-down bitch. You don't stop fucking with me, I'm going to the man for some protection against your crazy ass. I'm warning you, bitch—back off. I mean it, Luella."

Luella noticed that Tino didn't show up for work Tuesday. Wednesday, Thursday, and Friday, the same thing.

After receiving her paycheck, she left to go shopping at Northland Mall. It was the twenty-first day of August, and every store in the mall had summer sales. When she returned home, there was a process server on her doorstep who handed her a restraining order. It instructed her to stay at least fifty feet from Valentino, and the same distance from his property.

"That sucker don't know who he's fooling with." *No one ever refused this pussy and I ain't about to let a two-way bastard be the first. The son of a bitch will be begging to suck this pussy when I get through with him.*

Luella was genuinely hurt. All the thoughts about her being laughed at when she was in grade school—all the ridicule she had suffered for being fat, bald-headed, and gap-toothed—surfaced. Her pituitary gland had been fucked up, though doctors didn't know why. She hadn't cared why; she had just wanted to look normal.

She sat alone in her bedroom and removed a picture from her wallet. It was a photo of her at age sixteen. It wasn't a sweet-sixteen kind of picture. This was a reminder of how she'd looked before she spent thousands getting her stomach clamped—had a section of her intestines cut out in order to make her stomach smaller. In twenty-eight months she'd lost a hundred and twenty-eight pounds. That's when she met and married Omar. When she later gave birth to their two sons, she gained and lost eighty more pounds. But her quest for beauty hadn't ended there. The dentist bills to fix the gap in her teeth and get them capped was next. In two more years she would have all the bills paid off. She put the picture back in her wallet, then smiled. Ron would never know how much they truly had in common.

That same night, she called on one of her old acquaintances. She promised him an evening of sex games after he gave her the information she needed about Valentino. She learned from the weak fool that Valentino repaired televisions on the side. She also learned that on each and every Saturday and Sunday evening, around seven o'clock, he delivered those repaired sets to his customers. This is when, Luella decided, she would pay a call on his wife.

22

Hello, Cy," Sydney said, hugging him. "I'm so glad you stopped by before you left on your trip. There's so much we need to discuss. The courts have granted Jarrod joint custody of Graham. That means he'll be spending three months at a time with Jarrod in London. What am I going to do?"

Cy could tell she was holding back tears. They were in Sydney's main office, located in her biggest Champion dealership. Outfitted in sumptuous brown leather, the office looked more like an English drawing room than a place of work. "I think the only thing you can do for now is not make it difficult for Graham and then appeal the case. I'm sure a good lawyer will be able to convince the judge that spending that kind of time in England would be disruptive for Graham."

"It appears not." Sydney went to the wet bar and poured them both a drink. "I hope this isn't too strong," she said, handing him a double shot of Chivas on the rocks.

"Fine," he said, downing the drink in a single gulp.

"Are things that bad at home?" Sydney's voice was edged with sarcasm rather than concern.

Cy took a seat on one of the armchairs. "Things are bad

everywhere. They're screwing me over at Champion." He sighed. "And I'm disgusted with myself for not apologizing to my wife before I left to go on this business trip."

"Cy, I don't know why you keep resisting going into partnership with me. Things are all set to go." She downed her drink and refilled both of their glasses. Sydney took a seat opposite Cy and crossed her legs. She stared at him. And continued to stare until Cy looked away.

"I told you, Sydney, I'm not ready for that move yet. And I don't know if I'll ever be."

Sydney's smile stretched across her face before she spoke. "Circumstances might work out better than you expect, Cy." Her expression changed to a wicked half-smile. "Thyme might not pose a problem by then."

She made him so uncomfortable he wanted to leave. Instead, he shook the ice cubes nervously in his glass before taking a long swallow. Maybe he was imagining things. "Sydney, are you suggesting something? I've told you before; stay out of my personal affairs. Thyme and I have loved each other as sweethearts. We even loved each other as baby sweethearts. We share something I'm sure you can't possibly understand," he added bitterly.

"Is it her black skin that turns you on and makes you so obsessive about her?" She swirled the brown liquid around in her glass and leaned toward him. "Maybe you haven't met the right white woman yet."

It was funny, he thought, looking at his sister's bone-dry face. When had she lost her capacity for tears? "Passion comes in all colors. My wife happened to be the one that made me feel that one's color doesn't matter. And what about you, Sydney? Did you ever feel that kind of passion for Jarrod?"

Sydney laughed. "I don't give a rat's ass about sex. It's a

waste of my energy when I could be doing more productive things. All I care about is my son and money."

Cy set his glass down. "I never knew you were so cold, Sydney." Everything Thyme had said about his sister was true. Why hadn't he listened?

No wonder Jarrod had tired of her so quickly. Sydney's first husband had left her five Champion dealerships when he died. Now she was worth seventy to eighty million dollars. All that money and she was still miserable.

Throughout the twenty years he and Thyme had been married, he'd never been able to bridge the gap between his sister and his wife. Thyme's hatred had fueled Sydney's prejudice. But he had tried hard not to take sides, not wanting to alienate either woman he loved. Maybe now it was time to make a stand. And he had to side with his wife.

"I've got to go, Sydney. I'll talk with you when I get back." He set down his glass and rose to leave. He kissed Sydney on her eyebrow and headed out of the room. "Give Graham a kiss for me and tell him maybe I'll even visit him in London." He wanted to get the hell out of there.

"Cy?" Sydney said. She was following him out to the parking lot of the dealership.

He was anxious to leave. "What is it, Sydney?"

She approached him with her dry, passionless smile. When she kissed him softly on his forehead, Cy cringed. He pushed her back. "Good-bye, Sydney."

Sydney smiled and leaned against the door. "One more thing, Cy. I wanted to ask if you were going to see Graciella and the kids while you're in Mexico."

"No. It's over."

"I'm not your wife, Cy. I know what's best for you. I would never hurt you." She crossed her arms at her waist and followed him down the steps to his car. "I've known you for nearly fifty years—I knew you in the womb. I know you as well as you know yourself. Believe me, Thyme isn't for you. She's not PLU—people like us."

Cy's eyes narrowed before he put on his sunglasses. "Sydney, stay out of my life. We're not children anymore, and I can fight my own fights." He started his car, but before speeding away her final words echoed ominously. "As I said earlier, Cy, things might turn out better than you expect."

To his further disgust, when he was cleaning up the last of his work before leaving for Mexico, a familiar face peeped inside.

"Hello, Cyrus." It was Audrey, giving him her special smile. Cy figured Audrey had been upstairs visiting her aunt Candice-Marie, or maybe that was a ruse. "Aren't you leaving for Mexico today?"

He picked up the phone and began dialing his wife. He didn't care how rude it was. "Mm-hm. In a couple of hours. I had a few things to do here first." *Get off my back, Audrey. You're wasting your time.*

"Is your new pager working out okay? We've updated the global feature a bit."

"Perfect." Thyme's phone was ringing. His heart began beating faster as he put the words together that would make everything right again. When the machine came on, he left a message.

Looking up at Audrey, he thought about how he'd been wearing blinders. He was beginning to recognize that the white women working in corporate America totally understood that white privilege exists. Audrey was a perfect example. She had few skills and even less drive. The main reason she held her position with Champion was because of who she was related to. And it wasn't even a prestigious job—working in the electronics division, it was a joke, just something that enabled her to say "I work at World Headquarters."

Suddenly Cy saw Thyme and her case in a whole new light. Thyme was right, she had more education than most of the people he worked with. She deserved to win the case against Champion, even if it cost him his job. If upper management was ever put in the spotlight, the company would look ridiculous based on the bimbos they promoted and continued to promote over those who deserved it.

After Audrey finally got the hint and left, he shut down his computer, then gathered up his additional paperwork. As he did so, his mind stayed on his wife.

Just as he was about to leave, Sandler filled his doorway.

"I see you're all packed and ready to go." His cockiness and high-pitched voice were unnerving. "We have complete faith in you, Cyrus. You know how much this Mexican facility means to the company."

"What do you really want, Sandler?" Cy no longer had the energy to force politeness. Right now he hated everything about Champion.

"We're beginning to lose faith that you will be able to influence your wife, so we've come up with another option. We would still like to promote you."

"Face it, Sandler, at this point you have to promote me."

"Don't push it, Tyler. We will, but we're moving you to Manufacturing."

"Manufacturing?" It was a much less visible position and a political slap in his face. Cy paused and then continued. "Sandler," he said, "I need to understand something. If you're about to move me to Manufacturing, why the hell am I being sent to Mexico now? This isn't business; this is personal. You're trying to separate me from my wife when you know she's under a lot of pressure."

"Cyrus," Sandler said calmly, "you're not acting like yourself. Take it easy. I'm sure Thyme's lawsuit has put an unfair burden on you."

Cy took a deep breath. It was too late to stop now. "So I'm stressed! Why?" Cy laughed bitterly.

"Cy, watch yourself. You of all people know how much change we're going through. You are not invulnerable. You are part of a team."

Cy was fuming. "What fucking team? Fuck you and your team!" Cy clicked his briefcase shut and walked past Sandler, not looking back.

An hour later, Cy was at the airport. Cy realized he could be fired, but it would be better if he resigned.

Thyme had been right all along. White did prevail, and he was sick of it. But how could he make up for generations of wrongdoing? There was no way. The only thing he could do was show Thyme how much he loved her.

He called her office from the plane. Thyme wasn't there. His heart sank like the *Titanic* they'd seen on the stage. Maybe she'd gone home early. He dialed home again and again. Still no answer. Home. Thyme *was* home. She represented all he knew as home. She was all that mattered in his life. Sydney could find another husband. She could get another business partner. He would never again in life find another woman like Thyme, and he didn't want to lose her. He dialed her again.

At that moment he knew he would have to sever his ties with Graciella. Children. Affairs. Sex. Secrecy. No more. Although he cared for her, his history with Graciella had to end. Now he knew he could summon the strength to give up his honeytrap. He'd been greedy and selfish, and he had hurt many people in the process.

Cy called his wife one last time using the plane phone attached to the seat in front of him.

No answer. *Where are you?*

Even without you here beside me, I can still feel your sweet caress. Taste your tenderness. Moving, so sweetly

*together, to satiate each other's needs. All I want to do is to
hold you in my arms and feel us caress each other, silently.
Feeling the silence envelope us in a deeper realm than we
ever felt before.*

*I love you, Thyme. More now than ever before. You're
more precious to me than all the jewels in Krandall's jewelry store. I don't want to lose you. Maybe I didn't make it
plain before. But it's time you knew.*

You're irreplaceable.

23

Khan knew that the saying was "Thank God it's Friday," but all she could muster was "Thank God's it's Wednesday, because I might not make it until Friday." The weatherman said that today, August 26, had broken the old record of a hundred and one degrees in 1929. It was so hot in the plant today many of the workers had left early. Now Khan knew why they called them the dog days. Regardless, she and Valentino had put in twelve hours and were finished by two o'clock. They were hot, musty, funky, and tired.

It may have been a hundred and one degrees outside, but it was nearly a hundred and fifteen in the plant—a great day to go to the beach. Khan hadn't been to the beach all summer and was looking forward to going. She had made plans to meet Valentino, Sarah, and the baby at MacArthur's statue on Belle Isle by four-thirty. They'd still have plenty of time to relax, eat, and chill out in the water before they all had to haul ass home to get a good night's sleep so they could do it all again tomorrow.

Sweat continued to pour off Khan's brow as she stepped outside the plant. Damn, this must be what hell feels like, she thought, putting on her sunglasses. By the time she made it to the employee parking lot she felt light-headed. Just as she was opening her car door, she noticed Daddy Cool standing against the rear entrance of the building.

Daddy Cool was a young sixty-three-year-old maintenance worker who always smiled. He had reason to. Because of his age and "disabilities," Daddy Cool worked just two hours a day cleaning the plant.

Daddy Cool had everyone fooled. There was absolutely nothing wrong with him. He often kidded with Khan that his job was so easy that he would probably retire around age eighty.

"Daddy Cool!" she hollered. He didn't hear her. Getting inside her car, she started the engine, letting it idle for a minute, then pulled up to the door. "Hey there, old man, it's hot out here. You waiting for a ride?"

He grunted and muttered something profane as he staggered with his cane to her car. Resting his hand on her opened window, he said, "My ride must've came to the wrong entrance. They were supposed to be here by one-thirty."

It was ten after two now. "Get on in. I'll give you a ride."

"Baby girl, you don't know where I live."

"I know you live on the west side. That can't be too far from me. Look, it's hot, and if you don't get in right now I'm going to leave your crippled butt here."

When Khan let Daddy Cool out, she was surprised to see where he lived. It was a fairly new subdivision roughly five miles from her condo. Not bad, Khan thought. Daddy Cool must have saved his pennies. As she was backing out of the driveway, she noticed Buddy and three teenage boys in the next-door driveway, washing his car. She stopped and rolled down the window.

"Hi there. It's too hot to wash a car today. Too cheap to go to a car wash?"

Buddy smiled. "I don't frequent car washes. I prefer to wash my own car." He squatted down to wash his rims. "Are you following me? How did you know where I lived?"

"I bribed your Aunt Viola," she kidded.

Knowing he was probably too young to have sons that age, she asked, "Are the boys yours?"

"No." He came toward her car. "I'm a volunteer at Big Brothers. But today the guys volunteered to help me wash my car; otherwise they'd refused to ride in it again."

Coo points for you, she thought. "Hey, nice seeing you. I gotta go."

"Don't leave yet. C'mon inside. I've got a pitcher of lemonade in the refrigerator."

"I'm going to the beach. I'll see ya'." She had started to pull off when she saw him waving his arms in the rearview mirror.

"Wait! Wait!" He was out of breath from running after her. "Care for company?"

"I don't know." Khan hesitated, not sure that she wanted to mix a new friend with her family.

When he smiled, his perfect white teeth looked like a Rembrandt toothpaste ad. They positively sparkled in the white sunlight. It was the first time she'd really taken an honest look at him, and he was certainly cuter than she remembered.

"Look. We're just friends, okay? Friends have as much fun as lovers. Hey, I can bring my own blanket, towel, and food. And I can be ready in fifteen minutes." That pretty smile again.

"Okay, but if you're late I'm leaving you." She put the car in Park, kept the air conditioner on.

Buddy suggested that he drive. His pickup truck was indeed more practical than Khan's compact car. They arrived at Belle Isle at four-twenty. Valentino and his wife and son were already there.

Jahvel made the introductions first. He ran toward Buddy and grabbed his bare legs. "Hi!"

Buddy scooped Jahvel up in his arms and rolled his knuckles softly around Jahvel's fat cheeks. The baby giggled and cooed.

"I think he likes you," Valentino said, laughing.

"Hi, I'm Sarah." Sarah introduced herself and the baby to Buddy. Sarah rarely made small talk, let alone introduced herself. Khan noticed the proud look on Valentino's face as he listened to his wife brag about their child to Buddy. Khan was impressed by Buddy's relaxing influence.

"I hate to interrupt y'all, but fellows," she said, directing her conversation to the men, "one of you get the fire started, and the other unload the truck. Otherwise we'll never eat."

While the men got busy, Khan and Sarah spread out the tablecloth over the picnic table and began setting out the food. A short time later, steaks were sizzling on the grill with foiled potatoes and ears of corn layered against the sides. Exhausted from playing with Buddy in the water, the baby had fallen asleep.

Khan and Sarah went to the rest room to change into their bathing suits, while the two men chatted away. Strange, she thought, Buddy seemed so comfortable with her family. R.C. never had—the few times he'd met them, anyway. While they were in the bathroom Sarah surprised Khan by speaking up again.

"Did you know that Ida threatened to put Ron out? He didn't come home at all last weekend. She thinks he spent the weekend with his woman. They've been fighting and arguing about it ever since."

Was it Elaine? That bitch. Could it have been Luella? "So, it's gotten that serious?" Khan remembered what she had seen at the July Fourth barbecue. She hadn't realized it was still going on.

"Ron is so paranoid he accused Tino of siccing Luella on me. Tino cussed his father and then Ron went after Tino."

Khan tied the side knot on her cover-up. "What did Tino do?"

"He told Ron that if he ever touched him or his mother again, he'd kill him. And Khan, Tino ain't kidding. It scares me."

"Ron's a dog," Khan said slowly, trying not to cuss around Sarah. "I've got to do something about this. I'm not sure what yet. But I'll figure something out."

Thursday turned out to be hotter than Wednesday. It was so muggy inside the plant, it was no wonder everyone's nerves were on edge. When the plant reached a certain temperature, the company provided tanks of cold lemonade for the workers in every break area. Today no one cared. By nine-thirty the vats had barely been tapped. Everyone wanted to get their work done and get the hell out of there by lunchtime.

Khan's mind drifted to Buddy as she went back to her unit. While they were at the beach, he'd told her that he owned his own shortening company. It was a small business, but it was building. She'd had no idea that he was the third-generation owner of a family-owned business. He seemed so low-key. Khan wondered what else lay beneath the surface of his beautiful smile.

As soon as Khan got back from the break, she was flanked by five workers from two other units. "We got trouble, girl."

"What are you guys talking about?" Khan asked.

They took her down to the far end of the plant. Two mid-size car lines were being dismantled. The people who worked in the units were being sent home by their supervisors. Nobody was told why.

"This doesn't make any sense," Khan said out loud. Where was Thyme? Khan felt a rush of anger toward her friend. She's probably so caught up in winning her lawsuit she's forgotten about her real job, Khan thought.

Khan stopped by the closest break area and dialed Thyme's office. Elaine told her that Thyme would be out of the office until Monday.

Meanwhile, back in the unit, like nothing else in the world was happening except their greedy asses, Luella and Valentino were back to their same tired routine. Their supervisor, Allister, was turning purple he was so mad.

"Look, Luella," he shouted, "Valentino's working the overtime tomorrow. And that's it. Take your grievances up with Ron." He stormed off.

Luella bumped into Khan as she turned to leave the unit. "You can thank your friend Thyme for all the problems here."

"What are you talking about, Luella—"

"No. Fuck that. That bitch is a liar like the rest of them white folks. The A-team is still getting all the overtime. How long do you think the rest of us are going to put up with this bullshit?" Her words cut too close to Khan's own suspicions about Thyme and scorched Khan's soul.

Khan looked at Tino and could feel his rage. Damn, Thyme had told the Employee Involvement group that she would troubleshoot these problems for three months. Had Thyme become so selfish that she didn't even do her job anymore?

Tino and Khan watched Luella walk out of the unit. "Just so you know, cousin, I've had it up to here with Luella's bullshit. I filed a harassment complaint against her in the city of Detroit."

"But Tino, was that necessary?"

"Come on, you see how she goes after me every week! Now she keeps calling my home and threatening my wife and kid. I'm sick of her shit. I filed a restraining order against her." He stormed off.

Khan shook her head. She couldn't blame Tino, but she knew that this latest move was only going to add fuel to the fire.

No sooner had Khan sat back down at her machine than Valentino returned.

"Mom called. They've rushed Ron to the hospital."

"What happened?"

"They don't know—maybe a heart attack."

Khan could see the fear in Tino's eyes. She could guess the questions he was asking himself. With all the anger in their family lately, the worst thing that could happen was not having time to say they were sorry.

"Wait," Khan said, grabbing her purse. "I'm coming too. Luella can have both of our hours today." Khan knew she'd probably be charged the hours as well, but she didn't care. Family came first.

Twenty minutes later, they arrived at William Beaumont Hospital. Tino was ushered in with his mother to see Ron, and Khan went to the ICU waiting room. When Tino emerged with his mother, both were weeping.

"He's waiting for you, Khan. He didn't have a heart attack, but they say he should really be off his feet for a while. You can only visit for a few minutes. I have to take my mother home. We're not allowed to stay in the ICU." Ida stood there clutching Tino's hand, unable to speak. Valentino kissed Khan, hugged her tightly, then left with his mother.

When she saw her Uncle Ron with tubes going into his chest and arms, she freaked. She'd only visited a hospital once before, when her Grandma Pearl was sick with pneumonia. She'd hated the sterile smell then and, twelve years later, the sickly odor was more unbearable than she remembered.

Khan kissed him on his forehead, then took a seat beside his bed. "If nobody else tells you this, I will, Uncle Ron. You're sick. You look like you're about to die." Her eyes scanned the plastic tubes and IVs that gave his body life.

"Oh thanks, I needed to hear that right now."

"I'm real pissed at you right now. The plant's going to fall apart without you there to supervise everyone. You know how lazy the committeemen are. They're probably at the bar now, getting drunk."

"Really?" He forced a grin. "Not without me, I hope."

"That's my uncle talking. I'm gonna come back later and sneak you in a bottle of Seagram's." She winked at him.

That got him to rally a bit. He told her he'd be out of there before the weekend was over. He had to get back to head the union negotiations.

"Khan," he said, his weakening voice telling her she should leave, "did you save money for the strike like I told you?"

"Uncle Ron, chill. There ain't going to be no strike. They're still saying that General Motors will be the strike target. That's what Thyme said."

"She's one of them and don't you forget it. Thyme's hiding the truth from you. Lots of Troy Trim's sewing jobs are being sewn in a Mexican trim plant. Why do you think her husband goes to Mexico every month? Thyme is quite tight-lipped, you know. But I don't want to break up the high regard that you hold for your friend. There are some things you need to learn on your own."

"But Thyme wouldn't keep something like that from me.

Where are you getting your information from, Uncle Ron? Elaine?"

But Khan didn't want to push her uncle too far. He had to get better.

Khan was in a tizzy for days, sitting there alone watching *Oprah*. She couldn't stop thinking about R.C. and the night they had made love. She hadn't heard another word after that night. *What does he think of me? That I am some kind of sex freak and he could run in and out of my pussy anytime he feels like it?*

Her saving grace was the frequent calls she received from Buddy. It seemed that he could sense when she needed to talk. She never got too personal, but he seemed to know when to change the subject, happy to talk on and on about his family business. Her respect for him was building.

She was beginning to count on Buddy showing up at his aunt's and then casually easing down to her place. It was as if he could read her mind and acted on it before she could voice her thoughts. And the wonderful part was that he was so subtle about it. There was no pressure and no kisses. Just friendship. And that made it special between them.

Khan finally consented to go out with Buddy one pleasant Sunday evening.

"I shouldn't have let you talk me into this," Khan said, smiling at Buddy. "I'm going to be exhausted at work in the morning."

"Don't overdress," Buddy had said when they made the date. "Most everyone will be wearing jeans. Just concentrate on having some laughs. You've been too serious lately."

Her bed was full of tossed-out outfits. "I can't wear this; he'll think I'm trying to seduce him. I can't wear this; I look too childish." *Damn! What the fuck am I going to put on?*

Buddy picked her up at seven-thirty. "You look great,

Khan," he observed. She wore a powder blue sleeveless duster and pencil-legged matching pants. She felt her confidence building because of the blue Erykah Badu–style turban wrapped around her head. Her earrings made the ultimate statement. They were silver replicas of carved African warrior masks.

Buddy looked up at her turban, then looked back at her bashful face. "I like it."

"What?" Khan acted as if she didn't know what he was talking about.

Their date began with an elegant dinner at Pegasus. Khan was beginning to realize how much of his own man Buddy was. She felt R.C. slowly fading from the forefront of her mind and heart.

By nine-fifteen they were waiting in line on Woodward Avenue for the attendant to show them where to park their car. The first comedy act was set to begin at nine-thirty. Suddenly Khan froze. Just fifty feet in front of them she saw R.C. exiting a white limo with his wife. His arms were wrapped all around her. There was no mistaking what they represented: love and marriage.

They were third in line to park. "Stop, Buddy. I can't go in. Let's go."

"Khan?"

"Take me home." Her eyes were beginning to fill with tears and she didn't want Buddy to know why.

Buddy waved to the parking attendant and got his attention. A few moments later, the two cars behind him backed up enough to allow Buddy to get out of line.

"Where are we going?" she asked. "I don't live this way."

"Relax, Khan. I know where I'm going."

Khan had her eyes closed. When she opened them she and Buddy were parked on the north end of Belle Isle.

"Now tell me what's wrong. It's not going to hurt. And I won't judge you. Just talk, okay?"

Khan started slowly. She told him about her relationship with R.C. August was the month they were to be married. She tried not to think about it, but when she saw him tonight with his bride, both of them decked out in all white—even the limo—it was too much to take. She'd omitted the part about sleeping with R.C. recently. And also the part about the ring, which she had put away and never looked at again after that fateful night when he'd taken his pleasure with her and then walked out.

It was eleven o'clock when she finished. Her turban had fallen off; her face was flushed, her makeup ruined.

Buddy started laughing.

"Buddy? What's so funny?"

He pulled the lighted mirror down on her side of the truck. "Nothing. You're too young to be so serious. Fix your makeup. We're going to the comedy club. The second set starts at eleven-thirty."

It was two in the morning before Khan made it home. Surprisingly, she wasn't a bit sleepy. She set her alarm for four and headed for the bathroom. On her way back to the bedroom she heard a knock at the front door.

"Buddy?"

"No. It's me."

She let him in. "What are you doing here, R.C.?"

"I felt I needed to see you face-to-face."

You're such a goddamn liar.

"I'm going to bed, R.C. It was a mistake, you coming here." Just like that, he thought he could walk up to her door anytime. What did he think she was running, a saloon?

When he embraced her and cupped his hands beneath her buttocks, she struggled to push him off. "No, R.C. I ain't doing that shit with you no more. When you get rid of that yin-yang bitch you can have some. Until then, you can whistle for a piece of this pussy."

"You don't mean that," he said, reaching for her again.

Khan had to admit she was weakening. Her ass was hotter than gunpowder. But no way would she be some man's bitch. She was worth more than that. She pushed him away from her. "Back off, blood."

"You know you want it. I want to rock with you tonight, baby." He grinned. "For old times' sake."

You low-down son of a bitch. Once she had overheard her grandma saying to one of her friends, "Grandpa can't fly his kite 'cause Grandma won't give him no tail." Now she totally understood that line.

Khan felt downright cocky now. She stepped back two steps and placed both her hands between her legs. She lowered her eyelids a half-notch and cocked back one thigh. "You need to understand something. My pussy, it's one of a kind and hard to find. It's hot and it's tight all the time. Ain't no other pussy like mine. If you get it once, you're going to want it again and again. You know that, blood, better than anybody. But now, hey, I'm tired of listening to your excuses about your Japanese wife. You think about something when you leave here tonight: My pussy could have changed your life. But instead, I hope your mind will be so fucked up that you won't be able to make love to your wife. Your dick will soften like a sad melody, and every time your wife wants to make love, you won't be able to, because your mind will be on fucking me. 'Cause I got that snatch-back pussy."

"Khan," he said, his lips wet, eyes hungry.

She narrowed her eyes and eased down her pajama bottom, revealing her bushy blond vagina. "Naw, blood. I can't help you. Because, as I said before, brother, there ain't no other pussy like mine. It's blond and it's fine, and it's all mine. Now get out."

R.C. was still stroking his erection. She could swear she saw a wet stain on the front of his pants. "Don't leave me like this, Khan."

She was hot, but the thrill she felt turning him on and leaving him feeling hot and hanging was far more satisfying than any orgasm.

Opening the door, she told him once again to go. Feeling herself weakened by his pleading, she knew she had to make him leave before she lost all respect for herself. Her voice was strong and hard. "I won't ask you again, R.C. Go."

She wasn't prepared for R.C.'s final move. He shocked her by unzipping his pants and whipping out his penis. It glistened in the half-darkness of her narrow foyer.

He stroked the beautiful penis that she had grown to love until it grew so huge she thought it would burst. "Kiss it, baby. You know, the way you used to."

Other women might not understand it, but nothing was prettier to Khan than a hard, black dick. Especially one that had brought her so much pleasure. The seconds it took her to react to his invitation weakened her knees. She could feel the crotch in her pajamas growing damp. Khan knew that if she didn't put him off now, she'd melt. She took a deep breath then said, "I've sucked enough dick to go around the world seven inches at a time, brother. When you send that bitch back to Japan, you call me."

She pushed R.C. outside her door while he was still holding his dick in his hand. Locking the door behind her, she took a deep breath, her heart burning as if it had been scorched.

I'll fuck myself before I let you fuck me over.

24

Luella woke up Monday to the trill of the alarm clock. She whistled while she showered and dressed. But the real reason for her good mood was that last night she had paid a visit to Valentino's wife, Sarah. Luella smiled to herself as she relived the confrontation.

She hadn't been the least bit nervous when she knocked on Tino's door, knowing he was out delivering televisions. Luella had suspected that Tino was married to a quiet type, and she wasn't wrong.

Exactly as Luella had predicted, a wide-eyed creature answered the door. "Hello?"

At first Luella hadn't uttered a word; she was too busy noticing how tiny and innocent looking the little bitch was.

"Are you looking for someone, miss? Can I help you?"

Luella had begun huffing as she remembered Valentino's mistreatment of her over the years. She could hear the sound of a baby whimpering in the background. *If you think I'm going to have some sympathy for your teeny-weeny ass, you wrong*. Luella had then grabbed Sarah by the neck and yanked her outside. Knocking Sarah down, she kicked and punched her with all the anger and frustration she'd been building toward Tino.

Luella dressed in a long, yellow print dress and tied her hair back with a purple ribbon. She felt great, now unburdened of her own pent-up anger toward Valentino.

She drove to work with the window down and let the wind whip the back of her hair in the fresh air.

Her first stop was to the cafeteria to withdraw four hundred dollars from the Comerica cash machine. As she headed out the door, Tom, a committeeman, was on his way in.

"Is the office locked, Tom?"

"No. Need to make a long-distance call?"

"Yeah." Luella thought about Omar in Colorado. His message on her pager said he was going to be delayed coming home because his rig was broken down. What did she care? "I won't be long."

She felt a sharp pain in her heart as she pranced up the steps to the union room. Sooner or later, she thought, she would have to stop taking two Dexatrims a day. Her doctor had warned her five years ago that continued use of the diet drugs would bring on early heart problems. One day, maybe tomorrow, she'd take his advice.

Even though the ashtrays were emptied and the office looked clean, the room reeked of cigarette smoke. A fine layer of dust and film had settled on the bookcase and file cabinets. Even the beige plastic cover on the computer was stained an angry yellow. After turning on the radio on the bookcase, she took a seat in the desk with a matching beige captain's chair and dialed Omar's cell phone. No answer. Crossing her legs and swiveling around the chair, she studied the picture of Walter Reuther on the wall behind her as she waited a moment, then dialed the number again. It was busy. *The fool must be trying to call me.*

She picked up the phone again and dialed Maintenance. Daddy Cool answered the phone. "Hey, Daddy Cool, is Eugene around?"

There was a short pause before Eugene came on the line. "Luella. Daddy Cool said it was you. You got my money?"

"Yes. Do I have a year's guarantee on that unit?"

"Luella, I been installing air conditioners way before you were born."

"Then why ain't you retired by now, Eugene?" She glanced at the UAW calendar on the wall. "If you had let some of that young pussy alone, your drunk ass could have retired two years ago."

"Now let's not start talking about folks this early in the morning, Luella. I already told your husband when I finished on Thursday night that I'd guarantee my work for a year. Now s'pose you tell me why your husband said I had to ask you for my money?"

"Eugene, you know I'm in charge," she said angrily. "Now you hurry up down here. I'm upstairs in Tom's office. You hurry up now, 'cause I ain't gonna wait long."

After she hung up the phone, she took out her purse and began counting out Eugene's money. Just as she was about to try Omar again, she heard someone running up the stairs. That couldn't be Eugene already, she thought, as Valentino bolted into the room.

His face was lined with anger. He was wearing a long shop coat over wrinkled jeans. Luella thought that was odd, given how hot it was, but the sick look on his face frightened her and the shop coat was quickly forgotten.

She tried not to show the fear in her eyes. Kicking Sarah's ass last night had felt good. But she hadn't hurt the bitch that bad. If she had, she thought, she would have heard from Valentino last night. Half the plant knew where she lived.

Noticing that he kept looking back over his shoulder,

Luella nervously glanced around the room at the door, listening with every pore in her body for the sound of Eugene coming up the steps.

"You shouldn't have touched Sarah. Why you mess with my wife! My wife!"

"I told you not to fuck with me, Tino. You should have given it up. We could have settled our differences long ago. Anyway, I didn't hurt the little thing that bad."

"You made the worst mistake of your life. The last mistake, bitch!" Tino began moving toward the hat rack to his right. "I told you I'd fuck you up."

Luella knew he'd be angry, but she hadn't anticipated that he would go off on her. All kinds of shitty words came to her head, but something told her to keep her mouth shut.

"You fucked up my dad's life. My mom's. My *wife's*. Why you keep messing with the Lamotts? You crazy, girl? You think we some kind of fools? You think we ain't men?" He pounded his chest with his left fist. "You destroying a family—you deserve to die, bitch."

Luella's beeper went off. It was the first time in years she wanted desperately to talk to her husband.

Her mouth gaped open in horror when he removed the .38 special from his back pocket.

"Tino! We can talk about this. I'm sorry. I was wrong."

"Hell no! Fuck no!" Tino yelled. "I'm going to fuck you up. Yep, fuck you up. Crazy 'ho' like you messing with good folks' families. Good folks. You come to a man's house. His own house! Just because I didn't want none of your wore-out pussy! I wouldn't let my dog fuck you!" His eyes suddenly looked blank; it appeared as if he were talking to himself as he whispered, "There ain't nothing else I can do."

"You crazy, Tino. We can settle this."

"No. It's too late, bitch." He raised the gun and cocked it. "A low-down bitch like you deserves no pity."

At that point, Luella knew there was no way she was going to get out of this alive. Tears began to fill her eyes. He was right. She had no excuse. Still, she didn't want to die. Her body began to shake as she watched him aim the gun and pull the trigger.

The first shot hit her in the chest. Luella bounced out of the seat with both hands up. He shot her again, this time in the shoulder. She felt the taste of lead in her mouth, the pain in her chest as hot as molten lava. She fell back against the wall, gasping for air.

She could barely hear his words as he came toward her screaming, "Bitch! Crazy bitch!" He stopped at point-blank range and shot her in the stomach.

She collapsed on the floor with blood pumping from her wounds.

There was no sound.

Her eyes grew as wide as hope. "I'm sorry," she whispered. Her eyelids began to feel heavy and she tried to fight against it. *Oh Lord, my sons. And Omar, dear God, Omar. . . . I'm so sorry, baby.*

Neither Luella nor Valentino noticed Ron standing in the doorway. The realization of the tragedy swept across his face like a raging storm at sea.

"Not good enough, bitch. You dead, bitch," Tino said, shooting her one last time in the forehead.

Luella could feel numbness traveling to her arms, as if she had a pinched nerve. She fought once more to speak, trying again to say "Forgive me," but only bubbling blood erupted from her mouth. A waste of breath, a waste of years, behind, in balance with this life, this death.

"Tino!" Ron shouted, followed by gasps behind him from Eugene.

Her empty eyes stared ahead, her stiff arms sweeping the

bills to the floor as she fell back against the wall. A stripe of blood smeared the wall as she slid down to the floor.

Twenty-dollar bills were strewn beside her lifeless body, coated with blood.

25

"Gunshots!" Thyme shouted into the receiver. Doug Bierce, head of Security, informed Thyme that an employee had just been shot in the committee room. "I'll be right there."

He hadn't said who was shot. Was the person dead or injured? Jesus, why hadn't she asked him more questions?

It was 5:43 A.M. When the call came in from Bierce, she'd tried to get Ron on the phone, but the line was busy.

What the hell was happening?

Grabbing the walkie-talkie on her way out the door, she called Bierce back.

"This is Thyme Tyler. Have the police been called in yet?" The connection was jagged, fragmented.

"That's affirmative, Mrs. Tyler. They're on their way. You better get here quick, though."

Static on the line.

"Has Ron arrived yet?" She adjusted the Squash buttons back and forth but couldn't get him back on the radio.

Damn!

Thyme had been warning upper management to increase the budget for Security for over a year now. She'd even asked for metal detectors. "No," upper management had said, "Troy Trim is on par with other factories. Detectors would choke the flow of workers because of the metal parts and tools that continually flow on and off the factory floor."

Driving through the truck door, then through the roll goods warehouse, she noticed how eerie the plant looked. Not a soul was there. But she heard the screams and cries ahead. She made a left at the east break area. The committee room was located just past general stores, a hundred yards ahead. When she saw the crowd she realized she'd never get the cart through.

Parking her cart by the bathrooms, she began to push her way through the crowd.

"Let me through!" she called to some of the workers she knew. "Juanita, let me through." A path opened a few feet. Farther ahead: "Tony, it's Thyme. Can you help me get through, please?"

Hundreds of employees stood in the aisleways hugging each other and crying. The closer she got to the union office, the more wildly her heart beat.

Doug Bierce and five other security guards had temporarily cordoned off the area in front of the upper union offices. With Doug's help she was able to get to the steps that led upstairs.

Halfway up the steps she stopped, out of breath. Just then the door opened and Ron was there. The front of his shirt was covered with blood.

"Thyme." His voice was flat. "Luella's dead."

Thyme couldn't tell if he was angry or upset. She tightened her face and tried not to faint. Then she recognized a man's low moan a few feet away. He sounded like an animal that longed to be set free.

Her heart began to pound harder. The deadly smell of gunpowder was still in the air. She could feel the hard steel-mesh steps echoing against the clicks of her heels as she climbed the stairs. When she reached the top and went inside Tom's office, she wasn't prepared for the horror of the scene. Luella's bullet-riddled body lay on the floor approximately six feet into the office. The back of her head had been blown off.

Thyme grabbed a trash can and vomited. She sat down in the nearest chair and looked at Ron frantically, wanting an explanation. "Why? What happened here, Ron?"

His tear-stained eyes turned to the man she'd heard sobbing just before she entered the office. Valentino was crouched down in a chair in the far left corner with his face in his hands. His body was shaking violently, and a .38 special lay at his feet.

"They've been at it for months. I should have known—"

Thunderous steps pounded on the stairwell. The police entered with force and took control of the situation. Thyme would have to wait, like everyone else, until the interrogation was over to learn the entire truth.

Luella? Valentino? How were they connected? she wondered.

Then it hit her.

Overtime. She'd promised the Employee Involvement team weeks ago that she would monitor the overtime. She had truly planned on following up; how had the entire thing slipped her mind? She was so wrapped up in her discrimination lawsuit and her problems with Cy that she'd forgotten. *Oh my God.*

And now. A killing? A death? Was she to blame? Could this tragedy have been avoided?

Somehow Khan got through the crowd. Thyme looked up at her friend's blotched, red face, her eyes swollen from crying. Thyme started to call out to her, but the hatred she saw on Khan's face stopped her.

"You! You are the cause of this shit." Khan sounded hysterical. But her words were cuttingly true.

"Khan, listen."

"You should be ashamed to call yourself a black woman. I thought you could identify with us. The blue collar workers. Even though you held a white collar position, I still thought you were one of us, 'cause you was black. Because you knew about us."

"Please, Khan—let me expl—"

"But you all the way white, girlfriend. Just like that white man you married to. I bet you wished your skin was white. As lily white as your sister-in-law Sydney's." Khan began to sob in pain. "You gonna wake up one of these days and realize you ain't no better than the rest of us."

"I—" Thyme stopped. What could she say? She could only pray that Khan might regret her words one day. Still, she had to try to make her understand.

"Khan. I love you. We've been friends since you were a little girl. Please let me . . ." She stopped.

"No. No more. We ain't friends no more." Khan stormed out. And each step of her tiny feet down the stairs felt like a nail driven into Thyme's heart.

Thyme's feelings of guilt magnified. If she had taken the time to visit Ron when he was in the hospital, maybe he would have impressed upon her the seriousness of the problem. And she had done nothing, as a friend or colleague, to unravel the problems she could help with.

Was she entirely to blame? She wasn't sure.

She thought about her lunch with Khan three weeks ago. Khan must have known what was going on with Valentino and Luella. But Thyme hadn't let Khan get a word in edgewise. All Khan did was listen to Thyme go on and on about her marital problems and her lawsuit. Thyme felt her guilt crushing her skull like a two-ton bag of sand.

The self-loathing Thyme felt couldn't be ejected into a trash can or toilet. It went too deep.

Doug Bierce approached her. "Luella's family needs to be notified, Mrs. Tyler."

"Certainly." Thank God there was something for her to do.

"You need to speak with the employees. We don't want a riot to break out."

Thyme turned. She glared at him. Did Doug assume that because most of the employees were black and a black employee was slain they'd riot? Was that it? Was it different when a white conflict occurred? "I'll handle it, Doug."

"All four television networks are outside demanding information. They'll be bringing the body out soon. What should we say?"

The tears that burned her eyes couldn't compare to the hatred she felt at that moment. She hated herself, and she hated white people because they and their factories had caused this. And yet she was married to one. That hurt even deeper. "I'll handle that too, Doug."

All of a sudden, she realized how ridiculous she was for filing a discrimination lawsuit, a suit about money. Upper middle class. Fine homes in the suburbs. Was that all she was about? Had she lost her soul on her way up to the top? Was she turning a lighter shade of black with every step she took? Was that the color she wanted to be? White?

She couldn't answer. No—she didn't want to answer.

She heard from Cy just after lunch. She was still in shock.

"Hi, sweetie. What happened today? I received a message on my pager about the shooting."

She still felt so numb, even toward her husband. "I'll speak with you about it when you get home."

Nothing would ever be the same again. Not with her friends. And not with her husband. Everything in her life had changed because of that shooting. It was a wake-up call for all those who tried to play both sides. One couldn't be new collar and a blue collar. One couldn't be a Democrat and a Republican. One couldn't be black and white. It was a time for those pretending to be both either to acknowledge their actions, to choose a side and be willing to change, or to let the bullet of truth shoot them dead.

26

Bang! Bang! Bang! Tomiko woke with a start.

"R.C.?" she half-whispered. She checked the clock and saw that it was ten minutes to four in the morning. More bangs. No one answered.

Three more bangs. She hurried out of bed and ran to the door.

He shouted, "Tomiko, let me in!"

She was certain he was drunk. "Just a minute." When she opened the door he stumbled into her. The sour smell of vomit on the front of his shirt and pants made her turn her head away in disgust.

"Why'd you lock the door? I couldn't get in."

"Sorry. C'mon," she said, turning on the lights, then wrapping his arm around her shoulder to help him inside the room. How many nights had he come home in this condition? She helped him sit down on the sofa, then began removing his clothes. "Why do you do this to yourself?"

"I'm not drunk, Tomiko," he said laconically. "Sure, I've been drinking. I had a late dinner at Elias Brothers' Restaurant around twelve. Left there by one-thirty. Had a double shot of Jack in the car before leaving the parking lot.

I was on my way home then. No way could I make it, my stomach was bubbling and churning like a sump pump. I pulled over to the side of the road on Woodward Avenue. Must've been food poisoning. I've been vomiting for hours. And I'm mad as hell. I'm thinking about suing the place." He breathed heavily. "Sorry I scared you."

By then, Tomiko had removed all of his clothing except for his underwear. "I'm glad you're home." She kissed him on the forehead. It was still hot. Maybe he really did have food poisoning. "C'mon, you could use a shower." Taking him by the hand, she led him to the bathroom.

R.C. brushed his teeth and gargled while Tomiko turned on the shower. The tiny beads of water pounding against the metal tub sounded like bacon sizzling on a grill.

Seconds later he removed his boxers and began to step inside the glass stall, then stopped. Tomiko was sitting on the matching bed bench near the whirlpool tub watching him. "How about joining me?"

As sultry as a Siamese cat, Tomiko slid the straps off her shoulders, letting the navy satin gown slip off her lithe body. Her eyes penetrated his as she stepped inside the shower and let the pulsating water splash all over her body. She felt the heat of him as he joined her, and closed the door behind them.

"You feeling any better?" she asked her husband, her face strained with worry.

Wrapping his arms around her svelte figure, he held her tight, then whispered in her ear, "I was scared that I wouldn't make it home." He closed his eyes and placed his chin in the center of her neck, then kissed her. "I was trying to make it back to you."

"Hush, baby. Hush," she whispered, sinking deeper into his embrace. "I never realized until now how good it feels for you to just hold me." She wilted against him. "Does that sound childish?"

R.C. looked at her for a long time before he said, "You're not a child. You've proven to me how much of a woman you are by your patience. I'm even beginning to enjoy the sex games you can't seem to stop playing." When he looked at her, the smile from a second ago had faded. "I've been an ass, Tomiko."

His kiss on her eager lips felt like strange star-pulses, throbbing through every vein in her body, and seemed to last an eternity. The strength of it made her weaken. From six angles water streamed over their skin. They rarely took a shower together, their schedules were so hectic, and now Tomiko couldn't have been happier.

She was enjoying this small moment of pleasure, the first she'd had in months—maybe the first ever. It didn't matter. He was here with her now. In the end, that was all that really mattered.

Reaching for the shower gel, she squeezed the cool liquid on a purple sponge and shampooed him with spicy sandal-wood scent, using a stroke that was a cross between massaging and washing. She felt pleasure and tenderness as she lathered his body. R.C. relaxed against her as she adjusted the shower jets to rinse him clean. Even without the benefit of the sandalwood filling the air with its spicy aroma, she still knew the natural scent of his body and she took pleasure in inhaling the raw smell of him. She felt her body become aroused and wondered whether she'd feel close enough to R.C. one day to tell him how his scent turned her on.

Tomiko dried her husband's body, rubbed him down with lotion, and oiled and brushed his little Afro. Afterwards, she helped him ease on a pair of pajama bottoms and slipped into bed beside him.

"Tomiko?" he said ever so softly. "I need you. Please tell me you won't ever leave me."

She could hear the tremor in his voice. It was the first time he'd let his vulnerability show. He'd never exposed himself, his fears, to her before.

"I'll always be here, R.C. Right here."

And they fell asleep, her back against his belly, two spoons, a peaceful satisfaction on their faces that only love can provide.

"I don't know whether to laugh or cry." R.C. looked down at the woman's picture in Tuesday's early edition of the newspaper.

"What is it, R.C.?" Tomiko asked as she took a bite of toast.

R.C. lifted the corner of his mouth in a half smile. "This bit—" He cleared his throat. "Thyme Tyler, the woman I told you about at Champion that cost me all that money. Well, she's in the paper. It's her turn now." He handed her the page, which showed a woman's horrified face and the headlines that began with the word murder.

It was just past eight in the morning, and they were enjoying breakfast. R.C. had called his office and said he wouldn't be in until this afternoon. Tomiko's photo session didn't start until three o'clock.

Tomiko could smell the champagne in his orange juice. She knew from the young people in Japan that they called the mixture mimosa, and how much Americans enjoyed the drink at brunch. Somehow she felt that if she and R.C. were ever going to have a good marriage, he would have to cut down on his drinking. It was key to their commitment. Next was his gambling habit. She couldn't say which one was worse.

Even though everything appeared to be going well with

them today, she knew if he was drinking this early in the morning, things were still not all right in his world.

When R.C. was through with the paper he left the room to shower. Tomiko picked up the paper and scanned the article about the murder at Champion Motors. She shook her head at the thought of such violence. She placed the paper back near R.C.'s favorite chair and went to find him in their bedroom suite, where he was dressing.

"How awful about the murder at Champion. That's why I never wanted to go inside a factory. The people there seem vulgar. Especially the women. Maybe this woman did something to get killed," Tomiko said, sitting on the edge of the bed as she watched R.C. dress. "Some people say the women in factories act like whores, fighting over men."

R.C. laughed. "Where did you hear that nonsense from?"

"Oh, from some of my friends in Japan. And reading the American newspapers. These women have no pride. They have no knowledge of how to take care of their man. They think that making the same amount of money that they do will make them equal." Tomiko shook her head. "That will never happen. Stupid women."

He finished tying his necktie and came toward her. R.C. reached out and touched her hand. "You're special, Tomiko. It's what I love about you." Releasing it, he added, "But you've got a few things to learn about American women. There's such a thing as survival. My father worked at Chrysler for thirty-eight years. And my mother worked at the same plant for thirty-two years. Both of them retired from Chrysler in nineteen-eighty." He stopped and looked out the window. "All their hard work was for one goal: They wanted me to have a better life than they experienced. And it was especially important for them that I didn't follow in their footsteps and work in a factory like they had."

Tomiko was fascinated. He'd never spoken about his past

to her before. It made her think it was time she shared her own dilemma with him. "R.C.?" she asked in a timid voice.

"Yeah." His back was to her as he adjusted his tie.

"If someone from your past was trying to contact you . . ."

"Tomiko, are you speaking about yourself? If you are, be direct."

Her almond eyes widened but she kept silent.

R.C.'s tone was conciliatory. "You're not old enough to have had a past. But then again, let's say someone was trying to get a hold of you. Generally, most people have an ulterior motive. I don't care how genuine they appear to be. There's something at stake that they stand to gain." He shrugged. "Otherwise, what's the point?"

"But what if they were trying to find someone they lost?"

R.C. clicked off the television set. "You've seen too many made-for-TV movies." R.C. patted her head and left the bedroom. "I have some errands to run. I'll be back by noon. We can have lunch."

After Tomiko said good-bye to her husband, she didn't have a clue what to do.

Her need to get the truth about the letter ebbed and flowed. She was scared to pursue the truth, but she also couldn't walk away from it.

The best place to start was home.

Tomiko checked her watch. It was nine-thirty. In Kyoto, it would be late, but her parents were still young enough to stay up, she thought, and didn't mind her calling at such hours.

"Mother, how are you?"

"Tomiko! We're all well. It's so good to hear from you. And how is your husband? Are you helping him with his horse farm?"

"I'm trying, Mother. I called for something else, though.

I wanted to know about my father, my real father. What happened to him?"

"Tomiko, what's happening to you there? You are Japanese. Nothing about your so-called father matters."

"But Mother, I am also dark-skinned."

"You are Japanese first. What is this about?"

"I want to know about my father, what happened to him. You've never told me."

"I told you that he died and left us. He didn't love us. That's all you need to know."

"Did he have any parents?"

"Well, everyone has parents."

"Mother, did you know my father's parents?"

"What kind of question is that? Of course not. They are from America. They never cared about us. Now you focus on your marriage and making your husband happy. He is a good husband."

"Okay, Mother." She still hadn't worked up the nerve to be honest with her mother. But one day she knew she would.

"Good-bye, Tomiko."

When Tomiko hung up the phone, tears brimmed in her eyes. All she had been told was that her father was Afro-American and that he had died. She had always suspected that her mother withheld information. Now she was convinced. *But why would my mother lie to me?* Maybe she had a whole other family to love. Tomiko looked at the mysterious photos. She stared into her mother's young face and the face of the young handsome black man dressed in a military uniform.

Finally, moving quickly so she couldn't change her mind, she got in the car and drove past the Johnson's house in Holly. It was just approaching noon when she drove up to the house. The neatly manicured lawn showed that the owners took pride in their home. *Could these people be my grandparents?* When she rang the doorbell, she thought her heart would stop. It was as if her heart's blood were turning to tears. She suddenly felt as if her entire future, not simply her past, depended on this one moment.

An elderly, gray-haired woman with cheeks like apples answered the door. "Yes?"

Tomiko froze. Up close, she didn't look like the woman she'd seen in the photograph. She gulped. "I'm sorry, I've made a mistake." Turning, she ran down the steps, her hair flying behind her.

"Wait! Is that you, Tomiko? It's me, Grandma Johnson."

Stunned, Tomiko stopped, then turned around. The woman sounded so sure. Tomiko looked again.

"Please. Wait, Tomiko. Don't go. I sent you the letter. Is that why you're here?"

"I—"

At that moment a man using a beautiful cane came out on the porch. Except for the addition of the cane, he looked exactly like the man in the picture. It was all too simple. This was not a fairy tale, and she wasn't the little girl in *Swiss Family Robinson* who lived happily ever after.

Tomiko stood still and took in the plea in the woman's eyes. Her legs weakened. Then the man she thought might be her grandfather spoke her name with so much love she thought she would faint.

"Tomiko, it's Papa. Please come on in. We've waited so long to see you."

That sound. That voice sounded so much like one she'd heard before. Was it her father's? It was so long ago she couldn't be sure. No. Her father was dead. But the sound was comforting enough to take a chance.

When she went inside the home, she was uneasy. She wished that her husband were here with her now. R.C. would know how to relate to these people. Tomiko looked around the house. She could hear the soft sound of mewing kittens from the back of the house. Nothing seemed familiar, but there was an inviting warmth that made her begin to relax. Before she took a seat, a cat sauntered in from the back hall and took a seat beside the front doorway.

"That's Ms. Tibbles," her grandmother said, smiling. "Last month she had a litter of kittens. Would you like to see them?"

She took Tomiko in the back room and showed her the kittens that were just three weeks old, and beautiful. Afterwards, her grandmother made some sandwiches and brought out some iced tea on a pretty silver tray. She sat close to Tomiko on the sofa, while her grandfather sat nearby in a big easy chair. He lit a pipe. The scent of the sweet tobacco brought tears to Tomiko's eyes. It calmed her.

When she looked toward the door, Ms. Tibbles seemed to be pondering her. Then her grandmother brought out several neatly cataloged photo albums filled with pictures of her father growing up. As Tomiko flipped through the pages, her grandmother began the story of Kip Johnson, Tomiko's father.

Tomiko's grandfather was in the navy during World War II. He and Grandma Johnson were stationed in Japan and stayed there after the war. When Kip, their only child, turned eighteen, he also joined the service and then married a Japanese woman. Kip's parents were planning to return to the United States once Grandpa Johnson retired. But when Tomiko was born, Kip's wife, Kumiai, wouldn't leave Japan.

Tomiko turned to the whining sounds of the kittens in the back. Ms. Tibbles left, obviously to feed them, then returned to her same spot.

"Your mother wouldn't turn her back on her country. She is a very proud woman, Tomiko. We understood this, so we decided to stay in Japan. We didn't want to leave you or our son.

"Kip was sent away on duty a lot and we wanted to be around to help your mother with her new infant. But she wouldn't let us. After a while Kumiai rarely let us see you. Then Kip died." Grandma Johnson's deeply lined face lost its composure and tears spilled onto her cheeks.

"He was our only child, our son."

"But how did he die?"

"He died in a plane crash. He was on a mission to an undisclosed destination in Southeast Asia," Papa Johnson said in a flat voice.

Grandma Johnson began again. "After Kip died, your mother refused to let us see you. Eventually, we moved back to our country. But we never stopped trying to reach you."

The older couple sandwiched Tomiko on the sofa and hugged her. She knew their tears were full of love, remorse, and relief. And Tomiko cried with them.

Then Grandma Johnson handed her some letters. Sniffing back tears, Grandpa Johnson excused himself from the room. There were eight letters written in her father's hand to her mother. Her grandmother insisted that she read them in privacy. She felt that because the letters mostly spoke of Tomiko they belonged to her. She would learn from the letters how much her father had loved her. Her mother had returned these letters to them after his death.

Tomiko thought of her mother telling her that she didn't know her grandparents.

Her grandmother kissed her softly on the cheek. "We love you, Tomiko. My husband and I are old. We only want to do right by our son."

Grandpa returned, holding a new kitten. He handed him to her, then stuffed his hands in his pockets. "He's the only one we haven't named yet."

"I never had a pet before." She ruffled his furry ear. "I suppose you'll get stuck with the name Kip." She turned back to her grandfather and hugged him. "Thank you."

Tomiko broke down in tears, hugging her kitten, then both of her natural grandparents. For the first time in her life, she felt embraced for who she was. She felt proud, and prouder still, now, to be black.

27

People conceal much inside, blinding us to their secrets, using mirrors to reflect what they want us to see. America grants us this freedom, but perhaps some people take it too far. We are free. But free to kill? Khan wondered. Whatever bubbled to the surface within Tino had made him lose control.

What kind of lies lay behind Valentino's facade? Luella's?

Ethics seemed a roller-coaster ride inside one's heart, Khan thought, a ride that most people lived on. If only all of us could put our mirrors down and show our honest needs. If only we realized that we don't need most of what we so desperately scramble after, like Valentino and his damn overtime.

Like her own obsessive attachment to R.C.

Now Valentino was in a courtroom, awaiting his hearing. Luella lay dead, her husband and two grown sons left without her. Khan thought of her Mama Pearl and prayed for wisdom to understand the chaos around her.

But Khan also felt anger surfacing. Some of this violence and self-destruction could have been avoided. On Tuesday,

September 1, the hourly workers were notified that Champion's River Rouge Assembly Plant had become the strike target. And in two weeks, on September 14, the union had to agree on a national contract. What more could happen?

The union's strategy was to target Rouge Assembly, one of Champion's key plants. Eventually Champion Trim would be shut down and the workers would be laid off because of lack of storage space. Because Champion operated on a just-in-time system, there was no room for stockpiling. This action, the union felt, would allow their members at smaller Champion plants such as Troy Trim to be laid off eventually and draw unemployment benefits, which was approximately six hundred dollars weekly, instead of receiving the hundred-and-twenty-dollar strike pay.

These thoughts and more moved across Khan's mind in the empty moments before the morning session began in Judge Robert O'Jay's courtroom. The sound of spectators' whispers could be heard as anxious moments of anticipation ticked by. Khan winced when Tino was brought in with shackles on his legs. His wrists were handcuffed to his waist and he looked unkempt. When he turned to acknowledge his family's presence, sadness filled his face.

Khan sat next to Ron and Ida while they waited for the judge's decision on Tino's arraignment.

As they waited on the hard benches of the dingy courtroom, Khan heard her aunt and uncle arguing.

In order for Ron and Ida to secure an attorney for Valentino, Ron had to put a lien on his property for the fifty-thousand-dollar fee. Now he was furious.

Khan couldn't believe it. After all the lectures he'd given her about putting money in the bank and saving for the strike, Uncle Ron was nearly as broke as she was.

Tino's hearing was over quickly. Valentino was charged

with first-degree murder and sent back to his cell in the Oakland County Jail in Pontiac.

Ron couldn't wait until they were out of the courthouse before he blew up. Ida and Khan trailed after him. "That stupid son of a bitch!"

Ida stepped in front of his face. "Don't you call my boy a son of a bitch unless you're calling me a bitch." She narrowed her eyes, and when she did, they were filled with tears. "Are you calling me a bitch, Ron?"

Khan could hardly breathe. *Please take it back. Please, please, Uncle Ron, don't go there with Aunt Ida.*

"No."

Khan sighed in relief. "C'mon Uncle Ron, Aunt Ida. We can talk about this at home."

But Ron was still furious and wouldn't let up. "I knew some stupid shit like this would happen. That boy's been having trouble for years trying to prove that he's a man."

"Uncle Ron, don't—" Khan pleaded.

Aunt Ida stopped dead in her tracks; she was still wiping away the tears from their first argument. But her words were cold and cutting. "You impotent-ass bastard. Don't you start in on my child. Take it out on that lizard faced bitch Elaine you're fucking, if you're able to fuck her. You—you . . . limp-dick whore."

Oh my God! No, she didn't go that low in front of me! Khan was frozen in shock.

People were beginning to slow down as they walked by, listening. Everyone loved an argument, especially when the participants were hitting below the belt.

Ron didn't appear the least bit fazed at Ida's outburst. His darts of anger were clearly aimed at Valentino. "Your son's bisexual. I bet you didn't know that. I've known it for years. He's been using his wife and child as a cover-up for his gay activities. I heard about it. Yeah," Ron huffed, "I know a lot of people. I know a whole lot of shit that I ain't told you about."

Aw shit! Things are going to get ugly now.

"I told y'all to stop this mess. You'all ain't gonna embarrass me up in here. Let's go," Ida said, rearing her right shoulder back and sniffing back her tears. "Just because he ain't no whore like you don't make him gay."

"Fuck you, Ida."

"And motherfuck you, Ron. And tell you *mammy* I said so."

What's happening to this family? Khan began crying. "What's wrong with y'all? I ain't never seen y'all act like this before. Your son's in jail. Your daughter-in-law's in a terrible state, and your grandbaby is probably mixed up as hell because no one's there for him. How can y'all sit here and argue about some stupid shit like this! You better be glad I got any respect left for both of you." She brushed back tears that kept falling. "Now"—she gritted her teeth and balled her fists—"I said let's go." She marched off toward the car and didn't look back.

Shortly afterwards, Khan heard them following her.

Khan drove them home in complete silence. Not a word was spoken until Khan told them good-bye.

When she returned home, she listened to a message from Thyme, asking Khan to have lunch at work. Lunch? Who in the hell could think about lunch when in a few weeks they might not be able to buy groceries for their families? Khan couldn't get past the idea that somehow Thyme might have been able to do something to help prevent the tragedy of Luella's death.

Khan was so pissed she nearly knocked the phone on the floor when she snatched the receiver off its cradle to dial Thyme's number.

"Hello, it's Khan. You left a message." Khan tried to keep

her voice steady and give her friend a chance to exonerate herself.

"I thought it would be nice if we could go out for lunch."

"Hold up. Aren't you aware that Champion is the strike target? River Rouge is scheduled to shut down, Thyme! Fuck Champion Motors. Or are you going to lie about that too! You've lied to me about everything—the outsourcing, the overtime!"

"Khan, I still don't think River Rouge will walk, and anyway, I'm more concerned with getting some character witnesses for Valentino, and also about going to Luella's funeral tomorrow."

"Look, I'm not going to Luella's funeral. You go. I've already sent flowers and my condolences to her husband and children. The way I feel now, I could use a few condolences myself." Khan couldn't hold her temper a minute longer. "It's all your fault, you know. If you'd handled the overtime and monitored it like you said you would, none of this shit would have ever happened." Khan was so mad she spat into the phone.

"That's not fair, Khan."

"Bullshit! You're new collar and I'm blue collar, and you're giving me the blues. I don't want to have nothing more to do with your white ass-kissing, bitch!"

Thyme's voice got nasty now too. "Hey girl, don't get funky with me. Because up until now, you've been kissing up to some white folks too. That blond hair on your head— who you trying to be, Winnie Mandela? I hardly think so," she snarled. "Marilyn Monroe is more like it. And she's white, *ain't* she? Last I heard, black folks don't grow blond hair. I can read your broke blond ass like a Blondie and Dagwood cartoon, you're so fucking simple and outrageous."

"Say what?" Khan couldn't believe Thyme was talking to

her like this. They'd had small arguments before, but nothing like this. Things were getting too personal. "Let's cut this conversation right now, Thyme, before we say some things we regret."

"No. You started this shit. Now you listen." She measured out each word carefully. "You heard me saying, I'm sure: 'You know you ghetto when your country ass don't even know you ghetto.'"

"Who you calling country? You white bitch!" Khan yelled.

"No, you the bitch," Thyme said and hung up.

No, you didn't hang up on me. Khan picked up the phone and began dialing her back. She stopped. "Fuck her. She don't know anything about my life, no way."

Later that day, Khan was slumped on her sofa, feeling exhausted and dejected, when Buddy rang the doorbell. Khan was honestly glad to see him. They drank cold cocoa and talked in the living room. For some reason, he always sensed when she needed to talk. And he knew that now she needed to purge all the poison that had filled her heart with so much rage over the past few days.

"My cousin's in jail for murder. I've cussed out my best friend, and my uncle and aunt are about to call it quits. What else could go wrong in my life?" she asked him.

"Slow down, Khan. Think about it. The problems in your life are about other people. Not to say that they're not important. But what about you? What makes you happy? What gives you a moment or two of happiness that would make what you're going through now bearable?"

"I get what you're saying, Buddy. But I've screwed up my life, too. I ain't got nobody. The man I love is married to somebody else. I already told you about that. I don't know why I came to Detroit." Her voice cracked, and her eyes misted with tears. "I should have stayed home."

They were sitting in armchairs across from each other. But quicker than Robin could appear at Batman's side, Buddy was kneeling beside her before the first tear touched her cheek. Buddy pulled a handkerchief from his back pocket and patted both sides of her face. "Naw. Think about it. Then I would have never met you." He smiled at her and placed her hands in his. "Try and slow down, Khan. Everything seems to be stacked against you right now. But God is watching. You've got to take that leap of faith and believe that time will heal all. I can feel in my heart what kind of woman you are. Even your relationship with R.C. was a loving one. Still, it's time to let go of it."

Despite herself, she loosed her hands from his and wrapped her arms around his neck, hugging him tight. "I could kiss you. You always know what to say to make me feel better."

He looked her casually in the eye. "Why don't you kiss me? That would make me feel much better."

"I've always loved challenges." She kissed him softly on the lips. Half expecting for the kiss to be friendly, she was surprised to find herself giving in. The kiss felt luscious.

Apparently Buddy felt it too. He stood up straighter on his knees and pushed his upper body against her small breasts. His hands caressed her head, neck, and shoulders. The kiss deepened. She pushed her tongue between his lips until their tongues touched. And she was surprised to find herself falling back and welcoming the luxury of his tongue in her mouth.

Before she knew it, Buddy had slid on top of her in the chair and was pressing himself against her. There was no denying she needed the sex; she could feel the stresses of the day beginning to leave her body.

But suddenly she felt ambushed by her thoughts. Was she ready for another disappointment like the one she'd experienced with R.C.? No. She just couldn't risk falling for this man. Not now.

Khan pushed Buddy off her. "No, Buddy. Please don't."

He eased himself away. When he did, his penis pressed against her thigh; the sensation roiled over and through her. "I won't rush you, Khan. Especially now." He pulled back abruptly, appearing to be embarrassed. "I'm sorry."

"Buddy . . ." She couldn't even look at him. "It's my fault."

He gathered her hands in his. "No," he said, kissing her hands innocently. "It's mine. I was raised better."

I was raised better! Khan melted inside. Had he heard her talking to herself in his dreams? God, have mercy.

She tried once again to explain. "Buddy . . ."

He rose to leave. "Khan. You're upset and you're vulnerable. I knew that. I almost took advantage of you. I'm glad you stopped me. As a matter of fact, I thank you for stopping me. I don't want *us* to start out like this."

She couldn't speak.

"Like I said, you've got a lot on your mind. When I'm in trouble, I talk to my Aunt Viola. She's all I've got, and I know she'll be honest with me. Even when I'm wrong. It's the same with you and your Mama Pearl—why don't you go call her?" He kissed her hands once again and led her to the door.

"I don't know what to say. I just know I need a friend like you."

"Just promise me you'll call your grandmother. That's the most important thing you can do for yourself"—he winked at her—"and for me."

Khan was floating when he left. R.C. had never given her that much respect. They would have been fucking five minutes ago. She realized that Buddy valued and respected her. Khan wondered whether she deserved so much.

She knew he was right about Mama Pearl, and as soon as she heard him start his engine, she picked up the telephone to call her.

Khan explained everything that had happened over the past few days. Mama Pearl did not consider Uncle Ron family. Ron's brother had impregnated Mama Pearl's daughter and left. And no matter how much Ron tried to bridge the gap between his brother and Mama Pearl, Pearl had no use for him. She'd almost lost her daughter to heartache. She'd never met Valentino, or Ida, but she listened with her honest heart as Khan told her everything, spilling out all the interweaving stories, all that was coming undone. And, as icing on the cake, for the first time she was honest with her grandmother about her relationship with R.C.

But Khan felt lighter when she spoke about Buddy, as if suddenly Buddy had become the man in her life. Perhaps he wasn't that attractive on first notice, but the more she got to know him, the better looking he became.

"Time is passing so quickly, Mama Pearl. I feel like I'm fifty already."

"You can't see the passing of time, Khan. You can keep a diary of what you do, what you say, what your thoughts are. But it takes time to see the passing of time. You have to look back at it. You're too young to have experienced that, Khan. Enjoy life now. Because time, next to death, is what limits our lives. Both come too quickly, and can never be retrieved."

"Grandma—"

"Shhh," she said. "Time is endless, time is as wind, and as waves are we." She paused. "Can you hear it?"

28

Saturday. Thyme was leaving the church after Luella's funeral. She had slipped into the back row during the pastor's eulogy.

Thyme was surprised when Luella's oldest son, Cole, was introduced by the pastor to speak on behalf of his mother. He wore a rattan-brown single-breasted suit, white shirt, and a simple brown and beige tie. There was a proud smile on his face before he began. Cole spoke about the early days when his mother would take them to the Detroit Zoo and the Detroit Science Center. He told the small congregation that even though Luella had spoiled both of them, they always knew how much she loved them. That love had encouraged them to excel academically. Without her forcefulness and support, Cole said, he and Reese would not have become such successful students at Columbia University. At that moment, Reese, sitting in the front pew, broke down in tears. His father, Omar, weeping himself, tried to console his son.

Thyme was genuinely moved. And she was proud to see the enormous floral arrangements, mostly from Champion workers, that nearly overshadowed the coffin.

The atmosphere in the church was overwhelming, and

Thyme couldn't wait to make a quick exit the moment the service was over. The service left her feeling defeated, and the depression lingered as she drove home.

Thyme hadn't seen Khan at the funeral, though this wasn't surprising. Thyme thought back to her argument with her friend and winced. Thyme scanned the radio for news about the strike. She thought now that she'd been overly optimistic with Khan, assuring her that there wouldn't be a walkout.

Was it her fault that Valentino was in jail? That Luella had died? She was beginning to reassess her culpability. Although the A-team had been formed and endorsed by the union and operated with the full knowledge and consent of Ron, Thyme still felt she could have done more to address the stresses brought on by the issue of overtime. Thyme knew there was no way she alone could have dismantled the overtime system, including the special favors given to the so-called A-team, but if she'd been more involved, she might have prevented Luella from dying and Valentino from ruining his life.

But what hurt Thyme the most was that Khan now thought so badly of her.

As soon as she arrived home, Thyme made some coffee and turned on the TV for any news reports on whether the local union had reached a tentative agreement with Champion to renew its contract.

Later that evening, just as she finished watching the eleven o'clock news, the late-night anchor announced that the local union had agreed to ratify the contract. The union had quickly reached a tentative agreement long before the September fourteenth deadline. Thyme gave out a long sigh of relief and clicked off the set. The phone rang just as she was slipping into bed.

"It's me, Thyme."

"Cy?"

"I know it's late, but I was watching the late night news. Congratulations. No national strike."

"Yeah. It appears that everything is under control," she said, thinking about her settlement, which still was not *settled*. "When are you coming home?"

"Late next Wednesday night. I miss you, baby. Can you wait up for me? It might be one in the morning before I get in."

Thyme sighed. She so wanted to have him in her arms. But she still felt so betrayed, so angry. "Just come home."

"I miss you, sweetie. There's no one like you, Thyme."

"It's about time you found that out."

As Thyme's eyes shut and her mind closed in on sleep, she felt a glimmer of hope that all was not lost in her marriage.

A week passed quickly and when Thyme arrived at her office the Wednesday of Cy's return, Elaine handed her an envelope that had just been delivered by registered mail. Thyme opened it and skimmed the contents. Jack Cohen, the president of Local 1099, had called a membership vote the previous week. The union had voted overwhelmingly to strike Troy Trim two weeks from today, September 30. The main issues were (1) health and safety—lax security, causing Luella's murder, and operators' sewing accidents because of inferior parts; (2) the high sewing standards for the 1999 car lines; and (3) outsourcing the jobs from Champion Trim to Mexico.

She felt blindsided; it had never occurred to her that Champion workers would strike even though the national union had settled. She felt that the local issues could be worked out without a strike.

Damn! You could have warned me, Ron.

Thyme walked through the plant to speak personally with

people who had worked closely with Luella, including
Khan. She wanted to give them a chance to air their feelings,
whether they were sadness or anger. Thyme knew it was
important to give the workers a chance to voice or vent.

True to plant life, the gossip about Luella's death super-
seded talks about the upcoming local strike. But what good
would gossip do? Thyme thought. It happened. It was over.
They had to get on with their lives and hope that most
learned a lesson about the true price of overtime. It didn't
matter who was right or wrong. Neither Valentino's family
nor Luella's family would ever be the same.

The employees were dealing with the grief in their own
way, and most seemed to welcome work as a way to dispel
their frustrations. Thyme was relieved. If Champion would
negotiate with the union fairly, settling the local strike issues
would be a relief to everyone.

After lunch Thyme received an odd propfs message. As
was customary with electronic mail, several words were
always abbreviated—embrdy meant embroidery; ctns meant
cartons. It was so stupid. Why couldn't they just spell the
shit out?

MSG FROM: GCASTELLANPO14—TRY0006 USAET (UTC-
1:00) 9/16/98
Subject: Lear Matamoros
To: Ctyler 12—TRY0006
Hi Cy,
    ON YOUR DESK YOU'LL FIND TWO SHIPPERS. BOL#25779
WAS FINALIZED ON THE 14TH. NOTE THERE WAS NO AN
EMBRDY LISTED ON THE SHIPPER. ENRIQUE VARGAS CALLED
FROM ANOTHER MATAMOROS PLANT. THE SHIPMENT HAS
BEEN SITTING AT CUSTOMS FOR TWO DAYS BECAUSE THEY
DIDN'T HAVE ANY PACKING SLIP FOR THE EMBRDY THAT
WAS NOT ON THE TRUCK. WHAT HAPPENED WAS, THE SHIP-

PING CHECKER DIDN'T SCAN THE EMBRDY CONTAINERS
BEFORE FINALIZING THE SHIPPER.

I AM FAXING YOU A COPY OF THE EMBRDY LABELS OFF
THE CTNS. I AM ALSO SENDING YOU A COPY OF THE SHIP-
PER IN CASE YOU WANT TO REVIEW THIS WITH YOUR
CHECKERS.

YOU JUST LEFT AND I MISS YOU ALREADY! I KNOW
THINGS BETWEEN US ARE STRAINED, BUT WE'LL FIND A
WAY. THERE'S TOO MUCH TO GIVE UP.
Graciella
Matamoros Trim II
(525)355-0667, FAX #355-9455
==========END====OF====NOTE===========

What the hell is this shit about? Thyme wondered.
Somebody sent me Cy's e-mail. Who was Graciella? She
erased the e-mail and continued answering her memos. She
didn't even want to think of Cy right now; she needed to
keep focused on preparing for the strike, which now seemed
inevitable. She didn't even want to think about the outcome
of her lawsuit, the settlement of which she was expecting to
hear about any day now. Exhausted, Thyme decided to leave
the office a bit early.

As soon as Thyme stepped into her home, the phone
began to ring. It wouldn't be Cy—he'd told her he'd be getting in late. Who could it be? Then she smiled. Maybe it was
Khan and they would finally make amends.

"Hello," Thyme said expectantly.

"I heard my brother's coming home tonight."

"Sydney?"

"Yeah, it's me. Just thought I'd give you a courtesy call
and fill you in on what your husband's been up to."

"Listen, Sydney, we've never liked each other. I'm tired.
I'm beat. Let me say this clearly: You've got a fixation on

your twin. If you can't understand that old concept, Sydney, you should switch analysts. Any good shrink will say you're too close to him. Possibly that may be one of the reasons why your husbands leave and your kid is a mess. Jarrod will probably win custody and Graham will stay in London. You should direct your energy toward your own family and stay the hell out of mine!"

Sydney's voice was purposefully slow, the pulling of molasses. "Oh, honey. You may be joining me soon." Sydney laughed a vicious laugh. "Cy's got secrets. But twins can't keep those kinds of secrets from each other. And you know what?" She giggled. "I can't wait until you find out Cy's secrets."

"I'm hanging up on you now, Sydney. It's obvious you're drunk."

"Wait, Miss Black America. Your husband loves black skin, but black comes in many shades. Try Mexican. They're just as dark as you pretend to be. Night, *y'all.*"

At that moment, the name from Cy's memo leaped before Thyme's eyes: Graciella.

29

It had to end one day," Cy said to Graciella.

It was his last night in Mexico. Determined to move ahead for everybody's sake, he had stayed in Champion's suite at the Radisson for his entire visit, coming to the house only tonight to spend time with the children. Now the children were asleep, leaving him and Graciella alone. They sat opposite each other at the kitchen table. It had rained all day and still the rain came down, relentless. Even their affair appeared worn out by the rain.

"Why are you doing this, Cyrus?" she pleaded. "I'm happy with the way things are. I've lived with this for twenty years. You never heard me complain. I always accepted my role in your life. Why now? Why now!"

"I want you to find someone, Graciella. A man who will marry you." He ignored her protests and continued, "You're still young and beautiful."

"But my heart is with you, Cyrus. I cannot love another man. How can you ask me to allow another man in our lives? How can you desert Gregor, who so looks up to you? You can't expect him to accept another man's love when, like me, he only wants the love of his father?"

"That's not fair. You know how much I love the children. Don't use them to manipulate me."

"Then don't leave us." Her voice was a moan. "We need you. You need us, too. We're a part of your life, Cy."

"I won't be back, Graciella. I've made up my mind to resign from Champion Motors."

"And when will you return to see your children?"

Cy was silent for a moment. "There are still some details I have to get worked out back home before I come and see the kids again."

Her face was pale, but Graciella remained rigidly straight and stared at him with unblinking eyes. Her hand tightened around the arms of the chair so hard that her knuckles whitened.

"Graciella . . ." Cy began pleadingly. It hurt him to see her this way. As he looked into her face, her brown eyes, her heart, his heart ached with emotion. He would miss her. "I've set up an IRA for you and the children, and you will also receive twenty-five thousand dollars from me each year. As promised, I will also pay for the children's education." Cy had worked out the numbers and felt comfortable that the financial issues had been dealt with fairly, but he still had some doubts about his emotions.

"You can't buy me off!" Graciella said angrily.

"I am not buying you off. I'm taking care of you and our children."

"You cannot just get rid of me by signing a big check. No—no! I'll never let you go, Cy." Her hoarse voice rang through the small kitchen as she lunged out of her chair, pounding Cy's chest with both her fists. Tears streamed down her face and she fell against him, sobbing, pleading with him not to end the relationship.

"Don't do this, Graciella." His voice was very quiet.

He would not let himself give in to the soft feelings he felt for her, although he was tempted. As he had told her during the last trip, he would always care for her, but these feelings for her and the children were destroying his marriage. He pushed her away. And when he did, hate replaced the tears in her eyes.

Cy's rejection drove Graciella into a silent rage. She had never fought for what she wanted; now, for the first time, she was making a stand. She stood, slowly walking toward him, then slapped him with all her might. The sound echoed through the room. "You must be crazy if you think you can just walk out of our lives. I'll tell your wife about us. And that's just the beginning."

He grabbed her hand and held it. His eyes were direct, challenging. "No you won't, Graciella. Don't make this any more difficult than it has to be." Cy walked out of the kitchen and left the house for the last time.

Even as he heard her cries turn to screams, he continued walking toward his car. It was one of the longest walks of his life.

Cy felt weightless as he landed at Metropolitan Airport. Michigan greeted him with an onslaught of mid-September rain, but this was home and he was glad to be here.

Beads of rain hit him hard, like steel marbles, and Cy didn't have an umbrella with him. He started to get pissed as his suit jacket absorbed the water. He couldn't locate his keys in his briefcase; he then fished through his pants pockets, through his coat pockets, and, finally, nearly soaked, he found his keys on his belt loop.

Standing alone in the darkened parking lot at the airport, he had to laugh. He felt cleansed. Free. How powerful the rain is, he thought, and yet how simple. Who but the Omniscient could have devised such an admirable arrangement for watering the earth and cleansing the soul? And once again he felt the pull of home. His wife was fifty minutes away.

Driving home, he tried not to think of Graciella, but it was almost impossible. He was hoping that the worst of their breakup was finally over and praying the memories would fade with time.

As Cy pulled into the driveway, he noticed that most of the lights were out. He crept into the house quietly and slipped into his bathroom to shower. He wanted to wash away the last trace of his guilt before he got into bed with his wife. He approached her sleeping form.

"Thyme, baby, I'm back. I've missed you."

"Cy—"

"It's me, baby. I'm home." Cy pulled Thyme into his arms, but he could feel her resistance. After a moment, he released her.

"What's wrong, Thyme?"

"Nothing. It's late and I've had an Excedrin kind of day."

"But are you okay? Is everything all right?"

"Sure," Thyme said and rolled away, pulling the covers up to her chin.

By the time Cy opened his eyes the next morning, he could hear Thyme speaking to him. As she handed him a cup of coffee, she said, "Your sister called me while you were away. Ordinarily, I wouldn't have taken her gossip seriously, but I received a strange propfs message. It was addressed to you. It came from Mexico."

Cy felt as if his world were crushing in on him. Oh God, no. He hoped the sudden rise and fall of his chest didn't betray his fear. "I don't see the connection."

"Does the name Graciella sound familiar?"

Cy shook his head yes. "That's one of the receiving supervisors."

"Well, the memo was signed Graciella, and she ended

with the comment, 'I miss you already.' Then Sydney said something about a secret, implying that you enjoyed other varieties of dark skin, such as Mexican." Thyme's voice was beginning to sound edgy. "Now you tell me, Cy: What would you think if you were in my position?"

Cy just looked at her and then said, "It's probably Sydney up to her usual efforts to cause problems between us. Let me take care of it, Thyme."

Thyme looked at him blankly, her face hard and absent of feeling.

Oh shit! How could Graciella have done such a stupid thing? And Sydney?

As soon as Thyme had left for work, Cy called Sydney at the office. "I'll be brief," he said. "I told you before I left that I didn't want you interfering in my personal life. You didn't listen."

"Who's telling you lies about me, Cy?" she asked in an innocent voice.

"No one, Sydney. It's the truth. You've finally crossed the line. I've warned you. No wonder you're alone."

"How dare you talk to me this way! I'm your sister. Blood is thicker, Cy. You always said so."

Cy cringed. "Well, that has changed. Because of you. You've changed. You're nothing but a bitch now, Sydney."

Sydney laughed. "It's funny, Cy. Those freaky bastards I married—all four of them—made me into the bitch that I am today. And you know what? I love myself now more than ever." Sydney laughed again; her laugh was worse than a wicked witch's. She sounded downright cruel.

"I never realized how sick you are."

"How's that, Cy?" she stammered. "Did you say sick? Who are you to sit in judgment when you've been living two lives? You're always yapping about how much you love your wife. If you love Thyme so much, how could you lie to her for so many years?"

"I'm warning you, Sydney, if you get between me and Thyme, I'll never forgive you. Never."

When he slammed the phone down, he felt his face coated with sweat.

Cy wasn't scheduled to return to work until Monday. It was suddenly clear that he had to do two things to save his marriage: resign from Champion and stay away from his sister. No matter how enticing becoming partners with Sydney had seemed, he now realized that it would never work. He was confident that he wouldn't have a problem securing employment at another company. He spent the morning in his home office revamping his résumé and made a number of calls. He was sure it wouldn't take long to find a good job.

He ran some errands, and by the time he returned, Thyme was home from work and in the family room on the chesterfield sofa with her reading glasses on. Beside her were a pile of business magazines, including *Fortune*, *Forbes*, and *Business Week*. She looked like she had fallen asleep.

"Baby, you trying to get old on me," he teased, waking her with a kiss. He held a white paper bag in his hand. "Close your eyes," he said, removing her glasses.

"What do I care about G.I. Joe?"

"I *said* close your eyes." When she obeyed, Cy reached inside the bag and brought out a small plastic bottle. Unscrewing the cap, he dipped a plastic stick up and down in the mixture then removed a bubble wand and blew.

"That tickles." Thyme laughed. "What on earth are you doing?" she asked, jumping back and protecting herself. "That's not fair."

"Here," Cy said, handing Thyme her own bottle from the white bag.

"Good. Now it's my turn." Thyme began blowing bubbles in his face and he turned just in time. They tussled on the sofa until she managed to blow a few bubbles in his ear. Cy got up and, walking backwards, began blowing more bubbles in her direction.

Thyme followed him, picking up the pace, a smile on her face.

"Now let's see how fast those young legs can run," he said and took off.

"Uh-oh. Here I come." They ran all over the house, downstairs, upstairs, blowing bubbles after each other, giggling.

Thyme tripped on the steps, spilling hers. "Okay, I'm out. Game's over."

It was a relief to laugh. It felt good to both of them. They sat for a moment, exhausted, looking into each other's eyes and not saying a word.

They ended up back on the sofa after Cy helped her clean up the mess. "Baby, I'm sorry about the other day."

"It's not important." She touched a sticky spot on his face. "I love the bubbles. What made you think of it?"

He kissed her. "We've been way too serious lately. I thought it was a simple way of telling you how much I love you." He kissed her again, then pulled her head to his chest. "I admire you so much. I realize how much you're dealing with at work. I don't know how you keep motivated. You're such a strong woman. Don't tell anyone, but I've been stealing your strength for years."

Suddenly Thyme pulled back from him. "What, what's the matter?" he asked.

"Cy, I can't forget about everything. I can't forget you lied to me."

"But I told you that will never happen again. I love you, Thyme—you must believe me. You're my entire world. You've got to believe me."

"I want to, Cy, I want to." Thyme fell back into his arms and let him undress her.

On Monday, Cy arrived at work early. He wanted to turn in his resignation as soon as possible, but he knew he had to wait for the right moment. It might be weeks before he could do it right.

When he logged on to his computer, he saw that he had three propfs from Graciella and deleted them without reading them.

He also read an executive memo stating that in less than two weeks, six more of Troy Trim's units would be taken out of the plant and sewn in Mexico. By then everyone would know what was happening, including Thyme. Cy gulped; this news going public would only remind Thyme of how he had held back important information from her.

If the union workers found out about Champion's plans to close the Troy Trim plant, Thyme would be right in the middle of a wildcat strike. The recent violent death of one of their own would make the problem that much worse. Cy realized that by withholding the information he knew about the plans to shut down Troy Trim, he'd left his beloved wife twisting in the wind. Would she ever forgive him?

His instincts told him that regardless of any settlement Champion reached with the union, management would find a way to renege on giving Thyme the next available management position at World Headquarters.

The sale of Troy Trim at the end of the year looked inevitable, and he was powerless to stop it. The only way to save himself and his marriage was to get out.

30

Hot damn, we did it! The award is $1,270,000!" Stephen Kravitz yelled the figure as if it were his. "Where've you been? I've been trying to call you for hours."

Her voice was dull. "Troy Trim officially went out on strike today."

"I know you're upset. But Thyme, you're rich now. Laugh. Shout. Open a bottle of champagne!"

Thyme was unmoved. She'd spent the last week and a half praying the negotiations with the union would avoid the strike. But they hadn't. "I appreciate everything you've done, Stephen."

"My God, Thyme. We've won. We've cleaned their clock. Aren't you the least bit happy?"

"Yes, I am happy. I'll shout tomorrow. But not now."

What did money matter to her now? She felt more distant from Cy than ever, she'd lost her best friend, and to top it all off she was menstruating with huge cramps and the Midol wasn't working. What good would hundreds of pieces of green paper do? After all, it was just paper, and it provided no comfort. Her victory was in winning. But there was no joy. What hurt worst of all was that she couldn't share her victory with her husband because she knew he didn't support her the way a husband should support his wife, especially when she was right.

Thyme remembered being struck by a passage she'd read by the poet Samuel Taylor Coleridge: "As there is much beast and some devil in man, so is there some angel and some God in him. The beast and the devil may be conquered, but in this life never destroyed."

Reading those words, and remembering them now, she visualized her husband's two faces.

That evening, Thyme sat in front of her home laptop. Cy stood in the doorway. She kept her gaze focused on the computer screen. She'd just finished a video conference with three of her business associates. They were discussing the strike at Troy Trim and the possible implications for other trim plants that would be destined for the same fate. Everyone seemed reluctant to point fingers, but all agreed that the company was at fault. Greed was at the root of this problem. This situation could have been avoided.

"You okay, honey?" he asked. "I'm sorry. You're upset about the strike." Cy began walking toward the liquor cabinet.

"Why didn't you tell me about the sale of Troy Trim?"

"Sale?"

"Cy, I found out. Now we're not just talking Mexican workers temporarily taking our jobs. We're going to another level—workers, many of our friends, permanently losing their livelihoods, their homes. How can you continue to deny what you've obviously known for months?"

"Thyme . . ." he implored.

"How could you lie to me like that? What about my friends? They will never believe I didn't know months ago what was going on!" Thyme looked at the computer screen and wanted to scream. She tried to gather her strength.

"I was protecting you, Thyme. You have no idea what goes on at World Headquarters. It's bigger than both you and I. The automobile business has become global. It's dirty and extremely competitive. If Champion doesn't cut costs, there will be no Champion in the next century. It's that simple."

"And where does that leave us?" Thyme asked as calmly as possible.

"I'm working on that." Cy was quiet for a minute, as if he were trying to make an important decision. Finally he said, "Look, Thyme, I don't want to say more now. Just trust me that I'm taking care of everything."

What a clever way of saying you lied.

Without another word, Cy left. Thyme heard him get into his car and drive away. Thyme, for the first time, was glad to see him go. The moment he left she started looking through his jacket pockets, looking for anything else that might discount what he had told her. What she found was the pager that he had asked her to turn in two months earlier. Somehow, between the two of them its return had fallen through the cracks. She pressed the recall, and a number frequently dialed came up on the display. The area code was from Mexico.

Thyme dialed the number.

"*Hola,*" a young boy said in Spanish.

Thyme hung up quickly. Seconds later, her phone rang.

"Did you call my home?" a woman asked.

Thyme was shocked. Apparently they had return-caller ID in Mexico as well. "Yes. But it was the wrong number. Sorry." She hung up for the second time. But this time her instincts were beckoning her.

Lies, like truth, she knew, had a way of catching up with you. Either way, she would find out and hope and pray that Cy had told her the truth.

But didn't she already know he'd lied to her? Was it time

to be truthful with herself? He had lied about this Graciella woman, and he had lied about Champion. Things had broken down so badly between them, how would she react to yet more betrayal? Right now, she felt they would never be the same again.

It was time to take a good, honest look at herself and determine if she was ready to make a new life, one that may not include her husband.

She picked up the phone and dialed her attorney. "Stephen?" she asked hesitantly, "I'm interested in retaining the services of a private investigator. Do you have any suggestions?"

31

It was Thursday morning the seventeenth of September, and Khan sat in the break area with several of her co-workers, snacking on a Sprite and chips. At 10:30 A.M. everyone was waiting for the new work schedule to be posed.

Everyone was still arguing about who was at fault for Luella's murder. Some blamed Luella for being so hungry for overtime. Others blamed Valentino. No matter how justified, no one had the right to take another person's life.

Khan's feelings were mixed. Sure, she was saddened by Luella's death, but she was sadder every time she went to visit her cousin in jail. It hurt her deeply to see his forlorn face beaded with the sweat of frustration behind steel bars that seemed to be viciously stealing away his beauty. He seemed to brighten when Khan told him that Sarah and the baby were doing well, but the light soon faded from his eyes.

When the schedule was finally posted on the bulletin board outside the break area, everyone got up to look. As a reminder no one wanted to see, a picture of Luella along with her obituary was posted on the bulletin board next to the schedule.

"Look," one of the women in her unit called out, "there's no overtime scheduled for next week. The whole plant is on eight hours."

Another voice said, "Everyone except the A-team. Them fuckers always find a way to get overtime."

"Hold up," another said, "Look at this shit. Six units are down. What in the hell is going on?"

Khan got close enough to look. One man standing behind her said, "This don't look good. The plant hasn't been on forty hours since April."

"And six units down. What's up?"

Ron walked up just then. He was dressed in a red polo shirt and pale blue pin-striped slacks. "I'll tell you what's going on. The company ain't listening to our demands." He held newsletters, which he passed out to everyone. Listed on the newsletter were the dates and times each union member was supposed to picket, and where to pick up their strike pay. The strike was being called for September thirtieth, two weeks away. Ron called everyone to attention and explained that the union was calling for a local strike.

"You might as well know the full truth. As you may be aware, more and more jobs have been going to Mexico. Ultimately, Champion is going to close down Troy Trim."

"Hey, Ron," a man spoke up. "We just ratified the contract. I don't know about everybody else, but I ain't too keen on going out on strike over some stupid local issues. Even if what you say about closing Troy Trim is true, how do I know Champion won't find me another job?"

A big mistake! Khan thought.

"Brother, if you think the plant can go on forty hours, can keep shutting down units and that ain't serious, then I suggest you pull your head out of your asshole and wake up to the fact that these are not stupid issues. They are as serious as your next meal, your rent, your car payment. I kid you not."

"Where is your solidarity, man?" someone else shouted out.

"You might be working today, Wally, but you better be thinking about tomorrow. What'll happen next month if we're permanently out of a job?"

Wally lowered his head in shame.

Ron continued his speech. "If we don't stick together we won't have a union. That's what has made the union a force to be reckoned with—solidarity. Our brothers and sisters before us had to miss some paychecks, go out on strike in order for us to be reaping the benefits we're reaping today. The union struggle is a continuing struggle. We all have to stick together."

Now everyone was clapping, even Wally, who walked up to Ron and shook his hand. The newsletters that were previously glanced at were now sought after and looked upon like the Holy Grail.

"Amen!" a man shouted.

"Uncle Ron, I need a favor," Khan said.

"Yes?" he said, his chest poked out as proud as a robin's red breast and looking every bit like a plant chairman. Or so he thought.

"I finished early. How about taking me out to lunch?"

Ron stopped. "You're broke."

Yeah, and so are half the people I work with.

"My pleasure, Khan, though I did warn you to put money away."

Oh yeah, and what about you, Casanova? she wanted to say.

They had lunch at Cicero's on Long Lake Road two miles from the plant. A familiar eating spot for Troy Trim employees, Cicero's was a good place but the wait was long. It was nearly a half hour before Ron and Khan were able to sit down.

Khan knew better than to broach the subject of Valentino. Even though Ron appeared to be frustrated with his son, Khan knew how Ron worried about him. During the entire time Valentino had been in jail, Ron hadn't missed a day of visiting his grandchild and his daughter-in-law. He made sure they had everything they needed. Yet Ron refused to see his son in jail. No one could convince him that what he was doing was selfish. He was adamant; he could not condone what Valentino had done. At the same time, Ron knew his duty was to take care of his son's family.

Ron didn't stop talking. He started with the CAFE laws (the Corporate Average Fuel Economy standard). The law, established in 1975 by a Democratic and a Republican senator and called the Bryan bill, sought to increase the fuel efficiency of American-made automobiles.

So what? Khan thought.

Ron continued to eat and talk. Khan knew that all she was required to do was nod. And so she did.

"If the Big Four hike average auto mileage by forty percent, it would save two-point-eight million barrels of oil each day—four times the amount imported each day from Kuwait and Iraq before the Gulf War."

Khan still didn't get it. Why was he going on and on about this? What does this have to do with my life? Khan wondered.

"This is exactly why all nineteen ninety-nine models, according to government standards, are supposed to average twenty-five-point-six miles to the gallon." Ron exhaled. "In order to reach this goal, Champion has had to cut their costs in other areas to compensate for the growing costs of fuel efficiency."

"Mm-hm," Khan said.

Before Ron finished his sentence, Khan had nodded her head. She couldn't really retain the details of what Ron was saying; all she cared about was her job.

"I've got friends in pretty high places. And they tell me that our jobs aren't secure at Champion. They know exactly what they're doing. Every move they've made has been calculated. Just because they negotiated with the national doesn't mean they'll deal with us fairly on the local level. To put it bluntly, Khan, Champion is getting out of the trim business. Like I said back at the plant, all those divisions of each company are moving toward merger, and you know what merger always means."

If she'd been listening, Khan would have taken in the picture: everyone she knew at Champion was now at risk. But her mind was on simpler things. Buddy had promised to take her on a tour of his shortening company. The first time he'd taken her to see his home, she was astounded by how many trophies he had. Most were Boy Scout prizes. She thought his being a Scout was so cute. But when he added that he was on the national board of directors for the Boy Scouts of America, it wasn't cute anymore; it had opened her eyes to a part of Buddy she hadn't seen before. Lately, she'd been taking another look at this man. He was coming together like building blocks, and the more she learned about him, the more she was able to see his true shape and form. The more she did this, the more she admired him.

She thought about the night she'd seen R.C. and Tomiko at the theater. Thanks to Buddy, she'd finally gotten over R.C. She knew she really cared about Buddy because thinking about R.C. didn't hurt anymore. She also knew that she was falling in love with Buddy and was powerless to help herself. And the beautiful part was that he wasn't even trying to persuade her. His actions spoke for themselves.

She could feel her uncle's eyes boring down on her.

Apparently she'd missed something. "I'm sorry, Uncle Ron. What did you say?" But her mind stayed on Buddy. Khan wanted to call Buddy right then and talk to him. She was hoping she hadn't done anything the other night that turned Buddy off. She was beginning to see just how blind she had been; now she saw that many women would give their right arm to have a man like Buddy in love with them.

"One day you'll understand what I'm saying. Just know this: we don't have many choices. We need to face the facts; we may all be out of jobs soon."

"What?" Suddenly Khan heard what her uncle was saying. She realized that she'd been lost in her own thoughts, probably not wanting to listen to the reality facing her.

Throughout the rest of the afternoon, Khan began to take a serious look at her situation and began thinking about security for the first time.

Ordinarily, Khan would have been tickled by a message from Buddy when she returned home from work. But not this afternoon. She was plagued by what-ifs. What if the plant closed? How would she pay her mortgage? Her car note? The only thing she could afford to do was eat, and that would probably be sardines, or welfare cheese.

Shit! I knew I shouldn't have come here to Detroit. I should have kept my country ass home. The next voice she heard was Thyme's: "You should have stayed in college and finished your degree."

Trying to decipher everything her uncle had told her that day had given her a headache. By the time she finished writing out all her bills she was in a panic: $356.12 on Visa; $129.00 on American Express; $138.00 for her utilities. *Damn! That's almost $625.00 and I haven't even started on groceries yet.* She wrote out the checks, inserted them in their envelopes, and licked them shut, leaving a horrible taste in her mouth. Checking her balance, she had twenty-four dollars left to last until tomorrow, her next payday, which may be her last. Then what?

She wished she'd paid more attention to what her uncle had been saying. There was still a chance to avert the actual walkout. She prayed the plant wouldn't strike.

Later that evening, while Khan was eating a Healthy Choice fish entrée, Champion Motors headlined the evening news. The local issues between the union and the company hadn't been settled. The sticking points seemed to be outsourcing, overtime, and health and safety issues.

The next morning when Khan arrived at work, Allister handed her her weekly paycheck. But she noticed that half her co-workers received a layoff slip as well. Silence, like fate, fell upon the unit.

It was no longer a rumor that someone else had taken their jobs. Ron called Khan that night to confirm the union's plans. All talks had broken off, and they would strike a week from Tuesday at midnight. They all had their schedules.

By the time Tuesday night arrived, three hundred more hourly workers had been laid off. Tensions were high. When the clock struck twelve, a third of the workforce followed Ron inside the plant, including Khan.

"Let's walk!" he shouted.

Khan spoke her piece. "We're striking, people. Let's go!"

The sound of people whistling and shouting filled the air. No one was sad. Relief was apparent on all faces.

As the hourly workers formed a group and walked around the plant announcing the strike and building their ranks, Khan was scared. She'd never been involved in a strike and had no idea what to expect.

By 12:30 A.M., over six hundred employees had marched out of Troy Trim. It was as bright as daylight under the crime lights in the parking lot. The television cameras were rolling. One cameraman stuck a microphone in Ron's face. Khan blinked and stepped back.

"Mr. Lamott, you're the union chairman of Troy Trim?"

"Yes."

"And you've instructed your union workers to walk out tonight?"

"That's correct. Champion Motors is refusing to bargain with the union. They've cut off negotiations. We have reason to believe that the company is planning to ship four more of our units down to their Mexican operations. This has caused a recent layoff of over three hundred union workers in this trim plant. We won't stand for that. We demand fair treatment. We understand competitive wages. We understand helping developing nations. But not at the expense of our labor force here in Michigan."

"How long do you feel the strike will last, Mr. Lamott?"

"I can't answer that. Only Champion Motors can answer that."

They were cut off by cheers and whistles. A van arrived with the picket signs. Hourly workers picked up their signs and began forming a line on the street just outside company property.

"As you can see," Ron said, smiling, "our union brothers and sisters are behind us. We plan to strike until we have our jobs back and the company brings enough business back into this trim plant to keep our workforce employed." A confident grin. "We won't accept any less."

Khan, standing behind her uncle, saw Thyme's car pull out. She gestured to Ron. The newspeople had moved to talk to workers on the line.

"Don't blame her," Ron told Khan. "This was out of her hands. Sending these jobs to Mexico was an executive decision."

"You're telling me she's not to blame at all?"

"No, not for the outsourcing. I know she did what little she could."

"I don't get it, Uncle Ron. I thought you said that Thyme must have withheld the information? Where does Thyme stand, then?"

"I'm saying that she had no say about the outsourcing."

"But how do you know?" Khan insisted.

"I have my ways."

"Elaine?"

"Let's not get into that, shall we? For the record, yes, it was Elaine who told me. As Thyme's secretary, she is privy to some useful information at times." His voice was serious. "Thyme is in as bad a position as we are. Here comes Louis with the picket signs." He placed a caring arm on her shoulder. "You ready?"

"Yeah. I'm ready." Khan tried to sound tough, but out of fear her words sounded like a whisper, and more confused than ever.

Louis handed her a dozen signs that read in bold letters: UAW, AFL-CIO; UNITED AUTO WORKERS AMERICAN FEDERATION OF LABOR AND CONGRESS OF INDUSTRIAL ORGANIZATIONS, LOCAL 1099 ON STRIKE. Ron held others voicing the issues: STOP OUTSOURCING! JOB SECURITY! BETTER PLANT SECURITY! UNFAIR LABOR!

Khan checked her watch. It was fifty minutes past midnight. Tires screeched to a halt as hundreds of Champion employees arrived by the carloads. As if preparing for an all-out war, workers gathered and rationed out picket signs like ammunition.

As more and more workers joined in the unified effort, Khan felt proud to be a union worker. Among the crowd, there was a sense that they were waiting for something.

After an hour, Ron and Khan broke from the line to grab a cup of coffee provided by the strike committee.

Someone handed Ron a fax. As he read it, he frowned.

"Uncle Ron, what happened?"

"I see why Champion doesn't have that much motivation to settle."

"What do you mean?"

"This fax states that the company has hired scab workers to sew the new seats. They're coming in tonight. The union won't stand for this."

"What? Scab workers?" Khan knew this meant one thing: a fight.

"I didn't realize how much I depended on Ida until now."

Khan hugged her uncle and said, "Don't worry, Uncle Ron. Everything will work out."

"Don't let on to anyone what I just told you."

"Don't worry," Khan said as her uncle drifted away from her.

A third of the workers were armed with picket signs, and the others banged on the chain-link fence that surrounded the entire Champion complex.

Khan cringed inwardly. She felt an odd tension in the back of her neck that spread out along her shoulders. A part of her wanted to turn around and run back to the safety of her car. Standing on her tiptoes, she tried to find her uncle. Somehow, in all the shuffling, she'd lost him.

The first person she recognized in the darkness was Daddy Cool. "Hey, baby girl. Come on over here by me."

Khan stood again on her tiptoes, trying to see. "Have you seen my Uncle Ron, Daddy Cool?"

"He's down there." Daddy Cool pointed toward the guard shack at the east employee entrance.

That scared her. She could barely spot her uncle's thick body as he talked with two of the security guards. "But he knows that he's not supposed to be on company property. What's he doing?"

Khan fought her way through the pickets and down the ramp to the security-guard station. From behind her she could hear Daddy Cool warning her to stay back.

A few seconds later, she stood behind Ron and listened to him arguing with the security guards.

"Look, Ron. We don't want any trouble. You have to move back. You know the rules of the contract."

"Are we supposed to abide by the rules when the company is bringing scabs in here to do our work?"

"Ron," the security guard said, "you can do what you want in the streets, but this is private property. Don't make me have to physically remove you."

As the scabs began to file in, ten more guards exited the station and formed a protective line for the scabs into the plant. A line of vans had just come into view.

"I'm telling you to get back, Ron. Otherwise, I *will* call the police and have you arrested. I hope that won't be necessary."

Khan was feeling what her uncle felt now. Seeing the scab workers file out of vans, workers who had probably practiced her sewing job for the past two weeks somewhere while she was separating the jewelry she planned on selling to cover her bills, made her mind trip to the insanity level. "Fuck that shit!" she yelled, then stepped beside Ron. "Uncle Ron, who are these people? These people have no rights here."

"I'm sorry to say, Khan, but we could be those people unless we get this contract settled. These are our jobs and we're going to fight to keep them. These are our people— laid-off union workers—out of work trying to feed their families too. I feel sorry for them, but they can't have our jobs."

Ron pulled her small body back behind him and said, "Shhhush" under his breath so she wouldn't draw attention to herself. By that time one more van had stopped in the lot, and two more joined in, waiting.

Three committeemen whose role was to keep the union members in order came up beside them.

"Trouble, Ron?" one asked.

"No," he said, backing up. He smiled viciously at the guards. "We're going to do as the guard says. We're going to get off company property."

But Khan could tell by the sound of his voice that he had something planned. All five backed up the ramp slowly, all the while watching the guards and the van. The jeers from the union workers became louder.

Sweat trickled down Khan's face, and when Ron grabbed her hand she could feel the sweat on his hands intermingling with hers. The other committeemen were breathing hard and sweating profusely as well. She clutched her uncle's hand more tightly and began to pray.

Something was about to explode.

As doors of the fifth and last van opened, spawning more scabs, the union workers were propelled into action.

"Here they come!" a union worker shouted. "Scabs! Scabs! Assholes trying to take our jobs! Get out of here!"

32

The calls began coming in for R.C., first from his business manager, then from his bookie. They all wanted money. Tomiko was nothing short of astounded at how much debt R.C. had incurred. She'd been able to convince him to give up the alcohol, but she wasn't so sure of how much headway she'd made on his gambling habits.

Tomiko and Bonnie were in the kitchen feeding Kip milk from a bottle since he was too young to feed himself. "When the casinos are open next year in Detroit, I don't know what will become of R.C. I hope he realizes he can't beat the casinos before he loses the shirt off his back. Every day you read in the papers about people losing their homes, cars, jewelry, because of gambling," Tomiko said in exasperation.

"Here," Bonnie said, taking the kitten from Tomiko, "let me do that. You have to have a little faith, Tomiko. Mr. R.C.'s been in worse shape than this and pulled through. He's a survivor. I know he appears to be down and out, but don't give up on him. You're good for him. I found the eight hundred number for Gamblers Anonymous in his pants pocket. At least he's trying to do better."

When the phone rang, Bonnie answered and then reluctantly handed it to Tomiko.

"Hello," said Tomiko. "May I help you? This is Mrs. Richardson."

"This is Alexander. Tell your husband that he can't keep avoiding us." Alexander was one of R.C.'s bookies.

"Excuse me? Who is this?"

"His payment's overdue. He's got ten days or we'll get him good. He knows that." The line went dead in her ear. For the first time, Tomiko feared for her husband's life.

Tomiko calculated the days until October 1. She had just over three weeks. If only she could get R.C. to the ranch, maybe he would confide in her.

Things had been going so well between them. R.C. had even met her grandparents and told her afterward how meeting them actually made him feel closer to her. In the past weeks, Tomiko had renewed faith and hope for their marriage. She was determined not to let his gambling get in the way of this hope.

That evening, when R.C. came home, he handed Tomiko a check for twenty thousand dollars. She hid her disappointment that he was gambling for such high stakes; did he think he could hide from her that bookies were after him?

She told him about her plans to drive to Kentucky on Thursday. Trying to sound upbeat, she claimed that she needed to put some highway miles on her new car. She didn't mention the phone call from the bookie.

"No. Not alone. Kentucky's at least seven, seven and a half hours away. You've never driven that far alone."

They were getting ready to go see *The Man of La Mancha*, which was playing at the Fisher Theater. Robert Goulet was the featured star. Tomiko remembered reading the play in Japan in her eleventh-grade literature class. She always loved it and looked forward to seeing the play on stage.

"Friday then," Tomiko volunteered. "I could leave early Friday morning and be there by one."

"I can't leave Friday, either. If you wait until Saturday I can drive down with you."

A huge shipment of Mishimoto's Muresame sports cars was due in at two of R.C.'s dealerships on Thursday. And Champion's hot new Atlantic was a week overdue and expected to arrive at four of R.C.'s dealerships on Friday. Angry customers had been waiting for the cars they had ordered in July, and it was now September. R.C. was adamant that he wouldn't rest until his customers were driving their new vehicles.

"By then the weekend will be half over." She began undressing him. "Please. Please, R.C. This means a lot to me. I haven't had a weekend off in months. And you know we both could use some time off. C'mon, fly down Saturday night." She had him down to his shorts and shirt by then. "You can drive back with me."

He gave in, of course, and Tomiko figured it was the best she could do to get him out of Michigan.

Taking special care to dress, Tomiko slipped into a Louis Féraud black bugle-beaded bodice that exposed her midriff. The outfit was cutting-edge vamp. As she moved, she showed off her sexy ankles and shapely legs. R.C. was pleased. She'd even helped him pick out a new winter-white wool three-piece suit at Jack's Place in Southfield for the occasion. No one could tell the Richardsons they didn't look suave.

"You know what?" Tomiko teased. "You and I are looking so fine tonight, the actors in the play are liable to step off the stage and compliment us on our *slamming* clothes when they see us walking down the aisle."

"There you go bragging again. You beginning to sound

more and more like a soul sister when she thinks she's looking spiffy."

They arrived late and, sure enough, heads turned when they walked into the theater. But Tomiko stopped when she saw a face midway down the aisle.

It was like an itch that she couldn't scratch. She wanted to ignore it but couldn't. It was somewhat of a relief to see a man sitting beside the woman.

When Tomiko saw a blond-haired woman smiling at her, she slowed and nodded to the woman and the dreadlocked gentleman seated beside her. Though Tomiko had never seen Khan, she remembered Bonnie's description of her: "Darla" smile, short blond hair, and tiny body. Tomiko's instincts told her that this had to be Khan. Tomiko couldn't tell what R.C.'s response was, but he didn't miss a step behind her.

"Good evening," Tomiko whispered to Khan. The man sitting beside her with his arms around her shoulder smiled and returned the greeting.

Throughout the night, Tomiko barely watched the play she had so longed to see. Her mind and heart were on the woman behind them, the one in the background who had threatened their marriage. Was she still a threat? Tomiko wondered.

When the play was over and they rose to leave, she felt relieved to see that Khan and her date had already left the theater.

On Friday morning, Tomiko rose while it was still dark and had coffee with R.C. before he left for work and she headed off to Kentucky at five.

R.C. hesitated outside the front door after he'd kissed her good-bye for the fifth time. "I charged an extra battery for your cell phone. It's in the glove compartment, as well as the

Triple-A road service card in case you have a flat or something."

"You told me." She fell into his arms and hugged him tight.

"And the map. I've made several markings for alternate routes just in case—"

"You showed me." Tomiko opened the door and shoved him back inside. "Now I've got to get going. I'll be fine. I've got everything . . . more than everything I need."

R.C. pretended he was trying to remember one more thing.

She spoke in her sexiest voice. "I've got a surprise for you."

"What? Tell me."

"It's better if I show you." She felt his smile when he kissed her again. "I'll call you when I get to Cleveland, and the moment I cross the Kentucky state line. Okay?"

"Tomiko . . ." he said, softly stroking her chin.

"I love you, too."

Forty minutes later, Tomiko was on the interstate. The highway was clear except for some minor construction. And when she reached the Cleveland city limits, she kept her word to R.C., calling him at the designated times until she made it to the ranch by lunchtime.

The next morning she should have felt exhausted, but instead she felt exuberant. Sunshine coated the tops of golden and russet trees. The air was warm and sweet for autumn. She mounted the mare Caleb tacked up for her and they roamed the acres of countryside R.C. owned. And with each breath she took, Tomiko couldn't have felt freer. So free, in fact, that she hadn't noticed until the setting sun was as vivid as gold, orange, and purple on painted glass how quickly the day had passed.

Back at the ranch, the housekeeper was preparing a light

supper of chicken salad with homemade French bread. Tomiko could smell the bread baking in the oven the moment she finished riding the mare and exited the barn.

After taking a shower, she changed into a black brocade shift and cigarette slacks. By then it was just after seven. R.C. would arrive in less than thirty minutes. She spent the time standing by the window watching for him.

When she saw him, she felt a strange tightening feeling in her chest that she'd begun to feel each time they came together after a separation. At times, some of her former insecurity and distrustful feelings would surface. But when she saw his lovely smile greet hers, she couldn't have felt happier.

Later that night, Tomiko surprised R.C. with yet another game—this one called Sexual Secrets. She also had purchased Sinful Cinnomon Spanish Fly Aphrodisiac and Dirty Dice.

But R.C. was refusing to play.

After watching R.C. read the directions for a fourth time, Tomiko said, "What's wrong, R.C.?"

He was now on his feet, pacing in the large living room. "I've got to tell you what's going on. Four times this month I won between fifty thousand and a hundred thousand bucks. A couple of times I didn't spend it on nothing but gas and food, 'cause I lost it the very next day." He stood up, pacing back and forth, placing his hands in and out of his pockets and occasionally rubbing his head. He stopped. "I remembered asking God to help me. I promised that this would be the last time."

Tomiko smiled at him reassuringly. "I'm glad you realize how serious this is, R.C. I've read about all those people gambling over in Windsor having to file bankruptcy." She shook her head. "There are so many sad stories. People are refinancing their homes to feed their gambling habits."

"Not just that. They're losing their lives. A few weeks ago

a young man jumped off the Ambassador Bridge on his way home from the casino." His voice was quivering. "I knew that man, Tomiko. It hit home. I have to stop, or I'll be next."

Tomiko couldn't help it. She started to cry, shaking her head from side to side. Then she felt R.C.'s arms around her. "I love you, R.C. I always want you to be a part of my life."

"I went to The Male Health Center to see a Dr. Agnew. He's a urologist. I found out that I don't have that problem. You know . . . what you'd thought before."

"Are you okay?"

"Dr. Agnew said I've just been under too much stress. Gambling and the excessive drinking didn't help, either." She laid her hand against his cheek and caressed it. "Anyway. I'm fine now, so we won't be needing this." He took the Sinful Cinnomon Spanish Fly and tossed it in the trash can.

Tomiko took the cue and lay down on the bed. She stretched out her arms for him to join her. "We've toyed and joyed with each other, but my love for you goes much deeper."

The next morning she was awakened by the smell of coffee. When she entered the breakfast room, Tomiko saw that R.C. was already reading the paper. Wearing only one of R.C.'s sleeveless T-shirts that barely covered her thighs, Tomiko leaned down to kiss him. "Morning," she said.

He was working on a crossword puzzle. "Forty-two down, is . . ." She took the pencil from his hand and wrote in excitement, the answer to the clue, then sat across the table from him. "Mmm, that's how I feel this morning."

"Thanks." He reached over and stroked her naked thighs, then began to ponder another word.

"What?" she asked, pouring a cup of coffee from the decanter. "You need some more help?"

When she sat back down he said, "Tomiko? You should know . . ." He shuffled for the rest of the words. "My money problems are pretty serious. We're going to lose the ranch."

"I didn't marry you for your money, R.C."

"There's something else. You know my friend Oxford?"

Tomiko nodded. He'd called a couple of times over the last few months. Unlike some of R.C.'s friends, Oxford had always been very polite with Tomiko, always asking when she and R.C. would fly out to Seattle for a visit.

"Well, Oxford and I go back to the Vietnam War. Right after the war was over, I had to borrow money from Oxford to get my first business up and running. But I lost all of it. I was never able to pay him back, but Oxford let it go. When I started developing my horse business, I convinced Oxford to invest. I promised him he'd double his money. So now losing the ranch means I've screwed Oxford over again."

"Is that why you seem to avoid him?" Tomiko asked gently.

"Yeah. I'm avoiding my own buddy, and it doesn't feel good."

"R.C., we'll handle it together. I'm making good money now." R.C. didn't look as relieved as Tomiko expected. "What's wrong, R.C.? Is there something else?"

"No, no. You're such a sweetheart, I don't know what I'd do without you." He smiled, caressing her face.

When the doorbell rang, Tomiko jumped up to get it. Outside in the circular drive, she saw two green plain-looking cars. She could tell there was writing on the doors, but it was hidden by dust. The man standing in front of her held up a badge.

Tomiko noticed that they wore guns, but they were dressed in street clothing.

"Can I help you, sir?" She thought they might be there because of R.C.'s bankruptcy.

"I'm Special Agent Milford from Kentucky Immigration. Are you Tomiko Richardson?"

33

The heat was on. Everyone was ready. Including Khan. It was going to be ugly, but it was too late to turn back now.

"Are we going to stand for this bullshit? Scabs coming in here stealing our jobs?" one man shouted.

"Hell no!" A woman spoke up. "Fuck that shit. I got kids to feed."

Khan didn't know all her co-workers by name, but in the five years she'd worked at Champion she'd come to know their voices and their faces.

Khan's eyes wandered the crowd. She could see broken bottles and signs being held high in people's hands. When she turned back around she spotted Monica, a member of the Jehovah's Witnesses, which was a well-represented group at the plant. Standing next to her was Nelson, a member of the prayer group that sometimes opposed them. They were chatting with each other, holding up their signs. This is what Uncle Ron meant by solidarity, she thought. People whose personal lives may be oppositional but who came together in crisis; union brothers and sisters coming together for one goal. She forged ahead in love and prayer.

Ron elevated his strong voice above the noisy crowd.

"What are we going to do about it, then? Are we going to show Troy Trim that the union workers won't stand for this bullshit!"

"Damn right." Khan joined in. "Let's show 'em." Caught up in the moment, she was ready to fight. Being surrounded by so many people she worked with every day, now unified, was seductive. Everyone was adding to the momentum to keep that emotion going, that adrenaline flowing.

"I'm ready to kick some ass!" someone shouted.

"Let's do it! Yeah! Yeah!" the phrase reverberated through the crowd until everyone was shouting the same words: "Let's do it!"

It was the time to defend families and exact revenge. The strikers ran toward the closest scab van with vengeance on their minds.

By now several police cars had entered the scene. And in the far distance Khan could see more police coming on horseback.

There must have been twenty-five cops, many on horseback, trying to control the crowd, but it was futile. The union workers were growing in number every minute and already vastly outnumbered the police. The workers pushed against the line of cops. The cops pushed back. It was only a question of time before there came one push too many from either side.

Taco José screamed, "Let's cream those sons of bitches!"

A scab worker yelled from the van as the union workers surrounded it, "Hey, we've got families to feed too! Don't get mad at us. Your problems are with Troy Trim."

"Then get your own fucking job to take care of your families," a union worker shouted. Enraged, the union men hurled beer bottles toward the opened window.

Smash! The scab worker ducked inside, narrowly avoiding being hit. But the bottle connected with the window and cracked it. The scab workers in the van huddled together, knowing that the next bottle thrown would break through the glass and leave them utterly defenseless.

At that moment, Khan noticed more police arriving with sirens blasting, lights flashing. Squad cars and more police on horseback began to establish a line of defense.

Khan was terrified. She wasn't willing to challenge a twelve-hundred-pound animal. The sight of the mounted police trotting fearlessly near the fence only further fueled the anger of the men and women whose lives depended on the outcome of events here tonight. The union workers, black and white, were fighting for their rights. And if the big man refused to acknowledge them, it was time for war. This time everyone had something to lose. And color was invisible here. Salvation and survival reigned.

"We don't want to hurt anyone. Please, people. Get back!" yelled one police officer armed with a billy club.

It was too late. Hundreds of union members swarmed the scab vans, attacking with kicks and shouts. To her horror and amazement, Khan found herself among them.

Crash! Scab workers screamed. More union workers hurled bottles and whatever else they could find at the vans. Finally the first scab was hit. His limp body leaned against the broken window. At that moment more union workers swarmed the van. Feet, bats, fists, stones, and multitudes of bottles rained down, a monsoon, most directed at the already wounded man.

"We're going to war, motherfuckers. You are fucking with our gig!"

A sharp jolt shook the van. "What the hell are they doing?" one scab asked.

"We getting ready to kick y'all's ass," Khan yelled behind a horde of men who, with their backs and shoulders against the van, were now beginning to rock it.

"Omigod, omigod!" one scab shrieked. The others in the van soon joined her in panic as the van slowly rocked back and forth. The suspension of the van began to creak and bend. The angry mob pushed harder and harder, tipping the van a little more each time.

"They're going to tip us over—I have to get out of here!" Khan heard a shout and saw a man bolt for the rear door. Khan could see inside the van. Two men tried to restrain him, but his insane rage had served to strengthen him. He pushed them aside, leaping through the door and into the arms of the mob. The other scabs stared at the action, perhaps wondering what had been going through the poor man's mind. The beating he received was bad enough to bring even Evander Holyfield down.

The van was nearly overturned now; it needed just the final nudge. Khan stood watching the mob and yelling along with the rest. "Kill 'em, kill the bastards!"

An officer on horseback beside her stayed still, probably knowing he was powerless to stop the mob unless he shot at them. There were far too many workers. "Hey, why don't you go home, little nigger bitch." He sneered at Khan.

"Fuck you, pig!"

"Why you little piss-ant." He pulled out a can of pepper spray and squirted Khan in the eyes. She screamed. The pain, the burning were more than she could bear.

At that moment all she wanted was to stop the burning of her eyes.

Khan stumbled. All around her she heard screams and cries. The scent of pepper spray was everywhere. It filled the air. She pushed herself to her feet, took one step, and fell down again. Her hands frantically clawed at the pavement as she attempted to rise. Tears rushed down her cheeks as she struggled to breathe and clear her vision. The tears made the noxious spray burn even more. She felt as if someone had poured acid in her eyes. She opened them as best she could and ran toward the next van, eyes still burning but mad as hell.

Boom! She rammed her shoulder into it. The weight of her small frame added to the others' and the van tipped over. A mounted cop moved toward the overturned van. Khan swiveled, only to see a flashlight shining in her face and a horse rearing back on its hind legs.

To her right, she could see bodies climbing all over the vans like roaches. She could hear the thud of the policemen's billy clubs pounding against flesh, followed by cries of pain.

On and on it went. Khan lost all track of time. Red and blue lights flashed on the backs and faces of workers. Everywhere she dared to look, she saw people she knew lying on the ground. Their faces and bodies were dirty, and some were covered with blood. There was no way she could know if they were dead or alive.

The sky above took on the eerie glow of a wartime.

Where was Ron?

In agony, she knew she still had to forge ahead. She refused to lie down and give up the fight.

Between the workers and the cops, it was like a game of cat and mouse. The cops, union members themselves, treated the strikers as though they were criminals when they were just trying to protect their jobs, to survive.

Khan dived through the masses and pushed her weight along with the others, trying to stop the next van that was exiting the company premises.

From the corner of her eye, Khan saw three policemen beating a woman with a billy club. Then she spotted Uncle Ron just as the same three cops turned their attention to him. She left the van and ran toward him, against the crowd.

The vans were slowly retreating, but now the workers

didn't want the fight to end. Small groups began to chant, "Solidarity forever! We shall overcome!"

Sweat dripped from her nose and onto her lips. She quickly licked it off. It seemed as if that small little drop quenched her thirst. Full of anger, she moved forward.

"Fuck this shit! Bitch get over here, asshole!" someone shouted.

Blood spattered onto Khan's face but she didn't bother to wipe it off. She just kept pushing her way through the crowd.

Seeing all these angry people rushing to cause more violence just seemed to get in her way of getting out. And now just the thought of losing her job was making her angry. Annoying cries disturbed Khan's thoughts. Just hearing all the angry sounds made them seem like a brick wall in front of her.

When Khan thought she came to an opening in the crowd, police cars swarmed in, blocking it. Khan stopped and looked around the deranged crowd and spotted her uncle. She ran over to him and saw a policeman grabbing his collar. Khan heard the officer say to Ron, "Get out of here before I have to take you to jail."

"The hell you will," she said, stepping in and helping her uncle ward off the blows. The wallop she felt on the side of her head knocked her on her heels. Struggling for balance, she grabbed the policeman's sleeve.

Together, she and her uncle kicked and fought the policeman until he backed away.

Khan turned away from her uncle to see if she could spot anyone she knew who needed help. Then when she turned back, Khan noticed that Ron was battling with two more police officers. Sirens, shields, and sticks hadn't stopped the union members from defending their turf. More police cars arrived, but no one seemed to care. It was too late to stop now.

Somewhere a gunshot went off with a roar that reverberated above the cries of the crowd. Men and women scrambled, falling on the ground to cover their heads.

Everyone fell to the ground.

Another gunshot!

Frightened horses reared, their nostrils flaring, their huge black eyes rolling back in terror.

Immediately, Khan fell to her knees, trying to crawl toward the fence, fear driving her. She felt a woman's small hand tugging at her blouse behind her, trying to hold on. They had to get to safety.

When she touched grass, she tried to scramble to her feet. She had almost succeeded when a hand closed around her ankle, pulling her down. Crashing to the ground, her teeth bit into her bottom lip hard as she fell into a soft mush she realized was horseshit. She was dazed for a moment, but the taste of blood seeping onto her tongue assured her that she was still conscious. However, the man still held her ankle in a relentless grip.

Khan dug her hands into the grass, clawing out clumps of it, dirt encasing her fingernails. She held on. "Let go!" she said, kicking, trying to turn over on her side and ward the man off with her arms. "Let me go!" she screamed, kicking harder.

From a few feet away she could hear the thuds of fists pounding against the man's back. She turned and looked into the eyes of her uncle, who was now attacking the scab worker.

More gunshots rang out. Just ahead Khan saw a pregnant woman being carried in the air and passed across uplifted hands to the fence.

Please, Lord. Please, Khan prayed silently, don't let anyone get killed. Please Lord, don't let that woman lose her baby.

Blood was flying in every direction. And when the emergency vehicles tried to enter the scene, shouts rang out. The crowd encumbered their movements.

Someone else grabbed her once again from behind; she didn't know who. She felt a crushing blow against her shoulder, then heard a bone crack. She froze. Pain seized her in its vise and rushed to her spinal cord. She squeezed her eyes shut and felt tears singe her cheeks. She was certain either her shoulder or collarbone was broken.

Now someone kicked her in the abdomen, a punishing blow, and she doubled over in agony. The pain was unbearable. Suddenly, someone was pulling her back. Looking up, she saw Taco José lifting her up to the fence.

"Now you stay out of the way—you're hurt bad enough as it is. We'll handle this." He went back into the fight.

"This shit ain't worth it," one of the scabs shouted from beyond the fence. "Champion ain't paying us enough money for this shit." One scab worker broke away on foot and managed to run from the riot. Knives were stuck in tires, and the whoosh and bump of the vans lowering filled the air. Those inside stayed, powerless to move.

Veils of light peeked through the sunrise as darkness began to wash out of the sky. Khan heard the cry of the morning's first hawk. Then a group of birds swarmed, large ones, reddish brown, their wings arched. They circled lower, so low that Khan could see their yellow feet and eerie black talons. In this horrific setting, the sight frightened her.

When would the violence end?

Just then she heard a loud thud. A bottle hit one horse in the neck and it reared up, kicking its front legs wildly in the air. Khan attempted to shield her burning eyes from

the cop's blinding light, but nothing could protect her
from the horse's powerful legs and sharp hooves. *Thwok!*
She felt a searing pain in her forehead. Then everything
was darkness.

34

Both R.C. and Tomiko were handcuffed, read their rights, and arrested by immigration officers.

"Officer, do you realize who I am?" R.C. asked.

"Certainly, sir. That's precisely why we're arresting you."

Tomiko watched as R.C. was put into a separate squad car.

"Where are you taking us?" she asked the officer driving her car.

"To the police station here in Lexington."

"But what are we being arrested for?"

"You are under arrest for illegal immigration, and your husband for employing an illegal immigrant."

"But why?" Tomiko asked. "My papers are in order. My husband and I filed over six months ago. I have a green card."

"It's a forgery, ma'am."

"What?"

"You will be sent back to Detroit to be processed, and then you will be deported."

"Deported to Japan?"

"Yes, Mrs. Richardson. According to the United States Government, you are an illegal alien."

Tomiko was stunned. What was going to happen to R.C.?

Later that day, Tomiko, in prison scrubs, was put on a state bus and sent back to Michigan. Looking out the grimy windows, she felt embarrassed and degraded.

Once she arrived in Michigan, she was put in a lockup among women who obviously had been picked up for prostitution. Tomiko tried to make herself inconspicuous. After about an hour, her name was called.

She followed an enormous female guard to a small inspection room, where a female police officer waited.

"I'm going to strip-search you. It's procedure."

"What? Why? Where's my lawyer? This is awful! I'm not a criminal! I want to speak to my husband."

After a brief strip search, Tomiko was put in a private holding cell. Once alone, she burst into tears.

Anticipating deportation was like waiting for the executioner to throw the switch. She did not want to go back to Japan. All the racism she had experienced while growing up had embittered her to her homeland. And with just five months of being in her father's homeland, she knew this was where she belonged. And she wanted to be with her husband. She prayed that R.C. would find a way to straighten out the entire mess and get her home, to Kip, where she belonged.

Tomiko didn't know where or through whom R.C. had had her green card forged. But what was killing her was that he wasn't all to blame. Looking back, she realized that she had pushed him in her need to acquire fame, and that wasn't any better than R.C.'s greed for gambling at the crap tables.

It happened sooner than she expected. The door to her cell was unlocked and the guard said, "You're free to go, miss."

"What do you mean?" Tomiko asked timidly.

"The charges have been dropped and your husband is waiting for you downstairs. Here are your clothes. You can change in the women's room."

The tears in her eyes, which she didn't wipe away, felt good; they were tears of joy.

Twenty minutes later, she rushed into R.C.'s arms. "What happened? You had them drop the charges? How?"

"Whoa, slow down," R.C. said. "Thank your grandparents, not me."

Tomiko was surprised to see both of her grandparents coming from around the corner, each carrying a can of soda.

"Hi, baby," her grandmother said.

"Glad to have you back," her grandfather added.

"It's so good to see you two," she said, hugging them. "How'd you know I was here?"

"Your husband called us." Grandma Johnson looked sad for a moment. "It's all my fault."

"Take it easy, baby," Papa Johnson said to his wife, and helped her to sit down. "Let me explain, Tomiko."

Grandfather Johnson summed it up quickly. When Tomiko had come to their home the first time and they gave Tomiko her father's letters, they had neglected to give her something else: her original birth certificate. This document proved that Tomiko had always had dual citizenship.

It was part of the reason Tomiko's mother had refused to speak to them. The grandparents had filed a suit with the Japanese consulate on their son's behalf and were given the document. Tomiko's mother always feared that she would be taken away from her and had refused to file her true parentage with the consulate.

Tomiko felt transported by this news. She was truly reborn.

It was time to celebrate. All four left for the Richardsons'.

Bonnie and Kip were at the front door to welcome them back home.

Together, they all drank sake. R.C. had a thimbleful but refused to drink any more.

The evening was magical, with R.C. his most charming, affable self. Grandma and Grandpa Johnson were impressed with Tomiko's surroundings, but not overly so. Tomiko sensed strongly that these were people with the right values. And they were her people. That resonated inside her. The Johnsons were the kind of people she would search out from now on—to help her grow.

After they'd left with hugs all around, Tomiko and R.C. retired to their bedroom.

Knowing her husband pretty well by now, she could tell that he was happy that she was home but he was still with-holding something.

As Tomiko gathered up a newspaper R.C. had been read-ing on the bed, she noticed Sydney's picture in the bottom corner. She was leaving a courtroom. "I forgot to ask you something. Why do you hate Sydney so much?"

R.C. was taking off his clothes. "It's a long story. She had her husband fire me when I worked at Cadillac. She caught me shooting craps on company property. I was already enrolled in the dealer-ownership program, a much more suc-cessful program than Champion was offering at the time."

Tomiko was relieved. She thought they'd been lovers.

R.C. was stroking Kip now as they sat together on the bed. She knew he was about to reveal what he'd held back earlier.

"You're well aware of my gambling habits. I never tried to hide them from you. I've been a con artist all my life, though I never planned on hurting anyone. My dream was to become rich. And now I am." He cleared his throat. "I was."

Tomiko sat down beside him, listening.

"I had no idea how deep I'd gotten in debt until recently."
He stopped. "That's a lie. I did. I just denied it."

"A man called here last week. He said that you owed him
money and if you didn't pay—"

"Damn! That was Alexander. I paid him just before I
came down to Kentucky. But it must have been too late. He
must have turned you in already."

"R.C., is everything going to be okay?"

"No. I neglected to pay someone that I should have paid
first. The IRS. Because I didn't keep up with my payment
agreements with them, they wouldn't extend my payment
deadline. Now they've seized my accounts."

"How much do you owe them?"

"Millions."

"Can you cover it?"

"No. Not even after I sell the ranch." R.C. ran his fingers
through his short Afro. "I've been trying to think of a way to
come up with some capital."

"How about the jewelry you bought me? We could sell
it."

"I didn't want to ask. But thanks. That will probably have
to go, as well as some pieces I own."

"I have some money, R.C."

He hugged her close and kissed her on the forehead.
"Baby, you earned that money. It's not mine to take, but
thanks. What I get for the ranch will hold us for a while,
until I can get things worked out with the IRS."

"Will they take the house?" Tomiko queried. She thought
about all the memories she had here in so short a time and
how much she loved this home.

"I don't think so, if I declare bankruptcy. Even the IRS
has to allow us a home to live in."

He held her close to him. "Baby, whatever I lose I can get

again. I'm not scared to start over. But you want to know something?"

"Hmm?"

"I'm a little relieved. I feel like I got what I deserved for screwing Oxford. I'm free now. I'll probably sleep like a baby tonight. And then tomorrow I can finally call Oxford and face him like a man."

"Is there anything I can help you with?"

"No, just trust me, Tomiko. I've done some terrible things to people. Even when I tried to make people happy, it was for selfish reasons."

"Khan?"

"Yes, Khan. I truly cared for Khan, loved her in my own way. But I was never faithful to her, to anyone, not even, my love, to you. I never understood why fidelity was meaningful. Now that I've lost all I thought was important, I understand more about what matters."

"And now, are you and I going to make it, R.C.?"

"You know, Tomiko, I've taken you for granted. But no more. I always trusted you to be there for me. I thought of you as a child; the silly sex games you love to play that I've finally learned to enjoy. But you're a woman. A good woman. And I love you."

Tomiko looked at her husband, her eyes again brimming with tears.

"I bought you a welcome-home present."

She frowned. "R.C., we shouldn't be spending any money right now."

"I know," he said, kissing her. "But this is well-spent money. Hold on." He left the room and came back with a big wicker basket that had a small pillow inside. "It's a bed for Kip."

"Oh, R.C.!" She hugged him.

"We've got to break him of the habit of sleeping in our bed."

Tomiko took Kip and his new bed and set them outside the door. "I couldn't agree more."

35

The only thing black women are good for is fucking," Cy heard John Sandler saying.

"Excuse me," Cy interrupted Sandler and another man—someone he didn't recognize, probably from outside the company. "Was that meant for my benefit? Because I didn't see a damn thing funny about it."

Sandler grunted. "Oh, no. That was just an inside joke I was telling Murphy."

"Look, Sandler," Cy said, reaching inside his pocket for his letter of resignation. It was October 1, and Cy had waited weeks for this moment. He handed it to him. "There's something I've wanted to give you."

Sandler unfolded the paper and read the contents. "What the hell is this? Do you know what you're doing?"

"Positively. Hell, I was planning on giving the company the customary two weeks' notice. Fuck it. I might as well leave now."

Sandler spoke briefly to Murphy, who promptly left. Then Sandler said to Cy, "You should go back to work. You're making a big mistake. Do me a big favor, Tyler, think about this before you do something you'll regret."

They were in the executive cafeteria. The two of them were the only ones left in the area. They could shout to high heaven and no one would hear them.

"Not a chance. This mistake was made when you insulted my wife. We both know you were talking about Thyme."

"Pardon me, Cyrus. You've got the whole thing backwards. Maybe you haven't heard. Your wife—"

"Yeah. Yeah. I know. She won a huge settlement against Champion Motors."

"Hrrmph."

"I wish I had the balls my wife had to bring you bastards to your knees. She's got more guts than the both of us and you know it."

An odd look registered on Sandler's face before he spoke. "I agree that Thyme Tyler has guts, but it's a shame she's not one of us."

"What the fuck does that mean? She's worked her ass off for over twenty years for this company."

"The fact remains—"

"Oh, hell no. I get it. I knew it all along. You're planning on getting rid of her."

"We've had a meeting his morning. Frankly, Troy Trim has to be closed . . . Cyrus," Sandler said in the falsetto voice that Cy detested.

You son of a bitch.

"Your wife is as good as gone." Sandler held up his hand to silence Cy.

"You low-down son of a bitch." Cy grabbed John Sandler around his neck and tugged his tie tight, shutting off his oxygen.

Sandler pressed his hand into Cy's chest and fought to push him off.

Cy clamped his left hand beneath Sandler's neck and backed him up against the wall. Sandler was a good four inches shorter and forty pounds lighter. Cy lifted the smaller man's body up off the floor.

Sandler's face turned purplish red. Sweat began to bead on both their foreheads.

The terror Cy saw in John Sandler's eyes brought him back to reality. He relaxed his grip and allowed Sandler's feet to return to the ground.

Smoothing out the wrinkles from his suit, Cy eyed Sandler, who still looked as frightened as a horse in a barn on fire. Cy turned to leave, then stopped at the door and turned back around and smiled. "I'm giving you another notice, Sandler." His smile became broader as he gathered his thoughts.

Sandler was busily adjusting his clothes and hardly paying attention. "What's that?"

"My wife let you guys off cheap. I've got enough shit on this company to get you all fired. And John"—he paused— "I won't settle for under ten million." Cy saluted Sandler. "I always knew I'd retire early. Thanks, John."

He walked out whistling Dixie.

36

Later that same morning, Thyme was sitting in her office when the phone rang.

"Thyme, it's Jay Cutter," Thyme's boss said in a flat voice.

Before she could respond, Cutter continued in a rush. "It's just as well you should know: In all likelihood, this plant will close within the next year. Troy Trim has lost three million dollars. Operations continue to run in the red, week in and week out. Your people are on strike now."

He cleared his throat. "Despite our past . . . disagreements . . . it's clear we now have cause to ask for your resignation."

"You know, Jay, this is ridiculous. We both know why I'm being asked to resign."

"Thyme, it's a matter of poor performance. It's the rule of the marketplace."

"Bullshit!" Thyme said, her anger rising and then ebbing just as quickly. "You know, it's not even worth it. Fine, you have my resignation."

She wasn't surprised by her boss's request. Disappointed was a better word. Over the past few days, she'd begun clearing out her desk and taking certain personal files home. Her office already looked diassembled. She knew that she should finish cleaning out her desk, but for some reason she couldn't move. She stared out at the billowing smokestacks from a nearby plant.

Thyme picked up the silver-framed photo of Cy from her desk and held it in her hand. She was still holding it when the phone rang again.

"The union rejected the offer." It was Ron.

Ron quickly summarized the meeting with Dean Phillips, the industrial relations manager for Champion. Dean told the union the company would replace all the sewing machines with safer ones within two years. Place security guards at each entrance. All overtime would be okayed by the plant manager as well as the committeemen and Labor Relations on a weekly basis. Champion would review the indefinite layoff policy but would not agree to eliminate out-sourcing completely.

"Now what?" Thyme asked. This was not the time, she thought, to tell him that Champion had rejected her as well—

"I'm not sure. We'll have to wait and see," said Ron in a dejected, tired voice.

"Let's stay in touch," Thyme said and they hung up.

Thyme returned to staring at the smoke stacks outside, mesmerized. The smoke was rising upwards toward the heavens. There was a mystery in smoke, she thought, as it rose in the autumn sky. It was faint blue in color, the color of infinity and eternity. She felt the smoke, like her life, dis-appearing right before her eyes, and she was helpless because she hadn't started the fire, and she most certainly couldn't put it out.

Thyme left her office without looking back. Though she

felt badly for the workers, she wouldn't miss her job. And there was a huge settlement check to mollify the pain.

Thyme drove directly to First of America Bank. With her settlement check tucked in her purse, Thyme signed her name on the ledger and waited for the next available bank manager to handle her business.

"Mrs. Tyler," a young man said fifteen minutes later. "Follow me."

He offered her a seat and she handed him her check. He appeared to be very professional, and Thyme was positive she recognized him from somewhere.

"I'd like to open a new account."

"So," he said with candor, "this account will be solely in your name?"

"Did you read my application? It specifically states that this account will be opened for Thyme Tyler." She read the name plate on his desk. "Mr. Majors, do you have a problem with that?"

"Uh . . . Mrs. Tyler," he stammered, "you don't understand. Our bank is used to doing business with your husband. And because of the size of this check, I have to check with my supervisor."

Thyme leaned forward and laid her right elbow on his desk. "Mr. Majors, *you* don't understand." She snatched her check back. "This is not the only bank I can do business with." Thyme placed the check back neatly into her wallet and watched the man's eyes grow wide. "Obviously, you're more comfortable dealing with Caucasians than you are with African Americans. I'll take my business elsewhere. Good day."

And that was just what Thyme did. She walked across the street and opened an account at First Fidelity. The manager was happy to open her sole account, though, truthfully, to Thyme it felt heavy—like one piece of her was absent.

An hour later, she arrived home. Cy's car was missing from the garage, but Sydney's was there. Her heart dropped. As she unlocked the door, she wasn't prepared for the surprise that greeted her.

When she entered the kitchen she heard a child's voice.

What in the hell was going on?

She dropped her keys on the kitchen counter and Sydney entered the room.

"How did you get in my house?" Thyme demanded.

Sydney's voice was calculating. "Didn't Cy tell you? I've always had the code and the key."

Thyme was fuming. She poured a glass of water and swallowed it, pretending it had the calming effect of a shot of Hennessy. What the hell was going on?

"We've got company in the living room, Thyme. I'd like you to meet some of Cy's friends."

Thyme followed Sydney toward the sound of children's laughter. And suddenly she knew.

A beautiful Latino woman sat still on Thyme's pearl gray chesterfield sofa. Dark hair hung to her shoulders, barely showing the huge gold earrings caught in the thickness of her curls. She wore a white blouse unbuttoned to the fourth hole and a long, full dark green skirt. Thyme knew instantly that the woman was Graciella. The two children in the room with Sydney and Graham were her husband's. No one had to tell her. Even if the young girl hadn't possessed Cy's beautiful eyes or the boy the funny shape of his ears, her heart would have informed her that these two children owned pieces of Cy.

"Graciella," Thyme said before Sydney introduced them. Thyme extended her hand. "Hello. I've looked forward to meeting you."

If it kills me, I'll get through this.

Thyme's mind ticked like a time bomb. Had Cy sent for

this other family? The private investigator had told her all about Graciella and the children—Cy's children. But Thyme was not prepared for a face-off.

"So, Thyme. You've met Graciella?" Sydney asked. Thyme knew her brother well enough to read his twin. Sydney was pissed off that Thyme wasn't reacting, pure and simple. That gave Thyme strength. Sydney sat in a chair, legs crossed, eyeing both women boldly.

With all the finesse she could muster, Thyme answered quietly, "Oh, I've been hoping to meet Graciella—and of course the children—for a long time."

This broke Sydney's spirit. She was clearly hungry to see Thyme cry and shout like a typical geechee fool. It was evident from the distraught look on Sydney's face that she didn't know what to do next. She was obviously confused and had to think of another way to implement her plan.

Sydney spoke directly to Graciella in Spanish, which she assumed Thyme did not understand, but she was wrong. Sydney had told Graciella that Cy was afraid to leave Thyme. He was afraid she would cast a spell on him.

"Graciella," Thyme said. "In case you're uncertain, I'm Cy's wife and have been for twenty years. But I've heard so much about you." Watching the woman sitting on the same sofa she and Cy had made love on just weeks before, the same sofa on which he had made her laugh and on which, for the first time, he had seen her cry, cut her heart in half. It cut so deep she thought she would stop breathing.

Sydney looked as if she would burst into a thousand pieces; Graciella didn't look much better.

Thyme kept up the front. "I'm not sure when Cy'll be home. Why don't I page him?"

Thyme glanced into the hall library, where Gregor was checking out Cy's precious G.I. Joe collection. Meanwhile, Juana sat on the sofa staring straight at Thyme. Thyme could see the young girl's hatred in her pouting mouth, her knotted brow.

Thyme would deal with her own humiliation later. Right now, she promised herself, she would come out of this with her dignity intact. Later she'd get even with Sydney.

When the phone rang, Thyme picked up on the first ring. "You should come home right now. Your sister has brought Graciella and your children here." She was trembling but was careful to lay down the receiver quietly.

Seeing Cy's son, Gregor, hurt Thyme deeply, but it was Juana who crucified her. She looked exactly like Cy. The time they spent waiting for Cy to come home seemed like an eternity. Finally he walked through the front door. She heard his footsteps as he approached the living room, where all the women were gathered.

Cy looked first at Graciella then at Sydney, and finally his eyes met Thyme's. Panic lined his face.

Before he could speak Juana shouted, "I have something to say!"

"Juana!" her mother cried.

But Juana ignored her. "If it wasn't for you," the young girl said angrily to Thyme, "my mother wouldn't have been your husband's whore for the past twenty years. She would have been his wife."

Thyme wasn't angered by Juana's sharp tongue. She felt sorry for the young girl, who must feel so confused. Thyme remained silent. But the enraged look on Graciella's face replied louder than she ever could.

Juana wasn't finished. She had one last bomb to drop. "Do you all want to know what I'm really ashamed of? When my friends come over and my father is there, he and my mother are in the room making love like mad dogs. They're so loud my friends make fun of me and call them *los perros locos*, the crazy dogs."

Sydney, dressed in a three-piece red slacks suit, looked like a fox. She obviously loved Juana's little announcement. Both Thyme and Graciella lowered their heads in disgust. The child was humiliating both of them, and still she had more to say.

"What I'd like to know, my *señorita negra*, is if you make noises like that with my father when he's home. I think not, otherwise he wouldn't be so anxious to get in my mother's bed."

Cy looked like he would burst. "That's uncalled for, Juana." He grabbed her by the arm.

Juana snatched away from her father's hold. "You should be ashamed." She spoke now to Cy. "You're more of a whore than my mother could ever be. If I were either one of them," she said, pointing at her mother, then at Thyme, "I would tell you to go to hell."

Then Juana spat in Cy's face. At first Cy stood there with his hand to his cheek; then he slapped his daughter.

Immediately Graciella got up from her seat and held her daughter in her arms.

By now Gregor had come into the room. Everyone was still as a statue. Even Sydney appeared to be momentarily speechless.

"Gregor, Juana, go downstairs!" Cy shouted.

Juana glared at her father before leaving the room.

Sydney spoke first. "You need to know, Cy. I sent Graciella the tickets. I felt it was high time the truth of your life was revealed."

"Sydney, I'm ashamed that you are my sister. You've managed to embarrass me and hurt the woman I love more than anything in life. You also caused great pain to the mother of my children. These things can't be undone. But I have one thing to say. The last thing: Get the hell out of my house. Never come back. You're lower than any bitch I've known.

I never want to see you again." Cy was speaking to Sydney, but he hadn't taken his eyes off his wife.

Thyme stayed near the windows. She wanted to view the serenity, the beauty, the comfort of the waves outside that no longer represented her life. She couldn't bear to look Cy in the face. If she did, she feared she just might find herself jumping into those waves outside and praying for a quick death. She could feel Cy's eyes on her before she said a word. "I found out about Graciella and the children some time ago. What I didn't expect was for your sister to flaunt them in my face."

Sydney jumped in. "This is your chance, Cy. This is your opportunity to square things. You've got a beautiful woman who cares for you. Two healthy kids that adore you. What more can a man want?"

Graciella stood. She hadn't spoken a word before now. "I want to marry the father of my children. I love him, and I know that he cares for me, also."

Thyme's heart sank like a pirate ship that had just been shot by a cannon in the middle of the ocean. Never in her wildest dreams could she have imagined this happening to her—to them. Her soul was burning in an oven of rage. There was no hope for her marriage to survive. Her treasure, her love, was going to be lost at the bottom of the sea.

"This is fucked up," Cy finally said. "First of all, I never intended this to happen. Graciella, you know that. We talked about this." He turned to Thyme. "I love you." He looked at Graciella and then at Sydney. "Both of you know this. What did you hope to accomplish by doing this?" Cy looked at Sydney. His eyes were cold as dry ice. "What I said earlier I meant. Get out."

Sydney nervously gathered her keys and purse.

Graciella rose from the sofa. "Sydney, you can't leave me here."

Sydney looked at Graciella and then walked toward the door.

"Wait," Thyme called out. "Sydney," she said as she walked toward her sister-in-law, "I forgot something." Thyme snatched Sydney's purse and took the key to their house off her key ring. She handed her back the keys and purse, then, reaching back as far as Kansas, slapped Sydney across the face with all her strength. "Now get the fuck out!"

Sydney went pale with horror. She left without another word.

After Sydney left, Thyme stood with her back against the door. She felt she was suffocating as she waited for Cy to do something, say something.

Finally Cy spoke. "Graciella, you're going to take the children to a hotel. I'll find a room for you. I need to talk to my wife."

"You think you can just take care of things so simply!"

"I'll come by tomorrow."

"You will not. You will never see your children again!"

Nothing was settled. How could it be? A wife, mistress, children, deceit—no words could undo the destruction. It would take longer than a lifetime. And Thyme felt as though she had already lived one lifetime in a period of thirty minutes. At that moment she knew that her heart was dead to her husband.

Cy called the children to his side. "Daddy's going to take you to a hotel tonight."

Daddy? The sound of that word made Thyme want to vomit. It sickened her to think that her husband had an entire life with another woman. Why hadn't she known? Or had she chosen to ignore what now seemed so painfully obvious when he'd returned from Mexico? The weight gain. The refreshed look on his face. He wasn't working; he was fucking his ass off.

She knew what she had to do.

Several minutes later, she heard Cy's hurried footsteps coming back toward their bedroom. "Don't judge me now, Thyme. I can explain all of this. It's not like it seems. You know Sydney. She's miserable. And she wants you and me to be as miserable as she is."

Thyme allowed Cy to kiss her, then hug her tightly. She knew this embrace would be their last.

"We can talk about this, Thyme. I'm sorry. I'm sorry this had to happen, but it's over. No one matters but you. You're more important to me than anything."

Sure. Thyme was numb, her face without expression. She didn't have the strength to answer.

Cy left to take his Mexican family to a hotel. Thyme began packing her bags. How could he love her and yet still humiliate her this way? How did he define trust and love? Living a lie. Living separately, yet together. No. It was over.

The tears dried on her face as she snapped shut the last of her bags and set them by the back door. She knew she was doing the right thing. And for some reason she sighed in relief.

She went into the foyer and stopped, went back in their bedroom, and retrieved their scrapbook. Flipping through the pages, she stopped at their graduation pictures. Cy looked so handsome. And she didn't look bad either. The picture of them eating at McDonald's on their honeymoon and, later when they could afford it, a trip to Rome. And once again she reviewed the pictures of them together in Niagara Falls. She snapped the book shut. Warm tears slipped from her trembling lips. They'd been so happy. She opened her suitcase and slipped the book inside.

Khan. Khan. I should have listened to you.

Thyme finished packing her bags into the trunk of her car just as Cy pulled into the garage.

"What the hell are you doing?" Cy was as close to hysterical as she had ever seen him. "We can talk about this, Thyme. We've been together too long. Give me a chance."

Thyme slammed her trunk. "You know, Cyrus, I loved your white ass up until this happened. But you've got to remember something." She fought back the tears and exhaled. "When you lied about the bonus you got, I forgave you. When I found out you lied about the Mexican operations, I still forgave you. But you must know, my white brother, I cannot forgive another bitch, especially a bitch with two kids of your blood confronting me in my own home."

Cy fell down on his knees with tears streaming like water out of his eyes, begging Thyme to give him another chance, but she wasn't moved by his actions. For the first time she could see Cy for the low-down cheating dog he truly was. The only hurt she felt was for the time and dedication she'd wasted. And now she didn't feel an ounce of pity for him.

"Thyme—"

"No." Tears formed in her eyes and she willed them back. "Sydney was right when she told you that you should have married a white woman. Maybe she would have accepted her man having a mistress and children outside the home. But not me, Cy. Not me."

"Baby," Cy pleaded, getting up off his knees, trying to touch her.

Thyme pulled away. "You know what? Sydney did me a favor. I'm tired of looking at white folks and feeling inferior. I'm tired of feeling that I'm not good-looking enough, not skilled enough. I've had to put up with your lies, your cheating. Hell, Cy, you're not good enough for me."

"Thyme?"

"No, it's time that you knew how I felt all these years. I'm sick of the racism. I'm sick of black people talking about me behind my back. And I'm fed up with white people talking about me behind my back."

"It's not like that. . . ." Cy reached out to touch her and Thyme pulled back again.

"And I'm tired of trying to prove myself good enough for folks like Sydney to accept me, when I'm ninety-nine percent better than them anyway."

"You don't have to go, baby. Let me take your bags back inside. We can talk about this in the morning."

"Oh no. *Hell* no. If there's one thing we can't talk about, it's my black skin. Sure you love to feel it. You love to fuck it. But when it came time to respect and honor it, you turned your back."

Cy couldn't speak.

"Now I see that I've been acting white for over twenty years when my skin is as black as tar. I'm proud of who I am, Cy. And I'm ashamed that it took this fucking long for me to see it."

Cy was speechless.

"You've only seen me cry that one time, and you won't see me cry again." Her smile felt so fine to her now. It was like she held a special secret. "Did you know that fish are the only backboned animals with two-chambered hearts?"

Still he was silent, his moist eyes pleading forgiveness.

"One day you'll understand." Thyme got in her car and backed out of the garage. Then and only then did she let the tears fall. It would be the last time she'd cry over Cy. When she stopped at the gate, she pressed the code and watched the bar lift. And she knew then that she would never live behind closed gates again.

Two hours later, Thyme parked outside Khan's condo. She'd heard that her friend had been hurt in the rioting, but she also knew Khan would not welcome a visit from her.

Now, though, she felt it was time to try to bridge the gap between them.

When she knocked at the door, Khan opened it, her face showing surprise. Her left shoulder was fitted with a cumbersome cast, and there was a bruised welt the size of an apple on her forehead. She held a copy of *Solidarity News*, a colorful thirty-page periodical, in her right hand.

"Can we please talk for a few minutes?" Thyme tried again. Dressed in jeans and a sweatshirt, Thyme thought maybe part of Khan's surprise had to do with Thyme's ghetto look.

"Sure. Have a seat."

Thyme didn't know where to start. There was so much to say, so many things that needed explaining. Finally she started by reiterating that she'd had no idea about Troy Trim being closed. She explained that she knew, like Ron had suspected, that jobs were being moved to Mexico, but not the full extent of Champion's plan. "Believe me or not, it's the truth. I didn't want to believe that Cy had been lying to me all along. Now I have no choice but to face facts." Then Thyme admitted that she should have known and that it was stupid of her not to follow up and check with her sources about Mexico. Instead, she'd put her energies into trying to get new business at the plant. Now she knew why she couldn't get any new business: Champion hadn't wanted her to develop new business. "Please understand. If I had known, I would have tried to do something—anything."

Khan looked at Thyme flatly and said, "Okay, but that doesn't solve our problems completely. What about the layoffs? The violence? For God's sake, Thyme, someone was killed because of all the tension and stress at the plant!"

"I know, I know. I wish more than anyone that I could have done more about the overtime issue. But please, Khan, I am only one person and the problems at Troy Trim were

caused by many people. Not just me. You've got to understand that."

Khan nodded her head slowly.

Thyme was as still as a glass cat. Even her forced smile
froze on her face. "The real reason I stopped by is more personal, Khan. I've found out that Cy has a mistress and two
children in Mexico. In fact, Sydney brought the Mexican
woman into my house with her two kids."

Khan slammed her magazine on her lap. "What? You've
got to be joking! I'll be damned. I knew it. I was willing to
bet that if that ol' boy wasn't servicing you regularly, he had
to be taking care of somebody else." Sensing that she was
out of line, Khan softened her words. "I'm sorry, Thyme. I
know you must be hurting now. What are you planning to do
about it?"

"I don't know. I'm still dealing with the fact that I've been
living a lie."

"Hmm."

"I was saying that Cy lied to me—"

"So what, Thyme? So what? You're not the first woman
this has happened to and you certainly won't be the last. You
would have known to expect shit like this if you had any
common sense. I know that sounds harsh, but I think the
sooner you get to the baseline truth the better off you'll be.
Cy was not the man you thought you married. Your best
friend should be your husband, and he turned his back on
you. Now you've got to go to yourself. You've got a healthy
bankbook and a lot of *you*."

"Still and all, Khan, I'm trying to persevere. I've sent out
résumés hoping I'll get hired somewhere. Anywhere but
Champion Motors."

"But honey child, I read in the papers about your lawsuit.
You were already rich. Now you're richer, bitch. It appears
the last thing you need right now is a job. A friend would be

more beneficial. You should try and find a friend like yourself, Thyme. Somebody who thinks white. Maybe they'll sympathize with you. I don't have much sympathy left for people like you. I'm struggling just to make ends meet. You have no idea what that's like. But what's sad is that you are still struggling with which side to take, white or black, new collar or blue collar. Until you make a decision where your loyalty lies, you won't know what you are really about."

"I know I'm black, Khan. I have always known what color I am. I just gave my love to a dog and he hurt me. You've helped me to see that clearer than anyone."

"No, I think you're confused. Real black people don't act like you do. They stick together. Especially during tough times. When Valentino was accused of murder, you could have shown your support to his wife and family. You didn't even call Ron, did you?" She threw her hands in the air and brought them back down, then slapped her thighs in frustration. "All you did was show up at the festivities—make a grand appearance."

"You're right," Thyme said in a low voice. "Lately my life has been about as organized as goat shit."

"Black folks like you have Grey Poupon holders in the backseat of their car"—Khan cut her a snide smile—"and live up in the Bloomies with those white folks, behind big gates to keep out the undesirables. If you weren't married to that white man they wouldn't have never let your black ass get up in there. Sure, it's a gorgeous house. Remember how I couldn't get over how pretty the birds sounded the first time I went to your house? I hadn't heard a bird sing like that since I left Mama Pearl's house."

Thyme couldn't help but smile.

"Still, I like how the birds sound where I live—the pigeons and crows."

Thyme couldn't come back with a decent rebuttal.

Momentarily, there seemed to be a slight chill in the room.
Thyme hugged herself and still said nothing. It seemed like
an eternity until she finally spoke. "I can't offer any more
excuses. I won't ask for your forgiveness. I only know that
you are a true friend." Thyme leaned over and kissed Khan's
cheek, holding her close. "I love you, Khan."

We say things with our mouths when our hearts feel
something different. Thyme could still feel Khan's loving
arms around her long after the door had closed behind her.

37

Nothing was the same for Khan after the riot. She'd been hospitalized for almost a week, during which time her uncle told her that after the second round of negotiations, the union members finally agreed to go back to work. Khan's shoulder had healed, and the bump on her forehead from the horse kicking her was barely visible now. But with the union gaining so little ground, the wound penetrated into her heart, the source of her courage.

One fight the union had managed to win was for the mounted police to be outlawed during union strikes. Eighty-three people had been injured in the scab fight. Five people had been hospitalized, primarily suffering from injuries caused by the policemen's horses.

She missed Thyme. Where had she gone? No one knew. Cy wouldn't return any calls and had not been seen since Thyme had left.

Thyme seemed to have disappeared into thin air. Maybe Khan had been too hard on her. After all, they'd been friends for years. Khan felt she was to blame. No one had been as hurtful to her as she had.

The silver lining surrounding the strike nightmare was

how much closer she and Buddy had become. They were now inseparable.

Ordinarily, Sunday was the day Khan rested. In spite of her promise to Mama Pearl, she had never attended church. One night after they'd left the movies, Khan asked Buddy his thoughts about going to church.

"I don't go every Sunday. But I try to make it at least twice a month. On those Sundays I don't attend I send in an offering."

"Maybe I'd feel less guilty if I did that," Khan muttered. "Working five and six days a week, I use Sunday as a day to rest."

"Wait, let me rephrase that. What church does for people is this: It teaches people to learn more about the spirit of God that's inside all of us. The church teaches us to become better husbands, wives, and children. We'll work and get along better with other people, be more straight-up businesspeople, interested more in people than in profits. But I don't think this requires going to church every Sunday."

"I hadn't thought about it that way," Khan said. She was in awe of this man's maturity. How had he achieved such wisdom at such a young age?

The following weekend, Buddy asked her out for a "special time," as he put it. "It won't be a traditional date." Buddy hesitated. "Anyway, it's special to me, Khan. I hope you can understand."

Khan was certainly surprised when they pulled into William Beaumont Hospital. With little conversation or pre-amble, Buddy took her hand and led Khan to the third floor, where his Aunt Viola was recovering from surgery.

"Aunt Viola," Buddy said. "Do you remember Khan?"

Aunt Viola looked up at Khan through rheumy eyes. Khan could see that the medication may have taken away the old woman's immediate pain but not all of her suffering.

"Yes, I remember."

"Aunt Viola, your nephew has told me so many wonderful things about you. You mean so much to him," Khan said, barely able to contain her emotion.

"He was a good boy, and now a good man."

"Yes, he is," Khan said, looking at Buddy with pride.

"He knows how to treat his people. I think he's a godsend."

After they left the hospital, Khan couldn't help thinking about Mama Pearl. She vowed to send her a plane ticket as soon as she was able.

The weekend was a blur. Buddy ran back and forth to the hospital, and they snatched moments to be together. By Sunday night they found time to talk. They discussed his aunt's declining health and talked about their childhoods and how it felt growing up without the benefit of parents. There was no self-pity, just gratefulness that another person came along to love them just as much. Khan couldn't remember having such a personal conversation with R.C. Buddy was filling more and more of her heart. He wasn't pushy. Their relationship wasn't sexual. They hadn't even exchanged more than a kiss. But what a kiss.

And Buddy seemed to understand how important her job was. Because R.C. was so wealthy, he had always considered Khan's job a joke. Buddy, struggling to make his family business work, knew better. He also seemed to understand that for Khan, her job wasn't just about money, and he implicitly respected her need for independence. What woman in her right mind wouldn't love a man who supported her independence? The simplicity of that fact was completely seductive. And her emotions grew.

Khan continued visiting Tino in jail at least once a week. Last week when she'd visited, Uncle Ron was already there.

Tears came to her eyes as she remembered the conversation she'd witnessed between father and son.

"Tino, you are my son and I will always love you."

"Dad, we are different. But that doesn't make either of us less of a man."

"I think I understand that now."

"And Dad, thank you for standing by my family."

"Thank you for standing by yours. That's the true test of any man."

On the day of Tino's sentencing, without even being asked, Buddy had taken a day off work to accompany Khan to the courtroom.

They arrived before Ron, Ida, and Sarah. Tino looked tired, but he still had fight left in his face. When the judge read the verdict, "Guilty as charged," and then sentenced him to ten to twenty years, everyone cried. But they were tears of relief. The psychiatrist had discounted Valentino's original plea of temporary insanity. When his attorney entered a plea of guilty, the prosecuting attorney was ready to deal. Valentino would be out in three and a half years. He was led away by the bailiff but not before mouthing "I love you" to the bench where his family sat.

Later, everyone congratulated Sarah when she told them she was three months pregnant. Her future, her son's future, and now her new baby's future were with her husband. And all four would wait patiently, with prayer, until he was released.

As Khan and Buddy prepared to leave, Khan turned to Ida. "Do you two want to meet for dinner later?"

Ida cuddled against Ron. She couldn't answer; her smile was wide.

"We've got a date three aisles over. We're going to make it legal, Khan." Ron took Ida's hand in his and nodded.

Khan knew she would remember this beautiful moment between them no matter what valleys her aunt and uncle might have to cross.

"Wish us luck," Ida said finally, laughing. "Our honeymoon might be on *America's Funniest Home Videos*."

Ron slapped Ida on her rump. "Shut up, Ida." It was good that they had chosen this day to make joy happen. It was fitting in some way.

Tragedy had turned into triumph.

On their way back to her condo Buddy asked her a question that caught Khan off guard. "Did you read about R.C. in the papers?"

"No." Khan felt her face flush.

"He filed for bankruptcy. It appears the IRS has confiscated all his assets. In short, he's broke."

Khan knew that Buddy was gauging her response. It was a test she knew she would pass. Her conviction that she would always care for R.C. was now a part of her past. "That's interesting, Buddy." She snuggled against him and wove her fingers through his.

But later that evening Khan hesitantly called R.C.'s home. Tomiko answered.

"Hello, this is Khan."

"I recognize your voice," Tomiko said. "R.C. isn't home. Can I help you?"

Khan gulped hard. She was a bit apprehensive, but certain that she was doing the right thing. "I've never sent you two a wedding gift. Could you tell R.C. that a present from Khan is in the mail?"

"I don't know what to say. Thank you."

She took a deep breath and counted on her decency to continue the conversation. "I wish you all the luck in the world, Tomiko. I truly mean it." Khan's voice began to break just as she hung up. Sorrow filled her and she cupped her hands over her mouth, trying to keep it inside. Old love was hard; new love was, too—you never knew where the truth ended and deception began. How could she trust her flowering feelings for Buddy?

After calling Tomiko, Khan sent R.C. all the jewelry he'd given her. With the strike resolved so quickly, she'd never needed to sell it. He needed those things more now.

She was still crying minutes later when Buddy phoned. His aunt's condition had worsened. She desperately needed a kidney transplant. She was losing the window of time for a successful transplant operation.

The following four days were hell. Khan was finally back at work, but production was slow. The union was still waiting to hear about the fate of Troy Trim. Now with Aunt Viola near death, Khan found it even more difficult to concentrate on work. She turned down overtime and hurried home, waiting for Buddy's call. Even though she hadn't known Viola that long, her allegiance to her was strong. The older woman was Buddy's closest link to his family.

By week's end, Viola's health had deteriorated even more. In the interim, Buddy learned that his kidney was a match with his aunt's.

"Khan, I've agreed to donate one of my kidneys to my aunt."

But what about us? "Where does that leave you if something were to happen in your life? I'm worried about you."

Buddy was calm before he spoke. "My life means nothing to me without the love of my family. My Aunt Viola is the only family member I have left on this earth."

What about me?

"People live with one kidney all the time. Try to understand how I feel. I never told you before, Khan, that I love you. But I do. If your life was at stake I'd do the same thing."

This didn't seem the time to tell him that she loved him. The only thing left for her to do was pray. "I understand, Buddy." She held back tears. "Do what you have to do." Her mouth was trembling.

When Khan went to work Monday morning, she moved through the plant like a zombie. At lunchtime she stopped by the Bible study group. She asked for them to pray for Viola Robbins. Even though she'd never sat in on one of their meetings before, they greeted her eagerly. They wouldn't let her go until she joined hands with them and they could pray for her as well. Khan was genuinely touched.

After lunch, she called home and retrieved her messages. The first message was from Buddy. His aunt had died.

Khan felt relieved, and guilty.

Later that same day, Ron called. It was official: Troy Trim was being sold to Mishupont by the first of the year.

Ron went on to say that when Mishupont took over, the hourly rate would drop by two dollars. High-seniority workers with twenty years or more could bump to another Champion plant. Those left would get the first option of employment with the new company.

That left Khan out in the cold with only five and a half years' seniority.

The killing part was that there would be no union. With thirty years' seniority, Ron was considering retirement. Ida probably would retire as well.

What was Khan going to do? She had some money saved, but it was clear she could no longer count on Champion. She thought of Thyme and wished her friend were nearby to give her advice. Maybe it was a sign that it was time to get her degree. Maybe it was time to take off that blue collar.

Khan helped Buddy with Aunt Viola's funeral. Khan perceived from all the mementos in her home that the elderly woman had loved her house. It was her life.

It hurt her to see Buddy struggling with the small details, going through his aunt's closets to select a dress she'd soon wear.

"Maybe I should buy her a new dress," Buddy said.

"No," Khan said. "I think she would want to wear one of her own dresses; she has a closet full of beautiful clothes. We'll put an orchid in her hair and she'll look beautiful. The same way she does in that picture on the wall."

They both looked up to see a portrait of Viola at age twenty-five. She had aged well. Khan thought of Mama Pearl and missed her more than ever.

After the funeral, in the early evening, as the late October day faded, Khan waited for Buddy. Soft trickles of rain had begun to fall. The doorbell rang and Buddy handed her a small bouquet of African violets before he stepped inside.

She touched the dreadlocks that she had come to love and said, "Thanks." Then, taking his hand, she led him inside.

"Blondie, it sure smells good in here. Matter of fact, it always smells good in here. What is it?"

"My new fragrance, Amazon." She went over to him and held out her wrist and let him inhale it. "There's a little bit of cedar, coconut, cloves, and I won't say what else. Like it?"

"Mm-hm."

With a dish towel in one hand and the violets in the other, she led him into the living room and placed him in front of the television, handing him the remote. "Look, CNN is on." She kissed him on his forehead. "Now sit down and be quiet until I finish."

"But, Blondie, this ain't the kind of sport I'm interested in right now." He stared at her cleavage. There was no mistaking his intentions.

"You dog, you." She plopped his face with the dish towel and gave him a dirty grin.

Just then, thunder cracked outside. The sky had begun to darken and they could hear the wind reeling through the bare branches of the trees outside and whipping them back and forth.

Khan was in the breakfast area stretching out a tablecloth over the table. She placed a candle holder in the center and completed the two table settings.

"I love it when the sky grows dark like this before a storm." Buddy was standing looking outside the living room window.

The sky had turned surreal, its colors dark gray, black, silver, and iridescent white; it looked as if God's face were being stitched across the sky. The sky had become a quilt of the day: death and now new life.

Khan stopped what she was doing and stood beside him. "It is beautiful, isn't it?"

"Yes. Like you. Your eyes. They sparkle like angels." His voice was thick and husky. Buddy turned away from the window and came toward her.

Khan immediately stepped back. She could feel the intensity of his gaze on her. Also noticeable was the way his eyes blatantly feasted on her body. "Let me get the dinner on the table," she said. "I know you're starved." But she knew that rock Cornish hens and dressing wasn't the type of banquet he had in mind. *He wants my ass.*

The thunder cracked outside and the lights blinked off and on.

Still feeling his eyes on her, Khan felt more nervous than she ever had around him. When she sat, the dishes clinked and clattered on the table. *Shit.* She dropped the silverware on the floor and went back into the kitchen to get clean ones. Still she felt his eyes watching her at every turn. Khan filled both their plates with generous helpings of hen and dressing, mashed potatoes and gravy, French string beans, and cranberry sauce. Just as she'd filled two glasses with ice cubes Buddy called out her name.

"Khan."

The simplicity of hearing him call her name made her weak. She waited. He called her again, his voice more sultry.

"Khan."

Outside, the pounding rain was building and the cracking sounds of thunder were stronger than before. As the sky closed in around them, the darkness descended upon the house.

"Everything's ready, Buddy." She placed two gold candles in the center of the table, then stood back to appraise her work. Getting her mind off Buddy and sex to eating dinner was quite a feat. *What if he couldn't screw? What if he had a little dick? Ah, hell.* "Do you have any matches?"

He patted his pants and breast pockets. "No." Just then his penetrating eyes pinned her. They were like the eyes of a falcon and she had to turn away, the connection was so strong.

Outside, there was the sound of incessant rain, combined with a whoosh of thunder breaking into the scene as if the moment deserved a thread of kinetic energy. It conveyed such power, the power that crept into Khan's soul and spread down through the most private parts of her body.

The thunder cracked again and the lights suddenly flicked off. In the darkness she felt Buddy coming toward her.

His first touch, his fingertips against her face, felt as soft and caressing as a melody. It was ten times stronger than any verbal or emotional contact she had ever felt before. He stroked her eyes, nose, lips, and brought his fingers down beneath her chin, hesitating in the center of her breasts and pressing his splayed fingers against her breastbone. Then he stopped.

She savored the heat and heaviness of the hand that lay against her breast and raised her hand to touch it.

Her brain issued an SOS when she felt him disengage. But that touch was immediately replaced by another: his soft lips enveloping hers. He kissed her gently, then pulled back. "Baby, I need you tonight." Buddy wrapped his arms around her and pressed his body against hers.

Khan shivered. She could feel the pulse of his penis pressing against her thigh. No, she thought, he did not have a little dick. Desire unleashed months of pent-up passion. She lowered her hands and gently massaged his penis until she could hear his sharp intake of breath on her neck. He unleashed his hot tongue along her neck then inserted it into her mouth.

His kiss, as they shared one breath, sealed the chamber of her body to her lover, fusing their souls as they continued to drink from the wells of each other's mouths.

When the kiss deepened even more, she eased her thigh between his and began grinding her pelvis bone against his rock-hardness. She felt him beginning to move, and she reached down and unbuttoned the top of his jeans. Now she felt like the predator.

He stepped back, and she could hear him unzipping his pants and shedding his heavy clothing.

And when she reached out for him, touching him, lower and lower, until she felt the power and strength of him, it was like reaching into a chrysalis. She felt an unspeakable delight. At first she stroked him there. Then, feeling his need, she slid her fingers down the length of him, massaging him in slow, sweeping strokes.

"What'd you say the name of that cologne was, baby?"

"Amazon," she teased. "I was told it brought out the Tarzan in a man."

"Mmm, a jungle woman. Just what I need." Buddy

undressed her with considerable swiftness. And they stood in the middle of the living room, reveling in the freedom of their nakedness. There was no music to charm the moment, and they didn't need any. Lightning pulsed through the window. Their only orchestra, the rain outside, provided a natural melody.

Buddy's eyelids twitched ever so slightly in the heat of the moment, his pelvis moving with the beat of her nimble fingers into a comfortable rhythm of orgasmic ecstasy.

And their pelvic bones merged together, creating a louder noise than the one they heard seconds earlier.

Khan loved the way Buddy avowed the deliciousness of her sex without shame, and she felt the same.

"There are as many ways to make love," Buddy said in the throaty, caressing voice she had come to love, "as there are stars in the sky."

As he exquisitely stroked her buttocks, she gasped. And his fingers touched, ever so gently, the two secret openings to her body, time after time, with a soft little brush of fire.

"Mmmm. Ahhhh. Ahhhh. Hhhssh." Buddy exclaimed against the side of her dampened face. Together, they slid to the floor.

Buddy lowered his head past her abdomen and past her blond bush. He stopped at her ankles, delicately kissing the moist beads of sweat there. She felt his tongue move up the exterior of her thighs and her breath quickened, anticipating the ecstasy. She held her breath. Her mind begged him—no, willed him—to go farther. Inches closer. And then finally, when she felt his tongue touch the outer lips of her vagina, she shuddered.

Khan lifted her head and looked down at him. His mouth touched her soft mound and she prayed that he wouldn't stop.

He grabbed the curve of her buttocks. His tongue, in short

brushstrokes, dipped inside and outside her flaming lips. Her heart beat more thunderously than the storm outside her window. Her knees grew weak and fell open like an oyster revealing its prized pearl. When she felt his hot breath blow against her desire-fevered vagina, pressure rising like black steam, she lost all thought.

Khan's hands gripped his head and pressed it deeper within her, inviting further his erotic exploration of her throbbing vagina. Her bones quivered. And then she felt it— exquisite torment. A thrill like she had never experienced before ran through her. She broke like a pane of glass, then relaxed, soaked from pure joy.

The whole surface of her skin was stimulated, the way swimming naked made her feel. Only what she felt now was compounded by sensuality. All the hairs on her body moved like seaweed in an ebb tide, and the current was guiding her with his persistent fingers exploring every part of her nerve endings. The sweat on her feet felt like a squish of wet between her toes. She was drenched in an orgasmic tidal wave, and nothing could stop the torrent. The buoyancy of their bodies blended in one long and delicious tremble, like a chord, and for a moment, the light of their souls shone like living torches.

When they paused to take a breath, the thunder outside had stopped.

The cool wind howled outside, and white flurries had begun to fall.

Afterwards, Khan kissed him slowly on the lips. Her breath was like new-mown grass. "I love the taste of you," she said to Buddy.

She had no recollection of lying down, but there they were. She reached up and raised the blinds, letting the moonlight flow over their naked bodies. They were so comfortable with each other. Everything felt so right, so new, so fresh.

"I know it's early, but I wish it would really snow. You know, like ten inches or so."

"It's not even November yet, Blondie."

"Still, I love fall. But my favorite is winter. That's why I love living in Michigan."

"Tell you what, they've probably got fourteen inches of snow in Aspen, Colorado. I'll call my travel agent and book a trip. If not there, then we'll go to Minnesota—Or maybe we'll say fuck the snow, and spend a week in the Sahara Desert."

"Stop kidding! Someday I'd love to travel all over the world."

"It's a great experience. But only if you share it with someone. I spent five lonely years traveling the globe after my parents died."

"Why?"

"Because I was angry, and alone. But now I've found you, and I'm not lonely anymore." He kissed her ever so gently.

Her own smile felt good to her as it slid across her face.

Buddy pulled her back down next to him. He eased his hand down lower and lower over her sweaty body and pressed his palm over the hub of her vagina.

Khan felt the lips of her vagina swelling, anticipating, waiting, demanding full entrance. Relief came seconds later, when slowly, ever so slowly, he slid his fingers back inside her.

Her eyes took on a dreamlike quality and her breathing became harsh. The corners of Buddy's mouth widened in a satisfactory smile. "I've got a helluva lot to do with Mother Nature, Blondie."

"Amen, brother." She led him to the bed. "Don't stop

now." She was in the midst of a caravan of pleasure. And she didn't want the trip to end.

And it didn't. Not for a while.

Later, they lay in each other's arms feeling the pleasure of remembering their pleasure. It was a feeling they would share for years to come, a special feeling. One they knew would last a lifetime, no matter what else happened.

Stripped as they were, both Buddy and Khan began to talk to each other from that place deep in the soul.

"I want you with me always, Khan. Not just tonight, but every night."

Khan was afraid. She wasn't sure what he meant. Did he mean marriage? Or did he mean a live-in relationship? She decided to play it safe. She didn't want Buddy to hurt her like R.C. had.

"You know, Buddy, it's strange. When I hired on at Champion I didn't plan on being there long. I would work a few years, find a rich man to marry me, and retire by age twenty-five. After the first year I noticed how many people *didn't* want to retire. There were so many people with thirty-five, forty, and forty-five years' seniority who seemed afraid to retire. Then I found out why. The people who had retired kept coming back to the plant every week like they were desperate for company." Her eyes were moist with tears. "I never wanted to be like them. Now, here I am praying that I can go back so I can maintain my little hut here. You know, take care of my bills and send my Mama Pearl a few dollars." She sniffed, and more tears began to fall. "I know it's a simple little job, but I think now I want more. I just don't know if I'm up for it. Working at Champion brought me many things: love, happiness, and oh yes, I found hurt. I spent some of my darkest days at Champion. But it wasn't until I went outside the scope of the plant that I was able to find you."

"That's sweet, baby." Buddy's voice turned serious. "I've got a job for you, Khan. It doesn't pay as much as Champion. But the wages are fair. And it'll allow you to take any classes you need." He grabbed a tissue from the night-stand and wiped her tears.

She dried her eyes. "How much?"

"Fifteen an hour."

It was seven less than she made at Champion. She frowned, and her body shrugged as well. She could tell that Buddy felt her displeasure, because he spoke quickly.

"If you take into account our combined incomes, we'd gross about thirty grand a month."

"What are you talking about?" Khan was stunned. "Did you say thirty—thirty thousand a *month*? You make that much money?"

Buddy lifted her chin up toward his and smiled. "Sure do. Up until now, I didn't think it was important for you to know."

In a flash, she thought about R.C. and his broken promises. She thought about Mama Pearl and all her advice. "Well, it isn't, but—" Then her hopes died, and her voice reflected her worst fears.

"What is the job?"

"You'll be working for the shortening company," he said with a smile.

"What exactly are you asking me?"

"I don't want to spend another night without you. It took me this long to find you, and I don't ever want to let you go. Living together isn't for me, Khan. I want to marry you now, while your Mama Pearl is still alive. I don't want her to miss out like Aunt Viola. Mama Pearl deserves to see her grand-child walk down the aisle, don't you think? I want to devote the rest of my life to loving you and making sure you're never lonely."

Khan couldn't help but think back on her Aunt Ida's words: "Lust, love, devotion," and she knew she held the world in her arms.

The relief she felt was overwhelming. She couldn't bring herself to believe. "Are you serious?" Lord, it was just like her Mama Pearl said it would be. "Buddy—"

Buddy pulled her toward him and stripped the sheet from her body. His naked eyes lusted over her body like lasers until she felt that the heat was unbearable. She started to speak, and he stopped her with a touch of his fingers over her open lips.

"I forgot to ask, Khan. Will you marry me?"

Epilogue

One Year Later

Let me tell you about Tomiko and R.C. Well, as you might have guessed, R.C. lost all but one Champion dealership, the used-car lot he started with. He lost the ranch in Paris, Kentucky, as well. Even so, you know how much sister girl loved her R.C.: so R.C., well, he's hooked for life. Tomiko's modeling career has continued to build, and the couple is doing okay.

Now what do you think is up with Thyme? I'll let you take a peek at the letter Khan received from her just before Thanksgiving:

Hello, my friend. You're probably wondering where I've run off to. I'm in Ghana. Yes, girlfriend. In Africa. I'll bet you're laughing now. But Khan, I'm serious about my life, more serious about who I am—about being black and living black. I hadn't realized that by marrying Cy and living the life we did, how far away I had turned from myself and my blackness.

I've filed for a divorce from Cy. I love him. And I would venture to say that he loves me. But it's over.

I'm sure a lot of women who date or marry white men don't have a problem holding on to themselves. I pray that they don't. But I wasn't able to separate myself. No, that's not true—I wasn't able to be myself, because I was too busy trying to gain acceptance. Truly, Khan, I wasn't ashamed of being black. I merely wanted recognition. Recognition for my talents, my education, and for who I was. That didn't happen. I had to sue to get respect from a company to which I gave over twenty years of my life. The money doesn't matter. Because it can't buy respect.

Cy's written to beg me to come back home. There's no way. I can never go back to lies and deceit. And those children won't disappear, I don't care how far away they are or how much Graciella believes she can keep him from seeing them. They'd always be between us. No, it's better these days. I'm hurting, but I'm taking control of my life and not looking back.

I'm loving where I am. I'm working at Atheneum Enterprises as their new operations manager. I also head the Small Plastic Parts Division. They've set me up in a beautiful home just outside the city, and I have a maid, driver, housekeeper, and the best cook I could hope for. And, as you might expect, I'm no longer a size six. I'm closer to a ten, and I've gotten rid of all my permed hair. And you know what, I'm happy and I'm home.

You won't believe this: I'm pregnant! Forty-six years old and pregnant! Can you believe it! I plan to

marry my child's father in June. I hope you can come
for a visit when the baby is born in December.

Enclosed are my address and telephone number, and
a ticket good for one year. Khan, there's also a ticket
for Buddy. I hope by then the two of you will be married.

Wishing you love and happiness.

Love always,
Thyme.

Now tell me you weren't surprised. You knew that fine-
looking black woman had to find her a hot-blooded black
man who would bless her with some younguns, didn't you?

As for Khan, well, Mama Pearl indeed saw her granddaugh-
ter's wedding. Buddy and Khan put on a fine show. The
newlyweds decided to take a whole month off work. Then,
after a nice long vacation, Khan returned to work—this time
for her husband. But Khan ain't no blue collar worker, no
sir. She's got new collar status now and she's right up there
in the office working with Buddy every day. And don't let
me forget about children. You know they want some, but
that's a long way away.

You didn't think Khan forgot about her friend, did you?

Right now, they're planning a trip next year to Ghana to
visit Thyme. Khan returned the tickets, however, explaining
why they didn't need to take them—and in the same letter
informed her friend it was too late to hope they got married
because they already were!

And what about Cy? Well, Cy opened up his own engineering firm and is very successful. Presently, he's holding on to
another woman—a black one.

Now, you know he's gotten used to that dark skin. But

anyway, he wasn't all bad; he really did love Thyme. God must've given the brother a break and forgiven him for his sins, because Cy didn't sue Champion for ten million dollars. They gave him twelve.

I know what you been really waiting to hear about: Ron's implant. Yes, the man is still screwing his ass off with other women. Did you think he would ever change? 'Course, Ida ain't concerned. She took out a $250,000 insurance policy on Ron and made his two grandsons the beneficiaries.

Yeah, yeah, Sarah had another boy. But this one ain't too pretty. He looks just like his grandpa Ron. After the baby came, Sarah thought the best way to keep busy until her husband came home was to get a job. And where you think she headed straight for? You got it, the repair shop. She'd been watching Valentino repair those sets for years, though he didn't know it. And when he comes home in a couple of years, they might just be able to swing opening a small shop of their own.

Hold up. You wondering if Valentino is in the brick bitch switching his booty like some he-she. Naw. Valentino's learned his lesson after killing Luella. If he'd admitted the problem he was having then, trying to figure out who he was, and accepted himself, he might have never killed her. He has pictures of his sons pasted on every wall in his cell. One day he will sit down and tell them what it takes in life to be a real man.

Guess what! You won't believe what Graciella did. She took the kids back home to Mexico and moved to Mexico City. In less than a year she had moved a twenty-two-year-old matador in with her and opened up a chain of soul-food restaurants. With their newfound wealth, it didn't take long for Graciella and the kids to forget about Cy.

Oh yeah, don't let me forget about Sydney. Well, the bitch

is still sizzling about Cy and his new black chick that dresses like an African queen and is three shades darker than Thyme. She's sick over the fact that her brother has broken all contact with her. Hmm, she deserved as much—don't you think? Sydney even took Thyme up on her suggestion to see a shrink. She's been through three more of them. She's still a size two. You didn't think she'd get all depressed and gain weight, did you? Gracious no. The hussy spends money on personal trainers, face-lifts, tummy tucks, liposuction, collagen treatments, and skin peels. She'll keep fighting truth and what's real forever.

But you know what? Even though she's worth seventy million bucks, that's one miserable bitch!